THE VESSEL

By

Barbara Caldwell-Pease

Printed in the United States of America

ISBN: 978-0615899596

Aoweth Books

7516 West 95th Terrace

Overland Park, KS

Library of Congress Control Number: 2014907957

Drunemeton, *Ériu,* 121 CE

The women and men of the priesthood stood between her and the people. Their faces were set, as if they did not hear the relentless thunder of hoof beats, the clang of metal and the meaty thunk of swords cleaving human flesh.

Despite the frost on the leaves beneath her bare feet, sweat trickled down her spine. Her tunic stuck to her back. Her hair, whipped in the cold wind, lashed her arms and her chest. The ring of office on her left forefinger felt like a band of fire.

Part of her wanted to pull the ritual knife from her belt and try, once more, to sever her finger. Anything to stop the burning—to stop her destiny.

She had been chosen, though, because she would not give up. She would bear her fate with honor. How would it feel waiting thousands of years in darkness? When she woke, would she remember?

She would have to remember. Even now, images from the recurring nightmares clouded her vision; great hulking beasts of iron, swallowing the land, metal tubes exploding, blackening the sky, the earth reacting, storming, breaking, erupting, wailing, roiling masses of people, children twisted, raw and screaming—Rome's ultimate legacy that only she could stop.

Before she could shake her dreams, the soldiers burst into the clearing.

"Nobiscum Deus!" Cried the Roman general.

He and his soldiers drove their broad horses through the silent wall of people. Swords flashed left and right, up and down, slinging blood through the air, splattering the sacred oaks, anointing the Sentinels. On cue, acolytes plied axes against the gory trunks, ringing a sharp counter-rhythm to the rattle of hooves, the thud of falling bodies. The people offered themselves to the swords, blocking the path to priests, acolytes and her.

The mingled odors of horseflesh, sweat and copper overpowered the bright scent of fresh-cut wood. Steam rose from the animals' nostrils and the soldier's bloodied blades. Warm, heavy drops fell on her head as the chanting of her priesthood surrounded her.

The soldiers worked swiftly, shouting and cursing, fogging the air with the blood of druids. Hot fluid rained over her, soaking her hair, coating her skin.

The Sentinels screamed in her head, their trees creaking as they fell away from their roots. Her priests maintained their cadence.

The gathering power fed into her. Wave after wave of Sentinel magic blasted her until her knees buckled and she swayed half upright. The force roared in her ears, overpowering the dying grunts of her people and the dwindling chorus of her priests. When she died, the power would be drawn into the ring she wore, but the effort of temporarily holding the raw energy ripped the fabric of her being.

It seemed a millennium until arcing metal stopped the final chanter. By then, her bones were liquid flame.

Without ceremony, an anonymous blade bit her neck and she welcomed the relief. A final smile curved her lips. Somewhere in the forest behind her, The Circle waited to incinerate her bones and send her to oblivion.

When she woke, and they would see she did, she would repay Rome for her people and she would cleanse the earth with a fire beyond comprehension.

CHAPTER ONE

When she recognized the flash of yellow around the long curve, past the dripping overhang, Shan stepped behind a screen of laurel branches. Where was Isaiah?

She parted the wet leaves trying to see the next bus stop through the downpour. It would be just like him to get on the bus anyway. Thinking he would fight their school's nastiest bullies. Thinking he'd be some kind of hero. God! Boys were such a pain.

She couldn't see him, but his dark face could be lost against the rain-darkened tree trunks. She'd never skipped school in her life and if she skipped for his boney ass and he got on the bus anyway—if he survived Gary and Matt's beating—she'd finish him off herself.

A hiss announced the bus slowing at the road to Shan's house. Her heart thundered. She gave herself a mental shake. She was seventeen. She didn't even *have* to go to school. She needed to chill.

After a short wait, the bus slid beyond the dense undergrowth and Shan watched the passing faces. Distorted by the rain streaked windows, they looked like Van Gogh paintings; pale, twisted and unreal—from another world. Shan crossed her fingers and watched the vehicle approach Isaiah's little white house. The bus inched to a stop.

She imagined Isaiah watching behind his mother's lace curtain, weighing the certainty of punishment for skipping school against the threat of Matt and Gary. She squeezed her eyes shut. *Just stay put.*

Finally, the driver seemed to accept Isaiah's absence, gunning the engine with a roar. As soon as the red lights disappeared around the next curve, Shan slipped from her hiding place.

Granny Kat wouldn't have noticed whether Shan got on the bus. Granny wouldn't be looking up at the road. No doubt, she'd be pouring her second glass of Kentucky Deluxe by now. Shan flipped her sodden hair back with one hand and started toward Isaiah's house but the purr of another vehicle forced her to duck behind a stunted pine.

Holding the scratchy branches off her head, she watched the road. The dark, unfamiliar car floated toward her. Then, without signaling, it turned onto the dirt road leading down to Granny's house.

Shan stood up, catching her hair and clothing on the prickly pine. Who'd be visiting her granny? No one had written or visited for as long as Shan could remember. Her father, Granny 's only child, had rested for thirteen years in his hillside grave right beside her mother. As far as Shan knew, Granny had neither friend nor other relative.

The driver had taken the turn deliberately. The sleek machine rolled to stop in the yard, bumper almost touching the single porch step. A woman emerged from the car. The woman's short hair, high heels and red, pencil skirt shouted "Big City." Her dark hair was cut in a sharp wedge, bangs falling over perfectly arched brows, the kind available in expensive salons somewhere beyond the hills.

Shan held her breath. Granny came out of the house and stood, arms crossed, in the doorway right between the pile of throwing rocks and the upturned washtub. Granny didn't pick up a rock and she didn't yell at the woman to get off her property. She just stood still. Not typical Granny behavior, at all.

Clutching a black case under her left arm, the stranger stepped gingerly across the muddy yard, her nose wrinkling, and walked right onto the porch. Granny turned and stomped through the front door, leaving it open. The city woman's crimson lips curled in a mocking grin and she followed Granny inside.

A chill lifted the hair on the back of Shan's neck. She desperately wanted to slip back to the house. But, she'd promised Isaiah she'd be over as soon as the bus left.

She *had* to go to Isaiah. Groaning, she fought her panic, jerked her clothing free of the branches and stalked the rest of the way to Isaiah's house.

Before she could knock, the door flew open and Isaiah grabbed her arm, pulling her inside. "Mom's going to *kill* me!"

"Yeah, but it'll be a lot less painful than what Gary and Matt have in mind!"

Isaiah's strength always surprised Shan. How could such a skinny boy hide so much muscle? Maybe Isaiah would be a large man someday. Right now, though, despite the fact he was nearly a foot taller than Shan, beneath his skin, his bones looked as delicate as a bird's.

3

Which is why *she* had to keep him from getting himself killed.

Shan dropped her book bag on the floor and scraped her shoes against the stiff rug by the door. Marie Farris kept her house spotlessly clean. Muddy tracks on the polished wood floor wouldn't help Isaiah's case when his mother got home.

"If you'd just tell your mom what's going on, I bet she'd understand." In the year since Marie had moved back from Chicago, Shan had grown to like her. Granny said it took a mighty stupid woman to bring a half-black child back to the hills. Shan thought it took a very courageous woman to stand against ignorance and do the right thing for her son.

"Yeah, she'd understand alright. She'd send me to Chattanooga to live with Aunt Jolene." Isaiah trudged into the living room.

Starved as always, Shan downed a handful of peanuts from a jar on the side table and, dropping onto the couch, knees first, leaned her head against the window, shoving the nuts into her mouth all at once. She should be able to see her house.

"She'll probably ship me off anyway." Isaiah exhaled.

Because of the rain and the light behind her, Shan could see nothing but a transparent reflection of her own pale face. She ran her fingers through her hair, pulling dark strands off her forehead. Catching the long, wet mass in one hand, she tried to twist it into a knot, but it wouldn't stay. "Hmmm."

You're not listening!" Isaiah pushed her. "What you looking at? Oh, Lord, the bus isn't coming back is it?"

"God, Isaiah!" Shan turned around to face the boy. "It wouldn't come back *that* way *that* fast!"

Isaiah laughed. "Sorry. Mom's blonde, you know. I must've inherited some of it. I just know I am going to be grounded until I am thirty!"

"I know those boys will hurt you. Bad."

"I can't stay home forever, Shan. Eventually, Mom's going to get called." His nostrils flared and his eyes narrowed. For just a moment, he seemed much older than fifteen. "Maybe, once they beat me up, they'll leave me alone."

"Isaiah, listen to me." Shan looked directly into his brown eyes, "Those boys will kill you."

Isaiah shook his head. "You're just getting all worked up."

"This is the hills. People get killed. Nobody does anything."

Isaiah looked away, his mouth tightening. "I guess I'll have to go to Chattanooga."

"You won't. We'll figure something out." Shan crossed the room to the small side window and tried to lean over the antique writing desk to look at her house.

"Are you expecting the cavalry or something?"

Shan glanced over her shoulders. Isaiah's hands were spread in front of him and his brows were drawn together.

She sighed. "There's somebody at my house."

"Oh. No wonder you're worried." Isaiah's rolled his eyes.

"No. *Really*. Think about it. Nobody ever visits Granny. Somebody drove in just after the school bus passed. It's a car I've never seen before."

She swiped the window with her palm. She could see the weathered gray boards of her own porch and the patch of solid black past the blowing weeds. Branches from the two willows at the corner of her yard snapped in the wind, hiding the front porch. Thick clouds obscured the distant hills and patches of mist hung around the lush green mountain backing her house.

"How's this more serious than my situation? Maybe it's some long lost relative? Lottery official? Your Granny's got a secret lover?"

Shan couldn't help laughing. "If Granny had a secret lover, he'd be too blind to drive."

"Or, if he fits with your granny, too drunk!" Isaiah laughed with her. Then, his voice cracked and he stopped laughing.

A mantle of dread settled over Shan. "It's a woman anyway."

Clearing his throat, Isaiah said, "Go on. Go check it out, Shan." He looked away, squaring his shoulders, "Shiz, girl. I don't need no babysitter."

"I'll be right back." Shan crossed the room and opened the door. "I'll just sneak up to the kitchen and see what's going on. I don't want to get caught skipping."

Shan circled behind Isaiah's house, grimacing at the mud seeping into her shoes. The weather had been crazy lately, hot as the desert one day, raining like they were on the equator the next. Holding tree trunks and rocks, she walked along the hillside to crouch beneath her kitchen window. The car waited in the driveway. Water coursing over the windows made it impossible to tell whether the vehicle was occupied.

Even in the coldest weather, Shan kept the kitchen window cracked open to vent the endless smoke from her grandmother's cigarette habit. Shan crouched beneath the sill, her hands splayed against the wall, listening. The strange woman spoke with a northern accent.

"I know who she is, Katherine."

"It don't matter what you think you know." Granny pounded the table.

"I know it won't take much to prove you're no relation to her." *Her?* Who were they talking about? Shan's blood roared in her ears. She could barely hear.

"Get the hell out of my house!" A chair scraped.

"You can't order me around, old woman. You know what she is. I would prefer things to be done quietly and smoothly. I don't want to take her by force, but, mark my words, I will."

"I raised her!" Granny's bellow sent shivers down Shan's spine. They were talking about her!

"Yes. You've wasted a lot of precious time, Katherine. You're too damn drunk to realize what you had. Did you think you could hide her forever?"

"Fuck you." Something crashed to the floor. "You'll have to kill me to get to her."

"Whatever it takes."

Shan gasped. Footsteps clicked across the room.

"You don't scare me." A chair tumbled. Glass broke. Granny's boots thudded out of the kitchen.

7

The unmistakable explosion of a shotgun sounded from the front of the house. Shan jumped, banging her head against the window frame. She fell backward. Before she righted herself in the slippery mud, the screen door slammed. An engine rumbled, tires growled in the drive and dirt pelted the house as the stranger wheeled her car and sped up the hill.

Heart beating so hard her chest hurt, maintaining balance with her fingers on the unpainted outer window sill, Shan scanned the kitchen. The galvanized water bucket blocked her view. She moved sideways, looking past the stained white cotton tablecloth on the water table. She saw the bare lath ceiling and the cracked, unpainted sheet-rock on the other side of the kitchen. The cityscapes calendar she'd put up in April hung crooked on the wall.

Shan raised herself more. Gaze traveling down the wall, she took in the upturned dishpan, still draped with the dishrag she'd used that morning and the frayed, cane-backed chair against the wall where she'd left it.

Angling sideways, aligning her sight with a weak ray of light from behind her, Shan saw that a spreading liquid had pooled, darkening the bare plank floor.

Screw it. She couldn't breathe. She could explain skipping later. She had to check on Granny. Pushing the window all the way open, Shan hoisted herself into the kitchen, scowling at the muddy trail she left on the window frame.

One of Granny's crystal whiskey glasses, a gift from Shan's father, lay in shards on the wet floor. The Formica kitchen table had been knocked askew, its far edge almost blocking the narrow doorway between the dining room and the hall. The jar holding Shan's wildflowers had fallen and the dirty water described an elongated comma in the center of the table. The fifth of Kentucky Deluxe, still half full, had scooted to one side.

Granny's chair stood near the water table in its usual place. The smell of gunpowder wafted from the front of the house. Stepping with care, Shan skirted the table to enter the hall.

She'd meant to replace the burned-out light bulb the previous winter, but now, the hall was dim. She put her hand against the tar paper wall to keep from stumbling. Granny hated people seeing inside her house from the road, so a heavy quilt hung over the front window. Shan couldn't see the corner with Granny's rocker. Fingertips trailing the rough wall, she moved forward.

"Ah!" Granny shot up from the rocking chair, rooting Shan with the shotgun. "What are you doin' home?"

CHAPTER TWO

Shan leaned against the door frame, worried her trembling legs might give way. "Who was that?"

Granny lowered the gun, settling it across her knees. The long, black barrel seemed oddly appropriate against the weathered gray of the cotton dress she wore. She pulled a cigarette from the pack in her faded apron pocket.

"You're supposed to be at school." Granny's hands were shaking so badly she couldn't light her cigarette. "Don't I get no privacy?"

"You were talking about me." Shan crossed the room and snatched the cigarette from her grandmother's fingers. She tossed it into the empty coal bucket. "You have to tell me. You owe me that."

Glaring at Shan, Granny pulled out another cigarette.

"I don't have to do nothin'." She straightened her shoulders and lit the cigarette. "I don't owe you a damn thing. You owe me."

Granny's wrinkled face, surrounded by the colorless scarf she always wore, had become a stranger's face. Her brown eyes, beneath bristled steel gray brows, were unreadable. Her lips formed a straight line, expressing nothing but iron will.

She pulled a half-pint from another pocket, unscrewed the lid and took a long drink. She rested the bottle on the flat side of the gun stock.

"I raised you. I fed you. A lot. I sent you to school. What do I get in return?"

"I didn't ask you to raise me!"

"You didn't leave, neither!" Granny scowled. "Your mother married my son when she was pregnant. For all I knowed, you was his."

Shan's words, as she formed them, seem to come from far away "I'm not?"

"Oh, David told me. He was a good man. A real good man." Granny's eyes filled and she took another pull on her bottle. After swallowing, she cleared her throat. "We're in big trouble, Shanleigh, and you do owe me. It's what your mother would've wanted."

Mind blank, Shan crossed the room, stopping automatically to straighten the braided rug. She stepped behind the cold heating stove and lifted the heavy wooden stool, placing it inches from Granny's knees, sitting where she could stare directly into Granny's eyes.

"None of this makes sense."

Shan wanted to ask questions but she didn't know what they were. She didn't even know what to call the woman she'd always known as Granny.

"I can't fight her, see?" Granny's watery, bloodshot gaze locked Shan's. "I ain't got no legal claim, but it's right." The old woman tipped her head back, swallowed another shot and glared at Shan. "Your Mom chose my David as her champion!"

Shan blinked. The word "champion" sounded wrong coming out of Granny's mouth.

The old woman laughed, shaking her head. "I don't even know how to say what you are. Don't know the right words. It weren't supposed to be me."

For a moment, the floor seemed to tilt. Shan put her palm against her forehead. No, the room around her was right but nothing about the conversation seemed real. "What I am? Who was supposed to tell me what?"

"That's the thing, ain't it?" Granny barked a caustic laugh. "They's two ways of lookin' at things, two stories, and you was only supposed to hear one."

Granny took a drag on her cigarette and started coughing. Her face reddened and she slapped her chest. Shan half rose to get a glass of water as she always did when Granny's coughing got the best of her. Granny's hand caught her knee. She squeezed hard enough to make Shan wince. Granny's talon-like nails were sharp, digging in through Shan's jeans. Shan settled back on the stool, waiting.

Granny hacked a few more times, sucking air between coughs. During the entire episode, her eyes never left Shan's. Finally, the old woman's grasp relaxed and she slumped back into her chair.

"You have to help me." She croaked, looking away.

"Help you what?" The words came out as a whisper. Shan slid off the stool. She knelt beside the rocker. Her stomach growled and her face heated. She didn't know whether to be angry, scared or exasperated. Her thoughts formed with agonizing slowness. She couldn't remember one hug, one affectionate gesture from Granny. Yet she'd never been without food or clothes. She even had a computer and the internet. Come to think of it, she'd always had everything she needed—except freedom.

Gradually, one idea rose to the surface. This woman wanted Shan enough to hide her for seventeen years. To fight for her now. *But why?*

"Help me save you." Granny's tone carried an unusual, desperate note. Her distant gaze seemed to penetrate the far wall.

"Save *me?* From what?"

"From them."

CHAPTER THREE

Watching Granny's face, Shan's fingers curled into fists. Her nails dug into her palms. "Them who?"

Granny sighed. She took a long drag on her cigarette and chased it with a swig from her half-empty bottle.

Shan pulled herself up and took her seat back on the stool. She'd often wanted to shake Granny in the past. She wanted to, now, more than ever.

"Coral Morgan and her Circle. Coral's your Mom's sister."

That city bitch was her aunt? Shan mentally compared the one photograph she had of her mother with the elegant stranger. Long ago, Shan had memorized every detail of Amelia's photo. Surely her mother couldn't be related to Coral Morgan.

In the yellowed snapshot on Shan's nightstand, Amelia Amos faced the camera with a slight smile . Her hair, dark like Coral Morgan's, like Shan's, cascaded over her thin shoulders, almost obscuring the butterfly sleeves of her soft, floral dress. Her heart-shaped face, devoid of makeup, seemed innocent compared to Coral's. Shan couldn't imagine Coral Morgan wearing jewelry like the Yin-Yang symbol hanging from a ribbon around Amelia's neck or the braided friendship bracelet on her slender wrist. "I can't believe that woman's related to my mother."

"They are different." Granny nodded, "but they're sisters, too. Blood and blood bound. But for all the right in your mom, Coral Morgan has twice as much wrong. Didn't realize it at first."

"At first?"

Shan couldn't wrap her head around the situation. Life had always been centered right here, at Granny's house. Seasons turned on the hills. Stark gray and forbidding in winter, the mountains changed to soft green, dogwood white and purple in the spring. Undulating shades of velvet green in the summer morphed to fiery crimson, deep purple, amber and copper in autumn. By the time she started school, Shan could not only read but she could hoe potatoes, train beans on cornstalks, gather eggs and catch crappie, bluegill and brownies with an improvised fishing pole.

She could shoot tin cans off the washtub and she could make gravy and biscuits. She remembered standing on a stool to wash dishes in water heated on the wood stove by a fire she made. She knew every nook and cranny of Granny's hillside yard and the densely wooded mountain behind the house.

Prior to starting school, Shan rarely saw anyone but Granny. The frontier nurses came every year, sometimes on horses, sometimes in their green jeeps, to give Shan medical check-ups and provide vaccinations. They prodded Shan and held her arm with ice cold fingers, saying little to her and even less to Granny who glowered at them from the corner of the kitchen. At least Granny's antisocial attitude made sense, now.

Granny finished off her bottle and straightened in her chair. "When I met 'em, Amelia and Coral, they was the strangest people I'd ever seen. They showed me things. Things you wouldn't believe."

Shan leaned forward, curious and afraid. Granny's eyes were bright brown marbles, her expression unfamiliar.

"Like what?"

Granny sucked her upper lip. "I seen your Mom fade into the wall an' disappear."

Spine tingling, Shan stiffened. "That's impossible."

"I ain't no liar, Shanleigh."

"It had to be a trick."

"I aint no fool neither." Granny spat. "Them women could float in the air. They could hide in plain sight. They could bring clouds or sunshine. Make you see people not there, like ghosts, and hear music when they wasn't none."

Shan could tell Granny believed everything she said. It had to be some kind of drunken hallucination. But Shan had never known Granny to hallucinate. She'd never known her to be fanciful in any way.

"That's…" She clenched her teeth, reconsidering her response. She wouldn't get more information by arguing. "That's shocking.

"Didn't expect you to believe it." Granny put her shotgun on the floor beside her chair. "If I raised you right, you don't believe it. But it's true."

Granny exhaled loudly, closing her eyes. She sighed again and opened them. "I got to give you something. Help me up."

Shan jumped to assist Granny. Just as she had so many times before. Except this woman was no longer her grandmother. Had never been her grandmother.

Granny levered herself to a standing position and pushed away Shan's arm.

"Wait here." Granny pointed at the floor and left the room.

"I probably shouldn't." She mumbled as she entered the hall. "But if I don't, they ain't no hope."

Shan heard the slam of Granny's bedroom door and the creak of the old wardrobe drawer. There was quiet for a few seconds and the wardrobe drawer squeaked again. Shan's thoughts were too disorganized to sort, so she just listened to Granny move through their little house.

When she came back into the room, Granny's fist was clenched inside her apron pocket. "I was s'posed to give this to you. Rather hold it 'til David could give it to you. But he died and there's them two schools o' thought. I just didn't know what to do."

Granny stretched out her hand, palm up, and opened her fist one finger at a time. Shan inhaled sharply. Nested in the well of Granny's palm, out of place on nicotine stained whirls and wrinkles, lay a twist of golden ring with several large, colored stones. A ruby against a topaz formed an acorn and five emeralds formed an oak leaf. The stones looked genuine. The gold, though, was thick and unevenly formed.

"Don't just stand there. Take it." Granny thrust her hand out, twisting her wrist. Shan caught the falling band in her right hand. The weight of it surprised her. She almost dropped it.

Without thinking, she steadied The Circlet with her left forefinger, and, of its own accord, the ring slid past her knuckle. Instantly, the band heated. Crying out, Shan tried to pull it off.

It wouldn't move. She pulled harder, panicking.

"It ain't coming off." Granny punctuated her words with a single shake of her head, "Not long as you're livin'."

CHAPTER FOUR

Shan stared, open mouthed, conscious of the ring's heat traveling up her arm. This had to be a nightmare.

Granny watched for a moment, arm's crossed, mouth tight. Then she shook her head. "We thought we could keep you from it."

She turned away and picked up her shotgun. "Thinking we could save the world, we was just as much fools as them thinking they could bring back the dead."

It had to be a dream. Who used the phrase "save the world?" Shan's stomach growled and she placed her hand against it. Did people get hungry in dreams? "Wait. What are you trying to tell me?"

Granny looked back, her expression level. "Right now, I done told you enough."

"You've told me nothing." Shan pulled at the ring. "Why did you give me this? Why won't it come off?"

"I got to get a drink." Granny left the room, asking, over her shoulder, "Ain't you got something you should be doin'?"

Shan stood, feeling the strangeness of the ring's weight on her finger, the unreality of the day. She wondered if she was in shock. She took a step toward the kitchen and stopped. Experience had taught her she would get nothing out of Granny by arguing or by begging.

She'd promised Isaiah she'd come back. She picked up her book bag and went out the front door.

The rain had stopped, but water dripped from every weed and branch Shan passed. The forest had changed, somehow and Shan kept hearing snatches of unfamiliar music like a choir practicing on a distant hill. But when she stood still, trying to locate the direction, the song faded into the wind. By the time she'd made her way across the hill parallel to the valley between her house and Isaiah's, her clothes were soaking wet and she was certain she was losing her mind.

A little path ran from the briars at the edge of Marie's property, down to her sagging porch. Shan walked between the brown ranks of dead marigolds and slipped through the back door.

"Hello?"

Nothing.

"Hello?" She said to the silent house. "It's me."

No response.

Shan lifted a soft towel from a rack between the back door and Marie's white microwave. Splashing water on her face, soaping her hands, she listened for Isaiah. She rubbed her hands and face, relishing the clean, sun dried scent of Marie's towel. Everything at home smelled like smoke.

After devouring a few leftover biscuits on the stove, Shan flipped her head down and wrapped the towel around her hair. Coming back up, she tucked the towel ends behind her right ear.

"What the fu-fuzzle is that?" Isaiah stood in the hall, a holding a metal baseball bat in one hand, pointing at the ring with his other. Before she could answer, he dropped the bat against the wall and crossed the room.

"Let me see that." He caught the band in his long fingers and tugged.

Heat flared across Shan's hand.

She jerked away and Isaiah stumbled back at the same time.

"Damn!" Isaiah blew on his fingers. "What was *that*?"

Shan pulled out a chair and dropped onto it, propping her elbows on the table. "I don't know where to start."

"Start with why you wearing a heat lamp on your finger, girl, and go from there."

She lifted her hand to him. "Try again."

Isaiah leaned away from her, tucking his hand under his other arm and shaking his head. "Uh, no. That burns."

Shan got up and retrieved the damp washcloth she'd just used. Sitting, she tossed it to Isaiah. "Use this."

Shaking his head, Isaiah folded the rag several times. "This better not be a trick."

"Please." Shan's voice cracked. Isaiah's shoulders stiffened and he grabbed the ring with the cloth. Heat spread up her arm, enough to get her attention but not enough to burn her.

Grimacing, Isaiah pulled so hard Shan thought her finger would come out of its socket.

"It's no use." She said.

Isaiah let go, dropping the cloth on the table between them. A tendril of smoke curled from the material and Shan noted the scorch marks in the shape of an oak cluster.

"Let me see your hand." She reached across the table and grabbed Isaiah's wrist. Pulling his fingers open, she saw angry marks on his palm.

"I'm sorry." She touched his wrist with her forefinger and he yanked his hand away as if her touch burned, too.

"I'm fine." His eyes were darker than usual and he scowled at her. "Butter or soap won't help, either, I'm sure. Why'd you put it on, anyway?"

"You won't believe me."

Isaiah glanced at the burnt rag and raised one eyebrow. "I might."

"That woman. Coral Morgan. She's my aunt on my mother's side. It turns out I'm not related to Granny."

"I thought this was going to be bad news."

Shan glared.

"I'm sorry." He sighed. "Go on."

She told him about David being Amelia's champion and that Granny believed Coral and Amelia could do magic.

"Magic?" Isaiah snorted. "That's bull. Tricks. Illusions. Some shizzle like that."

"Granny said they could walk through walls and float in the air."

"Like David Copperfield?"

"She believes it, Isaiah." Shan tilted her hand at him. "And there's this. Is this a trick?"

22

"Next you'll be telling me you got a Hogwarts letter or," He nodded at the ring, "you need a fast plane to Mordor."

"I'm serious!" Tears blurred Shan's vision and she kicked the table leg. "Coral wants to take me away!"

"That's stupid." Isaiah pounded the table. "You're seventeen. You're a senior. She can't make you go. Can she?"

"I don't know." Shan held up the ring. Even in the wan light of the kitchen, the stones sparkled with convincing brilliance. "I could be able to ask for emancipation or something, but," Shan recalled the calm certainty in Coral's threat to take Shan over Granny's dead body, "I don't know what she's capable of."

Granny had seemed certain that Shan's relatives could perform magic. Granny did drink quite a lot, but she'd always been a grounded, no nonsense kind of person. Still, if it hadn't been for Coral Morgan's presence and the ring, Shan would've believed Granny was going crazy.

Isaiah watched her with hooded eyes. A muscle at the back of his jaw pulsed. For a second, Shan wondered if he knew what she was thinking. She went cold at the thought of him believing she was some kind of freak.

"I don't want you to go, Shan." He spoke slowly, his voice husky. His luminous eyes made Shan's face heat.

"Granny wouldn't tell me anything more." She put her left hand under the table. She didn't want the ring between her and Isaiah. "Maybe she has something in mind."

Isaiah said nothing, then, exhaled. "Do you want to stay with your granny—I guess she ain't your granny, though. Do you want to stay with her, anyway?"

With her right forefinger, Shan traced the lighter whorls in the table's golden grain. It was a slight distraction.

The browns and creams of the wood pattern reminded Shan of the sink-pools in the Laurel Fork River. They were only visible when the river was muddy. There was no sign of danger when the water was quiet. Every few years someone, a child, usually, would try to swim in the inviting, glassy green pool only to be sucked under and drowned. For a while afterward, everyone would demand signs be posted but there were never any signs.

"This is my home. If I wanted to go with Coral, I wouldn't be over here, would I?" Shan ran her palm over the glossy surface of Marie's table, but, of course, the whorls didn't brush away. "I mean, yeah, I want to leave someday, but not now. Not being forced out like this."

"We'll think of something." Isaiah covered her right hand with his larger one. Her pale fingertips were just visible under his mahogany skin and the warmth of contact was comforting without pressure. Usually, when a boy tried to hold her hand, it was a short prelude to something else.

They both jumped when the phone rang. Isaiah leaped to his feet, knocking his chair over.

"Don't." Shan slid half across the table to catch his hand. "You're not home, remember?"

"Oh. Right." Isaiah grimaced. "Are we skipping tomorrow, too?"

"I have an idea." Shan licked her lips. In the light of the morning's discoveries, she'd forgotten about her plan, "But you've got to give me a day to work it out."

"Meaning?" One of Isaiah's eyebrows went up.

"I go to school tomorrow..."

"But I don't." Isaiah cut her off. He slumped over the table. "I swear, you're going to get me killed trying to save me."

"I need time to convince Matt..." Shan hesitated. It had all made sense last night. She'd pretend she was interested in Matt, making sure he understood she wouldn't date anyone who wasn't nice to Isaiah. Matt was stupid and conceited enough to believe her, and whatever Matt decided, Gary did.

"I need time to convince Matt to be nice."

Isaiah lurched back, his face contorted in fury. "Oh, hell no. You're not pretending to like him to protect me."

"He'll kill you!" Shan stood, trembling.

"I don't care." Isaiah's eyes were narrow and his mouth twisted. "I'm not pimping you out."

"What do you think you're going to do?" Shan wanted to kick him but she didn't dare touch him. "It's nothing. It's not like I'll really hook up with him."

"So you'll convince him you like him without letting him touch you?"

Of course she couldn't, but what could Matt expect on campus? "Oh, for heaven's sake. He'll kiss me. Big deal."

"No." Isaiah turned his back on her, wrapping his arms around himself, hunching his shoulders.

25

"Do you know about Arlo Hoskins?"

Isaiah nodded.

Two years earlier, within days of people discovering Arlo liked boys instead of girls, he was found hanged in Black Pine woods. The sherrif's office had called it suicide, but everyone knew there were rope burns on his ankles and that his hands had been duct-taped behind his back. Matt's uncle was a deputy. "They'll kill you, too."

"I'll tell Mom I want to go stay with Aunt Jolene. I won't go back to school and I'll leave tomorrow or the next day."

"I don't want you to." Tears stung Shan's eyes. She tried to imagine life without him. Before Isaiah, her best friends had been in books. She got along with people at school, but she lived with crazy Kat Amos. It didn't take long for new students to learn Shan Amos wouldn't spend the night, wouldn't go to parties and would flatly refuse all dates. She chatted and kept in loose contact with casual friends on Facebook, but she'd always been an outsider, until Isaiah moved next door.

"Go home, Shan." Isaiah didn't turn around. After a few moments, realizing Isaiah needed time to consider his options, Shan left through the kitchen door.

The clouds had parted and the meadow sparkled in the sunlight. Queen Anne's lace, milkweed, cornflowers and bluegrass swayed in the soft breeze, sporting glittering droplets like jewels. She almost turned to call Isaiah outside, but he probably wouldn't come. She started forward, glancing up at her own house but a movement at the edge of the forest caught her eye. She whipped her head around, seeing only the dark shadows between the trees. Goosebumps spread up her arms. She could've sworn there had been someone there.

She shrugged. All of it—Isaiah, the ring and the crazy talk about her mom and Coral—was actually getting to her. She pushed through the weeds, spraying water as she went. It was possible Granny had come up with a plan. Or, maybe, she'd be drunk enough to be more forthcoming but not drunk enough to pass out.

Shan went through the back door, into the kitchen and found Granny slumped over the table, snoring. The spilled water had been cleaned up and the jar Shan used for a vase stood on the side board.

Shan helped herself to a drink from the water bucket and, taking peanut butter and a loaf of bread with her, headed to her attic bedroom. Maybe she could find something on the internet about emancipation. She wasn't ready to leave the hills, just yet. Of course, if Isaiah left…

It wasn't like she hadn't planned to leave. The acceptance letter from Boston College, hidden under her mattress, gave the lie to any different pretense. But that was a year away, a year to plan and to arrange. Not leaving now with some stranger.

She set up her laptop on the battered dresser which served as her desk and vanity. While she waited for the computer to start, she stared her reflection, looking for signs of magic. Of something different, anyway. The face gazing back from the spotted mirror, though, was the same pale oval she saw every morning, except that her eyes were bloodshot and her hair hung over her shoulders in tangled strands. She grimaced, her heavy, dark brows and wide mouth emphasizing the expression. She stuck her tongue out. She liked having her mother's river green eyes, but why couldn't she have inherited Amelia's delicate features?

She glanced at her mother's picture across the room, wishing she'd gotten a closer look at Coral. The thought of that woman made Shan hot all over. She'd spoken as though Shan were a piece of property.

Shan's stomach growled. She slapped together a few peanut butter sandwiches, punched a question into Google and ate while the search engine brought up the links.

Her research returned the unwelcome news that to become an emancipated minor, she'd have to prove she was self-supporting. She dug deeper, but found no viable answers.

"Really!" She said out loud, snapping her computer shut. She'd just have to tell Coral Morgan she wouldn't go. What could the woman do? Force her into the car? All for the nine months until Shan turned eighteen?

She took the remainder of the peanut butter and bread downstairs. If Granny was awake, she'd tell her she had no intention leaving. Shan put the food away and found her grandmother in the living room, smoking in the semi-darkness.

"I'm not going anywhere with Coral Morgan." Shan announced, curling on the end of the small couch beneath the window.

"Well," Granny drawled. "As far as I'm concerned you don't have to. Don't know what she's got up her sleeve though. Your Mom should've signed guardianship to David and he should've signed it to me."

She puffed and stared at the dark corner behind the stove as if she were addressing someone hiding in the shadow. She went on, "Didn't want no paper trails, though. Thought she'd never find us."

Shan nodded her understanding of why Granny had kept her so isolated. But she didn't have time to dwell on it. Too many questions vied for satisfaction.

"What did Coral mean about you not knowing what you had?"

"You heard that, huh?" A sliver of light from the edge of the quilt illuminated Granny's face. She frowned, clamping her teeth down on her cigarette.

"I heard everything."

"You take after your Mom." Granny exhaled loudly. "You able to do like them."

"Do like them?" Shan chewed her lower lip. "Oh, you mean magic?"

She almost said *bullshit*, but if she did, Granny would close right up and she'd learn nothing. And there was definitely more than Granny had shared so far.

"That doesn't make sense. You said you saw Coral and my mother perform magic. Why would she think you didn't know I was…like them?"

Granny ground out her cigarette in the tin ashtray on her side table. She took a swig from her pint bottle, lit another cigarette and grunted with her first, smoky exhalation.

"You expect me to know what that crazy woman's thinkin'?" She snorted, rocking back and forth.

29

Shan recognized the stubborn set of Granny's jaw. Normally, she'd have walked away. But she couldn't help trying again. "Granny. Please, tell me what this is all about? I need to know."

Granny took two more puffs and shook her head once. "If we lucky, you don't need to know a damn thing."

"And if we're not?"

"If frogs had wings their butts never would touch the ground." Granny shook her head again and lifted her bottle. "Ain't nodody, not even Coral Morgan, can hurt you with magic while you got that ring on."

Granny took a long pull and sighed, closing her eyes. Shan waited, watching the red hand on the simple clock above the door move with faint clicks. Granny just rocked with a slowing rhythm and, soon, her breathing turned to snores.

Sitting in the dark room, Shan realized she would get nothing from Granny. Goaded by a surge of anger, she pushed off the couch, whirling, balancing with her hand. She glanced down at the ring, almost falling when she noted a glow within the topaz. She stood staring at it. The light pulsed, moving around the stone in an irregular pattern. The hair on her arm stood up and her breath stilled. It was as if some trapped, living creature paced within the gem.

She didn't doubt Isaiah was still upset, but she had to talk to someone. Holding her hand in front of her, she stepped off the porch into the steamy heat of the afternoon. Despite the heavy air, she ran across the meadow, keeping the white boards of her best friend's house in view. Snatches of faint, wordless music rose and fell with her steps, heightening her unease. When she found Isaiah's front door locked, she kicked it hard enough to hurt her toes.

"Let me in." She said, through clenched teeth, when Isaiah opened the door. Water blurring her eyes made her angry and itchy. "Can I please have a coke?"

She dropped into the armchair Isaiah's mother used, and stared at the blank TV screen while he left the room and returned with the cold soda.

"Close the curtains and look at this thing with me." In her heart of hearts, she knew she shouldn't be ordering Isaiah around, but she couldn't give him time to resume the morning's discussion.

"Nag, nag, nag." Isaiah muttered as he drew the heavy drapes, turning the bright living room into a dim parlor. "Why the new drama?"

Shan leaned forward, flattening her palm on the coffee table. "Look at this."

Isaiah sat on the edge of the couch, bowing his head over her hand. He jumped back. "Shizzle!"

"Is it some kind of computer chip?" Shan lifted her hand toward his face.

Isaiah shrank back, but his eyes narrowed and he watched the stone for a few minutes.

"I don't think so." He looked up, "The movement doesn't repeat like a program would."

"That's what I thought." Shan watched the glow settle into the upper curve of the amber stone. "Look. It's like a caged animal. It's been pacing and now it's going to sleep."

"It could be a long program." Isaiah tilted his head. "You can get some powerful processing, now in miniature electronics."

Shan rested her hand on the chair arm where she and Isaiah could observe the ring. She had a sinking feeling there was no computer chip, but she had to make sure. The spark didn't move and her gaze flickered to Isaiah's face. His eyes were bloodshot and his thick lashes were damp.

Her heart lurched. His life was changing, too, and she was so busy with her own concerns, she'd forgotten his. She whispered. "I'm sorry."

"Me, too." He looked into her eyes for a few seconds, before his gaze dropped to her hand. "I know you were just trying to help."

"I wish I had some other way of helping." Shan spoke to the top of his head.

"I can't see another way." Isaiah glanced up, "You know, I never wanted Mom to come here. I'm not really clueless. I read about the hills and how some people think. But Mom was so relieved when Gran left her the house."

Shan stared his face, throat tight. She wished she did have magic, so she could stop Matt, Gary and all the others like him from hurting her friend.

"Chicago was awful." Isaiah continued, watching the ring. "The only place we could afford to live, we had to step over crack heads to get to the bus stop. Sometimes, we sat in our apartment just looking at each other 'cause it sounded like Afghanistan outside."

"I'm sorry." Shan whispered, watching his face. She could see the scared little boy in there. The injustice

32

made her furious, the fact she could do nothing about it made her desperate. "I wish it were different. But people here take a lot longer to change than the rest of the world."

He looked up, his narrow face hardening. "I don't think anywhere is that different."

"What do you mean?"

"I got hated on in Chicago 'cause my Mom's white. I get hated on here 'cause my daddy's black. She thought I'd get killed in Chicago." Throwing his head back, he barked a short laugh. "You say I'll get killed here."

"You will." Shan whispered. But Isaiah was no longer listening. He stared at the light which had resumed flickering around the topaz.

She watched him study the movement, listening to the ticks of the settling house, the rustle of a squirrel on the roof and the thudding of her own heart. Finally, he raised his head.

"It's not a computer program."

What now? She tucked her hand under her leg. Isaiah leaned back on the couch, a small frown between his eyes.

Before she could ask what he was thinking, he stood quickly and went upstairs. He came back wearing work gloves, holding wire pliers in one hand and a screw driver in the other. "Let me see that ring again."

"You sure?" Shan lifted her hand.

"I'm ready." He raised his gloved hands.

He pushed her palm against the chair, latched onto the ring with the pliers and touched the screwdriver to the edge of the topaz. Light flared from the ring and Isaiah's tools went flying.

Shan jumped to her feet, catching his arm. "Are you alright?"

He pulled away and nodded. "For now, but that screwdriver broke my third grade picture. Mom's going to shoot me."

"I thought you hated that picture."

"I do, but Mom loves it. Anyway, it's just the frame." He glanced at Shan's left hand. "I don't know how we're going to figure out what that is."

"Don't worry about it." Shan fell back into her seat. "I'll find out from Granny, eventually."

"You better tell me." Isaiah retrieved the tools and emptied the broken glass from the picture frame before sitting back down. When he did, he ran his hands over his face at sat scowling at the covered window.

"Are you thinking about leaving?" She had to ask.

"I was wondering what could make that light in that rock." He sighed. "And, yeah, I was thinking about leaving. If I believe you, and I guess I do, I don't see as I have a choice. I'll sure miss Mom, though."

Shan stuck her tongue out at him, pretending a levity she certainly didn't feel.

"And others, too, of course." Isaiah grinned, but the corners of his mouth trembled.

"Mr. Wilson?" Mr. Wilson was the biology teacher who'd convinced the school board to let Isaiah do his freshman and sophomore classes at the same time, so he'd graduate a year early.

"Yeah," he laughed, "but definitely not Coach Baker. He's still mad at me for being the only black boy he ever heard of who can't play basketball."

Silence stretched between them, heavy with half formed thoughts. Shan sighed.

"They'll see how smart you are in Chattanooga, too." She forced a smile. "You'll be telling me all about some trig or chemistry teacher there, and probably hooking up with some Tennessee belle before summer."

"I won't be hooking up with anybody." Isaiah's stared hard at her and looked away. "And you ain't got a phone. How're we going to talk?"

"I'll come over and call from here. Plus, we'll chat on Skype every day until you come to Boston, too."

"That's almost two years." He blinked.

"I know." And she couldn't even guarantee she'd still be in Salt Creek in a few days. She opened her mouth to tell him what she'd discovered about emancipation, but decided it was too much.

"You'll have to tell your mom something about why you, all of a sudden, want to go to Chattanooga."

"I been thinking about that." Isaiah rubbed his palms up and down his thighs. "I guess I'll tell her part of the truth. I'll say some boys been trying to start stuff and that's why I skipped today. I'll say it made me realize that I want to be somewhere I can kick with some bros."

Shan smiled. Isaiah's vocabulary was usually as good as her own, but he thought he stood out less when he talked like his peers. Shan liked being different, but, she guessed, for Isaiah, it was a lot easier to be as much like everyone else as possible.

"You got any more ideas about that ring?" Isaiah asked.

"I think Granny might, but I've got to get her to tell me." Shan stood. Catching Granny in her lucid moments was normally harder and harder as the day progressed.

Isaiah followed her to the front door, the corners of his mouth turned down, his eyes moist. Shan turned away, pushing the door open. If she stayed one more minute, she'd burst into tears.

"You coming back today?" Isaiah called as she stepped off the porch.

"Just don't leave before I do." She shouted, not looking back.

She could feel his eyes on her until she rounded the corner of his house. She thought she heard the front door close, but it was hard to tell through the buzz of jar flies, crickets and bees. Birds whistled and cried with the insects, their songs interspersed with the strange music she kept hearing.

There it was again. She stopped. Maybe it had something to do with the acoustics of a specific place. No, it was gone. She backed up. Nothing.

A jay crossed over her head and, after he passed, she heard the haunting melody again. She didn't move, but the sound faded as quickly as she detected it. She faced the wood. The melody had seemed to originate on the mountain. Should she investigate?

At the thought of entering the woods, an uncommon sense of dread enveloped her. She took a step forward and the dread increased. No doubt she was letting everything skew her common sense. She knew those woods as well as she knew her own bedroom. She started toward the hill with grim determination, but the band around her forefinger grew warmer the closer she got to the forest's edge. The heat grew from uncomfortable to painful and, shaking her hand to cool it, she stopped walking. She could see faded berries on the briars marking the edge of the meadow, and the tarry bark of the row of pines behind them. A small path went between the bushes, worn by feet crossing the hill long before Shan's birth, but she didn't take it.

She had a bigger mystery to chase. Granny was going to have to tell her about the infernal ring or she'd— she'd threaten never go to school again.

But Granny was in her own bedroom with the door closed. Shan groaned and her stomach grumbled back, reminding her it was time for dinner. There was a time when Granny had done all the cooking, while Shan did the dishes, but, in the past year, Shan had been doing both.

She found some fatback in the refrigerator and sliced two generous helpings. She started the oven and pulled down two cast iron skillets from the pegs over the propane stove Granny had ordered a few years back. While the oven was preheating she slid the meat into one of the pans over a medium flame. Waiting for it to start sizzling, she dropped a few hands full of self-rising flour into the biscuit bowl and added grease from the saver on the stove. When she'd cut the grease in with her fingers, she washed them and got out the jar of milk Charlie Hall left at the mailbox every Saturday morning. A thick layer of cream rested on the top, and Shan felt a twinge of guilt. She used to skim it off to make butter and the buttermilk

Granny loved, but with the college applications, schoolwork and Isaiah, she'd stopped.

She remembered sitting on the porch in the summer, shaking the canning jar full of soured cream, churning butter, while Granny talked about finding and using ginseng, crow's foot, willow bark and other herbs. There'd been a time when Granny would've scolded Shan for shirking her duties, but now, Shan wasn't sure her grandmother noticed she no longer made butter. Marie brought margarine every month with the groceries she picked up for them, so it was possible Granny just didn't care.

Standing at the stove, stirring the gravy, surrounded by familiar smells and sounds, the earlier part of Shan's day seemed like an unpleasant dream. But the ring, stones partially obscured by flour, was evidence that it had all been real. She just couldn't make Coral Morgan and Granny's stories fit the reality of the little kitchen with its chipped Formica counter and galvanized water buckets. Could anything be further from magic?

The gravy thickened and Shan removed it from the flame. As she pulled the biscuits out of the oven with folded flour sacks, she heard the shuffle of Granny's feet.

"Biscuits and gravy, huh?" Not waiting for an answer Granny set the table and poured two glasses of milk. Placing food items with studied casualness, Shan tried not to stare. Granny drinking milk instead of KD for dinner? She took the seat across from her grandmother, heart thumping. Was she about to get an explanation?

"What you doing so long at that boy's house?"

"Just talking." Shan barely refrained from an eye roll. "He's leaving tomorrow or the next day."

"In the middle of the school year?"

Shan nodded.

"What for?" Granny's brows drew together, her eyes suspicious.

"He's moving to Chattanooga."

"Figured he'd leave soon." Granny crumbled a biscuit on her plate and spooned gravy over it. "I'm shocked he lasted this long."

"Isaiah's a genius." An instant surge of fury nearly overwhelmed Shan. The woman had the gall to talk about Isaiah when she'd been drunk as long as Shan could remember?

"Don't get your britches in a bunch." Granny snorted. "People 'round here are like chickens. They see somebody different, they want to peck 'em to death."

"That's true." The anger drained away, all at once, leaving Shan feeling tired. She helped herself to a second biscuit.

Granny concentrated on eating, sipping milk between bites. When Shan began to think the woman was going to say nothing more, she took a deep breath.

"I know," Granny said before Shan could speak, "You want to know about the ring and your family."

"I do." Shan said trying to keep the urgency out of her voice.

"I don't know there's much more I can tell you." Granny patted her apron. She shook her head, removing her hand from her lap. "I don't know nothing about that ring, except it's s'pose to protect you and that once you put it on, it'd stay on long as you lived. Seems to me that's enough for now."

"What does it do?"

"Like I said," Granny finished her milk in a long drink and lit a cigarette. "It protects you from magic."

Granny's voice had the cagey ring to it that said she was hiding something.

"What *else* does it do?" Shan rested her left elbow on the table, holding her hand out so Granny could see the ring.

"I couldn't rightly tell you."

"But it does do something else?"

"Could be." Granny blew smoke out of her nose and mouth. "The likes of Coral Morgan don't take people like me into their confidence."

"But D—David must have." Shan almost said Dad. David Amos had been Dad her whole life, but he wasn't her Dad. Just like Granny wasn't her Grandmother.

"If I think you need to know anything that passed between me and David, I'll tell you."

"I'm old enough to decide what I need to know!" Shan didn't care that she was yelling. "Fifteen years and you couldn't tell me any of this? That I have a father somewhere else? An aunt? That I own a priceless ring with some kind of powers?"

"That I ain't your Granny?"

Shan stared at the woman who'd raised her. A thought slammed into place like a metal door. "You'll always be my Granny."

Granny bowed her head but, after a second, pushed back from the table and left the room.

Shan waited but, when Granny hadn't returned after ten minutes, Shan got up to look for her. Granny was back in the rocker, in the dark, working on a fresh pint. She didn't look up when Shan entered the room.

Settling on the couch, Shan fixed Granny with a glare. "You can't just leave me hanging."

Granny's thin shoulders rose and fell. She kept her face averted.

"I'm not going to leave." Shan said softly.

"You might not have a choice." Granny didn't look at her.

"I'm nearly eighteen. What's she going to do?"

"I wish I knew." Granny sighed. "But, mark my words, she ain't going to let it go without a fight."

"She's fighting on our turf," Shan's laugh sounded nervous to her own ears. "She'll not get much help from the authorities here."

Granny turned to face her, eyes wide, face grim. "Everybody's got a price, and, whatever it is, Coral can afford it."

"Are you saying she can buy me?"

"I was referrin' to our esteemed sheriff, but, you got a price too." Granny sighed again, shaking her head. "We all got one."

"I don't care how much money she has, she's not buying me!" Shan's hands curled into fists.

"Money." Granny snorted, took a drink and puffed her cigarette before continuing. "Don't imagine you could be bought with money, but she's got a talent for knowin' what people *can* be bought with."

"Not me." Shan tossed her head, but a tendril of dread curled in the pit of her stomach. Shan had seen Granny face down rattlesnakes, a bear and a burley, trespassing hunter armed to the teeth. Yet Granny was worried, now.

"Ain't much we can do, girl." Granny's words slurred together, "Except shoot her."

"You can't do that!" Shan meant it to sound like a joke but her voice squeaked.

"Do what I want." Granny's words slurred together, her eyes closed and she nodded.

Shan stomped out of the room and banged a pot onto the water table. It would be different if she was eleven, or even fifteen, but she was almost an adult. She filled the pot with water and put it on the stove to heat. Despite installing a bathroom with a water heater for Shan, Granny wouldn't have running water in the kitchen. Water coming through pipes tasted nasty to her.

Granny! She must've known this was coming. Why hadn't she told Shan?

Scraping the dishes and dropping them onto each other with clinks and clatters, Shan fumed. How was any of this fair?

She'd always obeyed Granny. Where other girls would've thrown fits or run away, Shan just accepted her forced isolation. While her classmates were out partying, going to the mall in London or weekending together, Shan was in her bedroom reading, or quilting by the heating stove in the living room. Even after Marie and Isaiah had moved in, Shan was always home to cook dinner.

Her insides were in a knot by the time she'd tempered the hot water in the dishpan with cold. Her whole life had been a lie and Coral Morgan could show up at any time, demanding Shan leave with her. Shan didn't really believe Granny would shoot her aunt, but there would be trouble when the woman did arrive.

Maybe she could broker a deal with Coral. Visit her on weekends from Boston. Hearing that offer would be a shocker for Granny, too. She had no idea Shan had applied for college. She couldn't say much, now. Funny, Granny had never talked about the future. Shan was a senior and Granny hadn't said a word about what would happen after graduation.

Opening the window to dump the dishwater, Shan remembered thinking, just yesterday, as she'd done the same chore, how, this time next year, she'd be surrounded by city lights. Free to visit libraries, go shopping and eat in restaurants. Did Coral Morgan offer the same kind of freedom? Recalling the woman's strident tone, Shan doubted it.

She grabbed the water buckets and went out the back door to the well. The sun had already gone down behind the hills, leaving the hollow in lavender shadow. Shan saw Marie's white Ford truck in the driveway and her eyes watered. Had Isaiah already told his mother he wanted to leave? She stood, holding the buckets, watching the Farris's living room window. She couldn't go over now. Marie and Isaiah would need time to talk. She'd IM him as soon as she went upstairs.

The weeds and wildflowers in the meadow swayed in the growing wind and, as Shan put her hand on the crank, she heard the rise and fall of the elusive melody from the hills. She looked at the tree line. There was only the shadows of the trees and the gently shifting underbrush. She drew water and tipped it into one of the kitchen buckets. Lowering the rope, again, she listened to the music on the wind. She couldn't distinguish voices, or even notes, but it was clear enough it couldn't be a figment of her imagination. She drew water to fill her second bucket, and dropped the draw bucket onto the curb. The band on her finger heated and her skin prickled. She wanted to go inside.

As she turned with the heavy containers, she saw something moving at the forest's edge. She twisted her neck for a better look. Silhouetted against the light from Marie's back porch, a black, hunched figure stood in the grass, its misshapen, horny head raised, blunt nostrils flaring to sniff the air. Shan inhaled, gripping the buckets, unable to move.

At her gasp, the creature turned its head, fixing its yellow, glowing eyes on her. Shan lurched toward the house, sloshing water all over her jeans. Inside, she kicked the door shut, dropped the buckets on the floor and pulled the deadbolt. She slammed the window by the door, locking it and the one over the sink.

"Granny!" She shouted, running to secure the front door. "Granny?"

But Granny and her shotgun had left the living room. Shan crossed the hall and knocked on Granny's door. There was no answer, so she did something she'd rarely ever done. She opened the door. Granny's room was dark, but there was enough light to see her snoring on her side.

"Granny."

Granny turned over, regarding Shan with a bleary, unseeing gaze and fell back asleep. Shan backed out of the room. Granny would be no help.

She stood in the hallway, trying to breathe slowly and carefully. What the hell was that thing?

Not for the first time, Shan wished they had a phone. She could really use Isaiah's intelligence. His wiry muscles would come in handy, too. After making another pass, assuring herself that all the windows and doors were locked, she grabbed the poker from behind the stove and climbed the stairs to her room. She opened her computer and started Skype. Isaiah was online and responded to her IM.

"Thought you were coming back over."

"Your Mom was home by the time dinner was done. I didn't want to interrupt. I just saw something outside."

"?"

"It looked like…" Trying to find words to describe what she'd seen, Shan felt foolish.

"It looked like a man wearing a Halloween mask." She typed.

"When?"

"five minutes ago."

"Where?"

"By the woods on our side."

"BRB."

Shan bit her lip, waiting for Isaiah to return. Nervously, she approached her bedroom window and looked out at the rapidly darkening hills across the road. Of course, she couldn't see Isaiah's house, or the back wood where she'd seen the...thing. A pop announced an IM and she went back to the computer.

"Nothing out there but some bullfrogs."

"I saw it."

"Not there now. Maybe imagination?"

"NM." The idea she could've imagined it annoyed Shan more than Isaiah's doubt. Isaiah looked at everything through a scientific lens. Of course he'd doubt. "Did you talk to your Mom?"

"Yes. Going to TN on Sat. Come over the minute you get off the bus!?"

"You know it."

"GTG. Mom rented a movie."

"See you tomorrow."

"TTYT"

Shan stared at the screen for a few seconds after Isaiah signed off. Had she really imagined the creature in the wood? Despite her extensive reading, Shan couldn't recall a single instance, before today, of having an overactive imagination. Could it be the damned ring?

She looked down at it. The glowing spark moved languidly across the center of the amber. As she watched, it stopped just past the middle and waited. Shan had the eerie feeling it was looking up at her. She turned the ring to the inside of her palm. She may not be able to take the thing off, but she wasn't going to let it take over her life.

She rose to change out of her wet jeans. Every movement jarred her. She couldn't shake the image of the beastly head scenting the air. She should go to bed, but the thought of turning off her light made her pulse race.

Isaiah had seen nothing. So, maybe, the thing she saw had moved on. Or it could've been an animal, a buck, maybe, and she'd let her worries twist it out of proportion. Shaking her head, Shan hung her jeans and collect her nightclothes.

After a quick shower, during which she repeatedly turned off the water to see if there were noises downstairs, Shan dried her hair and dressed for bed. She had chosen stretch pants and a t-shirt she could wear outside in an emergency. Still not ready to settle down, she stared around her room.

She didn't feel like surfing the web, or reading vapid posts on Facebook but the manila envelope from Boston was still under her computer. Taking it to her bed, she pulled out the acceptance letter, the scholarship award letter and information about the liberal arts programs she was considering. There were three glossy brochures; Literature, English and Archeology. She didn't know what she wanted to be, but she knew it involved discovery, books, different cultures and world travel.

So why was she so adamant about staying in Salt Creek, now?

She collected the brochures and dropped them back into the envelope, bending to tuck it under her mattress. It was simple. She wanted leaving to be her choice.

She settled into the bed, propping her pillows and picked up her latest library book. It was an old Agatha

Christie mystery the librarian had recommended, and, to Shan's surprise, she found the characters and plot vibrant enough to provide distraction.

Gradually, she stopped straining to hear every little noise, and her eyes closed.

They opened again, almost instantly, and she was no longer in her room. She walked through the clearing whispering the names of each of the sacred Sentinels, names she somehow knew as intimately as she knew her self: Choughain, Maedar, Rane, Ellyng, Daer. Low voices responded inside her, their individual tones filling her with joy. A fawn brushed past, his body granting temporary warmth to the hip he touched. Birds flitted nearby, so close, sometimes, the breath of their wings stirred the curls on her cheek.

She stood before the Mother, Gaiaes. The oak's trunk was so wide four acolytes together could not stretch their arms around it. Gaiaes's profuse, tangled branches stretched far overhead, tips touching at least one limb of each of the Sentinels. As she did every morning, she knelt to greet her Mother with an open palm. A question jarred her peace, why did her arm look wrong? Copper bracelets fell back from her freckled hand and sunlight glinted off the red-gold hair on her forearm. The fingers were long, knuckles stained dark, but the ring was *her* ring, and when her palm met Gaiaes's living bark, energy shot through the ring, dragging her into a dark, spinning vortex.

She landed hard on her feet in the middle of a desert town. Adobe houses with gravel yards sported cacti and plastic garden gnomes. The neighborhood looked the same all around her. In the distance, behind her, the gray outline of a large city shimmered on the horizon. Contrails crossed the bright blue sky.

The sun was hot on her back, the air still. A small boy on a dented bike paused at the intersection to look at her. His cropped black hair stood up in the back and his brown eyes were mildly curious. Her lips parted, but, before she could speak, a low rumbling began somewhere behind her. The boy's gaze shifted past her, his eyes widening. She turned to see the city disappear behind rolling dust and black, jagged cracks splitting the desert soil, speeding toward her. The ground undulated beneath her feet. She turned to grab the boy, but the shockwave had already lifted him. His small body came down, wrenched over the frame of his bicycle. She screamed.

Shan woke sitting up, drenched in sweat. At first she didn't know where she was. Her bedside lamp was still on, and the rising sun added its wan light to her room. Her room. She could see her face in the old mirror. Still, her heart thundered. She'd never had such a vivid dream. She looked at her hand. It was her own, of course, fingers slightly crooked with short nails, skin pale and unmarked, the back of her wrist brushed with fine, dark hair.

The yellow stone glowed when she looked at the ring. Was it hot? She touched the topaz. When her fingertip made contact with the warm gem, the sun beat down on her once more and the bedroom started fading into a desert town. Shan moved her finger, breaking contact, and her own room settled around her. She breathed slowly, keeping her eyes on the mirror.

"It was a dream." She whispered to the wild-eyed girl in the glass. She stared at her reflection. Straight hair, not curly. A big t-shirt, not a woolen robe.

It was a dream. A nightmare.

But it had felt so real. She squeezed her eyes closed, yet she couldn't shut out the image of the little boy's twisted body. She looked at her clock. Four-fifteen. It was too early to be up, but she didn't dare fall back to sleep. She should probably get on with her day. She made her bed, took down her dried jeans, tossing them into her laundry and headed for the bathroom. The house was absolutely silent. She hugged herself and turned on the lights over the bathroom counter as well as the overhead light.

After she took a shower and dressed for school, it was only five. Too early to start coffee for Granny. Isaiah wasn't on Skype, so Shan scanned Facebook, looking for local news. She couldn't keep her mind on the various break-ups, fights and party details chronicled on her feed. Everything seemed off kilter.

Maybe she had changed, somehow.

No. Actually, it was life which had changed, leaving her feeling powerless. She hated it. She couldn't stop Isaiah from leaving. There was the threat of Coral Morgan's return hanging over her head. Would she be any more able to halt Coral's plans than she was able to stop Isaiah's?

She pushed back from her desk. What good did it do to worry about it? She shut down her computer, closing the cover, and slipped her library book into her book bag along with the algebra homework she'd done, with Isaiah's help, a day ago. In another lifetime.

Impatient with her own jumbled thoughts, Shan hooked her bag over her shoulder and went downstairs to start the coffee. Although Granny usually didn't get up until almost time for the bus, Shan always fixed breakfast and coffee before leaving.

The coffee was done and she was pulling out biscuits when Granny came downstairs. Shan almost dropped the heavy pan in surprise. Taking a cup out of the dish drainer, Granny poured herself some coffee and tasted it with a satisfied grunt. Granny liked her coffee hot.

She got herself a plate and spooned gravy over a biscuit before taking it to her accustomed seat. Shan quickly dropped two sausage patties into her own plate of biscuits and gravy and joined her at the table. Granny was up early. Clearly, she wanted time to talk before Shan went to school. Good. Shan wanted to talk about what she'd seen the night before and about her dream.

Just as she'd settled her plate, wheels crunched on the driveway.

"It's Coral." Granny said. "Go. Give me some time to try reasoning with 'er."

"But…"

"Go!"

Granny left the room. Shan lifted her book bag and went to the side window. Sliding it open, she waited a moment, listening to the tap of Coral's heels crossing the porch. She should have been going through the field to Isaiah's house, but she strained to hear the voices from the living room.

"This is a court order giving me custody." Coral's icy tone seemed to suck the color from the world.

"How do I know it's real?" Granny, still defiant.

"You know it's real." Coral laughed. "And you knew I could get it done."

"She ain't here."

"I know she wasn't in school yesterday. Where is she?"

Shan's heart raced. She started to climb through the window and noticed the marks from the previous day's muddy entrance. She snatched the rag from dish pan and wiped away the dirt.

Shan scooted out the window, careful to hold onto the sill. She stood on tiptoe to pull the window back down. Her left hand felt clumsy with the unfamiliar weight of the heavy ring. Rage boiled to the surface and she slung her hand behind her, but the band didn't move. She gave it another tug, then, hearing voices in the middle of the house, she crouched.

Coral and Granny spoke in conversational tones, but Shan couldn't make out their words. Granny was being reasonable? No doubt, it was a ruse to give Shan time to get away.

Shan held onto the wall, crab-walking until she was behind the house. In the sloping back yard, she stood, sprinting up the hill, grabbing vines, ferns and tough weeds to keep her balance.

Remembering the beast she'd seen—or thought she'd seen—the night before, she stayed just beyond the forest's edge, running as fast as she could toward the path down to Isaiah's back door. She knew Maria had already left for work because the truck wasn't in the driveway. Assuming Isaiah would still be asleep, she pushed the back door, but it only gave a quarter of an inch.

Ugh. Someone must have engaged the hook and eye. After she'd used a folded piece of paper to lift the latch, making as little noise as possible, she poured a cup of milk from the refrigerator and pulled out a dining chair.

"Hey."

Shan jumped, dropping the cup, spilling milk all over Marie's table.

"Isaiah. I thought you were asleep."

"It's not necessary to break and enter for a cup of milk." Isaiah hooked a wet cloth and began wiping up the spill. "I'd have given it to you, anyway."

"Coral's back over there." Using a clean dishtowel, Shan dried up after Isaiah.

"Yeah, I saw the car from my window." Together, they went to the sink. Isaiah turned on the water to rinse the milk out of the dishcloth while Shan hung the towel. Arms nearly touching, they worked side by side with an easy rhythm. The familiarity of the moment caused Shan's chest to constrict. In two more days, Isaiah would be on a bus to Chattanooga and she would be—

They both jumped when a knock sounded on the front door. Isaiah slid toward the hall, knocking his chair over. He grabbed the baseball bat on his way to the living room.

Despite her thundering pulse, Shan almost smiled. Trust Isaiah to be Isaiah. Her amusement passed quickly.

"Who's there?" Isaiah called through the door.

Shan didn't need to listen for an answer.

She knew Coral had found her already and that life would never be the same.

CHAPTER FIVE

"Open up, son." Coral's tone brooked no argument.

"Just open it." Shan told him.

"I'm not supposed to open the door if Mom's not here." Isaiah replied, loudly enough for Coral to hear. He added, in a high-pitched whisper. "I'm stalling so you can get out of here."

"You don't want me to call the police." Coral rattled the knob.

Shan stepped around Isaiah, opened the door and stood face to face with her aunt.

Close up, Coral was shorter than she'd seemed in Granny's yard. Without her heels, she might be only a few inches taller than Shan. Coral's hair was the same as Shan's, black with red highlights, and the short fringe of her bangs fell over eyes the same water-green. Looking at the long, curling lashes and the same thick brows as her own, Shan couldn't deny her blood relationship to the woman.

"Can I help you?"

"Shanleigh," Coral held out her arms as if to hug Shan. When Shan stood stiffly, Coral's hands fell to her sides. She slipped a cellphone back into her patent leather purse and squared her shoulders. "Obviously, you know who I am. That woman," Coral spat, "Kidnapped you when you were a baby. I've spent the last fifteen years looking for you."

"I'm fine." Shan crossed her arms. Coral's gaze flickered to the ring and Shan tucked her left hand under her elbow. Too late.

"I see you're wearing it." Coral's words rang strangely, almost as if she were confused.

"So?"

Coral laughed out loud. "Oh, yes. You're a Morgan. Training you is going to be interesting"

"*Training* me?"

"Don't pretend you don't know you're coming home with me. You'll love New York. You'll have private tutors. A car at your disposal. You already have your own suite in the Bellingham, my home. *Our* home. It's been waiting for you since you were born."

"Thank you, but I'm fine where I am."

"I'm sorry, Shan." Coral's face was set. "You have to come with me."

"What if she doesn't want to leave?" Isaiah scowled.

Coral closed her eyes and sighed. For a second, she looked almost human. "I'm sorry. I know you have a life here and it's natural for you to have feelings toward Katherine Amos. But I have to do what's best for you. Even if it makes you angry."

"She's seventeen." Isaiah's defense warmed Shan.

"I know that." Coral snapped. She looked at Shan, her eyes narrowing. "I could have Katherine arrested for kidnapping."

Shan stared at her aunt, unmoving. Coral pulled the cellphone out of her purse.

"Do I have to leave right now?" Shan exhaled. Out of the corner of her eye, she could see Isaiah's open-mouthed stare. "Can't I have some time to get used to the idea?"

Coral's mouth tightened, her gaze narrowed. "I'm not going to leave you another night in that alcoholic's home. But I will let you have until seven tonight to get your things together and say your goodbyes. "

Relief must have shown on Shan's face because Coral added, "If you aren't here when I get back, if you aren't ready to go, I *will* call the FBI. Katherine Amos will go to jail for a long, long time."

"I assume," Coral looked at Isaiah, "your mother has a phone."

Without waiting for conformation, she handed a small card to Shan. "This is my number. If you have any questions or problems, call me."

Shan pushed the card into her pocket as Coral turned to leave. The woman stopped in the driveway, and spoke over her shoulder. "Don't bother trying to get the ring off. You'll only hurt yourself."

"Or somebody else." Isaiah said, under his breath.

The corner of Coral's lips curled upward as she turned away.

Shan stood with Isaiah, watching her aunt cross the small log bridge spanning the creek which, halfway up Marie's yard, curved across the drive dividing the Farris land. Any other time, the sight of the elegant woman walking between seeded grass and milkweed pods, would've seemed strange, but now, it didn't faze Shan.

"This," She closed Isaiah's door, "Is going to be one of those days I'm just going to have to do on auto-pilot. Unless you want to pinch me and wake me up, now."

"If this is a nightmare," Isaiah shook his head, "It's mine. But don't you pinch me!"

Shan crossed to the kitchen. Her mouth was too dry to talk.

Isaiah followed, watching as she helped herself to an apple from a bowl on the counter, took a cup from the drainer, filled it and downed the water.

"Are you leaving, then?"

No! Shan wanted to shout. She'd negotiated with Coral for more time, hoping to come up with some idea, some argument that would allow her to remain at least until graduation. But no matter which way she looked at it, she couldn't figure out a way to block Coral and still save Granny. Refilling her cup, Shan took sip after sip of water, waiting for the cold to spread down her throat, into her stomach. "What else can I do? I know she'll call the FBI on Granny."

Isaiah shrugged, looking out the small window over the sink. *Damn.* She wouldn't get to see Isaiah off. She couldn't even promise she'd be able to stay in contact.

Without intending to say anything, Shan blurted, "Come with me!"

Isaiah blinked and looked away. "That'll never happen."

"You don't want to?"

58

"Of course, I want to go with you. But I can't afford private tutors and suites in fancy houses. Besides, I just told Mom I was going to Chattanooga."

"So, she's ready to let you go." Shan closed the distance between them, and, putting her hands on his shoulders looked up into his eyes. "You won't back out will you? Promise me. If you don't go with me, you'll be on the bus to your Aunt Jolene's Saturday!"

Isaiah stepped back. "I want to go with you, but Mom's not going to let me go off with strangers."

"I'm not a stranger." Shan ran her fingers through her hair. "Besides, how do you know Chattanooga's any more progressive than Salt Creek?"

Slowly, Isaiah nodded. His jaw clenched and unclenched. "If I have to go…" He swallowed, "if I have to go, I'd rather go with you, if your aunt will let me. But we have to sell Mom on it."

"I bet I can get my aunt to let you. She wants something from me, so she'll be willing to negotiate. Besides you can share my tutor if she needs to save money." Shan went to the phone on the writing desk and pulling the card out of her pocket, dialed the number.

"Shan?" Coral's voice held a note of anxiety. "What is it?"

"Do you have room in that big house for my friend? Just for this semester, to help me settle in?"

Coral said nothing. Shan wondered if the woman could hear her heart beating through the phone. The silence continued so long, she began to think the connection had been broken.

Finally she heard a soft sigh. "Yes. That might be a good idea. If you can get his mother to go for it."

"Thank you." Shan's words were stiff. When Coral clicked off, Shan had the weirdest feeling she'd just lost a battle.

She went back into the kitchen where Isaiah sat at the table, fingering an empty plastic mug.

"Thing is; what've I got to lose?" He shrugged. "I was listening. I know your aunt said I could go. If I can get Mom to let me, I best do just that."

"Tell her the truth." Shan said.

"I can't take this place away from her."

"You think she really doesn't know?"

"Why do I have to keep reminding you she's blond?" Isaiah laughed. "She has no clue."

Shan knew how to sell Marie. "Tell her it's an educational opportunity. That you'll be living in a grand house, going to museums and concerts."

"Leave it to me." He exhaled. "I'll make lunch for her and when she comes to pick up, I'll talk to her. I got work to do. Shoo!"

As she went out the front door, Shan crossed the fingers on both hands holding them up for Isaiah to see.

She walked up the hill to the road and back down the driveway to her own house, aware she was taking the reverse path of Coral Morgan's black car. She dreaded facing Granny. She knew Kat Amos wouldn't want her to leave. Granny wouldn't care about Coral's threats. She probably wouldn't even believe them.

Shan went through the front door but the living room was empty. She checked the kitchen, grabbing a left over biscuit on the way, and knocked on Granny's bedroom door. No answer.

Maybe the older woman had gone back to bed. Shan couldn't stand still. Half to keep her thoughts at bay, half to fill the time, Shan cleaned the kitchen. Trying not to think about it being the last time she was likely to do each task, she swept the house, straightened the living room and mopped the kitchen. Finally, when there was nothing left to do, she knocked on Granny's door one more time. When there was no response, she cracked the door open to find the bed neatly made and the room empty.

Granny must have gone up the mountain. Shan went through the back door and found her would-be protector on the small back porch. Granny sat smoking, staring up at the tangled hillside.

Shan settled beside her. When the woman hadn't spoken after a few minutes, Shan addressed her.

"Granny?"

"She found you, I guess." Granny didn't turn around.

"Coral? Yes. She came to Isaiah's."

"She figured you was there before she come here. She knowed neither one of you'uns went to school yesterday."

"I have to go to New York." Shan pulled a dry blade of grass and held it up to the wind. The blade bent slightly, pointing over Shan's shoulder. Wind light and to the north.

"No. You don't." Granny finished her cigarette, grinding it into the soil. "But I 'spect you will anyhow."

"If I don't..." Shan began but Granny cut her off.

"She'll do what?" Granny spit to her left, away from Shan. "She'll throw me in jail?"

Shan nodded. She knew Granny better than anyone else in the world but they were complete strangers now. This woman who'd raised her, who'd wanted her enough to steal her, was as much an enigma as Coral Morgan.

"It ain't about me, you know." Granny faced Shan. "It's about you and that." She nodded at the ring.

"Can't you tell me what this ring is for?" Shan's eyes burned, "before I go?"

"Ah. Coral's right. I ain't sober. I'd just mess it up." She shook her head, her shoulders slumped. "Like I messed this up. I did have a plan. But I had to play it safe. If David hadn't died..." She opened a bottle sitting beside her and took a swig. Granny's throat bobbed and Shan could hear the sound of it moving. She looked away.

Granny continued. "He did though. Still. Thought I'd have time to get somebody else to tell you the right way."

Granny paused to take another drink. "True believers don't see nothing but what they believe in. Coral and her bunch, they're believers. But you ain't got to be."

Without warning, Granny turned and grabbed Shan's forearms. "I ain't never asked no favors, except for my boy, and that didn't help, but I guess I got to. If you're bound to go with her, do me one thing?"

Granny's fingers hurt, but Shan didn't pull away. "Yes?"

"Don't believe everything they tell you. I mean the why and the wherefore, yeah, but not the how. Will you do that? Listen and learn, but don't decide 'till you hear from everybody."

Shan frowned. *What was Granny asking?* Shan's lower arms tingled from her grandmother's hold, and the ring was warm. "Yes. Yes. I will. I promise."

Granny let go and snorted. "You ain't got no idea what I'm talking about, but I reckon you will have, soon enough."

Shan knew there was no arguing with Granny, especially when she was drunk. She knew better, too, than telling Granny about the possibility of Isaiah going along. The woman seemed to have a deep dislike for Isaiah. Maybe it was because he was black. Then, again, what other friend of Shan's had Granny met? Maybe she'd hate them all equally.

Granny drank and smoked in silence. Her eyes drooped and she slumped against the porch rail. Shan wanted more from Granny—words, information, regret. Something. It didn't seem right to just walk away from seventeen years, her entire life, with nothing more than a drunken request. But Shan had learned, long ago, that life was never like books. Too many feelings, worries and fears crowded her thoughts.

"I'm going to pack." She stood, taking one last look at the forest which had been her childhood playground and the little old woman who had been her family.

Granny snored softly, her gray head angled against the rail, hair blending almost perfectly with the weathered wood. Shan slipped through the back door.

Shan's own room pulsed with memories of who she'd been two days ago. By the door, the little iron bed, which had been her father's—no—*David's*, was covered with a simple quilt she'd started on her tenth birthday. Granny had given her the squares, cut from clothes Shan had outgrown, and showed her how to start. Another, more ambitious honeycomb quilt lay at the foot of the bed, unfinished ends tucked under. She'd planned to complete it during the winter.

A painting, which had belonged to Granny's mother, hung over the bed. Natural branches formed a frame for the small oil. The picture, not much bigger than a five-by-seven photograph, depicted a clearing in the middle of a stand of oaks. At first glance, the painting seemed peaceful, but Shan had always felt that it was incomplete, as if the artist was never allowed to finish. She moved away, but as she did, out of the corner of her eye, she thought she saw the leaves on the right side of the painting shiver.

Kneeling on the bed, Shan looked hard at the section. Chills bloomed along her spine. There was no movement while she watched, but she could have sworn the shadows had shifted. The mood of the painting had changed, too. She couldn't explain it, even to herself, but Shan could tell the painting…*waited.*

She exhaled. If she kept focusing on tiny things, she would definitely lose her mind.

She stepped back from the bed and her knee brushed the battered side-table she used for a night stand. A small brass lamp with a yellowing shade fell over the photograph of her mother. She righted the lamp and picked

64

up the picture. Isaiah had promised to scan the photo at the school computer lab, to preserve it for Shan. Maybe Coral had other photographs of her sister, but Shan had grown up with this one. She lifted the picture, holding it close to her chest, and crossed the room.

She stopped at her single bedroom window and pushed aside curtains so old they had as little original color as Granny's dresses. She scanned the hillside across the road. Anything lurking there was well hidden by lush growth.

The mountain had been taller, Granny often said, before the mining company had stripped off the top. Though Shan had never seen the original, the flat top among a sea of graceful curves had always felt unnatural to her, like an amputated limb. To her right, toward Isaiah's, there were many flattops among the rolling hills fading to smoky outlines in the distance.

She stepped away from the window. To her right, a yellow curtain stretched across the corner, marking Shan's closet. She lifted the curtain and let it drop, realizing she had no suitcase. How could she pack anything?

She placed her mother's picture on her combination vanity and desk. The mirror behind her laptop reflected her frown. How many times had she stood at that same spot, searching her face for some similarity with Granny?

Where Granny's high cheekbones were angular and sharp, Shan's sloped smoothly. Her eyes slanted down at the outside while Granny's tilted upward. Granny's mouth was small and thin, her grin barely stretching past her flaring nostrils. Shan's mouth was full and too wide. Even now, seriously set, the corners of her lips ended under her pupils. Shan had often wished for Granny's gracefully winged brows instead of her own heavy ones.

She used to search Granny's pictures of David, tracing his face, looking for a resemblance. Granny always said Shan just took after her mother's side, but Shan had believed she must've gotten more from her father than a tendency toward thinness.

There had to be something from her paternal side, surely. Except, now, Shan had no idea who her father might be. If Coral knew, would she tell?

She heard Granny's cough, downstairs, followed by the steady thud of boots on the stairs.

"Here." The elderly woman stumbled into Shan's room, carrying an old fashioned suitcase. She dropped it on the floor. "Put your stuff in this."

Before Shan could thank her, Granny had turned her back. She paused at the door and said, "You can take that paintin',too. Call it my partin' gift."

Shan didn't look at the painting. She certainly didn't want to pack it. But she would because Granny wanted her to have it. She didn't doubt Granny's assertion that she had taken Shan to protect her and she would do nothing to hurt the woman.

The years ran through Shan's memory in a rush, landing with a staggering weight. Clenching her fists and teeth, she took a deep breath, interrupted by a stomach growl. She stifled a threatening, insane giggle and went downstairs.

Unless she was in her room, Granny was no longer in the house. Shan sighed and made lunch for them both.

Marie Ferris's truck, parked in her driveway when Shan started lunch, stayed while she ate. She crossed her fingers, wishing luck for Isaiah and for herself. Afterward, when Granny still hadn't made an appearance, Shan wrapped Granny's sandwiches in plastic and busied herself cleaning the kitchen. She cleaned the rest of the downstairs too. She didn't want to leave Granny with work she was no longer sure the old woman could handle.

When the house was clean, Shan finished off the jar of peanut butter and, as Granny still hadn't made another appearance, squared her shoulders and went back upstairs.

Shan lifted the case onto her bed. Damn, it was heavy. She put her mother's picture in one of the elastic side pockets and grabbed an armful of books from the makeshift shelf on her windowsill. She spread the books carefully, so they wouldn't be damaged. She packed a second load, leaving only her large dictionary and a few paperback romances Marie had given her.

Shan covered the books with jeans, shirts and sweaters she'd ordered online, throwing socks and underwear on top of them. The suitcase had more than enough room for all of Shan's clothes, except for last year's winter coat. She'd planned to get a new one in October, so she left the puffy, bright green jacket among the empty metal hangers.

Shan's mascara, foundation and lip gloss were already in the makeup bag she pushed down beside her clothes. Two perfume bottles remained on the dresser beside her computer. Ordering them online had been reckless. Since she disliked them both, she decided not to take them. After she was gone, would Granny throw them away?

Shan owned two extra pairs of tennis shoes and one pair of hiking boots. She shoved all the shoes into the lid compartment and allowed the case to fall closed. She surveyed the room again. She wouldn't be unable to take either quilt. Would she be back to get them, or, like everything else, were they part of a past that no longer mattered?

She snapped the latches on the suitcase but as she started to lift it, the painting caught her eye. Nothing seemed to move but the sense of waiting remained. Shan reached for it cautiously, holding it by the twig frame. The painting was lighter than she expected. She turned it over. Leather cord strapped the twigs to the painting through small holes in the wood panel.

Resisting the urge to touch the painting, she put it face down on top of her clothes and latched the suitcase. Shoving her computer and university packet into her book bag, she slipped it over her shoulder. Lifting the heavy case, she dragged it down the stairs and propped it on the small sofa. Once it was secure, she went to look for Granny.

Shan found her one-time guardian in the back yard, pulling faded blooms off the wild honeysuckle border. Shan crossed the small yard and, selecting a fresh bloom, plucked it carefully to preserve the nectar. She offered the it to Granny.

Granny snorted. "When's that woman coming?"

"Seven." Shan broke the base off the flower and drew out the stamen with its clear, sweet droplet. She sucked the nectar and tossed the flower into the bushes.

"I don't want to go." She said without thinking.

"I know that." Granny's gaze fixed on Shan's face. "You know I did what I had to."

"I do." Shan waited, but Granny turned back to the flowers.

"I'm going to go over and say goodbye to Marie."

"You mean Isaiah, don't you?" Granny scowled over her shoulder.

"I guess." Shan spread her hands. What could she say? Why had she thought her leaving would make Granny different?

Shan stalked across the yard and up onto the porch. Just as she reached for the door handle, Granny called to her.

"You want me to shoot her when she gets here?"

"I'd hate to see Sherriff Begley get hurt trying to take you in." Shan laughed, relief washing over her. "Anyway, I bet she can stop bullets."

"Hide's thick enough, that's for sure." Granny frowned, then her face became serious, her eyes instantly clear and focused. "We'll be seeing each other again, girl. One way or the other."

Despite the approaching dusk, the day seemed brighter as Shan crossed the field to Isaiah's house. The strange melody still rang on the air but she refused to be distracted by it. She moved quickly, though, trying not to look for strange shapes at the forest's edge. She made it to the border of Marie's yard before she pulled up short.

What had Granny meant by "one way or the other?" She turned on her heel to go back and ask but Isaiah's shout stopped her.

"Shi-zzle! What took you so long?" He bounded off the porch and came around the side of the house. "Mom's not happy, but she's letting me go. Provided you promise to pay my way back if things don't go right."

"I'll find a way even if I have rob Coral." Shan looked back at her house.

"It's Mom you have to convince, not me." Isaiah linked his arm through hers, casting a wary glance at her left hand.

His excitement was contagious. Shan's step was lighter as she walked with him. Still, she'd talk to Granny again before leaving.

In the living room, Marie wiped her TV screen with a white cloth. She looked up when Isaiah and Shan entered. The woman's blotchy face and red-rimmed eyes highlighted her grief.

"I dread losing my boy," She sniffed, sighed and then smiled at Shan. "But I can't thank you enough for giving him this opportunity."

"I'm glad to have him with me."

"Both of you sit down, now." Marie indicated the couch with a wave. "I made a plate of cookies for you."

Shan sat on the edge of the couch and reached for the fragrant butter cookies. It seemed nothing, not even a belly full of butterflies, could soften her hunger.

"I didn't even know you had a living aunt, then, when Isaiah starts telling me about her, she calls. She seems so nice." Marie blushed, "Said she understands the importance of a first-class education for kids like Isaiah."

Shan nodded, surprised and uncomfortable. Coral Morgan certainly took charge. Isaiah elbowed her. She elbowed him back. What could she say?

She took a stab. "Yes. Coral's big on education."

"Knew he'd go off to college early, he's so smart. I'm going to miss my boy, though." Marie shook her head, and sniffed again. Tendrils escaped the pony tail she wore to work. Dark stains marked her blue janitor's overall. The words White Oak Elementary were stitched across the left breast. The right side sported a name tag reading Miss Farris. Shan hated the way the school board insisted it be Miss instead of MS. but Marie never seemed to mind. Her sky blue eyes were bloodshot from crying, but a softness about her face made her look closer to Shan's age than thirty-three.

"Aw, Mom. Don't. You know I'll be back, probably for Christmas." Isaiah elbowed Shan, again.

"No doubt." Shan nodded, convincingly—she hoped. She eyed her friend. Isaiah certainly was more inventive than she'd realized.

Marie sobbed twice, blew her nose and set her shoulders. "Are you sure you got everything you need, honey?"

"Shiz—er—yes, Mom." Isaiah stood, and headed for the stairs. "I'll go get my bag now."

"Make sure you pack those warm socks Jolene knitted!" Marie called, "Weathers got all funky. Anyway, it gets awful cold in New York, I hear."

Isaiah groaned and bounded up the stairs.

71

A wispy smile played somewhere, in the back of Shan's mind, but it didn't reach her face. The gold-toned horse and carriage clock on Marie's mantel showed the time as six-ten. If the fifties timepiece was correct, Shan had forty minutes before she had to leave the only world she'd ever known with a complete stranger who had some secret agenda. Not to mention magic not only existed, but she had the ability to use it. Why did she just feel numb?

"Did you hear me?" Marie's voice penetrated Shan's thoughts. "I wondered why you'd never mentioned your Aunt before."

"We'd lost contact. She just found us again, recently." Shan couldn't believe how the lies just fell out of her mouth.

"Kind of like a fairy godmother!" Marie tilted her head, "They do say life is stranger than fiction."

Shan forced a smile fingering the ring. Coral Morgan, fairy? Maybe, but certainly not like the sweet godmothers of fairytales.

"Oh, I didn't see that ring. From your aunt?" Marie stood, leaning across the coffee table, and reached for Shan's left hand. Shan pulled back quickly, then, noting Marie's surprise, held it up, palm facing in, so Marie could see the ring.

"It's a family heirloom." Shan broadened her forced smile, until one corner of her mouth trembled. "Granny was holding it for—for my Mom."

Shan hoped Marie wouldn't ask to try it on as she usually did with jewelry, scarves, gloves, and, actually, just about everything wearable. Marie must've sensed

72

Shan's reluctance because she put her hands on the table and simply leaned in to look at the band.

"It's sure different," Marie frowned, "It looks old. And real. Must be worth a fortune."

She sat back down, her brows still drawn. "Your granny probably could of sold that for enough money to build a whole new house. Ain't it something she kept it for you, instead?"

"You know Granny. She doesn't care much for new things. Imagine her trying to cook a pot of soup beans in a microwave."

"Got you a computer, though, and lets you get clothes off the internet." Marie shook her head. "Always seemed to me it would've been easier to let somebody take you to town to shop."

"That's just Granny's way." Shan wished Isaiah would hurry. Marie Farris was usually easily distracted but when she focused, she could get bullish. "I appreciate you letting Isaiah go with me."

Marie's eyes watered, but she chewed her lower lip and regarded Shan. "She must really like your Aunt, to let you go with her when she wouldn't even let you go to the fireworks with me this summer."

Shan bit her tongue to stifle a bitter laugh. She couldn't tell Marie that Granny didn't have a choice.

"She's known Aunt Coral forever, I guess." Shan grimaced. She stood. She'd explain to Isaiah later. "I need to get back to the house before my aunt shows up."

"You'll pick up Isaiah after loading the car at your Granny's, then?" Marie asked, standing, annoyance passing over her face. Shan didn't take it personally. Granny's hostility aggravated a lot of people.

"Yes." Shan gave Marie a genuine smile, "Thank you for everything."

"I'll miss you, too, you know." Marie caught Shan in a hug. Shan's bones seemed to turn to ice. Before she could figure out how to respond, Marie let go.

"Me too." Shan mumbled, face hot. "Please tell Isaiah to be ready by seven."

"Bye, now!" Marie called as the door closed behind Shan.

Dusk had fallen on the hollow, washing the valley in shades of blue and purple. The hills were black shadows, only recognizable by the ragged outline of trees against the cobalt sky. Fireflies winked over grasses. Cicadas called, frogs sang and movement near the forest edge revealed the gray-barred wings of an owl, waking early. The mysterious melody was either gone, or drowned by the din of forest life. The earth settled around Shan. Surely, there was nothing unknown in the valley that could hurt her.

Crossing the field, she thought about all the years she'd wished for a normal life. Modern appliances, TV, a car of her own, the freedom to read at a library, shop in real stores and to visit friends. Funny, she'd always pictured Granny as a part of that dream. Angry and fussing maybe, and no longer in control, but always waiting for her to come home.

Shan's vision blurred. She stopped to dab her eyes with the corner of her sleeve and heard the sound of a car. She watched the road. Sparkling headlights, not the usual dirty ones belonging to Salt Creek residents, cut through trees and undergrowth marking the road's edge. Coral Morgan, of course.

Coral's lights swept over Shan as the car negotiated the drive. Shan couldn't tell if her aunt saw her. The windows revealed nothing of the vehicle's dark interior.

Coral parked in the yard, this time, without crowding the porch steps. The living room light came on, turning the door glass into a yellow square. Shan watched for Granny's silhouette to appear in the frame, but it didn't.

Coral popped the car trunk and got out, leaving the engine running. She'd changed clothes somewhere. Her dark slacks and black boots were more suited to the terrain, though Shan knew, from her online shopping excursions, that the shoes were pricey designer boots. Had there been a time when she dreamed of growing up to wear such clothes?

A fierce longing overcame her. She wanted to take it all back, to climb the hill and disappear into the forest. As the thought struck, she took a step toward the woods, but she stopped. Coral would make Granny pay if Shan didn't cooperate.

She approached the car, realizing her aunt was watching her. The woman stood, hand on the open door, one long-nailed finger tapping the frame.

"Ready, then?" Coral's voice held no particular emotion. "Where's your bag?"

"Inside." Shan walked past her aunt and started up the steps. When Coral moved as if to follow her, Shan added. "I can get it myself."

She didn't want to witness another exchange between Granny and Coral. She stared into Coral's dark, un-flinching eyes and the woman stiffened. They regarded each other without speaking until Coral shrugged. "Help yourself. Hurry, though. We've got a lot of ground to cover. And we still need to pick up your friend."

Shan went inside without word. Her suitcase was where she'd left it. She almost passed it to look for Granny when she saw a piece of rolled paper tucked beneath the handle.

Shan pulled it out, slowly, heart sinking. The house had the silent, dry feel of emptiness. Granny wasn't going to say good-bye in person.

Shan unrolled the single sheet of notepaper.

"*Shan,*" Granny had written "*I did everything for a good reason. I hope you will understand some day. I never told you you was supposed to be special but that aint why I kept you. Coral knows more than anybody alive today but she can't do nothing without you. Learn what you can but think before you do anything like I always tried to teach you. Remember, who you are is your choice not nobody else's. Yours Truly, Granny.*"

Shan folded the note, slipping it into her back pocket. She walked down the hall in silence, collected her book bag from the kitchen table, came back to the living room and looked around once. Granny's rocker, the heating stove and the small blue horsehair couch under the window seemed at once out of place and just right.

Inhaling deeply, Shan picked up her suitcase and walked out the door.

At the car, she hooked her book bag over her shoulder and heaved the suitcase into the truck. She pushed it to one side, hoping Isaiah had a more modern bag that would fit in the small space left by the ancient case. She closed the trunk and looked up at her aunt.

Coral pointed to the front passenger door and Shan slid onto the soft, leather seat, buckling her seatbelt while Coral settled herself in the driver's seat.

"Let's go get our other passenger." Coral put the car into gear and backed out of the driveway. As the vehicle rolled up the hill, the light from the headlamps moved down Granny's little gray house, until Shan could see only the small square of yellow light echoed all around by an army of fireflies.

CHAPTER SIX

Two hours later, as the black car turned smoothly onto I-81 North, Shan was further from Salt Creek than she'd ever been. She had to keep stopping herself chewing the ends of her hair. She wished she wasn't afraid to ask Coral to pull into drive-through.

Through the side mirror, she could see Isaiah, in back, looking out the window. He'd barely spoken since his mother's tearful goodbye, presided over by an embarrassed Shan and an impatient Coral. *Is he half as nervous as I am?*

At first Coral had talked almost continually as she drove. She said, about New York, "There are people everywhere. More than you can imagine. But you see no one. No one sees you. Don't forget that."

She talked about shopping, "Anything you can imagine can be had within the hour. You will eat better than you ever dreamed."

And she talked about the Bellingham. "It opened as a hotel in 1818 and was converted to apartments in 1880. Our family acquired it in 1902 and it's been our home since then. We're on a very large lot in an old neighborhood. You'll be quite safe and a short ride from everything."

Coral listed some of her favorite restaurants and Shan tried not to picture plates piled high with pasta, sizzling steaks and two-pound lobsters. Coral said they might attend Broadway shows. If it hadn't been for a strange undercurrent in her tone, she would've sounded like a tour guide. But, instead of pride, Shan sensed something stronger and darker. Any questions she would normally have asked stuck in her throat.

Isaiah responded to Coral, asking questions about the Bellingham, the neighborhood and restaurants. Shan didn't feel like being polite. If she couldn't have food, she wanted time to try making sense of everything she'd experienced.

A few scenes stood out, clearly; the oak cluster burned into the cloth, the rustling leaves in the painting and the blunt-nosed figure sniffing the air. How much had she fantasized and how much was real?

Certainly she'd imagined the changes in the painting. She hadn't imagined Granny discussing magic as if it were natural as rain. The creature could've been an animal, but the weight of the acorn ring on her finger was very real and there were real burns on Isaiah's palm. She was actually in a strange car with an aunt she'd never known, traveling north at a high rate of speed.

Coral pulled over, once, for fuel. She told Shan and Isaiah to use the restroom at the service station because they wouldn't be stopping again until they reached the hotel in Wytheville, Virginia. She said she'd order dinner then, but Shan borrowed money from Isaiah to buy beef jerky, almonds and Twinkies. She ate them standing by the ice container, guessing Coral wouldn't want food in her pristine car. Licking the crumbs from her fingers, she caught Coral watching with a mocking smile.

On the road, the radio played classical music, and the familiar Cumberland Appalachians gave way to the larger Blue Ridge Mountains. It was hard, in the darkness, to note major differences, but Shan could tell the peaks were taller and further apart than they had been at home.

Out of the corner of her eye, she saw Coral glancing her way from time to time. When Shan intercepted one of aunt's looks, Coral turned her eyes back to the road. Her expression had not been angry. Rather, she looked as though she had something important to say.

Would Coral be more forthcoming if Isaiah was not with them? Shan almost asked, when another question occurred.

"Why are we driving instead of flyng?"

"There are several reasons," Coral's eyebrows went up, "but, we'll talk about that later."

The words from Granny's note came back to Shan. No time like the present to start taking advantage of Coral's knowledge.

"Why won't this ring come off?" She asked, glancing at the side mirror. Isaiah's eyes appeared closed, but a gleam of white showed between his lashes.

"Because it was created to bind to one wearer. It's part of you now." Coral shrugged.

"Granny said for as long as I live."

"Did she?" Coral smirked. "I'm surprised she remembered enough to tell you."

Shan snapped. "She raised me. She fed me. She took care of me!"

"She stole you." Coral punched the accelerator and Shan gripped her door handle. "You're *my* niece. No relation to Katherine Amos."

"Look," Shan sighed. "She thought she was protecting me. Can we leave it at that?"

"If she was protecting you, why did she take the ring, too?"

"She said it was for me."

Coral laughed. "It was meant for you, but it has only one purpose. Which is strange since that purpose is what they claim they wanted to protect you from."

"Granny did want to protect me." Shan's chest felt tight. "Wait. *They? Who is they?"

"One thing I'm not going to do, Shan, is lie to you." Coral shot her a stern look. "Your mother, David *and* Katherine said they wanted to keep you from being who you were meant to be. From your destiny. If that's what they wanted, it still wouldn't have been right. But I don't believe that's what they intended because they took the ring."

"So what does this ring have to do with my…destiny?" Vague words like destiny annoyed Shan, especially when they were being applied to her future.

"I can't explain that right now."

"I don't understand why you can't just tell me." Shan crossed her arms and glared, but her eyes stung. "You want me to believe you instead of Granny but you can't tell me why the ring makes such a difference."

"Oh, Shan." Coral sighed. "That Morgan stubbornness is going to make this more difficult than I'd thought. I have to show you things before you'll understand the ring's purpose."

"Fine." Shan looked out her window. "Until then, stop trying to turn me against Granny."

Coral drove silently for a few minutes but just as Shan began to think the conversation was over, her aunt spoke again.

"I can't stop being honest with you. Very soon, you're going to have to make a choice and what you believe about Katherine can affect your decision. You'll just have to accept that."

Shan wanted to scream. Getting information from Coral was no easier than getting it from Granny. Shan wasn't so sure the two women weren't related. If she couldn't find out more about the ring and the whole magic thing, maybe, she could find out something else.

"Did you know my real father?"

"You have a talent for complicated questions." Coral shook her head once.

"What? Did my mother sleep with everybody?"

"No!" The word exploded from Coral's mouth. She breathed heavily, then, spoke with real warmth. "Your mother was the most innocent person I've ever known, and the bravest."

"What did she do?"

"She gave her life so you could live and grow up, so the world could be saved. She had so much faith, she never doubted people who wanted to take advantage of it."

Shan's throat tightened. "I wish I could've known her."

"I wish you could've known her, too." Coral's words rang true. "If you knew her, this would be so much easier."

"Granny said my mother didn't want me to…" Shan didn't feel right saying her mother didn't want her to work with Coral, so she just said, "Wear this ring."

"She listened to a man who didn't know what he was talking about."

"A lover?"

"She never had a lover."

Shan swallowed. "But she got pregnant with me. That takes a man, unless she was inseminated."

Coral's mouth twisted. "Inseminated. Your generation thinks you know so much and yet you know nothing."

"Enlighten me."

Coral laughed again. "Trust me. I will. But not until we get home."

"I am not five years old!" Shan threw back her head, "Tell me *some* fucking thing!"

"Do you think vulgarity will impress me?"

"What does impress you?"

"Wise people impress me." Coral arched a brow. "Be wise. Accept that this isn't the time for our discussion and enjoy the ride."

"So it's wise to expect somebody to meekly go along when you drag them away from the only life they've known?"

"Okay." Coral exhaled loudly. "One thing. Six people gave their lives to make that ring you're wearing, trusting you will appreciate their sacrifice and do the right thing when your time comes."

Shan wanted more than ever to pull off the horrible band. "How can you say that?"

"See?" Coral shook her head. "You can't understand this yet. Don't ask me anything else."

Coral wouldn't talk about anything personal the rest of the night. At the hotel, she took a three bedroom suite. Room service brought an elegant meal of shrimp cocktails, steak and Kentucky Derby pie. Coral had wine and ordered mineral water for Shan and Isaiah.

It took all the self-control Shan could manage to keep from shoving her food into her mouth with both hands. Still, she would've been happier back home, eating fried potatoes and pinto beans. Isaiah kept looking around the room and grinning. His appreciation made Shan grin, too, the knot between her shoulder blades easing.

"You act like you've never been out of Salt Creek, either." Shan laughed, shaking her head. "At least you have a TV."

"I've never been anywhere this fancy." Isaiah pulled the tail off his last shrimp, dragged it through the cocktail sauce and dropped the whole thing into his mouth.

Coral scowled, taking a dainty bite of her own food.

"Besides," Isaiah seemed oblivious to Coral's disdain, "the only place I ever saw a TV that big," He pointed to wide set in the suite's ornate entertainment cabinet, "was at the Wal Mart in Harlan."

"I guess there must be a TV at the Bellingham."

84

Coral smirked, "There's one in each of your rooms."

"In our rooms?" Isaiah's smile nearly split his face.

Something very much like scorn flickered in Coral's eyes before she answered. "Of course."

Shan finished her dinner, but it felt like rocks in her stomach. She winced at Isaiah's surprise when she wished him an early goodnight. In her own room, she opened her case to pull out her sleep shirt and her cosmetic kit before showering. The little painting on top of her clothes caught her attention. She lifted it and inspected it carefully. The swirls of umber, green, orange and red were just tiny brush strokes. They didn't move. Shan propped the painting against the mirror on the dresser. The rough twig frame looked ugly and crude against the dark, polished wood of the hotel furniture. Shan turned away and undressed for her shower.

After taking off her charm bracelet, automatically, Shan started to remove the ring. As she pulled, the band grew snug and she fought a twinge of panic. However, when she stopped pulling, the ring twisted easily on her finger. She stepped into the shower, but even standing beneath the flood of hot water didn't take the chills away.

The same thoughts kept running through her mind. Nothing she believed seemed concrete, anymore. Even her own body seemed unfamiliar. She told herself it was just the bright light and the spotless porcelain of the hotel tub, but her feet looked like a stranger's feet and her fingers, working conditioner through her hair, looked like someone else's fingers.

Wrapping the fluffy hotel robe around her, Shan took the hair dryer from its spot by the steam-fogged mirror and went into the bedroom. She sat on the end of the bed and started brushing her hair. Watching her own image in the mirror, the light glinting off the stones in her ring as she worked the brush through her tangled hair, Shan noticed a movement in a the lower corner of the dresser. The painting!

She rose, moving closer to the picture. Had the shadows changed?

There was nothing she could point to, but, now, the scene depicted a late, summer afternoon instead of the spring morning as she remembered it. Had there been so many red and yellow leaves, earlier?

She grabbed the picture and considered taking it to Coral. Halfway to the door, she stepped on her jeans and Granny's note crinkled beneath her foot. She stopped and looked at the painting again. It didn't move, but it was still an afternoon scene. There was definitely something strange about the picture but it was Granny's and, maybe, for the time being, it was best to keep Granny things and Coral things separate.

Shan placed the painting face down on the bed while she blow-dried her hair. She dressed in her sleep shirt and picked out a pair of jeans and an Abercrombie t-shirt for her first day in New York. No sense in starting her new life, however unwelcome, looking like a hillbilly.

Shan crawled into bed and pulled the heavy down comforter to her chin. Trying to fathom the new world she faced, drained by the day's events she fell asleep almost immediately.

When she saw the clearing again, the Sentinals and Gaiaes, Shan knew she was back in the dream.

Wake up! Wake up!

"Silence!" a commanding voice sounded in her head. The voice was in her head, but it wasn't her head. Just as the body kneeling before Gaiaes was someone else's body. The stomach-twisting worries about Roman encroachment were familiar and nothing she'd ever thought. She could taste the salty tears of grief for slaughtered friends in distant groves but it wasn't her grief. It wasn't her hand, either, that reached out to touch the Goddess, but she felt the electric shock and the pull to another place.

She stood, in rapidly approaching darkness, at the end of a cornfield spreading as far left and right as she could see. Summer dry sheaves slashed at her arms and she fought to keep upright against the fierce, hot wind. Before her, a two-story white farmhouse stood in an island of yellow grass amidst the sea of corn. The front door was open and the screen slammed repeatedly. To the left of the farmhouse, a wide gray barn came apart, lifting and separating, sucked upward into a swirling, black sky. The remnants of the barn flowed over the farmhouse like planks in a flash flood, and the house came apart, too. First the tin roof, then headboards, a refrigerator and a flowered sofa sailed toward the sky. A couple crouched in the bathtub, arms around one another, white heads pressed together. The end of the tub tilted upward, and the male flew backward, his wail and the woman's lost in the whirlwind. In an instant, Shan flew with the storm. She screamed as the farmwife dropped away, face twisted, arms still reaching for husband.

She awoke, breathing heavily, skin feeling as if she'd scrubber herself with sandpaper. The clock's glowing red numbers reminded her she was in a hotel. She snapped on the light and scrambled up against the headboard. The storm felt so real, the silence of her room was deafening. She stared at the lamp's light, reflected in the mirror, until her breathing slowed.

Two nightmares on two nights since Coral had arrived. Since she'd put on the ring. She hoped it wasn't an effect of wearing the cursed piece of jewelry. If it was, she'd have to give up sleeping.

The clock read four-forty-five. She didn't want to risk going back to sleep, so she took another shower and dressed for the day. Despite lingering nausea from her nightmare, Shan was starved. There was no food in the hotel room, but there was coffee.

Granny's thick, bitter brew gave Shan the jitters, so she rarely drank coffee. Deciding to make an exception, she used the small machine in her bathroom. While the coffee cooked with hisses and gurgles, Shan examined Granny's painting, unchanged from the previous night, and put it back in her suitcase.

The coffee finished, and she filled the plastic-wrapped stoneware cup. Once she had doctored the hot liquid with cream from the tiny cooler and all the sugar she could find, Shan turned on the TV. With the volume low, she sipped her drink and watched the news.

There was a heat wave in Iceland and a killing freeze in Greece. Floods had devastated portions of India and China. Shan leaned forward, listening closely to the newscasters and reading the ticker. She watched for a while, but, to her relief, there were no breaking stories about tornadoes.

Most of the news had little impact on her. It never had. She'd grown up in the dark circle of the hills, under Granny's watchful eye. Her classmates probably thought the same way. Throughout the years, they'd been asked to report on and respond to current news, but even her teachers seemed to look at global events as something once removed from their community.

She flipped through the other channels but found nothing that interested her enough to overcome the recurring mental image of the farm woman's face, the knot in her chest every time she thought of home and the angry tingle she felt. It was totally unfair of Granny to have kept everything from her. Coral was wrong, too, giving her no say in the matter of leaving, and no time to adjust. Most of all, it infuriated her that people she didn't know could ask her to give up her life for plans they made thousands of years ago. She'd thought herself nearly an adult, and now, it seemed, she'd never really be free.

Shan pressed the scroll button on the remote, rolling through the channels angrily. Finally, she stopped on MTV and watched music videos, mouthing the words to the songs to keep from hearing her own thoughts. At five-thirty, a soft knock sounded on her door.

"Yes?" She whispered and put her ear to the door.

"I know you're up." Isaiah turned the doorknob, pushing into the room.

Shan stepped back, cheeks flaming. "What if I'd been naked?"

Isaiah grinned, "I'd run out and buy a Powerball ticket 'cause it's my lucky day."

"Minors can't play the lottery." Shan gave him a light punch and closed the door. She picked up her night clothes, tossing them onto her suitcase, covering the painting.

"I never knew you got up so early," She said, looking around the room to make sure she hadn't left anything else embarrassing lying out.

"I don't usually. I never knew you drank coffee." Isaiah lifted her cup and sniffed it. "Smells disgusting."

"It is." Shan laughed. That was the great thing about Isaiah's friendship. The sun always seemed to shine when he was around. "But it's the only food I could find."

"Did you sleep like a queen, too?" He bounced on her bed.

"Did you sleep like a queen?" Shan faked a bright smile. Even with Isaiah along, she couldn't shake her fears. She certainly didn't want to talk about her night. "Is that a new way of coming out of the closet?"

One of Isaiah's brows went up. "Yeah. I'm gay and I'm scared. So is it alright if I sleep with you from now on?"

"Dream on, boy." Shan pulled a chair beside the dresser and took another sip of her coffee. "Is my aunt stirring?"

"I ain't—haven't heard a thing." Isaiah smoothed the cover, then looked at Shan from under his brows, "I know you miss your Granny, and I miss Mom, too, but this is just…wow."

Shan forced another smile. "The most elegant place I've ever been."

"I know, right?" He rolled his eyes. "Oh, man, and the food last night."

"It was very well done."

"Girl." Isaiah crossed the room, smiling from ear to ear, and took her by the forearms. "We hit the big time!"

"Watch my coffee." Shan held the cup aloft, trying to quell her sudden irritation. Why shouldn't he be excited? He didn't have someone telling him what his destiny was going to be. He didn't dream of people being tossed like ragdolls.

Kneeling beside her, Isaiah took the coffee from her and, after putting the cup on the dresser, lifted her chin, forcing her to face him. "You know, you're doing this. No matter. No way to change it. So why get pissed? Even if we're on the road to hell, we can enjoy the trip, right?"

The single brow was up again and he smiled with one side of his face. "Come on, now. You're always going on about how you're moving to the city when you graduate. I know you've got to be a little bit excited."

Shan stared into his caramel eyes and sighed. She had no idea what things would be like in New York, or even if Coral would really let Isaiah stay. But they did have the trip.

"Maybe a little." She smiled back, realizing she meant it. Though she should be worried about everything, she couldn't help a small undercurrent of excitement.

91

She'd be seeing places she'd only dreamed about. "Granny never let me go on a field trip. I want to go to the Metropolitan Museum of Art. And Broadway. Coral said something about Broadway, didn't she?"

Isaiah rocked back on his heels and stood. He cocked his head and spoke in his southern home-boy voice. "I hope she buys you some new clothes, though, cause they ain't gonna let you in like that."

Shan laughed. Isaiah wore ripped jeans and a plaid shirt over a black t-shirt. "You're one to talk."

"Oh, I can look any kind of cool." He raised his chin.

A sharp rap made them both start.

"I've ordered breakfast." Coral said, "Are you awake?"

As she spoke, Coral came through the door. When she saw Isaiah, her eyes narrowed. "What are you doing up already?"

"I woke up around four." Shan said quickly, "and Isaiah came in about ten minutes ago."

Coral lifted one silk clad shoulder and let it drop. "We need to eat and get on the road. I don't want to hit the city during rush."

Breakfast came on a silver trolley. There was bacon, eggs, sausage, fruit, toast, waffles, pancakes, potatoes, coffee, orange juice and water in crystal glasses.

"Now this is breakfast." Isaiah flopped into his chair. Shan caught his eye. He straightened in his seat, and following her example, spread his napkin across his lap.

"I want you to eat well, because there'll be minimal stops until we get home." Coral helped herself to fruit and coffee.

Isaiah shrugged and filled his plate with pancakes, bacon and sausage. Shan took scrambled eggs, waffles and strawberries, then, as an afterthought, added several sausage links. The coffee in the silver urn smelled different from the one in her room, so she poured a cup for herself. She shook the pot at Isaiah and laughed when he grimaced.

Coral watched out of the corner of her eye while scrolling through pages on her phone. Shan thought she saw Coral's rare, tiny smile at Isaiah's comical expression. For a moment, she breathed easier.

They were on the road by six-fifteen. Coral pushed the speed limit, handling the sedan as if it were a race car. She seemed fixed on reaching the city and said very little as she drove.

The Smokey Mountains reminded Shan of home and she wondered what Granny would be doing. It was stupid to wonder. Granny would be smoking and drinking in the kitchen, like she did every morning. But was she worried about Shan?

Shan had hidden Granny's note behind the frame of Amelia's picture. She didn't think Granny would approve of Coral reading it.

Her aunt drove with purpose. Shan spent the rest of the trip trying to understand her nightmares.

The weirdest part was that she remembered the names of the Sentinels and knew them intimately. Choughaim numbered the stars and charted the course of their power, Maedar's kingdom was the air and she commanded the wind. Rayne managed the red-blooded, earthbound animals, controlling them and the stones on which they slept. Ellyng presided over water and he drove all things that lived in the deep. Daer was a little frightening because she held the reins of fire, from the world's spitting, molten core to the invisible sparks of energy which crossed the land on storms, striking plant and animal alike.

How could she know these things? Were they stories she created herself, in her dream? But even the memory of the Sentinel's voices bathed her in a peaceful glow. They comforted her because she knew them. She loved them and they loved her. Somehow, she knew, too, that these Sentinels were not really trees. Or, maybe, that they had not always been trees.

Outside the car, hills became mountains, then hills again. Despite everything, Shan couldn't help feeling excited as they passed through Pennsylvania into New York State. Isaiah teased her a little for her silence and she responded with what she hoped was a light tone, thankful Coral allowed them very little time to socialize outside the car.

"There it is." Coral said when the approached the city.

"I see it!" Isaiah pushed the back of Shan's seat.

"How far away are we?" Shan compared the differences between the New York City skyline and the one in her first nightmare. The city in her dream had been a lot smaller.

"We've got another forty minutes to the edge."
Coral glanced at Shan. "It's a very, very large city."

"Da-darn straight." Isaiah pressed his forehead
against his window. "It's got a bigger skyline than
Chicago."

One corner of Coral's mouth lifted.

Shan watched the city loom closer and closer. Each
time they regained the view after losing it around a curve,
New York City seemed larger. After a while, the skyline
stood constant and clear in the distance. Her whole body
tingled and butterflies multiplied in her stomach. She'd
dreamed of visiting New York, but the closer she got to
Coral's home, the more she wanted to know. What did her
aunt really want? What would Coral expect of Shan?
What if she couldn't do whatever it was Coral wanted?
Would Isaiah really be allowed to stay?

Before they reached the city itself, traffic gathered
around them. Shan gripped her door handle and her seat.
Coral drove about seventy miles an hour, with her bumper
just a few feet from the car in front of her. There were
cars on either side of them and one way too close to their
rear bumper.

Coral didn't seem perturbed until they exited the
expressway. A yellow cab sped around from behind,
causing her to slam on her brakes.

"Fucking cabs!" She punched her steering wheel
without taking her eyes off the road.

Isaiah kneed Shan's seat again and Shan tore her
gaze from the street long enough to glance at him over her
shoulder. Looking out his window, he pointed up.

She had been too busy worrying about crashing to notice they were in a canyon of buildings. She had to twist her neck to see the sky.

They passed a large cathedral, bright orange metal sculptures and buildings with trees stretching over rooftops. The noise, even from inside the closed car, was deafening. Horns, sirens, shouts, roars, truck engines, squealing brakes and people shouting combined to form an endless crescendo. The sidewalks were teeming. People spilled into the streets at the light changes, a parade of every type of human imaginable.

Coral seemed unaffected. Through the side mirror, Shan watched Isaiah take in the details with interest, not alarm. She assumed, having grown up in Chicago, he didn't find the city as alien a world as it seemed to her.

They traveled for more miles than Shan could calculate and the towers still blocked the sky. Finally, after their progress slowed to a crawl, Coral took a series of turns and the skyscrapers gave way to older buildings, most no more than fifteen stories. After countless blocks, Shan noticed there were fewer people on the street and the space between buildings had increased. The windows of some buildings were boarded up. Graffiti marked the concrete walls, metal doors and even the sidewalks. At one light, a group of teenagers crossed in front of them, looking belligerently at the car. One boy looked directly into Shan's eyes and hefted his crotch. She looked away.

Coral said something under her breath. It sounded almost as if her aunt was humming, but it ended too quickly for Shan to discern a tune. It was odd, but the hum seemed to carry a static charge.

The light changed, and Shan looked up as the car started forward. The boy who'd caught her eye glanced toward the car and frowned. He looked up and down the street and back at the intersection, before continuing on his way with a shrug.

They stopped at several more lights and their surroundings grew seedier. But, though there were usually people nearby when the car slowed, no one else seemed to notice the black sedan.

As dusk approached, Coral turned the car abruptly, passing a crumbling apartment building with broken windows and metal riveted over the entrance. The apartment sat on an empty lot. Across the street, on Coral's side, was an overgrown field with a few trees. On Shan's side, past the lot, a high brick wall, topped by a tall, spiked fence, bordered the street. Though layers of graffiti covered the first floors of the crumbling apartment building, and debris littered the vacant lot, the stone wall was unaccountably pristine.

They followed the narrow road for about a quarter of a mile. The field gave way to trees and brush while the stone wall continued until it angled sharply along an uneven brick road. Coral signaled, taking the turn with care.

"There's the gate," She nodded sitting up straighter.

A few hundred feet ahead, the brick drive was blocked by a massive iron gate. The wall they had followed stopped at one side of the gate and another like it took up on the other side, stretching into the trees.

As they approached, Shan saw that wrought iron formed a wide, spreading oak, tangled branches touching in the center. The middle of the gate was two halves of a large acorn and leaf cluster, very much like the one on Shan's ring. Shan recognized the oak, too. It looked like Gaiaes, from her dream.

Twenty feet from the gate, Coral hummed under her breath and the doors swung wide, allowing the car to pass. Surely, there was some kind of electric eye or a switch on the dash but Shan could see no sign of either. The hair rose on the back of her arms.

They could walk through walls, Granny had said. It was one thing to be told magic did exist after all. It was another thing entirely to see it in action.

Shan felt Isaiah's hands on the back of her seat. She didn't look at him. Unwelcome or not, Shan didn't want to miss the first glimpse of her new home.

"You'll see the Bellingham when we top this hill." Coral sounded like she would be seeing her home for the first time, too.

She slowed the car as they crested the rise, and Shan drew a sharp breath. The broadened avenue leading to the house was bordered by oaks with branches nearly touching over the drive. But at their current position, the branches seemed to have purposefully grown in such a way they framed the Bellingham.

Fronted by a vine covered tiered fountain, the building was at least five stories high. Made of white stone, it consisted of two sides connected by a single-story center. Lush greenery thrived on the roof, behind the crenellated wall joining the taller sides. Both of the wings had rooftop Gazebos. Twin gargoyles, claws piercing globes, topped each gazebo. The face of the building's center portion was marked with half columns and scrolled concrete arched the wide entry.

"Oh." Shan felt that she had stepped completely out of the real world. "Do you live there alone?"

"Hardly," Coral laughed. "My associates and I all live in here. It makes communication in our work much easier."

As they drew closer, Shan could see that lights were on in all the front windows. "There must be an awful lot of you."

"We have twenty staff members and twenty five live-in employees."

"How many rooms does it have?" Isaiah asked, drumming his fingers on Shan's seat.

Coral drove around the fountain as she answered. "It was originally a residential hotel, then an apartment building, so most of the rooms are parts of suites. We use the main floor for offices, meeting rooms, library and private museum space. The top floor of each wing has been converted to a penthouse. The three middle floors have fifteen suites or apartments each, so there are ninety regular apartments."

She stopped the car in front of the double doors. The word "Bellingham" was etched into the concrete arch. The doors were made of dark, rough planks held together by studded metal bands and marked by a single, small, beveled glass window on each side. Shan wondered if the doors had been borrowed from a medieval castle.

Before she could ask, one of the doors opened and a young woman emerged. The woman's curly red hair was pulled into a low ponytail. She wore dark leggings, tall black boots and a forest-green riding jacket. She spoke into a cellphone and rushed to open Coral's door.

"Come on, children." Coral stepped out of the car, leaving the keys ignition. "Your—er—luggage will be taken to your rooms. It's time for dinner."

The young woman bowed her head when Coral stepped out. She whispered something Shan couldn't hear, but it sounded like "Mistress."

Shan stood at the car, surveying the entrance. Granny's house and yard would fit under the portico of the Bellingham.

"This is my niece Shanleigh," Coral said but it was more of a designation than an introduction. "And her friend, Isaiah."

"Megan is my assistant, one of the staff you'll see from time to time." Coral glanced at Shan and told Megan. "Put the boy in 412 and get both their sizes so someone can collect suitable clothing."

Coral started through the open door without a backward glance. Shan grabbed her book bag, and remembering the painting in her suitcase, turned to Megan. "Could you do me a huge favor?"

The young woman smiled, "Of course."

"Let me get something out of my suitcase before you take it up."

Megan spread her hand toward the open trunk. "Please, hurry. The Mistress doesn't like waiting."

100

"I know." Shan said with feeling. Isaiah helped her open the old case. She pulled out her mother's picture and the painting. She slipped them both inside her book bag and hurried to the front door.

Coral stood in the middle of a grand entry. Her booted foot tapped on glossy brown marble. Overhead, a bronze chandelier, made to look like branches of a willow tree, cast brilliant light from thousands of bulbs nestled between leaf-shaped crystals trembling with the stir of the closing door. Wide, flat steps led to each wing and the back wall was a stone fountain ending in a pool filled with living water lilies, ferns and orchids.

"What's that?" Coral pointed to Shan's backpack. "Why didn't you leave it with Megan?"

"It's my computer and some personal stuff." Shan shrugged, hoping she sounded nonchalant.

A man came out of a door to Coral's left. She raised a hand. "We'll be eating in the small conference room, Danny."

Danny was dressed exactly like Megan, so Shan assumed it was some kind of uniform.

"And make sure Allie knows we have two new residents instead of one."

"Yes, Mistress." Danny's look held Coral's for an instant, and her expression softened. Then his gaze passed over Isaiah. His look at Shan was quick, but uncomfortably penetrating. His pink scalp showed through the flaxen fuzz of his short hair and razor burn stained his broad jawline. He looked like the bad sergeant in every spy movie Shan had seen.

"This way." Coral led them up the steps to her right and down the hall to a plain, polished wood door. She touched the door with her thumb and forefinger and it clicked open. Shan felt the now familiar tingle and tried to see, as she passed through, if the knob had a security scanner. Coral kept her hand on the door, though.

They were in a room with soft green walls, a round table and six cushioned chairs. There were two impressionist paintings on the wall, both garden scenes. A flat, black-screened monitor on a swivel framework leaned over the table. Coral touched a button near the light switch. The monitor slid back and up into a ceiling panel.

Taking a seat at the head of the table, Coral pointed to chairs at her left and right for Shan and Isaiah. Shan took her seat, sliding her backpack under the table in front of her feet.

"We're going to have dinner, and I'll personally take you to your rooms. Normally, we eat in the formal dining room. Dinner's at six-thirty. You'll be expected to be prompt and you'll dress for dinner every day."

Shan gave Isaiah a warning look. She could just hear him saying something to the effect of, "I don't usually go to dinner naked."

The door opened, admitting two workers in white, uniforms. One carried a tray of crystal and china, another carried pitchers, cloth napkins and flatware. Coral said nothing while the pair arranged place settings and poured water for Shan and Isaiah. When the servers left, after pouring dark red wine for Coral, she spoke again.

"The staff will purchase suitable clothing for both of you." Coral sipped her wine and continued. Shan took a quick drink of water, ice rattling in the glass like hail on a tin roof. Coral's eyelids flickered but she didn't complain.

"I have an education plan in place for Shan." Coral shot Isaiah a tight smile. "Of course, we'll have something worked out for you, too. I take it you are in different grades?"

"I'm a junior." Isaiah cleared his throat.

"Really." Coral's eyebrows twitched. "Impressive for a fifteen year-old."

"Almost sixteen." Isaiah smiled, but Shan wondered that he couldn't hear the odd tone in her aunt's voice.

"You're a senior, then. Correct?" Coral waited for Shan's nod before continuing. "We're actually registered in the state as a private school and have education facilities in the basement. I've materials already on hand and tutors prepared to start your education. Arrangements are being made for Isaiah as we speak."

There was a basement? Isaiah's wide-eyed stare mirrored Shan's surprise.

The entrance of people carrying covered platters, baskets of fresh rolls and pitchers of iced tea, interrupted Coral. When the staff had uncovered herb salad, Cornish hens, blueberry stuffing, new potatoes and dishes of butter, vinegar and oil, Coral said, "We'll serve ourselves tonight, Antonio."

Antonio, a broad shouldered man with a shaved head and dark eyes, nodded and left the room with the rest of the staff.

Coral passed the food around herself, and when all had been served, she spoke again. "We don't normally discuss business while eating, but there are a few things I need to settle tonight to make sure we all start off on the right foot."

She waited for Shan and Isaiah to respond.

"Okay." Shan said, pulling a small leg off her hen. She thought Coral might protest if she lifted the whole bird the way her stomach wanted her to.

Isaiah echoed Shan's okay and picked up a roll.

"Good." Coral took another drink of wine. "First, Isaiah, I believe you'll be an asset here, so if you need anything, just let me know."

Shan had trouble swallowing the food in her mouth. She didn't like the term "asset."

"Shan, in addition to your regular education, you'll be working directly with me learning the lore of our people."

"What people?" Shan frowned.

"That's a long story and really not one I normally discuss in front of outsiders."

Shan watched Isaiah. His nostril flared, and he chewed slowly. Her own face heated. "If you want me to be some kind of skinhead, you can forget it."

"No, no. It's nothing like that." Coral smiled brightly, but Shan suspected the woman had intended the misunderstanding. "We're not a race based culture. We are part of an organization concerned with the preservation of the earth."

"Like Green-Peace?" Shan blinked.

"Far older," Coral's smile became genuine. "And far, far more powerful."

Shan took a bite of her roll. According to some things she'd read, Green Peace could be militant. What did her aunt mean by more powerful?

"If there's only twenty of you, how powerful can you be?" Isaiah put his glass down.

Coral's trilling laugh went straight through Shan's head. "There are many kinds of power. For instance, this entire compound is run off alternative power. We limit our use of fossil fuels to necessary transportation."

Shan swallowed with difficulty. "Are you terrorists?"

Coral waved her hand, turning her head. "Of course not. There are many, many more of us than those who live in this house but we don't resort to mechanized weaponry."

Shan might believe that her aunt's friends did not use "mechanized weaponry" but she doubted Coral had been joking when she claimed she and her partners were powerful.

"You mean money and influence?" Isaiah went back to eating and Shan wondered how he could take everything so calmly.

"That's a great part of it, yes." Coral ate a little of her food and continued. "We've been training, amassing wealth and power for nearly two thousand years."

Shan stared at her Aunt, "Training for what?"

"We'll talk about that later." Coral used her fork to pull at her Cornish hen. "But, while you're under my roof, you both will do exactly as I say and you'll contribute to the common goal, with or without explanation."

105

They finished the meal in silence, and, after the staff had cleared away the dishes, Coral led them up three flights of stairs.

"I guess they saved money on the elevators." Isaiah whispered.

"Stairs are healthier." Coral snapped.

Isaiah rolled his eyes at Coral's back.

They arrived at his room first. Isaiah had been assigned a large suite. The siting room had leather furniture and a flat screen TV.

"Don't turn the volume up too loud," Coral remarked as they passed into the next room.

A kitchenette had a small refrigerator, microwave, sink and dishwasher. Coral told Isaiah he would be expected to eat meals in the dining room but that he could snack in his room.

"Wash your own dishes," She added. "My staff won't be your personal maids."

In the bedroom, Isaiah's unpacked duffel was folded at the foot of a queen-sized bed. A black lacquer dresser matched the curved headboard and the nightstand beside the bed. A bench, padded in black leather, stood beneath a wide window. Grinning, Isaiah opened the mirrored closet door, revealing someone had carefully hung his jeans and t-shirts.

"This is what I'm talking about."

"Don't get used to that type of clothing. You'll be provided with a wardrobe more suited to your new lifestyle." Coral wrinkled her nose. "Always put your laundry in the bathroom hamper and don't leave your things lying about. I don't like my staff wasting time doing unnecessary chores."

"Damn!" Isaiah blurted when he saw the Jacuzzi tub in his bathroom. "I think I could get used to this."

"Excellent." Coral's mouth stretched to a wide smile. "I hope you do."

Shan grinned, but something didn't sit right with her. Coral didn't seem the type to do anything without reason. Why would she be so generous with a boy she didn't know?

"Someone'll be here to show you to breakfast in the morning." Coral stood in the doorway, blocking Isaiah inside his room. "Goodnight."

When Coral turned away, Shan offered a small smile to Isaiah's frown before the door closed between them.

"Your room's at the other end of the hall around the corner." Coral stopped walking and faced Shan. "I think we should get something out of the way right now."

Shan stiffened. *Here it comes.*

"What's your relationship with that boy?"

"Oh, *jeez*. We're just friends." Shan rolled her eyes. "He's only fifteen."

"I forgot what a difference a couple of years make when you're so young." Coral's head tilted and a wistful smile crossed her face. In that moment, Shan could see the resemblance to Amelia. "I trust that means I won't hear that you've been sneaking back and forth to each other's rooms."

Coral raised her chin and looked to her left. Shan, following her aunt's gaze, saw the discreetly blinking green light of a security camera installed just above the dark crown molding. She knew she wouldn't be visiting Isaiah's room at night just as she knew any resemblance between Coral and Amelia was superficial.

"We're *friends*. But would it bother you if we were having sex?"

"Only that I can't have you distracted." Coral stopped at a door just like Isaiah's, except the number over the security window was 426. "And, I most certainly can't have you pregnant."

She opened the door and waited for Shan to enter. Shan's apartment was distinctly Victorian. Her red sitting room, complete with a wide iron fireplace, was furnished with fringed antiques, Tiffany glass and Persian rugs. The ornate four poster bed was of rich, dark mahogany with a matching dresser and chest. Brocade drapes parted to reveal a deep window seat piled high with silk cushions.

Large, renaissance style paintings dominated the bedroom and living room walls. The subjects were woodsy scenes or people in simple, ancient dress. The deep colors of the artwork were accented by wide, carved frames in rich, gilded woods. A cut crystal vase on the nightstand held a large bouquet of violets, Sweet Williams, fern and Baby's Breath. Shan lifted the card propped against the vase.

"Welcome home," said the note written in a strong, flowing hand which had to be Coral's.

She turned her head. Her aunt stared at her, mouth slightly open, gaze fixed.

108

Shan buried her face in the flowers, inhaling the sweet, welcoming smells of a mountain summer. She schooled herself to smile widely and lifted her head.

"Thank you." She said before realizing Coral had left the room.

Shan found her aunt in the living room, straightening the lace on the black iron mantel.

"The flowers are beautiful." Shan said, clearing her throat. "The whole apartment's beautiful."

Coral's expression remained impassive. "I hoped you would approve."

Shan nodded, unsure what to say. She wasn't as adept as most southern girls at knowing how to politely express her feelings.

"Shan," Coral sighed, shoulders drooping enough to suggest an underlying fatigue. "I miss my sister every day and I've longed to have you back here since Katherine and David took you away."

Coral closed her eyes for a moment before continuing. "I've redecorated these apartments half a dozen times since then."

"Thank you." What else could Shan say? She couldn't apologize for being gone and she wouldn't apologize for Granny.

As if reading Shan's mind, Coral frowned. "Believe what you will, Shanliegh. I haven't lied to you."

Coral opened the exit door. "I want this door locked at all times until you learn to make a ward. Clothes will be brought to you in the morning. Please be dressed and ready to accompany me to breakfast at six forty-five. You'll find food in the kitchenette if you get hungry before then." She hesitated, then, straightening her shoulders, left with a simple, "Goodnight."

Shan turned the bolt and stood, surveying her room. The silence settled around her, heavy and dark. She didn't want to think of anything. Not Coral, not Granny, Isaiah, the horrid ring or nightmares.

After checking that her clothes were hung in the walk-in closet, noting the insignificance of her two pairs of shoes on the huge shoe rack, Shan put the painting under her dresser and placed the picture of Amelia on the bedside table next to Coral's card.

She toyed with the card. She just couldn't believe Coral was simply the concerned aunt she seemed. Her willingness to take control of Shan over Granny's dead body, her threat to call the police and her maneuvering with Isaiah's mother all added up to a very manipulative person. On the other hand, Shan couldn't ignore her aunt's sincerity when she spoke of missing Amelia. Granny had suggested Shan learn from Coral, but, despite Granny's consistent personality up to yesterday, Shan couldn't help feeling resentful. How could Granny, who claimed to hate subterfuge, have hidden so much from Shan?

She slapped Coral's card back onto the nightstand and crossed the room to look out the window. She could see little beyond the silvery green foliage of a very tall, lush elm.

Wandering through the kitchen, she opened the cabinets, noting they were stocked with bread, crackers, dried fruit, popcorn, nuts, herbal teas, several varieties of instant coffee and various energy bars. The refrigerator held milk, juice, mineral water, butter, sliced cheeses, fruit and vegetable trays, protein shakes and a selection of deli meats. Coral didn't eat as if she were as ravenous as Shan always felt. How had she known to stock so much food for Shan?

She wished she could run down to Isaiah's apartment and see if he had a ton of food, too. On an impulse, she unlocked and opened her door. Right away, she saw the security camera across the hallway, pointed directly at her door. She waved at the device and went back into her room. Was the camera there to protect her or to guard her?

Fighting exhaustion, she poured some milk, collected three granola bars and opened the Queen Anne cabinet in the living room. As she had suspected, the cabinet housed a flat screen TV. Taking the remote stored beside it, she curled in the corner of her velvet sofa and flicked through the channels.

Shan didn't want to watch the news again, in case there were stories which could trigger more nightmares. She'd watched so little TV growing up that she had no interest in sitcom reruns and, at the moment, she couldn't stomach music, either. Finally, she settled on a Travel Channel tour of Athens. Keeping the volume low, she watched scenes of brightly colored streets and crumbling architecture, marveling most at the difference between the bright blue Mediterranean and the glimpses she had caught that day of the gray-green Atlantic.

The TV's flashing colors and the soft murmur of voices with canned music washed over Shan. Her eyelids grew heavy and after a period of welcome darkness, she was in the grove again.

She recognized it this time, feeling, as well as hearing, the voices of the Sentinels. They urged her toward Gaiaes, and, on bare feet, she crossed the carpet of grass and moss to kneel before the great oak.

"Mother." She said, reverently. Well, the word she said meant mother, she knew that, but the voice and the language were not really hers. Her hand/the other woman's hand lifted despite Shan's terror and stretched toward the bark. The ring flashed ruby, amber and emerald fire as her palm made contact with Gaiaes's skin.

She spun, again, through the vortex, landing on her back in the snow. The sky was white and hard. Crystalline flakes stung her face and the exposed skin of her arms and chest. She pushed herself upright, the biting cold making her fingers instantly stiff. Snow clung to her wool robe, weighing it down. She crouched to stand on the hem putting some measure of protection between her feet and the frozen ground. Partially obscured by the driving snow, skyscrapers towered around her. They were not right above her, though. Trees coated in ice marked a boundary between Shan and the city towers. The space around Shan had no trees, but benches and shrubs rapidly disappeared beneath the icy onslaught.

Something moved to her right. She turned, her gaze raking dozens of hunched forms, until she faced a huddled man. His sky blue eyes faded to silver as she met his stare. She fell forward, wrapping her arms around him, but he was already stiff, frost filling the ridge of his upper lip. Cold from his body spread to her in an instant, and she could feel her blood slowing, but a massive weight moved over her thoughts. Unable to stop herself, she turned her head slowly to re-examine the forms around her. The crouching, kneeling and prone shapes were not ornaments and shrubbery as she had thought. They were other men, women and children, still clutching book bags, groceries and briefcases. The woman to her left had been caught with her cellphone to her ear. White frost quickly turned the lipstick on her open mouth from blue tinged crimson to rose-petal pink. Shan scrambled back, moaning, and woke to the warmth of her living room.

As soon as she could force away that last vision of the woman's blanching tongue, Shan touched the ring. The stones were hot, removing any doubt as to the origins of her nightmares.

Why me? I didn't choose this. I didn't ask for it. Shan pulled at the offending jewelry. The harder she pulled the tighter the band grew. The stones heated again, at her touch and she let go. Turning her hand so she could see view the stones, Shan examined them closely. The emeralds were smaller than the other stones so she could only see light reflected off the facets. Past the surface of the acorn's ruby cap, a steady light glowed. Shan could see through the topaz, to her bare skin, except where the tiny spark moved, aimlessly. The gem lent a red-gold tone to her skin and the tiny hairs on her finger. Remembering the arm that was not her arm in her dreams, Shan dropped her hand, looking away, but not before registering the little light's swift course across the amber surface.

Rubbing her bare arms, she stood, pacing the length of her living room. She'd never been one to give in

to imagined fears. Granny wouldn't have allowed it.
Granny!

Why hadn't Granny explained things to Shan from
the beginning? Why keep her isolated, controlling every
move, teaching her survival skills, if she never intended
for Shan to know the truth? Granny must've planned to
tell Shan, someday, or she must've believed Coral would
eventually arrive. But which?

In the light of everything happening over the
previous two days, Shan couldn't stem a rising flood of
anger. It would've been one thing to grow up knowing she
was different, that she was expected to shoulder this
responsibility. It was an entirely different thing to have
this weight dropped on her.

She stopped, glancing down at the ring. The truth
was, Granny had given her the ring. Not Coral. For all
Shan knew, Coral might've asked before giving her the
talisman.

She checked the time on the cable box. Five
minutes before six. It wouldn't be long until she would
see Coral. Surely, if the woman expected cooperation
from Shan, she would eventually answer some questions.

A discrete knock interrupted Shan's thoughts.

"Who's there?" Shan put her hand on the bolt.

"Staff, Miss Morgan." Shan blinked. *Miss
Morgan?*

Undoing the lock, she said, "I'm Shan Amos."

"The Mistress says you're Miss Morgan." Megan
smiled with one side of her thin mouth, but real humor lit

114

her pale blue eyes. "I've brought you some new clothes. I'll just hang them in your closet."

Shan stepped aside, automatically reaching for some of the bags Megan carried. Megan shook her head, ginger curls dancing, and walked around Shan.

"It's okay." Megan grinned, "I've got it. Want to come and see?"

Shan followed Megan. She recognized some of the names on the bags; Saks, Macy's and Nordstrom.

"You're to wear these clothes today." Megan dropped the bags on the bed. Her gaze raked Shan's figure and she shook her head, but the twinkle in her eyes didn't go away. "Thank goodness!"

With quick, birdlike movements, Megan unpacked slacks, leggings, blouses, skirts, lingerie, hosiery and several pairs of shoes. Shan touched one of the blouses draped across the bed. Her calloused fingers caught on the thin silk. Her cheeks warmed and she backed away, leaving Megan to finish unpacking.

Megan took boxes of varying shapes out of the last Saks bag. She opened each box and placed the little pots, jars and tubes on Shan's dresser. "Skin care. Clinique. I had to guess, but hopefully these will do until you can get your own brand."

Megan pulled out a white leather cosmetic bag, stamped "Chanel" and handed it to Shan.

"Body wash, lotion and perfume. The Mistress believes we should take proper care of ourselves so we can better manage our duties." She emptied the last package, another kit, this one clear, revealing white tubes of Leonor Greyl hair care products. "I'll let myself out. You should take your shower and get dressed. The Mistress will expect you to be ready when she comes down."

Megan collected the shopping bags and left. Shan stood, holding the two cases, until she heard the front door open.

"Thank you!" She called, but she wasn't sure Megan heard. Shan dropped the products on her bed and went to her dresser to look at the pots and tubes. She'd never thought of using most of this stuff. Foaming cleanser, toner, perfecting cream. She looked in the mirror. A touch of red from the sun crossed her nose and cheeks, but otherwise, she liked her skin. If she didn't use all this stuff, would Coral know?

She picked up a bottle of hand cream and opened it. The luxurious moisturizer felt like satin between her fingertips, immediately softening the rough patches which had caught on the silk. If she was going to wear the clothing Megan brought, she'd have to use the cosmetics. Otherwise, she'd go to breakfast looking as if she had climbed through a briar patch.

Shan carried the new items to her bathroom. Fluffy white towels, marked with an elaborate "M," waited on the towel rack. A soft, white robe hung behind the door, a pair of terrycloth footies clipped to the pocket. In fifteen minutes, Shan ran the waiting brush through her hair, surrounded by the mingled, exotic smell of her new conditioner and the bright, rich scent of Chanel.

She dried her hair quickly with the blow dryer she found under the sink and went to choose her clothing. She toyed with the idea of wearing her old clothes, but Granny always said people were more likely to listen to you, if you

116

showed you were willing to listen to them. Not that Granny followed her own advice.

Shan dressed in nude stockings, jeans by a designer she didn't recognize, a tailored white cotton blouse and soft, black flats. She rummaged through her jewelry box, but finding nothing befitting the new clothes, decided to go without.

She used the face cream and the hand lotion and added a touch of her own lip gloss. The girl in the mirror looked far more sophisticated than Shan had ever imagined she could be. She couldn't resist a surge of pleasure. Her hair gleamed, falling over her shoulders in black waves, garnet highlights catching the light. She smiled at herself, but the smiling stranger reminded her just how much she'd changed in the past forty-eight hours. She turned away from the mirror.

What would she find out today? What would she have to do? She considered taking out the painting to see if it had changed again, but before she pulled it from beneath the dresser, a sharp rap sounded from the living room.

"Coming." She cried sprinting to the door. There was no response so Shan turned the knob anyway.

Coral surveyed Shan then gave a nod. "Better. Stop chewing your lip."

Shan obeyed. Coral was more intimidating than she had been the day before. Dressed in a royal blue, tailored pantsuit, Coral wore a white scarf around her short hair and a gold toque at her neck, Shan thought her aunt looked like a CEO instead of the fanatic head of an eco-terrorist group.

"Let's go." Coral started walking and, pulling the door closed, Shan followed. Coral stopped, waiting until Shan had locked the door. "We need to get you some jewelry."

"No more like this, I hope." Shan waved her left hand.

"There *is* no more like that." Coral's lips thinned. "And let's hope there will never be."

"Why won't you just tell me what's going on?"

"This is not the place or the time." Coral glanced over her shoulder but kept walking.

"I'm sick of secrets." Shan stood still. "This ring gives me nightmares!"

Coral paused, her spine stiffened. Brows arched, eyes wide, she walked back to face Shan. "What kind of nightmares?"

"I'll tell you after you tell me some things."

Coral's mouth and right arm twitched at the same time. "I have to explain to you, in one day, what you should've been taught over seventeen years." Her eyes narrowed and she took a deep breath before continuing. "I can tell you're going to argue every step of the way. I think it would be easier on both of us if we had breakfast before commencing battle."

"Does that mean you'll explain today?" Shan waited, not moving.

"It's my top priority. However, I won't talk about it in front of your friend." Coral continued down the hallway. "Come now. Patience is a mark of maturity.

118

Shan followed her aunt past Isaiah's room. She was eager to see him and equally anxious to be alone with her aunt.

Coral pushed through the door beneath a brushed aluminum exit sign and trotted down the stairs with surprising agility. Shan was glad the noise of their shoes kept them from talking. She didn't want to talk about anything but her so-called destiny and the ring.

When they reached the first floor, Shan realized she was more winded than her aunt. She shook her head. Coral must work out. The dining room, behind pocket doors off the far wing, was bigger than Shan had anticipated. It could've held her high school cafeteria *and* the kitchen.

A gold-toned Persian carpet softened the museum cold of the brown marble floor. Beneath a wide, round, crystal chandelier, large silver candelabra marked each end of a gold brocade runner flowing down the center of a glossy wooden table. Shan estimated there were at least twenty chairs.

Along the far wall, a fireplace of white stone rose to the ceiling. The grate could have accommodated half a cow, easily. Staff, in their green and black livery, lined up on either side of the hearth. Isaiah stood off to one side, alone.

Seeing Shan, he flashed his brightest smile and marched across the large room. He looked older in his khaki pants, red Henley and black jacket.

"Shizzle, girl. You look like a movie star." He arched one eyebrow and spread his hands. "I'm about scared to talk to you."

"You look like an Old Navy ad." Shan waved her finger at him. "If Gary and Matt could see you now."

"I know." He shook his head, "they'd be in a whole lot bigger hurry to beat the crap out of me."

"Shan," Coral placed her hand under Shan's elbow, pulling her to the head of the table. "You'll sit to my right."

Coral touched the top of the second chair to her left. "Isaiah will sit here."

Shan sighed, closing her eyes. Of course they wouldn't be allowed to sit together. When Coral moved to her own seat, Isaiah winked at Shan.

Danny pulled out Coral's chair and Shan found a young, dark haired male holding the back of her own chair. She grasped the other side and pulled. The fellow actually looked at her aunt before releasing his hold. Shan rolled her eyes.

"That's fine, Liam." Coral nodded, then caught Shan's eye.

Lifting her napkin, Coral shrugged. "It's the purpose of society to establish patterns of behavior which allow humans to live together reasonably."

Shan noticed Isaiah seemed just as bewildered as she by all the dishes, glasses and flatware arrayed before them.

"Don't worry." Coral smirked. "You'll get used to it. Just watch us and do what we do."

People dressed in green jackets and black pants filled the empty seats at the table. They stared at Coral as if she were the queen of England. Servers in white

120

brought covered dishes, pots and baskets from a green door at the far corner of the room.

While they placed food and poured coffee and tea, Coral introduced Shan and Isaiah to all the members of her staff. Shan tried to memorize the names and faces while watching which utensil her aunt used for each dish. By the time the servers had cleared away the last pieces of fruit, Shan felt as though she'd climbed a mountain. Egg cup, grapefruit spoon, butter knife, pastry fork—Shan couldn't remember eating a single bite, though she must have. The only staff whose names she remembered were Megan, Danny and the brown-nosing Liam who sat beside her.

In the hall outside the dining room, Coral said she had business matters to attend to, asking Shan and Isaiah to follow Danny to the basement.

Shan ground her teeth. How much longer before she got answers?

"I'll only be a few minutes." Coral watched Shan with narrowed eyes. "I'd rather not be interrupted once we get started."

Coral and Danny shared a brief, intense look before she walked away.

A wooden door at the far end of the east wing hallway led to a white concrete foyer. Danny unlocked a gray metal door with a card and they followed him down a very long flight of metal stairs. They went through another locked door.

"We're serious about security." Danny clipped the card back inside his pocket. "No one gets in or out of here without a key card."

"Here" was a long concrete hallway with a distinct downward slope. The floor, walls and ceiling were white. Large, recessed light fixtures were covered by thick metal grills, illuminating the walkway with little squares of light.

"What about an emergency?" Isaiah hesitated. Shan remembered he didn't like tight spaces.

"Trust me." Danny's smile didn't reach his eyes. "This is where you want to be in an emergency. It's watertight, built to withstand a nuclear explosion and has its own light and water systems. It has everything you'd want in an emergency."

"Except air." Isaiah stood by the door.

Shan exhaled loudly then looked at Danny. "Does it have a fresh air system?"

"Of course." Danny started down the hall. "Classroom four's this way."

Shan patted Isaiah's arm. "You won't smother to death, Isaiah."

"Don't be a smartass." He pushed her lightly. "It's probably full of spiders."

Shan peered sharply at the corners. She couldn't tell if there were cobwebs. "Thanks, Isaiah. That's just what I needed, another reason not to sleep."

"Mr. Farris, this is your classroom." Danny held open a blue steel door. If the man had noted their banter, he gave no indication. "Ms. Jessie McGill will be your tutor."

A middle-aged woman, not much taller than Shan, held out her hand. "Call me Miss Jessie. Everyone does,"

Isaiah ducked and shook her hand. "Pleased to meet you, Miss Jessie."

Miss Jessie's silver-streaked auburn hair was cut short and tucked behind her ears. She wore no makeup and, across her cheeks, cinnamon colored freckles stood out against her pale skin. She offered her hand to Shan. "Miss Morgan, it's a delight to finally meet you."

"Nice to meet you." Shan shook the teacher's hand firmly. Miss Jessie's smiled and nodded twice with obvious deference. What had Coral told people?

"Will there be anything else?" Miss Jessie looked at Danny.

When Danny shook his head, the teacher swept her hand around the classroom, "Let me show you our state of the art learning center, Isaiah."

Shan watched Isaiah's progress while Danny waited at the door. Isaiah surveyed the room without comment. Shan could tell he was impressed, though, because he had that half-smile she'd learned to associate with his intense concentration. He leaned forward, rounding his back too much. When something had his complete attention, he forgot his efforts to look strong. She didn't blame him. Salt Creek high school had one computer lab with four obsolete computers.

Miss Jessie's classroom boasted several large desks, all equipped with computers, electronic microscopes, printers and calculators. The walls were floor to ceiling shelves filled with leather bound, hard back and paperback books. A Bose music system was tucked in a corner and speaker grills were visible in the ceiling around the room. A large display panel hung behind the teacher's desk and an array of controls stood to one side.

Isaiah chose a desk and Miss Jessie started the computer.

Isaiah shrugged and, with a grin, waved at Shan.

"Have a good day, Miss Morgan." The teacher leaned over Isaiah's shoulder.

Danny led Shan further down the hall. The downgrade continued and Shan realized they were going deeper underground. She didn't know which to worry about more, spiders or the possibility she was being led into a terrorist's control room.

"This is where you'll be." Danny stopped beside a set of double doors after Shan had followed him for about a mile. Though, she realized, she must be overestimating. Big as it was, the Bellingham couldn't be a mile long.

"After you." Shan held her hand out.

"We have to wait for the Mistress." Danny pointed to a discrete panel on the wall. There was no keypad, just a lighted screen. "That's a palm scanner. The Mistress has it set so she is the only one who can open these doors."

There were two small windows, but Shan could see nothing past the frosted glass. "Haven't you ever been in there?"

"Of course." He took up his post next to the security panel, feet shoulder-width apart, hands behind his back.

So what's in there? Shan wanted to ask, but she doubted Danny would give her a satisfactory answer. Hoping Coral would arrive soon, Shan started to sit on the floor before remembering she wore expensive new clothing. She leaned against the wall. The cool concrete had no hint of damp, but she detected an earthy smell, like the old, unused well behind Granny's house. For all Shan knew, they could be much deeper beneath the surface than a well.

The doors clicked open in front of her and Coral stood with one hand on her hip. "Ready?"

Shan straightened. Coral ushered her into the room and shut the door, leaving Danny standing in the hall.

"I have my own entrance, directly from my apartment." Coral touched a switch and the dim lights brightened. "This is where we work."

The space was bigger than the dining room but more utilitarian. Reflective black tiles crossed overhead, punctuated with recessed lights and the main wall was padded, floor to ceiling, in black.

"The work areas." Coral's arm swept around the divided space.

"Here is where we train our physical body." The far side looked like an exercise studio, with mirrored walls and a padded floor.

"This is where we hone our mental powers." The floor in the center section resembled the kind of polished laminate used in basketball courts. It boasted a weight bench, loose metal bars and stacks of concrete blocks.

"And this," Coral crossed to a black glass wall to her right, "Is where we train the spirit."

When Shan stood beside her, Coral waved her hand, murmuring, and the glass parted. Through the panel was a garden. They stood at the head of a path between two grassy sections. Coral went through and Shan followed.

Once they were both inside, Coral spoke again and the panels slid together. As Shan watched, a scene spread across the glass. It was like looking out a window at a dense forest. Trees grew close together, leaves dancing in an invisible breeze, while ferns, wildflowers and moss marked a forest floor disappearing beyond the trees.

In front of the screen, real trees grew in dark soil contained by natural stone. Water flowed down the back wall, over lichen covered rocks, and fell into a green pool surrounded by ferns, wild orchids and tufts of grass.

The remaining two walls were blocked by live trees and bushes. Stone benches and small fountains were installed at the border. From a bronze sundial, flagstone paths radiated to each section of the room. A narrow shadow on the sundial's surface made Shan look up. The sun, in the bright blue sky, shone far, far overhead. Shan's mouth opened.

"Incredible, isn't it?" Coral shaded her eyes. "It's a projection of the real thing."

Squinting, Shan looked for the place where the glass wall met the ceiling. After a few seconds, she detected the shadow of an angle. "It's beautiful."

"A good place to start, don't you think?" Coral took a seat on a stone near the pool. Shan sat opposite her aunt, thoughts whirling. If Coral ran a terrorist operation, the control room must be somewhere else and the technology must be beyond anything Shan had ever imagined.

"May I see your left hand, please?" Coral held her own hand out expectantly. "We'll begin with the ring."

Remembering the ring's response to Isaiah's attempts to remove it, Shan stretched her arm cautiously. Coral took Shan's fingers, leaning forward rather than pulling. She examined the ring for a moment.

Still holding Shan's fingers, Coral asked, "Do you see the light moving in the topaz?"

Shan didn't know how she should answer.

"You have to be willing to trust me a little, or the next few hours are going to be a waste of time for both of us." Coral's clear eyes gazed into Shan's. "If it helps, know this: It's vital to my purpose that you understand as much about all this as possible in the time we have."

Coral looked down. "This ring is nearly two thousand years old and it's a lot more than a piece of jewelry."

"Believe me, I got that." Frozen blue eyes and curious dark ones pushed at the back of Shan's mind. "What is it and why am I wearing it?"

Coral let go of Shan's fingers and Shan folded her hands in her lap.

"The ring was made for you." Coral ran her fingertips along the bottom edge of her hair, feathering it over her ear. "And you were made for the ring."

"A ring was made two thousand years ago for me?"

"Six spirits sacrificed their earthly bodies to make this ring so you could use it to restore the balance on the planet."

Remembering the living spark in the topaz, Shan pushed her thumbnail under the band, wanting to pry it as far away from her skin as possible. "Is there blood in it?"

"Ah, much more than that."

Shan would've felt better if Coral had simply said no.

"The stone was imbued with the magic of five individuals and—"

"Choughaim. Maedar. Ellyng. Rayne. Daer." Shan whispered the names and the voices resonated in her mind as they did in her dream.

"What?" Coral's eyes widened. Her face paled. "Katherine said she told you nothing!"

"She didn't tell me anything." Shan caught her own hair behind her back, crushing the ends in her fist. "I had a dream."

"You dreamed of the Sentinels?" Coral leaned forward, hands on Shan's knees "Did they speak to you? What did they say?"

Shan recoiled, icy chills pushing the warmth from her body. "I don't know!"

Coral leaned back, gripping her own seat so hard her knuckles were white. "Tell me what you dreamed."

Shan didn't want to remember but the scenes were there again, filling her mind as intense and vivid as they had been on the previous nights. She described them to Coral.

"Palax Lae's visions." Coral breathed. "I wonder if she's sending them to you—she has to be."

"Who's Palax Lae?" Shan's voice was hoarse. "Did Palax Lae have red curly hair and long fingers?"

128

"Palax Lae was the druid priestess who founded The Circle. In the first century. Gaiaes sent her visions of the future. Showed her the end result of Rome's policy of dominating the earth, training up people to ravage nature, claiming their god would give them a new earth." Coral rubbed her palms together, arching her brows, focus distant. "Palax Lae, interpreting Gaiaes's visions, founded The Circle. Then, she gave up her life to help create the talisman you're wearing. I have no idea what she looked like."

Something foreign moved at the back of Shan's thoughts. She shook her head, rubbing the ring against the soft material of her pants.

"Wait." She frowned. "Gaiaes. The big oak tree, right? Is she sending me those visions?"

"It's probably Palax Lae. Gaiaes is lost." Coral's eyes grew luminous, irises reflecting emerald depths. "The Romans chopped down Her tree and burned the wood. There were no priests or priestesses to perform a ritual, no vessel for Her to enter." It surprised Shan that, when speaking of Gaiaes, Coral's face reflected the same deep sadness it did when she talked about Amelia. "There was no place for Her spirit, so she's lost."

"Why did they chop down the tree?"

"Haven't you had world history?" Coral's words were strained, her lips drawn back like an angry dog's, "They created a god to rule the world. So they had to stamp out any opposing gods."

"How did they know about Gaiaes ?" Coral's reverence made Shan uncomfortable. She had only seen Gaiaes as a symbol—a huge tree.

129

"Because they tortured the druids, forcing sons to kill mothers, hurting children in front of parents, until they found out all they needed to know."

"Granny said you had magic." Shan leaned forward, heart pounding. "Didn't the druids have magic? Why didn't they use it?"

"We druids all have magic, but only a portion of what our ancestors had. Still, druid magic was created to heal and to build, not to tear down and not to kill." Coral tossed her head, "Not then."

"Not then?" Shan's mouth went dry. "They—*you* can kill with magic now?"

"Over the last two millennia, The Circle has learned to redirect druidic magic. If our purpose is pure, we can throw fire and lightening," Coral sighed, "with enough strength to kill one person at a time. Even now, we couldn't stand against an army."

"But," She sat straight, her shoulders square, her head high, "There is one druid who can, and that's why Palax Lae sacrificed herself and the Sentinels."

The presence fluttered in Shan's mind, again. She shook her head. "No."

"Don't you realize those dreams are real? Each one of those people you saw is *real*." Coral stood, throwing her hands out, "They're going to die, and millions more with them, if you don't do what you've been called to do."

Coral walked up and down the path in front of the fountain. "That child in your dream, those people, they're living and breathing right now. But the earth has been broken. For a long time, it has been reacting to rid itself that which is hurting it. Its response is escalating."

Shan remembered the increasingly strange weather back home, the news stories about heat waves, hurricanes and floods.

"Now that things have started," Coral shook her head, slowly, "Reactions will grow much more violent, very, very quickly."

"Granny said there were two stories about me." Shan swallowed, her throat sticking together.

"That's Katherine's interpretation."

"What do *you* want from me? What am I supposed to do?"

Coral stopped, wheeling to face Shan. "You're meant to save the earth."

Shan didn't feel relieved. There would be more. She knew it.

"Thinking like Katherine's is why the druids were slaughtered in the first place. I don't understand how people who knew what happened could forget. I guess Amelia was blinded by her natural love of her child, David by his love for Amelia and Katherine keeps her mind closed because she lost David." Coral's hands were on her hips. Her eyes narrowed. "There were druids who surrendered to Rome. They thought their people would be spared. There were so many who died willingly, thinking they would save others. But nothing stopped the Romans."

"I know enough history to know Rome fell, eventually."

"Ha." The gleam in Coral's eyes, her rasping laugh, brought back Granny's warning about fanatics. Coral started pacing again, her movements controlled, athletic, "the secular government fell. You tell me, Shan, what nation is the biggest world power, right now?"

"This one." Shan cringed. She hated playing to Coral's fervor, but the more she knew, the better her chances of finding a way out of this insanity.

"And who controls this one?"

"The people?" What answer would satisfy Coral? "Corporations?"

"You're smart. You almost have it," Coral, paused, holding up a finger, "Ostensibly, the people control the government. But who controls the people?"

Shan lifted her shoulders and let them fall. Several answers came to mind but she had no idea which would suit Coral.

"I suppose you don't watch the news, either." Taking her seat once more, Coral ran both hands through her hair. "Of course corporate interests control this government, and every other government, but how do they do it in this 'land of the free?' They tell people it's God's will. And who is in control of God?"

"The Pope? The Vatican?"

"So tell me again that Rome fell."

"Thank you for the history lesson." Shan crossed her arms, "But there's a ton of religiouns and they're always fighting each other. I don't see what anybody can do about it, especially me."

"It's not about religion," Coral smiled and Shan realized she had played into her aunt's hands. "It's about corporate freedom to make a profit on the destruction of the planet. It's about the death of every living thing on the planet. People are taught this world doesn't matter. Why

132

should they care about a world which is going to end when their messiah returns?"

Despite her antipathy, Shan understood. She nodded.

"So why not dynamite the ground for more fossil fuels? Cut down the rain forest? Why worry about emissions? Why control population? It doesn't matter, because, in the end, they think their god will give them a new planet."

"But one person can't stop climate change."

"With the right tools, the right person can stop the infection before the earth becomes uninhabitable."

Shan looked away from Coral's flushed face. "You think that's me?"

"I know it's you. It's why you were made."

"Made!" Shan slapped the stone, standing up. "I'm a person. I have rights. I get to choose."

"Oh, Shan." Coral crossed her legs, holding one knee. Her lips curved in a mocking smile. "You *were* made and you *are* allowed to choose. From two options: one way some people live, the other way everybody dies."

Tears stung Shan's eyes and she turned away from her aunt. "You can't put that all on me any more than you can make a person."

Shan wrapped her arms around her chest. She would *not* remember the nightmares. She wouldn't.

"Sit down." Coral commanded. When Shan didn't move, Coral shouted. "Sit down!"

Shan sat, clenching her teeth. Her aunt was crazy.

"You were created with magic. Magic from a lot of people including me, your mother, David and your

133

precious Granny. That's why she didn't tell you anything. She was in on this from the beginning."

"In on what?"

"Creating you."

"That's disgusting."

"It had nothing to do with sex, Shan." Coral spoke softly. "As far as I know, and I *would* know, your mother was a virgin. You're a moonchild. Created in your mother's womb through the earth's natural magic to be the receptacle for Palax Lae's reincarnation."

"I'm the reincarnation of Palax Lae?" Shan recalled the pale hand in her dream.

"You should've been." Coral's hand shot out, her fingers circling Shan's wrist. She didn't resist when her aunt pulled her hand forward. "But Palax Lae's spirit is still in the talisman. I see it there. I don't know whose spirit inhabits your body."

Shan pulled away. "This is nuts."

"Is this nuts?" Coral flicked her wrist and a flame danced above her open hand. She swung her arm and the flame shot out, forming a circle around them.

"A magician's trick." Despite her words, Shan knew it wasn't a trick, "Anyway, how's believing all this any different than believing in God?"

"I never said there weren't gods." Coral wagged her finger, "There was Gaiaes, but She's lost. Her children died to grant you their powers. Are they energies formed by the universal unconscious or are they beings who lived before us? I don't know and it doesn't change anything, either way." Coral's voice was high pitched and her expression more than a little frightening. The veins in her neck stood out, her eyes bulged. "The world's about to become uninhabitable. All living things will die." She exhaled. "That's what's important, what I care about."

"How do you do magic if you don't know?"

"It's the same as turning on the light without understanding how electricity works." Coral leaned forward, "You don't have to know where magic comes from. You only have to know which switch to flip for a specific result. And that is what I have to teach you."

Goosebumps rose on Shan's arms. Would she actually be able to do magic?

"But first," Coral's eyes narrowed, "I think you need to see more than my 'magician's trick.'"

Coral closed her eyes, mumbling in her singsong tone. The air crackled with the same charge Shan felt in the car and at the doors. The back of her neck tingled and her ears rang. The light within Coral's circle began to change. A blue-white orb, like one of those lightening balls from a science fair, formed on the path next to Coral.

Her chant continued and the lightening ball grew longer, wider. Shan's eyes were so dry, blinking hurt. The light coalesced into a shape and, in a fraction of a second, a woman stood on the path. About Shan's height, the woman wore a long white robe. Strawberry curls tumbled down her back. Her small-boned face was slender, her eyes wide and sapphire blue. She wore a crown of mistletoe and a gold circlet around her neck.

"Priestess Palax Lae." Coral lifted her shaking hand and bowed her head.

"Priestess Coral Morgan." Palax Lae's strong voice echoed as though she were in an auditorium. Her long, white fingers touched Coral's and she tilted her head.

"This is the child." Palax Lae whirled, her robes and curls dancing in a secret wind. Black clouds formed behind her, and her next words rumbled like thunder, "Who inhabits this body?"

"I am Shanleigh Amos." Shan stood, furious that she spoke without will.

"Who were you *before*?" The sound waves blasted through Shan.

Rocking on her feet, she crossed her arms. She wanted to run. Her blood thrummed through her body and she feared she would die. Her words came of their own accord, "I am Shanleigh Amos."

"Priestess." Coral rose, too, stepping over to Palax Lae. "She must be a new spirit."

"Who were *you* before?" Palax roared at Coral.

Coral swayed, her eyes glazed and she answered, "I am Taysine of Iceni."

Palax Lae faced Shan. "New spirit, this is not your body. Go."

Once more, the power blasted through Shan but her words were her own. "This *is* my body."

"Parasite!" Palax Lae raised her arms. Light flashed through the roiling clouds behind her.

"No, priestess!" Coral grabbed the woman's arm. "You'll destroy her."

"My mission comes first." Palax Lae shook off Coral's hand.

136

"We need her to complete that mission." Coral twisted her hands together over her stomach, "there is no time to make another."

Palax Lae's eyes glittered. She regarded Coral then Shan. "Show me the talisman."

Shan's arm lifted and Palax Lae caught the ring. She pulled, but the ring did not budge. Palax Lae pulled harder and harder.

"Stop!" Shan caught her own wrist with her right hand, squeezing to shut off the pain. The priestess crushed Shan's hand in her own, wrenching and pulling at the ring with determined might. Shan's bones cracked and she screamed.

"Blood and flame!" Palax Lae released Shan's finger. "It will not come off!"

Shan cradled her hand in the crook of her right elbow. With every heartbeat, white hot pain shot up her arm.

Palax Lae touched Shan's hand and the pain disappeared. She stared at the druid, stunned by the sudden relief and the ecstatic heat that flooded her body.

"Will *it* work with us?" Palax Lae, growing transparent, addressed Coral.

"She'll do what's necessary." By the time Coral finished speaking, Palax Lae had completely disappeared.

"I didn't expect her to be so strong." Coral touched Shan's left hand. "Any pain?"

"No." Shan backed away. "I thought you said druids healed instead of hurting."

"I'm truly sorry." Coral licked her lips. "But I said druid *magic* was created to heal and build. She didn't hurt you with magic."

"She's evil!"

"No," Coral said, "She's efficient. That's why she was a priestess."

Shan stared at her aunt. Palax Lae had called Coral "priestess." If the ancient priestess had been chosen for her ruthless efficiency, what kind of person was her current successor?

"Let's get to work then." Coral said without further explanation. She sat on her stone, curling her legs beneath her. "Remember I said that all druids have use of a natural magic? You do, too. Sit."

"Can Palax Lae come out of the ring on her own?"

"She's bound there and can only be brought out and held through the use of a great deal of power." Shan noticed, as her aunt spoke, that the woman's face and neck were slick with sweat. "Will you please sit?"

Shan obeyed. Her thoughts wouldn't settle. If she knew how to open the glass doors, she'd run from the room and keep on running. But, on the other hand, it seemed magic was real and she didn't know the world outside the room any more than she understood the one inside. She'd better learn what she could.

"Magic is simply directed energy. Learning it, for most people works like learning any other thing. At first, you'll find it slow and cumbersome, as we all did." Coral looked down at her hands. "However, the more you practice, the better your result."

Shan waited, hoping her aunt would be more specific.

"We start by learning to see our magic core." The corners of her mouth turned down. "Normally, this is where I would give an acolyte explicit instructions. But I can only give you generalities about finding the connection within. Once you can do that, though I'll help as much as I can, you'll have to find your own way"

"What? Why?"

"Because, normal druid magic creates. Our magic was given so that we could serve the earth's needs for renewal. We keep the balance by *making*." Coral looked down at the pool and a whirlpool formed. When she no longer watched, the surface settled to gentle waves. "You are, in a way, the anti-druid."

"Meaning?"

"You *unmake*." Coral picked a leaf from a small shrub by the pool. She pulled at the edges, ripping the green body from the stem. "No druid knows how that works."

"How do you know I—unmake?" Great. Magic was real, but, of course, Shan couldn't have the kind everyone else had.

"I noticed, even in your stress coming out here, you had quite a healthy appetite. But you're rail thin. Are you always hungry?"

Shan nodded. Even now, her stomach grumbled.

"Gaiaes gave her druids the ability to make and to heal, to keep the balance of nature. She gave each of the Sentinels, her children, the power to *unmake* the specific things under their control. Palax Lae and The Circle

139

helped the Sentinels sacrifice themselves, with Gaiaes's blessing, so that their powers could be held for you. When you put on the ring, the powers transferred to you."

"But I've always been hungry."

"Yes, your body was created to be a repository for tremendous power."

"Because I was supposed to be Palax Lae come back?"

Coral's head tilted. "There's more to it than that. In each incarnation, we druids occupy human bodies. We train for years, but, by the time we can use magic, these bodies are dying. They're draining. Therefore, we don't hold energy. We manipulate energy outside us for building and healing. If we tried to hold it, our bodies would die quite quickly."

"Won't my body start to decay, too?" Shan rubbed her thighs.

Coral bared her teeth in a grim smile, "Your body will continue regenerating, absorbing more and more magic. Your appetite for food is insatiable because your body's desire for energy is boundless. You draw power by your very nature. Unless you balance that influx by discharging magic, at some point, it will explode from you with all its destructive potential."

Shan stared at her aunt. "You're kidding."

"My dear," Coral patted Shan's knee, but her words and her actions seemed mechanical, "You'll soon learn that I don't exaggerate. Now, close your eyes and listen to me."

"You say I'm supposed to save the earth, but you're telling me my power is for destruction." Shan stood, arms crossed, chin high. "It sounds to me like Granny was telling the truth."

Coral exhaled with force. "You are to save the earth by destroying that which is killing it. It's really very simple and logical. Stop acting childish. Sit down and do as I say."

Shan took her seat again, but her teeth were clenched. There was some hope though. The druids had found a way to turn healing into killing. Maybe, she could turn destruction into healing.

"By the way, when I said your magic could explode from you, I didn't mean like a stick of dynamite. Think of it more like a nuclear explosion. Now, close your eyes."

Shan closed her eyes, shivering. The idea of accidentally releasing a nuclear explosion made her nauseous. She had to learn enough to prevent that, at least. Anyway, she couldn't help being excited about wielding magic, but she had no intention of letting Coral know that.

"Allow your hands to rest on your knees. Put your feet flat on the floor." Coral spoke slowly and rhythmically. "Inhale deeply, filling your chest, your belly. Feel the breath. Exhale slowly. Breathe in, again, this time counting to seven. As you count, you will relax more and more. At seven, you will be in a trance. Concentrate on your breathing. Send your breath to every part of your body. Push away all other thoughts."

Shan did as Coral instructed, noting the springy grass beneath her feet, the cool feel of cotton across her shoulders. She continued breathing, ignoring other thoughts, worries and fears.

"You're inside your mind. It's like a dark cave." Coral said, "You feel perfectly safe, but you can see nothing. You smell nothing and you hear only the sound of my voice. Spend a moment noting the safe, warm texture of the darkness."

Shan felt the satiny comfort of the dark.

"Look around and you'll see a door."

She saw the door as Coral spoke. It was far down a grassy path, and as Coral suggested, Shan imagined herself walking toward it.

"When you reach the door, take time to examine it."

Shan's imaginary door was barely tall enough for her and it was made of rough bark. A leather handle was knotted through a hole in the door.

"When you open it," Coral whispered, "There will be a bright light above a pillar. Don't be afraid. Just watch it from the doorway." She inhaled. "Open the door."

Shan opened the door and her imaginary world exploded. Intense light knocked her back. She opened her eyes.

"What happened?" Coral scowled.

"The light was too bright." Black dots danced before Shan's eyes. "It pushed me out."

"Let's try again," Shan's aunt sighed, "this time, look down as you open the door and just feel the warmth of the light."

"What is the light?"

"It's just your core power. It can't hurt you."

Shan followed Coral's directions again, and, again, the light's brilliance pushed Shan away. They started over and got the same result. Coral insisted they try again and again, until Shan's body was drenched with sweat and she was so hungry she thought about eating the water plants in the fountain.

"It throws me out!"

"It can't." Coral messaged her temples. Sweat dampened the fringe of hair crossing her forehead. "You're backing out. You're afraid of it."

"I'm not." Shan's stomach grumbled and her aunt winced.

"It's lunch time anyway." Stretching, Coral left the pool and, speaking in her singsong language, opened the glass partition. "We'll try again afterward."

"You used magic to open that door, didn't you? The air felt tingly."

"Good. You're detecting magic." Coral's expression relaxed. "Practice that skill. It'll prove quite useful."

"It's a little like static electricity."

"Soon, you'll be able to use your inner eye to see power, including other people's constructs and your own working."

"Did you use healing or building magic to open the door?"

"It's really the same thing. Pressure is a tool of healing and we adapt it to do other things. I create a wedge of pressure against the seam of the panels and push." She walked through the opening after Shan. "As the pressure wedge is pushed forward, it pries the doors open."

Coral spoke again and the door closed. "Closing that door required divided pressure points lodged against the back edges of the panels. When I allow the points to seek each other, the door is pushed closed with their effort to reconnect. Magic's just a matter of figuring out how to use the tools you have."

"What if I can't do it?" Shan dragged her feet.

Coral waited until Shan was beside her.

"You'll do it." Coral exhaled loudly, "You have to, or we're all dead."

She started walking again, briskly. Shan lengthened her stride to keep pace. "If you can't tell me how my magic works, how am I going to know what to do to save the earth?"

"We don't know the specific mechanics of how you'll do it, but we know *what* you need to do."

"I don't." Shan touched her aunt's shoulder. "Why can't you just explain everything to me and then teach me what I need to do."

"I can't explain what you'll be doing until you understand what you can do." Coral stopped at the classroom door and knocked twice. "If you want to know, I suggest you focus on learning to reach your magic. Most acolytes can do this in their first five minutes of training, and they come to us at twelve."

Twelve? No wonder The Circle needed a private school. Shan started to ask how Coral found her acolytes but Miss Jessie stepped into the hall, Isaiah behind her.

"Mistress." The teacher inclined her head at Coral and nodded at Shan. "Miss Morgan."

"Hello, Shorty," Isaiah waggled his brows. "Hope you've had half the fun I have."

"He's very interested in all the sciences." Miss Jessie beamed, "But he has an innate understanding of plants. We have another gifted botanist in the making."

"Hmm." Tilting her head, Coral appraised Isaiah. "Useful. Good. Lunch?"

She indicated Shan and Isaiah should take the lead.

"Botany?" Shan whispered, pulling Isaiah's jacket, "Slow down." She didn't want to get so far ahead she couldn't hear Coral and the teacher.

"Don't mess with the threads." Isaiah pushed his sleeve back in place. "You look like you've been playing dodge ball. What's the dragon lady been teaching you?"

"I wouldn't know where to start." Shan rolled her eyes. "Tell me about Miss Jessie. How does it feel to have one-on-one instruction?"

"Weird. But in a good way." Isaiah's eyes sparkled. "She's letting me explore right now, seeing where I'm at."

"I hope she's going to work on your English."

"I can write it, but I'm never talking like you in public, girl. There's already enough people wanting to kick my ass."

"Hmph." Shan folded her arms. "Nobody's ever wanted to beat me up for speaking properly."

"Huh." Isaiah's head jerked, "Boy's won't notice what you're saying, and girls, well, I guess they're all afraid of your granny."

"It's probably Granny on both sides," Shan laughed, "I'm not that much to look at."

"You are a bit boney, but all guys see is that everything's in the right place." He looked away in mock delicacy.

She elbowed him, holding her smile, wishing he could walk the dark corridor of her magic with her. "Anyway, what's this about botany?"

"We were looking at basic evolution. You know, cyanobacteria, colonization of land…"

Isaiah spoke with great enthusiasm, stopping only when they reached the stairwell door. Shan hoped he didn't know she'd missed everything he said. Coral and Miss Jessie were talking about her. She caught snatches of their conversation.

"Resistant." Coral.

"There's no time." Miss Jessie.

"Find a path…" The rest of Coral's sentence lost beneath Isaiah's words.

"Anyway," He concluded, "I just think it's interesting how plants seem more evolved than animals. How they protect themselves with oils and spikes and how they use animals to reproduce when they can't chase each other the way animals can."

"Very." Shan said quickly. She could hear the other conversation clearly, now.

"That's what our figures are telling us." Miss Jessie said as she and Coral approached. The teacher looked apprehensive.

"Acceleration isn't unexpected, Jessie." Coral stared ahead as if she could see through the basement walls. "We always have less time than we think."

"What if she isn't ready?"

146

"She will be." Instead of bolstering Shan's confidence, her aunt's certainty made her nervous.

Coral and Miss Jessie fell silent as they drew closer to Shan and Isaiah.

Lunch was in the large dining room, with the staff. The seating arrangements were the same as they'd been for breakfast, with Liam next to Shan.

"Good afternoon, Miss Morgan." Liam held her chair and she allowed him to seat her. She spread her napkin over her lap, hoping her stomach would remain quiet until she could start filling it.

"I trust you had an interesting first morning?" Liam's handsome face showed nothing but polite inquiry.

"I did." Shan wished the servers would hurry with the chicken she smelled and the dinner rolls. "Thank you."

She drank half a glass of water to avoid talking to Liam and to keep her stomach quiet.

"We're all looking forward to seeing you work." Liam's black hair fell across his forehead, highlighting the deep blue of his eyes. His bow-shaped lips formed a half smile which, on anyone else would have looked shy, but on him, was just cocky. Shan distrusted overly handsome guys.

"You *all?*" She finished her glass of water as a server placed a salad on her plate. She wanted to grab the salad with her hands, but she picked up her salad fork and selected a dainty bite. She had no intention of looking like a pig in front of Mr. Perfect.

"The staff." Liam manipulated the tableware as if he had been born a Kennedy. Actually, he could be a

147

Kennedy. Out of the corner of her eye, Shan thought she detected a resemblance to the political family.

"We've been hearing good things about you." He watched her face.

"Really?" She took several quick bites in succession. "How long have you been hearing these things?"

"It's part of our training," Liam laughed once. "We all have to know who you are if we're to support you."

"All of you know?" Shan looked around the table. Staff talked to each other, mostly. Megan laughed, apparently at something Isaiah had just said. Miss Jessie and Coral ate in silence. Danny ate mechanically, gaze moving around the room, only pausing when it met Coral's face.

"All twenty of you think I'm *who?*" Shan faced Liam.

"Twenty?" Liam's white teeth flashed. "There are only twenty who live here. We're the Mistress's personal staff."

"There are more people in The Circle?"

"Come on, now." Liam's brows arched. "You must realize there're thousands of us. Every druid who died in Drunemeton, all over Great Britain actually, has descendants in The Circle. After two-thousand years, that's a lot of people with druid blood."

"Druid blood? Isn't that like saying baseball player blood?" Forgetting herself, Shan stuffed half a roll into her mouth. She looked away, face hot.

"The original druids were mostly Celts," Liam didn't seem to have noticed her lapse. "But the Romans, and later the churches, systematically hunted and killed anyone they believed had the potential to become druids. Except for those hidden by The Circle. Since The Circle had to be so secretive, members tended to procreate with each other. So most druids now are actually descendants of those in The Circle."

"All the descendants of these druids can do magic?"

"Naturally." Liam leaned close. "There are probably others who can do constructive magic, too, but don't tell your aunt I said that."

He winked and went back to his food. Shan looked up to find Isaiah scowling at her. She finished her main course planning how to get Liam to tell her more and wondering what had annoyed Isaiah.

After their plates were removed and replaced with dishes of fruit, Liam spoke again. "I'm sorry. I forgot to answer your question."

"We all know you're Palax Lae." He didn't bother lowering his voice and several people looked their way. Coral, glancing at Shan, gave a slight shake of her head.

Shan kept quiet. Coral had said she wouldn't lie to Shan. Would she lie to her people? Why did Coral want them to continue believing Shan was Palax Lae?

After lunch, Shan met Isaiah in the hall where they waited for Miss Jessie and Coral. The staff remained in the dining room for, according to Coral, a short meeting.

"You already got a boyfriend, I see." Isaiah leaned against the wall, inspecting his nails with studied indifference.

"I do not!" Shan tossed her head. "Honestly, guys have one-track minds!"

"Just guys?" He laughed. "I saw you getting all chummy with Clark Kent. I'm not saying I blame you. Granny did keep you locked up tight."

"Liam was telling me about The Circle…"

"Oooh. *Liam.*" Isaiah interrupted, batting his eyelashes.

Shan kicked his ankle just as Coral and Miss Jessie exited the dining room.

"A little decorum, please, Shan." Coral sighed. "Sometimes, you seem younger than our newest trainees."

Shan didn't think it would be a good idea to point out that she *was* the newest trainee. Liam, along with Danny, Megan and several other staff members crowded behind Coral. Shan couldn't tell by Liam's face whether he'd heard Isaiah, but she knew he'd caught Coral's reprimand.

"Don't you have any new trainees other than me?" Shan kept her voice level, hoping the warmth in her face didn't mean her cheeks were bright red.

"There are fourteen at this location but they're field training in the mountains for the next few weeks."

"Why'd you send them away?" Shan took a deep breath, "And why don't you tell people that I'm not Palax Lae."

"What do you think I just did?" Coral hissed. She walked beside Shan, her posture rigid. "I chose to send the other acolytes away because we needed to focus our energy on your training. We have so little time."

"What do you mean?"

150

"I mean, in a few weeks, three months at the outside, all your dreams will start coming true."

CHAPTER SEVEN

Directing Shan to lie on the grass, Coral led her through a relaxing meditation before asking her to open the door to her magic, once more. It didn't matter. The brilliant light knocked Shan out of her trance and left spots dancing before her eyes.

She steeled herself, afraid Coral would start shouting. Granny would've. But Coral closed her eyes and chewed the corner of her upper lip. After a while, she spoke.

"Jessie suggested something interesting." Coral stretched her legs in front of her and started removing her shoes. "Take your shoes off."

While Shan complied, Coral said, "Jessie thinks, and she may be right, that you've had too many years drawing energy without releasing it."

Shan frowned. She couldn't have been drawing energy for years. She had no idea what it meant.

"So, let's try something." Coral stood and Shan stood with her. "Feet shoulder-width apart, flatten your soles against the grass. This is the actual earth beneath our building. Close your eyes and feel the grass beneath your feet, the earth beneath the grass."

"Can you feel it?"

Shan nodded. The grass prickled her feet beneath her stockings, but there was more. She sensed a cool, powerful…presence emanating from the dirt.

"Visualize roots going from your legs, into the earth. Allow the earth's energy to travel up those roots, filling your body. Breathe, focusing on your connection to the earth."

Shan breathed, counting as she inhaled, matching the count when she exhaled. Steady, cool energy washed up her legs. She allowed the comfortable essence to flow through her body. It was how she imagined a mud bath would feel.

"Now, Shan," Coral whispered, "envision that door you've been seeing and allow it to open, letting the light flow back down into the earth."

Shan's heart rate increased but she counted breaths, willing it to slow. She pictured the bark door and imagined it opening. The bright light shot through her and into the earth as quick as thought. The calming energy dissipated with the light.

"Keep breathing." Coral said before Shan broke the trance to tell her aunt she thought she'd done it. "When you've released the light into the earth, allow the earth's energy to flow back into the ground, and count five breaths before opening your eyes.

When she was done, Shan looked into her aunt's eyes. "I've never felt anything like that. But wasn't it just imagination?"

"Of course you imagined it." Coral picked up her shoes, "but that doesn't mean it didn't happen."

Imagining it didn't guarantee anything *had* happened, either. Shan picked up her shoes, following her aunt back to the stones by the fountain. Coral slid her feet into her shoes, but Shan placed hers beside her on the rock. She liked the touch of the ground beneath her feet.

"Everything begins in the imagination." Coral drew her hand through the pool, "From the conception of this pool to the creation of a nuclear weapon, everything made begins as an idea."

"But..."

"Ideas are just imagination." Coral spoke as if Shan weren't there. "It's what you do with an idea, how you focus energy, that creates the pool or the bomb. Magic's another way of focusing which turns an idea into reality."

Shan almost laughed. Her aunt sounded like an infomercial. Maybe The Circle was actually a cult. "Imagine it and it happens? Just like that?"

"What do you think Abraham Lincoln would say if you told him he could light an entire auditorium by flipping a switch with his little finger?"

"I could, and someday when I have the luxury, I *will*, talk to you about particles and the illusion of space, but, really, for us magic is imagining and willing. That simple."

"So you just imagine a wedge and use it to open the door?"

Coral nodded. "I actually envision directing the air to form the wedge and the wedge prying open the door while willing it to happen."

"You believe in it and it happens." Shan folded her arms. "Sounds like faith."

"I prefer to think of it as confidence and experience." Coral ran her fingers under the edge of her hair. "Faith implies belief without knowledge. I know magic works and so do you. Now let's get back to it."

Shan bit her lip. She dreaded trying again. What if she hadn't truly released the light? What if it was all in her mind, and no matter how hard she tried, she kept seeing the same thing?

"Don't start panicking before we even begin." Coral snapped before instructing Shan to close her eyes. The breathing section seemed to last longer than it had in the morning, and by the time Coral had talked her to the door, some of Shan's tension had ebbed.

"Open it now."

Shan obeyed and saw only a candle-sized flame dancing above a black pillar. The room around the column was dark. The small flame gave off little light.

"Walk up to the flame and let your breath flow over it."

Shan crossed to the pillar. She breathed over the flame.

"If your breath doesn't make the flame move, blow gently across it."

Shan did and the blue tip danced away from her. She blew again and again the flame responded. If she wanted to, could she blow it out?

"Now that you know you can manipulate it, I want you to push the flame to grow. Just a little."

Shan stared at the flame, willing it to grow. It didn't even flicker. She blew again, and it moved. She concentrated, feeling sweat on the back of her neck. The fire shot upward, like a gas torch and Shan retreated, willing it to shrink.

"Make the flame smaller, again."

"I already did." Shan opened her eyes. She arched her back, stretching her aching muscles.

"Don't just pop out of a trance like that," Coral sighed, "Until you're adept at manipulating matter, just changing your focus can result in someone or something getting hurt."

Shan ran her forearm across her brow, finding it damp. Her stomach contracted forcefully.

"I'm starved." She blurted.

"I guess you are." Coral opened the partition, and after rummaging through a cabinet at the far end of the double room, offered Shan an energy bar.

It was gone before she realized she'd opened it. "Are there any more?"

"Give that one time to settle." Pulling her cellphone out of her pocket, Coral dialed a number.

"It's time." She said and hung up. She looked at Shan. "You'll be learning basic self-defense from one of my staff, starting today. I had planned for you to take accelerated academic classes in the afternoons, but our time table has moved up, and for now, we have to focus on training essential to our mission."

"Granny taught me to fight a long time ago. Besides, if I can do magic, why do I need self-defense?"

Shan lifted her chin, "I want to do more than just imagine a flame. Teach me to protect myself with magic."

"Trying to teach you to use your magic defensively right now would be like trying to give a toddler driving lessons because he can hold a set of plastic keys."

"Do you expect me to be in danger before I learn to use magic?"

"Ah. Until now, I never realized the amount of patience my mother had. Am I going to have to explain every detail all the time? " Coral massaged the base of her nose with her thumb and forefinger. "Do you think I could slide the panels open with magic if I didn't know how they worked manually? You need to know the basics of self-defense to use any weapon, including magic. And I'm not willing to bet your life on Katherine's teachings."

Before Shan could tell Coral that, in a physical scrap between the two women, she'd bet on Granny any day, there was a discrete knock at the door. Coral opened it with magic. Shan bit her tongue when she saw Liam at the door.

"An hour, then she needs to get ready for dinner." Coral stepped into the hall.

"Do as he says." She said, over her shoulder and closed the door.

"Miss Morgan." Liam nodded. He wore a pair of black athletic pants, black soled sneakers and a black spandex shirt. "We're only going to play a little today, but from now on, you'll want to bring athletic wear so you can change for our sessions."

When he turned to one of the mirrored panels, Shan stuck her tongue out at his back.

He opened the mirrored door and drew out two wooden poles.

"Quarter staffs." He tossed one to Shan and held one across his body. "Hit me."

"Gladly." Shan came forward, pole high and ducked, aiming up at his stomach.

"Good." He deflected her blow just in time. "Some natural talent."

He brought up the lower end of his weapon, then, with a flick of his wrist, tapped her right shoulder. His tap didn't hurt. She doubted it even marked her blouse but his self-satisfied smile infuriated her. She swung hard as he backed up but he easily blocked her shot and flipped her staff out of her hands.

"Lesson one." He tossed the staff back to her. "Don't get mad."

Gripping her staff in the middle, she swung at his left shoulder, and, as his guard came up, she flipped his right shoulder with the other end of her staff.

"Lesson two," She said, sending a silent thanks to Granny for childhood training with hickory sticks, "Don't get cocky."

Liam's face turned a blotchy red. Shan laughed. Mr. America didn't like being shown up.

"I was told you had no training." He twirled his staff, watching her through narrowed eyes.

"You were misinformed."

He stood silently for a moment, while the red left his face. He inclined his head. "Noted."

"But I suppose I should practice."

"Yes, of course." He took a defensive position and motioned for her to attack. Shan couldn't hit him again, but neither did he get past her defenses. He didn't break a sweat, and, if he was breathing heavily, Shan couldn't tell. She realized that if he really wanted to, he could probably overcome her in seconds.

"Did Coral tell you to go easy on me?" Parrying a blow, Shan spoke breathlessly.

"No." Liam tilted his staff, pushing down the end of hers. "You're not dressed for fighting."

"So," She brought her weapon back up and stepped into a forward thrust. "I'll always be dressed in comfy clothes, if I am attacked?"

"I thought you'd want to avoid ruining your nice clothes unless your life *was* in danger."

"I guess Aunt Coral would be a bit pissed if I tore my blouse the first day."

"You really don't know the Mistress, do you?" Liam held up a hand, calling an end to the exercise. "Money doesn't matter to her."

"It never does to people who have it." Shan resisted the urge to slap her hand over her mouth. Liam's ease with seven course dinners, his patrician face and his posture all indicated he had grown up wealthy. He would probably faint if he had to sleep in a house like Granny's.

Liam bowed without saying anything. Shan bowed, too, though it was not something Granny had done.

She walked to the cabinet and put her staff in the rack where it belonged. Behind her, Liam reached around to replace his weapon. Waiting to put the quarterstaff on its hooks, he pressed the full length of his body against her back and she saw red.

"Don't touch me!" She wheeled, throwing her arm out. There was a flash of light and a resounding pop. Liam flew across the padded floor.

Shan's tongue tingled and darkness gathered at the edges of the room. She stared at Liam. "Did I…are you okay?"

"I'm sorry Miss Morgan." He got to his feet, eyes dark, face drained of color. A burn mark crossed his left bicep and his staff was missing.

"I was out of line. Forgive me, please."

"You *were* out of line." She meant to sound firm, but forming words was difficult. Black dots collected at the edge of her vision and she watched Liam through a tunnel. She held onto the door to steady herself.

"I assure you, it'll never happen again." He smoothed his hair back with both hands. "Please don't tell the Mistress."

She wanted to agree. It wasn't as if this was the first time a boy had come on too strong, but, before she could speak, blackness closed in on her.

She awoke with her head cradled on Liam's forearm. He pressed a straw to her lips. She tried to push him away, but she had no more strength than a kitten.

"It's Coke. Drink it." Liam's forearm trembled beneath her head. "You used magic and drained your reserve. This will help until you can eat something."

She grabbed the glass and drank so quickly, she inhaled the fizz. She coughed but kept drinking. The soda restored her energy and she sat up. "Food?"

Liam, moving around to sit in front of her, gave her an energy bar which she finished in two bites.

"More." Her mouth was full, but she didn't care. She thought she had been hungry before…

Liam handed her another bar. She finished a third before her head stopped spinning. "Thank you."

"Sorry about that." She pointed to the red mark on his arm.

"You destroyed my quarter staff."

"I just meant to push you away."

"Are you going to tell your aunt?" His gaze shifted back and forth.

"I should talk to her about the magic," Shan began, but when the color drained from Liam's face, she felt sorry for him. More importantly, though, she wanted an ally in The Circle's camp. "But I don't want to get you in trouble. As long as it never happens again. With any girl." She added, licking her fingers. "Does magic always make you faint?"

"Magic's never made me faint." Liam rubbed his chin, "But our magic's different from yours."

"Yeah, Coral said that." Shan stood on wobbly legs. "I don't suppose you have another one of those bars handy?"

"I think a protein bar, instead." He handed her one from the pack beside him.

She looked down at him as she ate. Gradually, the strength came back to her knees. "How does your magic affect you?

"We were trained for years before we could even use magic. For us, it's all about keeping a balance. We don't actually store power. We just direct it." He shrugged. "If we tried to store it, we'd burn up. We don't tap more than we need."

"I just reacted."

"I know." Liam laughed, standing, dusting crumbs off his knees. He smiled down at her, his eyes pleading, "Don't tell the Mistress why."

"I said I wouldn't." She frowned. "Do you expect girls to just fall into your arms every time you show your dimples?"

Liam's mouth opened and closed. His brow furrowed. "Honestly, I never thought about it. It just happens."

Shan laughed. "I'll give you this, you're honest, anyway."

He laughed once and glanced at his watch. "I've got a meeting. Are you ready to go?"

"Not yet." She didn't want to walk with Liam. If Isaiah saw and teased her, she was afraid she'd blow him up.

"See you tomorrow, then." Liam shrugged, "and don't forget the athletic clothes."

Shan hoped her sweat pants and Salt Creek High gym shirt would work. Unless Megan had done some more shopping during the day.

The door opened automatically for Liam. Wanting to give him time to get well out of her way, Shan checked the mirrored panels one by one. The cabinets held towels, exercise straps and bottled water. Shan closed the doors. Noting her pale reflection, she pinched her cheeks and bit her lips. It was useless. She looked half-dead. She ran her fingers through her tangled hair, dislodging flakes of chocolate and granola.

She pressed her forehead against the mirror until her eyes merged into one fuzzy green iris. She couldn't decide which bothered her more; the fact that Liam had tried to push himself on her or that she'd accidentally thrown him across the room. With magic.

As if reminded of spent energy, her stomach cramped. Surely Liam was far enough away by now she could risk going to her room.

She walked up to the door quickly, hoping it would open for her as it had for Liam. It did.

She followed the empty hallway, passing Isaiah's classroom. She heard his voice and Miss Jessie's reply. She hoped Isaiah would be finished soon so she could talk to him.

Danny waited for her by the stairwell door, "Miss Morgan."

"Hi, Danny. I hadn't thought about how I'd get through the security door."

"You'll have your own pass in a few days." He led her through the doors and up the stairs. Once they'd entered the main building he wished her a pleasant afternoon.

Shan peeked into the dining room. A woman in white polished flatware at one end of the table and a man stood on a ladder, dusting the chandelier. The large clock on the far wall read two-o-five.

She signed. If Miss Jessie kept regular school hours, Isaiah wouldn't be out before three at the earliest. Reaching the far wing, she wished for an elevator. She

163

wasn't sure her legs would carry her up three more flights of stairs. Finally in her room, she went straight to the refrigerator. Armed with a pack of ham, a jar of pickles and a Coke, Shan curled up on her couch. She'd eaten half the ham and several pickles before she could think of anything except slaking her hunger.

Her mantle clock said it was only two-fifteen. She considered turning on the TV but she wanted to know if the flame of her magic looked different now. She did exactly as she had with Coral, counting as she breathed in and out, finding the dark corridor. This time, though, the opening was harder to find because the light leaking from beneath the door was weak. Nervous, Shan opened the door. The flame over the pillar was noticeably smaller than it had been earlier in the day.

She willed it to grow, picturing it larger, and it responded immediately, but her head felt heavy and she backed out of the room. Counting down slowly, controlling her breathing, Shan brought herself out of the trance.

Darkness threatened her vision, once more, and the whole pack of ham was gone. How did people manage to perform magic without carrying a refrigerator with them?

She trudged back to the kitchen and pulled out another pack of ham. She ate it there at the counter, finishing with a glass of milk. Feeling better, she went to her room to take a shower. She found a deep green velvet robe hanging on the bathroom door, and matching slippers against the wall.

"Thanks, Megan." She said wrapping herself in the plush garment. After drying her hair, she put on a new pair of pinstriped dress pants and a red silk shirt. Her face still looked pale, so she used the blush, adding mascara and lip gloss. Though her hair was soft and shiny, it didn't have the rich luster it had that morning. At least she did look like a different person from the one who'd fainted in the training center.

When she'd finished her grooming, it was three-thirty. Surely Isaiah would be back by now.

She went to his room, sticking her tongue out at the security camera on the way. Isaiah answered her quiet knock with a toothbrush in his mouth. He wore a pair of sweats and a towel draped his neck. Waving her to the couch with his toothbrush he disappeared into the bedroom. The smells of spicy soap and minty toothpaste lingered behind him. Catching her reflection in the black glass of the television, Shan was surprised to see she was smiling. How would she have done this if Isaiah hadn't been with her?

He joined her a few minutes later, wearing navy slacks and a white polo. The gold chain his mother had given him for his birthday brought out the warm, brown tones in his dark skin. His long lashes were wet and his eyes were the rich color of summer honey.

"You look like—" She almost blurted he looked like a stranger. Instead she said, "You look older."

"I'm sexy and I know it." Grinning, he posed with one hip out, biceps flexed.

Shan laughed, feeling as though she'd just put down a heavy weight. "How was class?"

"Awesome." His smile was straight and confident. Without his cocky grin, he became the stranger again.

"Miss Jessie says I could actually finish high school this year."

"That's great. You'll probably graduate before I do." Wincing at the bitterness in her tone, she shook her head. "Don't mind me. I didn't even have class today. I don't know who's going to teach me."

"That's right. Don't be hating 'cause I'm beautiful." Isaiah flopped onto the couch, rocking it. He patted her shoulder. "Seriously, you're smart as me, just in different subjects. But, girl, what have you been doing all day? Did you see the terrorist lair?"

"I was in a training center. Just an exercise room and an indoor garden." Shan told him everything. She'd meant to omit her spat with Liam, but being with Isaiah again made her babble.

"I'll slit his throat." Isaiah leaped to his feet, his jaw set, eyes dark with fury.

"Oh!" Shan had never seen Isaiah look so angry before. "You're scaring me. Sit back down."

He exhaled loudly but she could feel the tension emanating from him.

"Did you miss the part about where I blew his staff out of existence and left a welt on his arm?" She touched Isaiah's hand. He jumped as if she'd pinched him. "Chill. We have more important things to talk about."

"I guess." Isaiah sighed. "Miss Jessie believes in magic. She says there's a scientific basis. She's absolutely brilliant. So, I don't know what to think."

"I believe in…whatever it is." Shan tugged a strand of hair. "Even yesterday, I would've thought it was crazy.

But the world's not what I thought it was. I wish I knew how I made that staff disappear."

"Didn't you feel something?"

"Pissed."

"I'm not sure," Isaiah's brow wrinkled and the corners of his mouth turned down. "That's a good thing."

Shan punched him lightly. "Of course it's not a good thing."

"Your aunt said you un-make?"

"Yes." She frowned, "Why?"

"That could be very bad."

"I get that." Shan bit her lower lip. "But what kind of bad?"

"It could be—like—nuclear." Isaiah scratched his chin. "If things come apart at the atomic level..."

"Wait." Shan told him what Coral had said about Shan absorbing energy and what would happen if she didn't expend the energy. "She said 'think nuclear.' She can't really mean that, can she?"

"Sure she can mean it. Doesn't prove she's right." He shook his head slowly. His voice went high. "But, girl, if it's anywhere near the truth, until you learn to control that energy, you're a walking time bomb."

A walking time bomb. She gritted her teeth, breathing through her nose to stop threatening tears. When she had enough control, she asked, "You think it's possible?"

"You want me to say I don't." His eyes closed. When they opened, he focused on a spot behind her. "But, Miss Jessie believes it, and what you did with that stick...we have to act as if it's true."

He looked back at her and she met his stare. "What am I going to do?"

"Hey," He smiled, "You're not by yourself. The question is what are *we* going to do?"

"Thank you, Isaiah." Shan put her hand on his, "You're wonderful. I couldn't have asked for a better best friend."

Isaiah glanced away, squeezed her hand and let it go. "Right back at you."

She frowned. Her chest tightened. She could barely inhale. She knew she'd made him uncomfortable, but she wasn't sure why. Unless…

"Do you believe" She spoke quickly before she could change her mind, "that I'm this thing, this moonchild?"

"A couple days ago, I would've thought you'd lost it, if you'd asked me that." He shrugged. "Today, like you said, it's not the same world."

"So you think I'm some kind of magic being?"

"*Part* some kind of magic being." His grin spread across his face. "We all have family issues. That doesn't mean a lot." He rubbed his head. "I'm part white, but that doesn't keep me from having nappy hair."

"Your hair's curly."

"There you go, getting jealous again." He patted his close cropped hair.

For a moment, Shan relaxed. "I guess if I'm part…whatever, it's not really new, is it?"

"So, you're still the Shan we all know and love."

Isaiah's look intensified. The atmosphere grew heavy again. Shan looked away, twirling her hair. Silence stretched between them.

Finally, Isaiah stood up. "Want to go explore the grounds?"

"Yes!" Shan said but, remembering that she would've been stuck in the basement if Danny hadn't been waiting for her, she added, "I hope we can get back in."

"They'll make sure *you* get back in." Isaiah snorted. He stepped into the kitchen, filling his pockets with granola bars. "You should hear the way Miss Jessie talks about your aunt. All of them act like she's the queen. Actually, she might *be* their queen."

"Queen. Be glad you don't work with her," Shan rolled her eyes, following Isaiah into the hallway, "She's more like a dictator."

"Better hope the cameras don't have sound." Isaiah indicated the device across from his room.

"Do they usually have sound?" Shan tossed her hair, "I don't care. If she doesn't like it, she should learn there's a difference between teaching and giving orders."

"They don't usually have sound," Isaiah laughed, holding the stair door for her, "but the security systems here are pretty sophisticated."

On the main floor, Shan looked around before opening the front door. She noticed Isaiah did the same. Surely her aunt wouldn't mind them exploring the grounds. Shan just didn't want any lectures.

No one stopped them, so they crossed the grass to the stand of trees opposite the house. The sun already settled low in the western sky. The expanse of green

separating the forest was deep emerald in the fading light.
A few gold and crimson leaves stood out in the green
shadowed by the evening rays.

Shan longed for the mountains. She missed the
damp coppery smell of the soil, the incessant chatter of
frogs, the buzz of cicadas and branches teeming with birds.
Strangely, she also missed the acrid smell of burning
tobacco on the cool evening air.

They entered the Bellingham's forest. The trees
were mature. Oaks, maples, spruce and walnut grew with
laurel, mulberry and species Shan didn't recognize.
Layers of decaying leaves carpeted the forest floor. She
placed her feet carefully to avoid stepping on small plants
which had pushed through the thick compost.

The trees seemed to grow further apart than the
ones back home, or maybe there was less plant life around
the roots. A few ferns created bright splashes among the
grays and browns of tree trunks. In Salt Creek, the
profusion of ferns, herbs, vines and bushes hid the forest
floor except where centuries of foot traffic had worn
narrow paths.

"I wonder if they planted these." Shan stopped to
wait for Isaiah who squatted to examine a group of red-
brown mushrooms.

"These are tawny milksap." He straightened. "You
don't plant them. They just grow."

"I meant the trees, doofus."

"A lot of these are older trees." Isaiah surveyed the
grove. "If somebody planted them, it would've been a few
hundred years ago."

"It's hard to know if there's a regular trail." Shan peered through the trunks. "I wonder if any of them walk in here at all."

"Look there," Isaiah pointed to his right, "past those two oaks. That's a trail. Nothing's growing on it."

"Let's follow it and see where it goes."

As they picked their way through the woods, Shan stumbled and her hand came up automatically. Her fingers splayed against the knobby bark of the nearest tree and it seemed to vibrate beneath her touch.

"Oh!" She jerked her hand back, heart racing. She stared at the tree. Though not nearly as large as the one in her dreams, the trunk was broad. Branches wider than Shan's waist grew out from the trunk, reaching skyward. Underneath, the mottled bark was almost black, whether with age or by nature, Shan couldn't tell. The outer layers were covered with white particles, red particles and small patches of moss. Overhead, leaves trembled in a soft breeze and she thought she heard the elusive music, again.

Shan couldn't help herself. Her hand moved forward slowly until her fingertips grazed the coarse husk. *Yes.* Her skin tingled with the contact. She flattened her palm against the oak's trunk and an electric hum flowed through her. The vibration coalesced into a song. The notes rang through her, low and sweet, deep and earthy rich. The song was a lullaby speaking of life sparking, building, growing, reaching glorious height and of an approaching darkness, of loss and emptiness. An endless night.

"Shan. Shan!" Isaiah gripped her shoulder. "What are you doing?"

His arm snaked around her waist and he drew her away from the tree. When she broke contact, she felt water cooling on her cheeks and tasted salt in the corners of her mouth.

"Shizzle." Isaiah, gripping her shoulders turned her to face him. "Are you hurt? You were stuck in a trance or something."

She didn't know how to tell him, so she shook her head.

"Why are you crying?" He wiped her face with his sleeve. "Are you homesick?"

"I guess." She drew a deep breath. Golden shards of sunlight jeweled Isaiah's face. Birds fluttered into the trees, their melodic voices mixing with rustling leaves and the huff of Isaiah's breathing. All of it was unbearably real because, she was certain, now, all of it would soon be gone.

Isaiah smiled nervously, his eyes searching her face. "Do you want to go back?"

Yes! She wanted to scream and *No. A thousand times no!* She wanted to touch every tree, to hear the story again, to feel the song. Most of all, she wanted to promise each of them she would save them.

"No." She said finally, shaking herself. "Let's stay out here a while."

"Okay." Isaiah shoved his hands into his pockets, pulled them out and held them at his side, fingers opening and closing.

"Let's follow that path." She sprinted across the clearing to the little trail. She ran between the trees, through alternating light and shadow, hearing the song's echo in the wind, knowing the melody rang in every tree she passed.

The path wound through the small forest, eventually leading to a lake. Shan and Isaiah perched on a large rock and watched the water. The lake's rippling surface reflected the cloudless sky. Water bugs danced across the top and, occasionally, silver flashes indicated life beneath the surface.

"Wish I had some fishing line and a paper clip." Isaiah's sidelong look still held uncertainty.

"Yeah," Shan grinned, "Can you see us bringing Coral a string of fish?"

"Now *that*," Isaiah lifted the hem of Shan's blouse, "makes me want to pull some thread and go for it."

"Out of my clothes?" Shan yanked her shirt free. "They probably only eat sea bass or shark anyway."

A kingfisher skimmed the lake and, after making a sharp dive, came up with a struggling minnow. Isaiah glanced at her, looked away, cleared his throat, and looked at her, again.

"Never saw you cry before." He muttered. "Sure you okay?"

"I can hear trees."

"Huh?"

"Trees speak to me." She told him about her nightmares, then. "I thought it was…" Shan didn't want to risk evoking the druid by saying her name. "Her in the ring. The one in my dreams, causing me to hear what she heard, but I touched that oak today and it sang to me."

Consternation, surprise and interest crossed Isaiah's face. But not disbelief. "It sang to you? Like words or music?"

"Like a humming voice. It was very deep. But the music told me things."

"What'd it tell you?"

"It, she, I think, talked about feeling the light for the first time." Shan struggled to find words that could explain the song's power. The sun inched toward the horizon, the lake darkened, sparkles on waves turned to soft, glowing ripples. The wind picked up, moving through the trees, strumming branches, rustling leaves.

Isaiah watched her until she continued. "It talked about all the trees in this forest, maybe in the world, and living a slow life." Her eyes burned and her throat tightened. "Then she was talking to the trees, not me."

He waited, his brow smooth, his patience offering strength.

"She was singing with the other trees." Shan touched Isaiah's arm. "All the trees are singing the young trees to sleep."

"That's amazing!"

"No. It's awful." Shan's vision blurred, "They're singing them to sleep forever."

Isaiah pulled her into a hug. She sobbed against his chest. He rocked her, his chin resting on her head. When she could control her tears, Shan pulled away. Isaiah seemed reluctant to release her.

"I'm sorry." She brushed the front of his sweater, worried she might have stained it.

"Shiz." He twisted away, his fists clenched on his thighs. "Leave it be, girl. It's cool."

"What am I going to do? I'm supposed to save them." She bit her lip. "And all those people, too."

"Come on superhero," Isaiah stood abruptly, offering her his hand. "We have to get back, or your aunt will kill us."

She allowed him to pull her up, but he let go of her hand and started walking as soon as she was on her feet. His gruffness hurt. "What'd I do?"

He stopped walking. His shoulders drooped. "You didn't do a thing." He looked back. "I'm...I just don't want to upset your aunt."

"I can deal with my aunt." She caught up to him and he matched his pace to hers.

"It's just, I don't want to get sent away." Isaiah shrugged, his head high so she couldn't see his expression. "Don't want you saving the world all by yourself, getting all the credit."

Smiling, she nudged him. "If there's a chance I can save anything, I know I can't do it without you."

"Be sure you tell that to the TV reporters."

Shan laughed politely, but she couldn't shake the fear that she wasn't up to the task the universe had given her.

CHAPTER EIGHT

Danny met them at the door, arms crossed, mouth tight. "Next time, you need to let somebody know before you wander off."

"I'm sorry." Shan put her hands on her hips. "Is there some kind of rule book I should read?"

"There's an understood rule book. It's called common courtesy." Coral came out of the building. "The idea of courtesy is to minimize any discomfort to those around you. Didn't you think I might be worried about you?"

Shan folded her arms. "Granny never made me tell her every time I went for a walk in the woods."

Coral's face reddened. "That's right. Katherine Amos is quite the example of parenting. Anyway, this isn't her house. Here, we treat each other with respect."

"By ordering everybody around?" Shan knew she should just apologize, but something about Coral sparked her anger.

"My position demands I give orders." Coral bared her teeth. "It's what everyone expects me to do, so I oblige. Now, get ready for dinner."

She turned on her heel and disappeared into the Bellingham. Tearing his gaze from the spot Coral had just vacated, Danny opened the door for Shan.   He held it until Isaiah had followed her inside.

"Girl," Isaiah whispered as they walked up the stairs, "Why do you have to fight with your aunt? You say she's the only one who can teach you to do your thing."

"I don't know." Shan remembered Granny's gray head against the weathered porch rails. "I don't know why she pisses me off. Maybe it's because she acts like I can just replace Granny with her, when, up to a couple days ago, I never heard of her."

"That might be because she's spent fifteen years thinking of you."

"Yes," Shan exhaled. "But, as what? A niece or a tool?"

Isaiah didn't say anything else until they reached his door. He sighed, and taking both Shan's hands in his, he looked into her eyes.

"So much is happening to you, Shan and I know it's hard. Sometimes all you can do is finish what's set in front of you and bide your time. Know what I mean?"

"I do." Shan let her hands rest in his. "I'm lucky to have you."

"Don't you forget it." He squeezed both her hands and let go. "If you're not going down with your aunt, walk mc to dinner, will you?"

Shan had trouble keeping her eyes open during dinner. Afterward, Isaiah teased her about her lack of attention and refused to sit in her room and help keep her awake.

177

"Your aunt would be furious. I don't think we'd like her furious." He said at her door. "Maybe the dreams won't come tonight, or maybe you won't remember them."

But a dream did come; a tropical city, teenage girls in leis swallowed by a sea of lava. Shan woke at dawn and sprayed her room with perfume in an attempt to dispel the remembered scent of scorched, rotten eggs.

The day went almost exactly as the previous one. Breakfast, training with Coral, sparring with Liam and dinner. After dinner, she and Isaiah told Danny they were going for a walk. Shan stopped at the grand fountain, pulling Isaiah down to sit with her on the curb. The tree lullaby wafted on the breeze and she knew the sound would be stronger the closer she got to the woods.

Isaiah talked almost non-stop about what he was learning, his ideas about magic and his growing worries about global warming. In the past, Shan would've teased him about joining a cult, but the plaintive melody in the air made his fears all too real.

When they went back inside, half an hour later, Isaiah said goodnight at his door and Shan went back to her room, dreading sleep and the nightmare to come.

The rest of the week followed a similar pattern, except Shan could feel her aunt's rising impatience with questions and hesitation. She began dreading the morning hours almost as much as she dreaded her nights.

On Friday, Coral came into the gym at the end of Shan's lesson. She could feel her aunt's gaze on her as she put away her staff and fortified herself with energy bars.

When Liam left, Coral spoke.

"We're having important guests for dinner. I've chosen a formal dress for you. It's in your room. Please wear it to dinner and be prompt."

Coral turned her back and opened the elevator before Shan could respond.

Shan's face heated and she had to stop herself throwing an energy bar at the wall. It was bad enough Coral bought Shan's clothes without her input, but now, her aunt had moved to telling her what to wear.

Shan stalked all the way up the stairs an into the hall, colliding with Danny. He caught her arms in his cast iron grip.

"Sorry." She mumbled between clenched teeth.

Danny's brows shot up and a, for a second, the light made it look like his eyes twinkled. It had to be an illusion. His hold didn't relax. She shrugged to free herself.

"No harm done, Miss Morgan." He released her and she swept past him.

Back in here room, Shan found a gauzy white dress hanging on her closet door. On the floor beneath the dress, was a pair of silver, sequined flats. Standing before the mirror, she held the dress up to her shoulders. The gown had spaghetti straps and a fitted bodice sewn with silver sequins. The double skirt flowed from an empire waist all the way to the floor. Shan had scarcely dreamed of wearing something so fine. Who was coming to dinner? Why did she care? She had half a mind to wear her blue jeans and t-shirt just to spite Coral.

She hung the dress back on the door and noticed a white, bow hair-clip on her dresser, atop a black leather case. She moved the clip, annoyed all over again that Coral would tell her how to wear her hair.

Her annoyance disappeared when she opened the case. A string of pearls rested on a cushioned bed of blue satin. Two matched pearls in the middle were post earrings. Shan lifted the pearls from their case, draping them across her arm. They warmed to her touch, taking on a pink and amber glow against her skin. She longed to wear them, even if it meant wearing the dress Coral had chosen.

An hour later, Shan examined herself in the mirror. She had parted her hair on the side, blow dried the ends under and pulled it back with the clip. Her eyes were highlighted with creamy pink shadow and a deeper pink blush touched her cheeks. Black mascara darkened her lashes and a hint of purple liner made her irises look emerald green. The pearls lay over her collar bone, lending their glow to her skin. She turned to leave with a final over-the-shoulder grimace at the woman in the mirror.

She had to admit the dress fit her perfectly. The bodice hugged her curves and the overskirt was so light, it floated with the slightest movement. She looked like she belonged in the elegant room, but her heart still beat like a rabbit's.

Isaiah waited for her outside his door. He wore a tuxedo with a smooth white shirt and a black bow tie. His smile didn't reach his eyes, though. They were dark with some emotion she couldn't place. Looking away from her, he started down the hall without a word.

"Do your clothes make you uncomfortable?" She asked.

"It's a monkey suit, all right." He scowled, looking down the hall. "But at least I don't look thirty."

She lifted the side of her skirt and kicked his shin.

He stumbled, glaring at her. "What? I can't help that you look like you're wearing your aunt's clothes."

"I *am* wearing my aunt's clothes." Shan snorted, "but, then, so are you."

He stared at her intently. Then, he laughed. "Damn. You're right!"

"Wonder if I'll be able to sneak some of your aunt's fancy liquor. You think they'd say anything?"

"The staff might not, but Coral would rip your head off."

"True dat." He tugged at his collar. "On second thought, I'll stick to water."

All Coral's staff, except kitchen workers, wore formal dresses and tuxedos. Coral's dress was a fitted red silk number with a beaded bodice and a fishtail skirt. A gold circlet, Shan would bet it was the same one Palax Lae wore, curved around Coral's neck and square rubies dangled from her ears. A heavyset man with silver hair chatted with Coral. The woman by his side looked to be the same age despite her blond up-do.

Catching Shan's eye, Coral called her over. "Lady Derring, Lord Conway, may I present Shanleigh Morgan, my niece."

Shan nodded, mumbling, "Pleased to meet you, Lady Derring, Lord Conway."

"Call me Mara, dear." Lady Derring squeezed Shan's fingers and let go. "We were so glad to hear about your rescue."

Coral's hand, flat between Shan's shoulders, stopped her from spouting an angry retort.

"And I'm Rory." Lord Conway lifted Shan's hand to his lips. Her smile faltered. She resisted the urge to dry the back of her hand on her skirt. He winked at Mara and turned to Coral "She has your beautiful eyes."

After Coral had introduced Isaiah as "A promising botany student," the meal began. When Shan had eaten enough to take her mind off her hunger, she turned to Liam. "Are Mara and Rory druids?"

"Of course," Not a trace of arrogance showed in Liam's expression when he looked up. If Shan hadn't known better, she would've thought him contrite. He smiled with one side of his mouth. "But that's not the main reason they're important."

Shan raised her brows.

"They provide The Circle with lots of cash." He looked left and right. "Everyone makes their resources available to the group, but some people have a lot more to make available. Rory and Mara have the most."

"Coral doesn't control it all?"

"The Mistress is wealthy in her own right, but, compared to Rory and Mara, she is almost poor."

"Do they have more say because they have more money?"

"We don't operate that way." Liam frowned. "You don't have to sign a pledge to be part of The Circle. You just have to hold your duty to preserve the earth above

182

everything else. If you see a need you can fill, physical, financial, educational, whatever, you fill it. We're governed by the Directorate, an elected body. Rory's on it. Mara has been in the past. "

"Do Mara and Rory come here often?"

"This is the first time in three or four years." Liam laughed, "They came to see you, of course. There'll be a regular parade of visitors, I'm sure, now that you're here."

Great. In the middle of learning how to control power she didn't understand, learning to live with a woman she didn't know, trying to avoid a malicious spirit who believed her a body thief, and oh, yes, concentrating on not blowing up the city, she was going to be trotted out like a prize dog.

She touched the pearls at her throat. Their warm, smooth texture soothed her. At least she could look forward to a lot of new dresses. And shoes.

Shan turned back to her meal, finishing in silence, allowing the polite chatter to wash over her. After dinner, Rory and Mara repeated their pleasure at meeting Shan, indicating they were looking forward to hearing about her progress.

Before Shan left the dining room with Isaiah, Coral took her aside.

"You did well tonight. I'm pleased."

"Thanks." Shan started to walk away.

"Wait." Coral touched the pearls on Shan's neck. "They're perfect on you."

"Thank you." Shan felt prickly warm. "Thank you for giving them to me."

"They're a gift from my mother, your real grandmother. She wore them more than any other piece of jewelry she owned. She willed them to her first granddaughter."

Shan's hand flew to her necklace. Her fingers traced the perfect orbs. "What was her name?"

"Maureen. Maureen Alyssa McCaid Morgan." Coral stared into the distance for a second, then, looked back at Shan, "We get our short stature and green eyes from her."

"Was there a grandfather, then?"

"I'll tell you about him later. I've got to get back to my guests. Goodnight, Shan."

As she left the dining room, Shan heard Lord Derring say, "Getting worse across the globe. There was an ice storm in…"

The door closed before she heard the rest. The melody of the tree lullaby went through Shan's mind. Her insides felt like ice. If the end was near, and she could do something, why did Coral shut her out of business meetings? If everything was truly coming to a head, why didn't they talk about it at the dinner table?

Isaiah walked back with Shan. She told him the origin of her pearls, not noticing his unnatural silence until they reached his room.

"Hey, what's the matter?" She reached out to straighten his tie. He brushed her hand away.

"I'm just wiped, Shan." He opened his door. "I guess I'll see you in the morning."

"Okay." Shan stopped herself from saying *whatever.* Isaiah had never let her down. He had just as much right as she did to miss his home and to feel intimidated by all the strangers. "I'll talk to you in the morning."

"Wait." He said as she walked away. "Wake me if you need me. About your nightmares. Anything."

In her room, Shan changed into a sleep shirt and gym shorts. She put the earrings back in the leather case, but she left the pearls around her neck. Fingering them, she resolved to ask Coral for a family history. Maybe her aunt had photographs she would share.

Since it was only eight o'clock, Shan fixed a snack and searched for a movie to keep her awake, to distract her from thinking about magic and disaster. Scrolling through titles, she recognized a few movies either from ads she had seen watching shows on the internet, or on TV at Isaiah's house. Just as she settled on *Ten Inch Hero* because the title amused her, someone knocked on her door.

Recognizing Isaiah's sparkling brown iris staring back through the peephole, she opened the door.

"Hey, silly. I thought you were tired." She swung the door wider. "Come in."

"I better not." Isaiah glanced back at the camera. "Your aunt might shoot me. And I am wiped, really. But Megan brought me a cell phone. It was a call from Mom."

Shan's heart lurched. "Is everything all right?"

"Oh, yeah." His smile was brief. "Teddy Hacker from the county garage has been taking her around."

"Is that a problem?"

"Nah. Teddy's better than most." Isaiah switched his weight to his left foot. "It's not about Mom. It's about your granny."

"Tell me!" Shan gripped her pearls tightly.

"She left the night we did."

"How? Who…"

"I'm trying to tell you." Isaiah rolled his eyes. "Mom said somebody picked her up in an older model truck. She couldn't see who it was, but when your granny didn't come back, Mom went over to check on her. The house is locked up tight and Mary Beth at the post office said the mail is supposed to be held until your granny picks it up."

"I can't believe she left." Shan hugged herself.

"I can't believe Mom went over there!" Isaiah spread his hands before him. "Ever get the feeling we don't know shizzle?"

Shan grabbed Isaiah's hand and pulled him into her room. She arched her hand in front of the camera, opening and closing her fingers as if she were operating a puppet.

"Talking." She mouthed and shut the door. Hopefully, whoever watched the cameras would understand.

Isaiah prowled around Shan's living room. "Looks like a museum in here."

"It probably is." Shan curled up in the couch corner. "Sit down."

"Yes, Miss Morgan." Isaiah rolled his eyes. She threw a cushion at him, but he dodged quickly. He looked at her, batting his eyes in mock fear.

"Granny left the night we did." Shan couldn't help the surge of excitement. "She didn't use Marie's phone?"

"Mom would've said if your Granny had come to our house."

"How'd someone know to pick her up?"

Isaiah shrugged. "Maybe it was something she already had planned."

"Too much of a coincidence." Shan leaned back crossing her arms. "This has to do with me and Coral."

She chewed her lip. If only she could talk to Marie. "Do you still have the cell phone?"

"Megan took the phone. She waited while I talked." Isaiah smirked, shaking his head. "I mean she's nice and all, but I *was* talking to my mother."

"Do you realize Granny could show up here any minute?" Shan went to her window. Isaiah followed as far as the bedroom door.

She could only see her own reflection in the glass. She looked over her shoulder, "Turn off that light."

"Uh." Isaiah stood with one hand hovering below the switch. "My luck, the minute this light goes off, your aunt walks in and thinks I'm sneaking into your bed. I bet you there's a dungeon around here someplace and I don't want it to be my new room."

"For goodness' sake." Shan angled her hand over her eyes and looked out the window. She shook her head. It was stupid to look for Granny out her window, anyway. It faced away from the drive. She climbed out of the window seat and pushed Isaiah back into the living room. "You go on back to your room. But be ready. If Granny shows up here, it's all going to hit the fan."

"Why would your granny come here?" Isaiah stood with his back to the door, his arms wide. "She has no right to take you. Coral would just have her thrown off the property and, besides, didn't she tell you to learn from Coral?"

"Coral said Granny was a member of The Circle." Shan knew she was grasping at straws, but Granny represented a normalcy that hadn't required Shan to be a living bomb. "Maybe she'd have to let Granny in if she showed up."

"Wondering is a waste of time." Isaiah's soft expression took the sting out of his words.

"A girl needs a little hope now and then." She elbowed him aside and opened the door.

"So does a guy." Isaiah grunted, his lips twisted.

Shan's chest contracted. Had Isaiah's earlier moodiness been about wanting to go beyond friendship with her. "Were you upset earlier about…?"

"Not what you're thinking." He scowled, then raised and lowered one shoulder, "Most people don't forget their best friend's birthdays."

"You're sixteen! I'm sorry. I didn't get you anything!" Emotions passed through Shan so fast she couldn't react. What would a normal girl do? She threw herself against him, flinging her arms around his waist. Her face was hot and her eyes filled. "Happy birthday."

He held her tightly for a moment and released her. "Don't beat yourself up. It's been the weirdest week in our lives. Shoot, weirdest in anybody's life, I guess. I should've said earlier." He ran his thumb under her eyes, "Please don't start bawling on me."

"What can I do to make it up to you?" She clenched her hands at her sides.

He looked into her eyes. His were dark with unspoken emotion. Shan's heart thundered. If he asked, how could she refuse?

"Just don't sing happy birthday." He grinned, "And we'll be even."

"Hey!" She laughed, relieved, "my voice isn't that bad."

"That's cause you don't hear it right, girl. The rest of us aren't so lucky." He shook his head. "Now let me get some rest. I've got a ton of work to do tomorrow."

After he'd gone, Shan tried to go back to her movie but she kept losing track of the plot worrying about Granny and forgetting Isaiah's birthday. Some friend she turned out to be. She told herself she'd been so distracted, she would've forgotten her own birthday. It was no excuse, really. She'd have to make it up to him somehow. Maybe she could ask Megan to pick something up the next time she went shopping. Then, again, maybe she didn't want Megan knowing. There was no way to fix her mess-up with Isaiah, right now. And there was Granny. How had she contacted someone to pick her up? Where had she gone?

What if she'd simply gone on with her life? No. She wouldn't do that. She'd promised Shan they would see each other again.

Frustrated with unanswered questions, Shan switched to a light classical music station and dug out her prized, leather-bound copy of *Emma*. Resolving to stay awake as long as possible, she stacked her pillows, settled on top of her covers and opened the book. Austen's prose immediately transported Shan to an orderly world of tea, parasols and hand-written letters. A place where the world was not about to end and magic was just a word. After a while, she closed her eyes just to rest them for a moment.

The next thing she knew, she was in the grove again, greeting the Sentinels. Their voices held a hint of urgency.

"Peace." She whispered to them.

Though she, too, felt that trickle of distress, she did not want to add to it. Maybe it was a result of them reading her mind, learning about the Roman attacks on groves in Iceni. Caressing each of the five trunks, telling them those attacks were far away, she passed around to the center. Dread gripped her heart as she approached Gaiaes but she could not stop Palax Lae's —*her*—hand from reaching out and flattening against the ancient, uneven bark.

She landed on a rocky beach. Her bare feet sunk into cold, wet sand. She threw her hands out to maintain her balance. The sun came through patchy clouds, illuminating stretches of wet shore. In the distance, a dark, violet sky blended with the choppy gray-green sea. Close in, white spray erupted against dark, wet boulders. A young man crouched on a flat rock. He wore dark work pants, a tweed cap and a thick, blue sweater. His eyes were alight. He looked past her, his lips curving in a welcoming smile. She turned, following his gaze, to see a girl approaching. The girl's bright green eyes touched Shan's politely before sliding back to the boy, her private smile for him alone. Copper bangs danced across her forehead. A thick braid fell past her wind-reddened cheek and flowed over the front of her left shoulder, bright against the gray wool of her overcoat. As the girl passed, a shadow flowed across the sand, rolling over her. She looked up, her mouth dropping open, her eyes widening. Unable to stop herself, Shan's head turned back, following the girl's gaze just in time to see the towering wall of water swallow the boy. The girl's scream was lost in the thundering roar as the wave ripped her from her feet. Together with the boy, the girl and Shan rose in the dirty, frigid water, limbs flailing. Tires, furniture, pieces of wood and cement blocks dipped and twirled as if they weighed nothing. Horizontal, spinning like a jack, the girl slammed feet first against the boy's chest, but his body rebounded, his head wobbling slowly, already lifeless. The girl's mouth opened but the lobe of a car-sized anchor grazed the back of her head and, catching her undulating braid, jerked her away. Shan tried to scream for the girl, but water flowed down her throat.

She awoke coughing.

She hugged her knees, waiting for the fear to subside, willing the faces to fade into memory. At least it was after five this time. She must've slept a few hours before the vision came.

She might as well stop fighting. No one could stay awake forever, no matter how much they wanted to, so she had to accept the nightmares. Clearly, they were a part of her life now. She considered talking to Isaiah but the dreams were sent to *her*. They were something she needed to figure out. Besides, she already asked too much of him.

Were the dreams more than just images meant to scare her into action? The first dream had warned about an earthquake in what appeared to be the United States, but, as far as she knew, the dream had not been prophetic.

The frozen park had been in some city which reminded her of the little she'd seen of New York, but the weather had remained warm. Though she had been watching the news, noting daily instances of violent weather, she hadn't heard of a flash freeze in a city like the one she'd dreamed. She'd bet there'd be no news of tidal waves today, either.

Anyway, Coral thought the visions foretold events that would happen if Shan didn't act. But if the dreams were not being sent by Palax Lae, why did they all start with her? Shan opened her laptop, which connected automatically to The Bellingham's WIFI. When Palax Lae returned no results, she googled The Circle and Coral Amos. Hits for The Circle had nothing to do with Coral's group but Shan found an abundance of information on druids. Much of it was contradictory and, when she closed her computer, she realized she probably already knew more about druids than anyone outside The Circle. However, at the first opportunity, she'd ask Coral about the human sacrifice legends.

Most of the articles had mentioned sacred groves. That little painting was of a grove. Shan got the picture and brought it to her bed. The colors appeared darker and a somewhat washed out, as if evening approached. But it was the grove from her dreams. The spreading oak in the center background was Gaiaes, she was certain. There was Maedar! And that was Choughain. She couldn't quite tell by the angle, but the next tree was probably Rayne. Ellyng and Daer were in the far right.

Coral had told the truth. Granny was part of The Circle. Otherwise, why would she have this painting?

She touched the representation of Gaiaes with her forefinger and a current shot through her arm. She dropped the picture. Retrieving it, she touched it again, and again, her arm buzzed with energy and she recoiled. But she hadn't had that reaction before. Of course! She'd never touched the canvas, at least not since putting on the ring.

Holding the painting by the frame, she scrutinized it. There was more to it than a depiction of the grove. But what was it? What did it have to do with her dreams and why did Granny want her to have it?

She could ask Coral but she wasn't sure she should admit she had the picture. As far as she knew, Coral hadn't asked Granny about it and she hadn't mentioned it to Shan. Granny's two stories, again. Shan would have to figure this one out on her own, too.

Megan stopped by at six thirty, dropping off yoga clothing, a gentle reminder that Coral expected Shan to work on Saturday and Sunday, too.

"How're you settling in?" The pretty red-head asked on her way out. "Isaiah tells me he loves it here. He's very excited to be working with Jessie."

Shan felt a stab of anger, but she quelled it. She should be glad Isaiah had someone to talk to besides her.

"It's nice, so far. Thanks for bringing the clothes." Shan closed the door slowly enough to give Megan time to step back. Which the girl did with a surprised blink.

Shan's face warmed. She wasn't angry, was she? Of course not. She was happy Isaiah was making friends.

After breakfast, Danny met Shan and Isaiah outside the dining room, giving them both plastic cards with magnetic strips.

"Now, you won't have to wait for me to open doors for you." Danny's tone was light, but his expression didn't change. "Don't worry, though. I'll still be keeping an eye on you."

"Man's a robot," Isaiah whispered as they went down the basement stairs.

"I know, right?" Shan responded, thinking of the artificial sun in the garden room. "Or a zombie, maybe."

"You don't know zombies." Isaiah laughed. "They *smell* and they go for your brains."

"What do ghosts do?" Is that what Palax Lae was? A ghost? "Can they break your bones?"

"One of those nightmares?" Isaiah's arm touched hers. "Did it hurt you?"

"No," She wasn't lying. It hadn't been one of her dreams. "Something else."

"Can't you tell me?"

They'd reached the classroom and Miss Jessie was at the door.

"Hi, Miss Jessie." Shan spoke before the woman gave her a deferential nod. "I'll talk to you later, Isaiah."

"You better." Isaiah's chin jutted, "See you at lunch."

"Good day, Miss Morgan." Miss Jessie held the door for Isaiah.

Shan continued down the hall. No one was outside the training center, so Shan leaned against the wall and waited. She was about to sit down and open her computer when Coral came out, wearing black spandex pants and a dark green, sleeveless tee.

"Come here." Coral allowed the door to shut behind her. "Put your hand against this panel."

When Shan obeyed, a blue light shot across the little panel and the lock clicked.

"From now on, just let yourself in." Coral went to the middle room and sat cross-legged on the floor.

Shan joined her and they went through the same procedure as they did every day, only Coral instructed Shan to imagine wind blowing over the flame she created instead of imagining herself blowing. When Shan could make the flame move, as well as grow, through will, Coral asked her to do it with her eyes open.

They broke for lunch and Shan had to promise Isaiah she'd talk to him after classes because Coral was anxious to get back to work. Once more, Coral took a seat on the floor in the middle room and Shan followed suit, wondering why they didn't use the garden.

She knew in a short while. Coral took her through a few more exercises of manipulating her magic without going into a trance before telling her to bring her magic into the center of her body. Shan willed the flame to migrate to her chest and within seconds she was aware of a tingling sensation there. Following Coral's instructions, she grew the flame until her entire torso prickled with energy. She made it smaller again, and held out her right hand as Coral did.

"Bring it along your arm until it is centered in the palm of your hand."

The electrical tingle traveled through Shan's right shoulder and took residence in her palm. Her outstretched hand pulsed with her heartbeats.

"Now, release just a tiny flame through the center of your hand, and hold it there."

Shan did, watching the space above her hand, feeling the energy travel, but half expecting to see nothing. When a tiny fire, the size of a small candle flame, hovered above her skin, Shan yanked her arm back with an involuntary squeal.

Coral took her wrist and held it, commanding her to raise the flame again. Shan did. This time, the flame was so tiny it only lasted a second. Coral ordered Shan to make another and hold it. By then, Shan's entire body trembled so she couldn't keep her arm still.

"Ugh." Coral stood, running her hands through her hair, making it stand out on one side of her head. "Get something to eat and a drink. But make it quick. We'll not finish today until you can at least control your magic while it's still connected to you."

After she finished two protein bars and gulped down a bottle of water, Shan felt less shaky. Seeing the flame above her own hand left her speechless. She was determined to do more but she was nervous. She didn't want to black out as she'd done with Liam. She debated telling Coral about the accidental release of her magic, and the result, but she hadn't come up with a plausible story that wouldn't break her promise.

Wiping her mouth with the back of her hand, Shan sat across from her aunt.

196

"Tomorrow, I'll start teaching you how to draw energy from the environment." Coral said. "It's a little tricky because if you draw indiscriminately, you can draw too much and accidentally release it.

"Will it keep me from feeling faint if I release too much magic?"

"Don't be silly!" Coral tossed her hair. "You've not done anything that should come close to making you faint." Her eyes narrowed. "Have you been feeling faint?"

"I just meant dizzy." Shan twisted her mouth, rolling her eyes. "I'm sorry. I was being overly dramatic."

"It's a bad habit." Coral frowned. "Now. Feel your magic."

After a few more tries, Shan was able to hold a steady flame over her hand. She maintained even breathing, trying to think of nothing but keeping her power steady. A little voice in her head, though, shouted with excitement. She was actually doing visible magic.

"Maintain even breathing. You're going to create a mental conduit between you and that crumpled paper on the mason blocks." Coral's neutral voice kept Shan focused. "Make it a clear pipe, whatever you like. Nod when you are sure can see a clear, unbroken circuit between your hand and the paper."

Shan tried to imagine a glass pipe, but it was difficult. She could picture the end of a pipe, or the beginning, but she couldn't hold the image of the entire length in her head. She counted her breaths, deliberately relaxing her muscles, and pushed away all other thoughts. She had it. A solid glass pipe started at her hand and ran all the way to the paper.

She nodded.

"Send your magic along that pipe to the paper."

Shan pictured the small stream of magic moving through the air and, withdrawing control, she let it go.

With her release the entire stack of blocks exploded. Coral fell back, scooting against the floor and Shan's vision darkened. She woke a few seconds later. The stack of blocks was gone and Coral lay still.

Trembling, Shan moved to her aunt. Good. Coral was breathing. "Coral? Aunt Coral?"

Shan inhaled, preparing to shout, but Coral moaned and opened her eyes. Gaze locking Shan's Coral sat up, putting a hand to the back of her head.

"No blood." She looked at her fingers, "But I've got a nasty bump."

"I'm sorry." Speaking required tremendous effort.

"You look worse than I feel." Coral rose to her feet, rubbing the back of her neck. She pulled some granola bars out of the cabinet and tossed them to Shan. "Eat."

Shan fumbled with the wrapper, too weak to tear it, so Coral snatched it out of her hand and ripped off the cover before handing it back. "That was totally uncontrolled."

"I know," Shan said with her mouth full. "I couldn't help it."

"You have to help it." Coral lowered herself carefully to the floor. "You could've killed us both. You have no idea the amount of power you're capable of wielding, which is why you should've been trained since childhood. But there's no remedying that, so you are going to have to learn now."

Shan spent the rest of the period learning to manage and hold power above her hands. By the time Coral called it quits, Shan was able to manifest her magic not only as various sized flames, but as cones of ice and energy balls. She could also divide and move the manifestations between both hands.

"Should I practice after hours?" Shan helped herself to a granola bar and water while Coral prepared to leave.

"No!" Coral shook her head. "You could kill yourself or somebody else. Until I say so, no magic outside this room." She held up a hand. "Come with me to the classroom."

Shan followed her aunt down the hall. They passed Liam on the way to the training center. His nervous gaze slid past Coral and fixed on Shan. She shook her head once and was rewarded with his dazzling smile which just made her want to punch him.

"She'll be back in a minute, Liam."

"Thank you, Mistress."

Oily. That was it. He definitely had an oily way about him. Did her immunity to his good looks mean there was something wrong with her or were there others who could see through men like Liam?

When Jessie opened the door to Coral's knock, Shan caught a glimpse of Isaiah bent over a microscope.

"I need Owen's treatise on directing power and the third through fifth McCallen workbooks. Jessie left the door open while she went to the bookshelves.

Isaiah looked up and winked at Shan before going back to his work. She saw he had been sectioning green leaves, but there were also yellow and brown leaves spread to his right.

"We're doing plant life cycles." Miss Jessie's gaze followed Shan's as she handed the books to Coral. "But I suppose you've already done that."

Shan nodded, though the only thing she remembered about biology was the smell of lunch cooking down the hall.

"Thank you, Jessie." Coral stepped away so Jessie could close the door. "Shan, I want you to read Directing Power tonight and start on the first workbook."

"Do not practice your magic until we're back together." Coral walked away.

In the training center, Liam waited while Shan pulled her hair into a pony tail. Tossing a staff to her, he said, "We'll practice more blocking, advancing and parrying techniques today."

He flicked his wrist and the end of his weapon rapped Shan's knuckles. The sting brought tears to her eyes, but she had learned from Granny, not to let pain cloud her judgment. Twisting sideways to provide a thinner target, Shan moved her injured hand, allowing that end of her staff to drop. When Liam lunged to deliver a torso blow, she flicked her wrist, turning her staff to bring it up under his. As the weapons collided, she brought back her other hand. She tried to flip his weapon out of his grasp with one end of her staff while allowing the other end to protect her body.

The force of both weapons jarred her muscles, but she didn't let go. Liam grinned and stepped in to slam the center of his quarterstaff against hers.

He started naming the moves as they did them. "Low guard. Parry. Hanging guard. Fencing lunge. Parry."

She repeated the names. Granny hadn't called them anything. She'd just made sure Shan could keep pace with her. Clearly, Liam was a more advanced fighter than Granny, but, while Shan had little fear she would end up in a stick battle, the exercise felt good.

Soon the pace increased so she could no longer talk and Liam fell silent. He had disarmed her twice, and left a welt on her right arm before their time was up. She didn't mind, though, because the knuckles of both his hands were bleeding.

If he was angry he didn't show it. He didn't flirt with her either, thankfully. She could've been another guy for all his expression. Good. As long as he respected her boundaries, they could work together.

Shan went straight up to her room for a shower and a snack before diving into *Directing Power*. The book was interesting enough. Some of the techniques Owen described, Coral had already shared, but Owen's directions on creating containments to hold and direct magic seemed promising. If Shan could build a field around her target, maybe the explosion could be contained.

However, All of Owen's techniques, as well as the first workbook, talked about building and repairing. The protective fields described were meant to hold cauterizing flames. In the section on repairing a torn leaf, the workbook included molecular models and drawings of repair mechanics.

If Shan had been a regular druid, the lesson would've been thrilling. It seemed repairing used mostly air and fire. Air pushed and pulled, sewed, trimmed and formed a barrier to prevent contamination while holding an injury steady during healing. Fire removed dead material, destroyed bacteria and sealed wounds.

Comparing the effort and knowledge necessary to repair a torn leaf with the mere seconds it took Palax Lae to heal her crushed hand made Shan dizzy. If she was going to be wielding more power than Palax Lae, how could she ever control it?

She thought, wistfully, of factor trees and linear equations. Could she ever learn all the theories of energy needed to control power? She thumbed through the other workbooks. They went through complex plants to animal organisms. Cleansing water, directing weather, visions and long range communication were listed in the index of the last lesson book. She looked at the chapter on visions, but it only offered lessons on how to receive visions. Shan had hoped she would find a way to banish them or to discover where they came from. Long range communication sounded like fun, but she had no idea how to locate the person she wanted to speak to or how to send lines of energy to their consciousness.

She slammed the book closed and went back to the workbook Coral had assigned. At the end of the first chapter were activities and questions. Since she wasn't supposed to use magic when she wasn't with Coral, Shan took her notebook out of her bag and opened it, to start writing answers to the questions.

The first spiral bound pages were filled with the outline for her essay on Mary Shelley. It was due today. Shan wished she was back in class, listening to Mr. Hallsby talk about the impact of popular fiction on modern culture. She tried to remember how it had felt back then to believe there was nothing wrong with the earth and that druids were just characters in video games.

In the notebook's front flap was Shan's packet from Boston University. She hadn't planned to tell Granny about her decision until after she turned eighteen, in May. By the end of the school year, she would've saved enough money from her allowance for a Greyhound ticket. Marie had already promised to give her a ride to Lexington to catch the bus and the scholarship had meant she could start without financial support from Granny.

She probably wouldn't need a scholarship now. If Coral would let her go to Boston. If Boston still existed in a year.

She sighed. She shouldn't dwell on the past. She found a clean sheet of paper and the mechanical pencil she always kept in the spine of her notebooks. Determined to get past the knot in her chest, she set to work answering McCallen's questions.

With the addition of written homework, the following week passed quickly. Shan practiced McCallen's visualization techniques under Coral's supervision. She learned to "see" the way the energy of her magic excited electrons to heat the paper until it ignited.

By the end of the week, Shan could incinerate a piece of paper while exploding just a few of the bricks around it. She adapted McAllen's containment technique, thickening the barrier she created around her target, to absorb her more potent magic. The repercussions were weaker, but, as her aunt pointed out, the destructive energy was much less than what Shan would be expected to produce. Coral worked very hard to be supportive, but her impatience was always there, coming out in sighs and gestures, keeping Shan agitated.

Saturday, Shan worked hard, learning to draw power instead of just using whatever her body had available. Coral taught Shan to see, with her mind's eye, the web of energy in the practice room. She guided her in recognizing the colors and lines of light energy, the heat and electricity within living things and the kinetic energy of inanimate objects. Shan learned to recognize the crackling flow of power as Coral pulled and directed magic. Shan went back to her room thrilled and exhausted.

On Sunday, Shan's first attempt at drawing magic resulted in dimming the lights and crumbling the concrete blocks in the work area. The power came to her so quickly, in such abundance, that she shook wildly with the effort of holding it to her.

"Release it into the floor now!" Coral shouted, eyes wide.

After the release, Shan felt as if the inside of her body had been scrubbed with steel wool.

"From now own, have a conduit in place for release until you learn to draw only when needed." Coral panted, "Always keep an eye on your core so you don't pull so much."

Shan practiced keeping her core, the conduit and her containment in place while directing her magic. Now that she could pull energy from around her, the core burned like a small sun inside her and it terrified her.

"You don't have time to be afraid of your own power," Coral snapped when Shan told her. "There are way too many other things to fear."

Coral didn't elaborate, so Shan assumed her aunt referred to climate change and the impending disaster.

While Shan worked and studied, Isaiah was allowed to roam the extensive grounds, collecting samples, working with botanist druids. Shan longed to breathe the forest air again, and she wanted to be out of the basement. At the same time, she feared being drawn to the trees, hearing the song. She didn't know if she could bear it. Not that it mattered. Coral wasn't going to allow Shan any freedom until she could control the raging power at the core of her being.

On Monday, Coral added lessons in English, algebra, world history and astronomy to Shan's workload. Her practice sessions with Liam were scheduled for after class. Her work was so overwhelming, she could only see Isaiah a few minutes at night. Every time she went to his room, or he came to hers, she feared Coral or Danny would burst in, demanding to know what they were doing.

Nevertheless, life at the Bellingham settled into a pattern. Breakfast, magic with Coral, lunch, magic and academic lessons with Coral, physical training with Liam, homework, dinner, quick chats with Isaiah, night and the inevitable nightmares. Shan began keeping a journal of them on her computer. There didn't seem to be a pattern to the second half of her dreams, but the first half, when she was Palax Lae, progressed like days. She felt Palax's fear as word of Rome's advance reached the grove. She knew the moment Palax realized the army was unstoppable, and she understood the woman's grief for her people. In her dreams, Shan shared Palax Lae's memories of Gaiaes's touch—joy, love, knowledge and peace beyond expression—and she began comprehending the woman's all-consuming desire to save humanity. Shan didn't know if Palax could sense her thoughts, or whether Palax Lae sent the dreams to her. But she didn't dare call the woman's name, even in her mind, for fear the druid would step out into reality and, without Coral there to stop her, crush Shan like a bug.

Isaiah heard no more news of Granny and Shan stopped expecting her to show up at the Bellingham. Obviously, she'd gone on with her life. It hurt to think, for all her words, Granny didn't care enough to at least try to stay in contact. Isaiah thought Granny was either somewhere drinking her troubles away or playing a long game. Shan hoped it was the long game. She wanted to know the other story Granny had mentioned. Though Coral still refused to tell Shan exactly how The Circle planned to use her destructive powers to save the earth, Shan had an idea it would be something she'd find objectionable. It'd be nice to know there was an alternative and Granny seemed the only person among Coral's acquaintances with any idea there was another way.

No matter how hard Coral pushed, Shan couldn't find a balance in her power. Either she released a harmless trickle or a wild surge that burst through her flimsy containment, obliterating anything it hit. Concrete blocks, steel pipes and even a huge portion of the laminate floor had fallen prey to Shan's magic. Coral had suffered another bump to the head before giving in and raising a shield when Shan worked.

No repercussion bothered Shan. At least she'd learned to draw and release power evenly enough to stop her fainting after directing magic. However, she feared she'd never be a useful druid. What would happen, not just to her, but to Isaiah, the forest and all the people in her dreams if she couldn't learn to control her power? Although her aunt tried to hide it with encouraging words, and stiff pats on the back, Coral's flared nostrils and the thin line of her lips revealed her frustration.

She did allow Shan more freedom, though. Saturday and Sunday afternoons, Shan walked the grounds with Isaiah. For a few moments each day she was out, Shan stood in the forest, listening without touching the trees. Even the faint humming, audible without physical contact, touched her profoundly. While the notes of hope and growth disappeared from the melody, replaced by gradual surrender, the song conveyed a joy in belonging, in mutual life that was beautiful beyond human words.

Isaiah waited for her on the bench by the lake, never mentioning her tears. Sometimes they met Megan, Liam or another staff member outside. Megan walked with them a few times, but the other staff members would greet them and move on. Shan knew Danny watched them.

She'd catch the occasional glimpse of his bright hair, or
see his shadow on the grass as they walked around the
Bellingham. She didn't mind. Danny protected them and,
as far as she could tell, kept their actions to himself.

Time passed so quickly, Shan often had trouble
telling the days of the week. The small, serrated leaves on
the elm outside her window turned from rich green, to
bright yellow. There were days or hours, when, as she
walked outside, leaves swirled in the wind like golden
rain. Each time, fewer and fewer clung to the light
branches, until the gray trees were nearly naked, limbs
cradling the occasional curled, brown body of a dead leaf.

Without her notice, someone, probably Megan,
added soft sweaters, long sleeved shirts, heavy denim and
jackets to Shan's wardrobe.

Isaiah seemed to be falling under the spell of The
Circle. When they met at night, instead of commiserating
with her worry about The Circle's plans, he talked to her
about the loss of the ozone layer. He told her that with the
melting ice caps and the systematic obliteration of the rain
forest, the earth was in a crisis state.

"Your aunt's right," He said one evening,
spreading a print-out on his dinette. "Look at this chart.
See here? See the extreme weather patterns?"

"Honestly, Isaiah." Shan didn't need a chart to tell
her what her dreams told her every night. "I believe
wholeheartedly in global warming. Where Aunt Coral and
I disagree is in how it should be handled."

"Oh, yeah." Isaiah scooted back his chair and got
up from the table. "We could try to cut down greenhouse
emissions. We could plant trees, recycle and stop using

208

fossil fuels. If we had a time machine." He came back to the table and leaned over to trace his finger along the sharp curve at the top of his chart. "But it's too late for that now."

"Isaiah!" Shan jumped up, knocking her chair over. She let it lay where it fell. "Are you telling me you think The Circle's right?"

"About?" He folded his arms across his chest. His enigmatic stare, without humor or mock fear, made him look different. Or maybe she hadn't looked at him closely in a while. His arms were not so skinny anymore and black hair dusted the curve his upper lip.

"About how we can stop this…thing."

"You mean how we can stop the earth falling apart? How we can save life in the ocean? How we can stop carbon dioxide from the dying rain forest destroying the atmosphere? Is that what you mean?"

"Isaiah." Shan stared open mouthed at her friend. "What's Miss Jessie been telling you?"

"Miss Jessie doesn't have to tell me anything. I've figured this out myself. She's just teaching me regular science and letting me use the equipment. " Isaiah shook his head and turned away. " Do you really think I'm stupid, Shan?"

"Of course I don't. Do you know what they plan to do?" Shan came up behind him, hooking her hand over his arm, pulling him around. "Do you?"

"I don't." Isaiah shook her hand off. "Really. Do you?"

"I know it's going to be something drastic. Using me." Her eyes filled with water, making her see his face as a blur. "I'm a bomb. I'm meant to destroy."

"That doesn't make sense." Isaiah shoved his hands in his pockets, his jaw working. "I don't think The Circle's hung around two thousand years to commit suicide now. Ask your aunt."

Shan looked down, blinking until her vision cleared. "I did. She said I was supposed to save the world. But my magic only unmakes."

"You said." Isaiah put two fingers beneath her chin and forced her to raise her head. "I thought I got the gist of it, but I checked with Miss Jessie. She said you were supposed to be able to unbind molecules."

"Like a nuclear bomb?" She swallowed.

"That takes splitting specific atoms."

"The point is I make things go boom." She shook her head. "So I'm going to save the world, according to Coral. But the only thing I can do is make things explode."

"You're not going to be alone, girl. The whole Circle is part of this." Isaiah rubbed her arms, his familiar grin appearing for a moment. "And you've got me."

"So what can I blow up that will save the world, Isaiah?"

His hands dropped and he turned away. "I don't know."

For the first time since she'd known him, Shan wasn't sure she believed her best friend.

CHAPTER NINE

Before Shan knew it, the first hint of winter arrived. Light snow dusted the grounds and she kept the fireplaces blazing in her apartment. The music of the forest had grown quiet, like a mother's voice approaching the end of a bedtime story.

In the Bellingham, along with their usual urgency, the staff buzzed with excitement about the coming holidays.

Coral ordered a grand feast for Thanksgiving and bought a green velvet cocktail dress for Shan. An accompanying necklace—a square emerald on a thin, gold chain—and a pair of gold hoops finished out Shan's wardrobe. After Megan pulled Shan's hair into a French twist, securing it with a mother-of-pearl comb, she felt up to meeting a large party of British Circle members.

While most of the elegantly attired people complimented Shan on her beauty, she got the distinct impression she disappointed them. Her suspicions were confirmed, when, after dinner, Coral came to her room, interrupting a discussion between her and Isaiah.

"Go to your room." Coral held the door for Isaiah, her expression icy. After Isaiah had left without showing any of the ire threatening to make Shan scream, Coral turned to her.

"The Circle thinks I can't manage you." Her aunt's words were short and quick. "They think I'm too soft on you. It's not that they don't like you, it's just there's the whole planet and here's my niece wasting time while I coddle her."

Coddle? Surely Coral was joking. Shan's arms crossed over her ribs and she bit her tongue.

Seemingly unaware of Shan's fury, Coral continued in the same cold tone, "You will start controlling your magic immediately, or I will be forced to make you."

"You know I'm trying."

"Not hard enough." Coral held onto the fireplace mantel, the tips of her fingers white.

" I've done everything you asked." Shan held out her hands. "All I do is work or study."

"You weren't studying just then." The corners of Coral's mouth turned down. "Maybe it's time I made better use of that boy."

A warning knell sounded in the back of Shan's mind. "Leave him alone!"

"Ah." Coral's eyebrows arched. "You *are* learning. Bravo."

"You wouldn't really hurt him. Would you?"

"Oh, my dear." Coral stepped closer, leaning in to touch Shan's hair. Her aunt's hot breath reeked of scotch. "You think I'm a sorceress, but I'm not. I'm a general. Wherever my soldiers can accomplish the most good for the common welfare, that's where they must be sent. I don't deny Isaiah's clever, and that he has more potential than either of you realize. But, if more good is

212

accomplished by putting him in a different position, then mark my words, I'll do it."

"Isaiah trusts you!"

"I know. But clearly, you don't." Coral waved her hand dismissively and tilted her head. "You don't believe I mean what I say."

"I do." Shan's heart pounded. Coral had something nasty in mind. Shan could see it in her aunt's eyes. She didn't doubt for a minute that Coral would do whatever it was. To Isaiah. "I do believe you."

"We'll see about that." Coral's head tilted the other way and she swayed a little. Of course. She was drunk. "If you can't show me some control in the morning, then I might have to let Isaiah help me do some convincing."

Without another word, Coral left the apartment, stumbling slightly as she crossed the threshold. When the door closed, Shan stood shaking, power running up and down her body, seeking release. For a split second, Shan considered letting it go. But she couldn't risk hurting someone. The staff person in the next apartment. The one below.

She breathed through her anger, letting her power seep down the walls, into the earth, tasting bitterness on the back of her tongue. For all the fancy clothes, the jewelry and the words, Coral only cared about how Shan could help her fulfill her ambitions.

Shan paced. She couldn't go to Isaiah. If Coral found out about her visit and thought Shan meant to warn him, there was no telling what she'd do. Besides, she knew what Isaiah would tell her. Coral was drunk. How many times had Shan let Granny's drunken words pass over her?

213

But drunk was Granny's way. Granny's actions were what stood out. In the years she lived with Granny, Shan never went cold or hungry. She never felt pressured to be anything except responsible for herself.

But in the light of what she knew now, how were Granny's actions different from Coral's? Shan faced the small voice in the back of her mind.

It was Coral's implied threat. For all her misanthropy, Granny never threatened anyone except in defense of her privacy. Probably to protect Shan's secret. But Coral had made it plain she'd be willing to use Isaiah. She hadn't said she wouldn't hurt him. She claimed to be a general and generals sent soldiers to die.

Shan wished she'd never asked Isaiah to come with her. If she'd let him go to Chattanooga, right now, he could be laughing with friends instead of sitting alone in a dark room surrounded by a deadly army.

All in all, it might be best if Shan appeared to lose interest in Isaiah. If she pretended she didn't care for him, would it stop Coral using him? It could work. Maybe, she could, at least, buy time for him go home for Christmas. While he was there, she could tell him to go to Chattanooga.

The next morning, at breakfast. Coral acted as if the previous night's discussion hadn't happened. Shan left the dining room quickly, going downstairs ahead of Isaiah. She hoped he would think Coral had urgent business with her.

In the training center, Coral took Shan through the normal exercises of gathering power, holding and changing it. But Coral's composure fractured when,

214

instead of blowing up a nail as instructed, Shan destroyed an entire stack of cinder blocks, with a power backlash that threw bricks against the mirrored shelves across the room.

Shan sat still, catching her breath, gathering the strength to try once more.

"You've got to do this. You're not a child!" Coral knelt over Shan. Her face was so close Shan could see the individual pores in her aunt's skin. Tiny beads of sweat formed at Coral's hairline and along the bridge of her nose.

"I'm doing my best." Shan whispered, breathing heavily, leaning away from her aunt. "You have to give me time."

"We don't have time. Focus! Why don't you make stronger containment?" Fury etched Coral's words. "If you were going for a real target, you'd kill us all."

"I'm doing everything I can."

"You don't want to take out a target, do you?" Coral was beside her now.

"No." Shan wanted to shout, but the single word was faint.

Coral's eyes widened, her lips turned down at the corners and, for a moment, Shan felt the woman was about to slap her.

"If you don't care whether or not you live or die, don't you care about other people? Isaiah? Katherine?"

"I believe there's another way." There. She said it.

"Because Katherine told you that?" Coral snorted. "You have no clue."

"Then give me one!" Shan leaned into her aunt. "Tell me what you want me to do and how it's going to work."

"There are well over seven billion people on this planet. If the planet dies, they all die. Every single one of them." Coral sat back on her haunches. "They'll freeze to death, be broken by earthquakes, shredded by tornadoes, boiled in lava. The ones who survive the primary events will be unable to breathe because there'll no longer be enough oxygen in the air. Unless we act."

"I know." Shan closed her eyes. "But how do you mean to act?"

"We are going to take out every energy plant in this country. All at the same time."

Shan felt dizzy. She had no idea how she could direct her magic in so many ways at once. But even if she could...

"What about the people working in those plants, or near them?"

"They're dead already if we don't act. As is Isaiah. Back to work." Coral rolled back off her knees and resumed her cross-legged position opposite Shan. "Sit up. Let's go back a little."

"Like me." Coral's hands were on her thighs. Her open palms and fingers forming cups. She closed her eyes.

Shan adjusted her position, took a deep breath. She couldn't think about what The Circle expected of her. She had to be successful this time. She hadn't forgotten the threat in her aunt's words. In Coral's mind, if Shan didn't cooperate, Isaiah was dead already. She closed her eyes.

"Focus on your breath. Relax." Coral's voice had an edge to it that made Shan want to run.

"Keep breathing. Feel the weight of your body against the floor."

Concentrating on her body was easy. Trying not to think about Isaiah, Granny and the people in her dreams was the hard part. Not to mention Coral's fury when Shan misfired again. The cold floor made her tailbone ache and her feet, tucked into her legs, were falling asleep. Shan gave herself a mental shake. Isaiah's well-being, if not her own, depended on her pleasing Coral.

Coral allowed Shan to keep breathing for several minutes. The knot in Shan's chest loosened and her heart no longer raced.

"Make your energy ball, now." Coral said.

Shan obeyed, watching the blue lights of her power crawl around the globe she constructed. The lights bounced against the perimeter as if seeking a weak spot through which they could escape.

Closing her eyes, Shan could feel the pent up energy pushing against control, clamoring for release. It was much more than the ball manifested before her. She had pulled power in her anger. Now, it wasn't a current of power. It was an ocean dammed only by her will. It roared to do what it was meant to do—destroy. And only she stood in its way.

"Look at the small stone on the bricks." Coral's voice seemed to travel from a far-away planet. "Visualize a thread of power unraveling from your ball of energy and traveling slowly toward the stone."

Sweat bloomed on Shan's body. She couldn't do it. She didn't dare do it. The minute she allowed a wisp of that raging power to unravel, it would all burst past her defenses

Power surged within her, running over her body like electricity over a pool. Shan's chest buzzed and a thousand pinpricks ran down her arms. Gritting her teeth she slammed her hands together, allowing the energy ball to flow back into her.

Coral watched her, gaze sharp like a vulture, tongue to her teeth. Shan scrambled back and stood, swaying. Coral stood, too, her face contorted in fury. "You're refusing?"

Shan knew if she had let go, everyone in the Bellingham would've been dead. A flood of nausea threatened and, clamping her hand over her mouth she ran, bumping Coral out of the way. The lock clicked as Shan approached and she slammed the door open.

"Stop!" Coral was right behind Shan.

Shan didn't look over her shoulder. Speeding down the hall, she swiped the card around her neck and bounded up the stairs. She made it to the fourth floor, hearing the beat of Coral's feet behind her. Shan wrenched open her own door, but before she could slam it, Coral caught it.

"You're hysterical!" Coral's hand came up so quickly, Shan felt the sting on her cheek before she realized her aunt had hit her. "What the fuck did Katherine tell you?"

"Get out." Shan's own voice sounded like it came from a tin can. She stood so her aunt couldn't cross the threshold.

"You'd do well to listen, Shanleigh. Katherine's plan of educating people didn't work. We're out of time. And if she plans to use you some other way, you might want to know your power will be deadly outside the protection of The Circle. We're not fighting just humans, you see. There are things in this world you've never dreamed of. And they're coming for you. Without us beside you, you'll be ripped to shreds." The corners of Coral's mouth turned down. "You think about *that* tonight."

Coral pushed Shan into the room and slammed the door. Shan heard a key turn in the lock and her knees almost gave way. *They're coming for you! Could it be true?*

She remembered the creature at the forest's edge, the blunted snout sniffing the air. For a moment Shan didn't move. Chills rippled over her body. With a shaking hand, she tried the door knob. Locked.

Shan wanted to scream and pound on the door, but that would be playing into Coral's hands. So she made lunch, and ate it while reading. No matter how hard she tried, though, she couldn't shake Coral's warning. What were the things she had never dreamed of? Until August, Shan had never dreamed she was anyone other than Kathleen Amos's granddaughter. Druids, rings with spirits and magic were ideas she'd never entertained. There was no way she could fathom what could be out there.

Shan slammed her book closed. She just couldn't concentrate. Her cheek still stung from Coral's blow. Granny had never struck her. Shan determined, right then and there, to leave the Bellingham. She would have to convince Isaiah, but he'd want to take Coral apart once he learned she'd hit Shan.

There was the planet, though, and, if Shan left the protection of The Circle, she couldn't use her magic. With the strange creature's image fixed firmly in her mind, she didn't doubt the truth of that statement. Besides, so far, her aunt had never lied to her. Could Coral withdraw The Circle's protection? Whatever was out there, could it be coming for Shan now?

Shan stood up, pacing. How could she just wait and do nothing? She retrieved her laptop from her bedroom and opened a search page. She found information about The Earth Mother, Gaia, Tara and other religions, surprised to discover many new religions had been born on the rumors of older ones. But, other than new conventions based on old names, she found nothing she didn't already know.

Because Coral seemed to hold the Catholic Church ultimately responsible for the demise of the earth, Shan researched there. The legends, societies and stories generated by the establishment of Christianity astounded her. The worst were the ideas of demons and dark angels. She found pictures of leathery creatures with spiked wings and jagged teeth. Their blunt-nosed faces made her go cold.

The name of a site connected to some of the images was Chronicles of the Sentinels. Skin prickling, she clicked the link. There was only a page of writing and images of angels and demons. There was no writer's name, no contact information and no advertisements. The page claimed that angels and demons were the same thing, capable of changing appearance at will. The creatures were, the article claimed, the result of forcing gifted people to perform miracles for gain. Misuse of their gift twisted them until they lost their humanity. The church, finding the creatures wouldn't die, began using them to hunt the gifted and to frighten the populace into the church. Finally, the author reported, the Church used the creatures to defend against supernatural entities.

Were these beings Shan's enemies? Had the church come after Coral, too?

She continued searching for a while, but she could find nothing else useful. The few references she found to the Chronicles referred back to the same page. Surely it was all a load of crock, as Granny would say. Coral probably just wanted Shan to fear something besides the end of the earth. But, Coral said she wouldn't lie to Shan. And despite the fact any illusions Shan had about The Circle having a benign plan were dispelled, she'd never known Coral to lie. But, if there were forces arrayed against the druids, why had Coral kept this information from her. Did Granny know about it, too?

Biting back a scream, Shan closed her computer. Night had fallen. What did Isaiah think about her absence?

Her room, with its dark paneling and heavy furniture, had too many shadows. The velvet drapes over her recessed window were pulled back revealing only a reflection of the desk lamp and blackness. If Coral meant to frighten Shan, it was working.

When, as a child, Shan had been too scared or upset to know what to do Granny would assign her a few routine chores until she'd regained emotional control. Shan took a deep breath and went to the dresser. Picking up her hairbrush, she pulled the velvet band from her hair and regarded herself in the mirror.

The pale face didn't seem any different than the face she'd seen in the flecked mirror back in Kentucky. But there was a difference. Did the magic show or was it the cosmetics? The large room behind her?

Shan dropped the brush. The mirror reflected a pair of glowing eyes in the window behind her. Her room was four stories up. Nothing natural could be looking through that window. *And they're coming for you.*

Terror galvanized her. She couldn't look away from the glowing eyes. *Coming for you, coming for you, coming for you.* The words rang in her mind, scattering her thoughts. The eyes didn't blink.

Slowly, feeling came back. Shan licked her lips. Anger heated her face. She'd asked for none of this. Not Granny's lies nor Coral's ambition and especially not this so-called power.

She wouldn't do it. No. Shanleigh Amos would not die with her back turned.

Picking up the hairbrush, Shan turned and faced the window. The watcher hadn't moved. Heart thundering, she advanced, gathering power and lifting her brush over her head. The lighted room made it difficult to see anything beyond the glass except the watcher's eyes.

Shan climbed on the wide window sill and, holding her breath, pressed her face against the glass. The glowing eyes were surrounded by a triangle of black face and a pale body stretched along a slender branch from the old elm.

All that fear for a little cat.

Feeling lightheaded, Shan raised the window. The animal regarded her without expression, its claws deeply entrenched in the bark of its tree branch. Shan stretched. She could almost reach the twigs at the end of the limb, but she doubted those would hold the animal. She sighed. The creature would never jump, and somehow, even if she had a phone, she doubted Coral would approve of calling the fire department to rescue a stray cat.

"What are we going to do?" Shan stared at the cat.

The cat let out a hoarse cry and straightened from its crouch. Taken aback, Shan slid off the window seat. The branch swayed with the animal's weight and the cat scrambled. Shan cried out, certain the creature would fall, but the cat gathered itself and sprang into the air. Landing with a soft thud on the window sill, it looked into her face with serious blue eyes, meowed again and leaped to her bed.

Shan closed the window and joined the cat. The animal turned around twice before settling on her pillow. She ran two fingers down his back and he purred. He had no collar, and, clearly, he was little more than a kitten. Despite his protruding spine, and the thin flesh over tiny ribs, Shan couldn't imagine such a beautiful Siamese being a stray. He belonged to someone.

"But I can keep you tonight." She said.

As if in answer, the cat placed one elegant, black paw on her arm.

Shan's worry seeped away. She couldn't talk to Isaiah, she couldn't avoid the nightmares, but, tonight, at least, if the demons came for her, she knew she would not have to fight them alone.

CHAPTER TEN

Sometime in the middle of the night, before Shan walked in her dreams with Palax Lae, she awoke to knock followed by a key turning the lock to her door. She sat up quickly, dislodging the kitten, who meowed in protest. Not wanting Coral to find the animal, she put him in the bathroom with a whispered apology and hurried to the living room to open the door.

Danny stood in her doorway, his face unreadable. "You're to come with me."

Shan looked down at her bare legs. "Can I put on a robe?"

"Quickly."

Closing the door to her bedroom, Shan wrapped her robe around her and filled a tray from her dresser with water for the kitten. Using her legs as a springboard, he tried climbing her robe. She stroked him once and pulled him away.

"I'm sorry." She said under her breath.

Going back to her hallway, she closed the bedroom door and followed Danny down the hall toward the stairs. She hoped they would not be gone long so the kitten didn't have time to make a lot of noise.

When Danny stopped at Isaiah's apartment, Shan assumed he was being summoned, too, until she walked into his sitting room. Coral, Miss Jessie, Megan and Liam stood in front of Isaiah's couch, facing it.

Shan couldn't see Isaiah but she knew something was very wrong. Moaning she lunged toward him, but Danny caught her around the waist.

"Not yet." He said. His voice was expressionless as always.

Coral glanced at Shan then stepped back. Megan, Miss Jessie and Liam moved with her.

Shan screamed. Isaiah lay on the couch, his face a mass of bruises. Blood oozed from his swollen lip and dripped from his crooked nose. A gash on his forehead revealed pink skin and a gleam of white. His eyes were closed and his arm hung at a twisted angle.

"Let me go!" Shan struggled against Danny's iron grip. "What happened?"

"I told you, Shan." Coral's voice was level and chilling, "You have to control your power. The Circle will accept no more delays."

"You bitch!" Shan charged, power flowing through her. Danny fell back, releasing her. Her magic snaked around the room. Glass and furniture exploded and Shan fell flat on her face. Crawling toward Isaiah she drew more energy. Reaching for the power, she could see the sparks flow toward her, but the same vision showed her that Isaiah, Coral and everyone around the couch stood inside a flaming barrier.

"Stop." Coral held up her hand.

Shan got to her feet. Power crackled around her, lifting her hair, burning her eyes. Her voice vibrated when she said, "I bet I can break that shield."

"Allow me to heal him." Coral leaned over Isaiah, placing her hand on his chest. She hummed and, with the rise and fall of her voice, Isaiah's injuries melted away.

"Why are his eyes still closed?" He looked normal. His chest rose and fell with the even rhythm of sleep.

"Send your magic away." Coral crossed her arms.

"Do as she says," Shan looked back to see Danny standing by the door, sporting a cut on his left cheek. "If you want him to wake up."

Shan envisioned conduit snaking down through all the Bellingham's floors, digging deep into the earth below. When she knew the lines were in place, she released her magic. The energy quickly drained to the ground.

She folded her arms across her stomach and tried to speak without sobbing. "It's done."

Coral didn't remove her shield. She spoke under her breath and Isaiah's eyes fluttered open. He sat up immediately. While touching his lip with one hand, he stretched his previously broken arm.

His brow furrowed. "What?"

He stared at Coral, Liam and Megan, his jaw working. His focus moved further out and he caught sight of Shan. His hands fell to his lap. His lips parted and his eyes widened.

She shook her head quickly.

"Are you alright?" She croaked.

He nodded. His fingers closed into fists and the color in his cheeks deepened.

"Don't do anything." Shan crossed the room, but she couldn't pass the invisible wall. She glared at Coral. "Take it down."

Coral's stare remained even. Her gaze didn't flicker as she removed her ward.

"I'm so sorry." Shan sat by Isaiah, putting her arm around him. "It's my fault." She didn't add that she'd make it right. But she *would* make it right.

"I'm okay." He said, leaning against her. She pulled his head onto her shoulder and he let it remain there for a moment. His hair tickled her neck and the sharp cedar smell of his soap made her feel bees had invaded her chest. It took all her concentration not to pull away.

Abruptly, as if he could read her thoughts, Isaiah moved back. He looked up at Miss Jessie, then, at Coral.

"Are you in any pain?" Coral asked before he spoke.

Shan jumped, ready to spring at Coral, but Isaiah's hand on her knee stopped her. He frowned again, concentrating, and said, "Nah. I feel…fine."

"Let me know if there's any residual effect." She raised her eyebrows at Danny who gave Isaiah a cell phone. "It only calls my number, but don't hesitate to use it if you need me."

"As for you," Coral turned to Shan, "Go to your room. Today, if you show me you mean business, things can go back to normal."

Shan gaped at her aunt. She was supposed to just leave Isaiah after what had been done to him? After what she'd seen? "You're crazy."

"Do you really want to try my patience again, Shan?" Coral's mouth tightened and pink tinged her cheeks.

Danny held the door open. Liam and Megan took positions on either side of the couch where Shan sat with Isaiah.

"Go." Isaiah patted her arm. "I'll be fine."

Shan stared at her friend. She couldn't read his expression. Did that frozen look mean he was resigned? Scared? She wanted to ask him but he avoided looking at her. She ground her teeth. He had every right to blame her. It was her fault.

As she left, she looked back one last time, hoping for some signal from him. He just sat stiffly, hands clasped on his knees, gaze focused on the floor. Miss Jessie stood behind him, her hands spread on the back of the couch, her eyes intent on Isaiah.

Liam and Megan went toward the stairs, but Coral walked with Shan and Danny back to Shan's room. Coral came in while Danny stayed outside.

As soon as they were alone, Shan wheeled on her aunt. "Who hurt him?"

"Staff," Coral shrugged.

"You had it done." Shan glared at her aunt, feeling power come to her. "You might as well have hit him yourself."

"Shan, don't be stupid." Coral raised a shield. "You're just as likely to destroy innocents as you are to hurt me."

"You're evil. I hate you."

"Hate me all you want." Coral crossed her arms and raised her chin. "I warned you."

"I tried!" Shan's fingers curled into fists at her side, nails digging into her palms.

"Your kind of trying will not save a single person, let alone the planet" Coral looked away. "Do you think a commander likes sending troops into battle? I hate hurting anyone. I did *not* choose to do this. But I do care. Why else would I dedicate my life to saving people?" She ran both hands through her hair and shook her head. "I have no family but you and no life but The Circle."

"Maybe you didn't choose your responsibility," Shan said between clenched teeth, "But you chose how you performed it."

"Ha!" Coral wrapped her arms around her middle, hugging herself. She took a breath before speaking hoarsely. "You're too young to understand, but there is no other way. Those before me tried. I tried. People just aren't motivated unless they have something important to lose. Besides, isn't pain better than death?"

"Are you threatening to kill him?"

Coral snorted.

"We," she enunciated carefully, "are all going to die if you don't stop it. Period. Isaiah, too."

"Are you going to hurt him again?"

"Are you going to cooperate?"

Shan's eyes filled with tears. "I'll do whatever you want if you don't hurt him."

"Shan." Coral's hand came toward her. "It breaks my heart to see you hurt."

"Don't lie to me!" Shan backed up, bumping against her coffee table. "You brought him here in case you needed to use him this way."

"I don't deny that," Coral blinked, "But I'm not lying. I don't lie to you. I hate hurting people. I hate making you look at me like that, but think about history. It's always been the way that a few must be sacrificed to save the many. We both must sacrifice."

"Why didn't you just have me beat up, then?"

"Because, if you lose control, we all could die, and with us, the only chance for humanity." Coral sighed. "And because I know the kind of person you are. I knew you'd be more motivated to save your friend than yourself."

Shan's throat burned and her nose felt as if she'd inhaled water. There was nothing she could say to her aunt, the zealot.

Coral glanced at the clock on the mantle. "I'll send someone to get you for breakfast."

She hesitated in the doorway. "I really am sorry it had to be this way."

Shan heard the lock click and she slumped, allowing the tears to come. Lying face down on the couch, she smothered her sobs. Her thoughts were not coherent, at first. She just kept seeing Isaiah's broken body, imagining the pain he must have endured.

She had to get him out of here. She sat up, drying her face with her hands.

Coral could only control her legally for a few more months. If she and Isaiah ran away, chances were good Coral wouldn't be able to catch them before Shan turned eighteen.

The ring caught a strand of hair. Pulling it free, noting the frantic movement of the spark in the topaz, Shan remembered her dreams. She didn't doubt the world was in danger, and she wouldn't turn her back on humanity, but she wasn't going to work with Coral. She tried to think how she could get Isaiah away from Coral and still save the world. Granny had hinted there was another way. That was it. They'd have to find Granny.

Yes, that would work. She only had to master enough control of her power to convince Coral she was really trying. Then Coral would let her out of her room. Three hours until breakfast. Shan went to the bedroom to get her books.

When she saw the closed bathroom door, Shan wanted to hit herself. The kitten—poor baby. Shan found him curled up on the back of the toilet. He had pushed her bath powder to the floor and pulled down the fluffy towel to make himself a bed. He yawned when he saw her, stretched and regarded her with his startling eyes.

He allowed her to pet him before climbing over her shoulder and dropping to the floor. Sniffing disdainfully at the water she'd left, he marched to the kitchen, looking back to make sure she followed.

He stopped in the middle of the room and let out a raucous meow. She picked him up again and put him on the counter while she quickly tore a piece of ham to bits. Cooing with relish, he devoured the ham in less than a minute, and demanded she carry him.

She wished she could spend a few more moments with the kitten, but there was so little time before breakfast. He bounced onto the bed and to the window seat. Meowing pointedly he looked out the window and back at her. Of course he wanted out. She had no box for him and no way of getting one.

But could he jump safely onto the branch? She had to let him try before someone heard his insistent *ree-oooow*. She opened the window, pulse hammering when she saw the gulf between the window sill and the trunk of the branch. He'd never make it.

But apparently, he had no such doubts. Gathering his weight over his hind legs, he sailed across the distance as if he had wings. He scrambled across the branch, and stopping once to thank her with a meow, he swung backward, spiraling down the tree trunk with the ease of a boy sliding down a stair rail.

"Thank you." She whispered. It was probably good-bye, but, she left the window open about six inches. Just in case.

She couldn't take time to even hope the little animal came back. She had to get her power under control.

What was she missing? Her conduits held to release power back into the earth. Why did they fracture when she directed the power at an object? Shan skimmed all the lessons in the books Coral had given her. Except, she already knew everything the authors had to say. She could've written a research paper on it without looking up a reference.

Her magic had erupted in Isaiah's room. Oh, Isaiah.

"Stop." She told herself. She couldn't afford to indulge her emotions. *Lesson one, don't get mad.*

Coral had made her get rid of the magic after she'd destroyed the furniture. Yet some of it remained. She touched it. It was still there, pulsing, living energy with a will. Too strong to be the residual she usually felt after a release. But she'd neither eaten nor drawn power deliberately since sending it back to the earth.

Coral had said her body was a receptacle for energy and she'd learned to balance what she allowed in. Therefore, she must've retained some control in that hour. She'd wanted to destroy Coral, Miss Jessie, Liam and Danny. But there had been Coral's ward. In the back of her mind, Shan hadn't wanted to be defenseless. She'd held onto her power unconsciously. Because she had a reason?

She had a reason to channel her power every day. It couldn't have been just the threat to Isaiah. She didn't doubt the visions, neither did she doubt the science Isaiah showed her. She had needed to control her power to save his life just as much yesterday as she had this morning. What, then, made the difference?

A scrabbling scratch startled her. She exhaled with relief when she realized her little friend had returned through the window. The fearless creature jumped onto the foot of her bed and stalked up her legs as if she were not a hundred times his size. Of course, he knew she wouldn't hurt him just as he knew he could reach the branch from the window sill.

That was it! In Isaiah's room, for the first time, she'd known she could bring the Bellingham down. She experienced the vastness of the energy about her, and knew just how to channel it to do as she willed. She hadn't doubted her ability to wield it.

She glanced around her room. There, in the trash can, an empty bottle. She had to try it, again. She created a pipeline between her body and the bottle. She connected the conduit to a containment box she built around it. She allowed her instinct to determine the size and density of the box.

Her power raged against the outlet she'd created, threatening to burst through. The kitten settled on her chest, tiny claws piercing her robe, pricking her skin. His purr was ridiculously loud for such a small thing. She relaxed a little, focusing partially on the warm spot in her chest, partially on the living magic inside her.

It might be living, but it was in her body and it was hers to command. She *could* control it. Thinking about keeping the magic in the conduit rather than destroying the bottle, Shan released it. In an instant, the bottle had blown to nothing and she dropped the pipeline, shutting off the outflow. The trash can rattled a little. Mentally, she surveyed her closure. It was solid. She could feel the magic swirling against the place where her conduit had touched, but it didn't break through. She'd done it!

Holding a hand beneath the kitten, she got up to look at the trash can. There was no scorch mark, nothing. It was as if the bottle had never been.

"I did it." She said against the kitten's fur, but he just purred.

She used her free hand to rip a piece of paper from her notebook, crumple it and drop it on the window sill. Remembering the trash can had rattled, she brought it across the room and turned it upside down. Dropping the paper onto the can's metal bottom, she retreated.

Sitting on her bed, she made another tube, feeling the force of the energy push against it. She pushed back, allowing only a thread to escape. She let the thread feed into one spot on the paper, until it began to smoke. She closed off the opening fully, and released the pipeline. A wisp smoke curled from the paper and faded into the air. She retrieved the paper, pinched the burned surface, grinding it to ash, and sprinkled it out the window.

"Twice." She spoke out loud, pulling current from the air to replace the little she had spent. She closed the window and settled the cat onto a pillow. He curled tighter into a ball, tucking his black feet around his nose.

Getting ready for breakfast, Shan marveled at how easy it'd been. Just knowing she could do it took away the fear. Trying to direct the flow while imaging all the terrible things that could happen had been like trying to thread a needle with her eyes closed. She just had to get past the fear.

She groaned. She could've kicked herself, instead, she ripped the band off her pony tail and threw it across the room.

She'd just proven Coral right. Bile rose in her throat. If Coral hadn't—hurt Isaiah, Shan may never have understood. But that still didn't make it right. Coral had as much as admitted she brought Isaiah to New York in case she needed leverage. Anyone who could calmly order something like that be done to sixteen year-old boy was a monster. Coral had no qualms about deciding who got saved and who got thrown under the bus. The best thing Shan could do was to get out.

CHAPTER ELEVEN

Liam came to walk her to breakfast. He knocked on her door, unlocked it and waited. When she came out, he nodded and started for the elevator.

"I hope you feel good for your part in hurting my friend."

"Isaiah," Liam said stiffly, "suffered no lasting damage."

"I guess you know that because people have beaten the crap out of you for no reason." She almost punched him, however, she couldn't afford to start the day with a brawl in front of Coral's security cameras.

"He was fully healed."

"Physically, yes. But what about emotionally?" Shan moved in front of Liam. When he started around her she walked backward so she could watch his face. "Isaiah came here because people back home were going to beat him up for being black. His mother took him out of Chicago last year because people were threatening him constantly."

Liam halted and looked her in the eye. "At least he's alive."

"You think my aunt has the right to choose who lives and who dies?"

"No. I think she's obligated to choose some people to die so everyone else can live." Liam stepped around her and continued down the hall.

Isaiah was already in the dining room, standing with Megan and Coral. His whole frame radiated tension and his expression had none of its usual animation. Coral touched him gently, and though some strange emotion flickered in his eyes, he didn't flinch.

Her aunt spoke to him and he nodded. Shan took her seat and Isaiah took his by Megan. From her own place beside Liam, Shan watched Isaiah. He ate without relish, taking only the food Megan offered him. Shan tried to catch his eye. If only she could telegraph her support, let him know it would be over soon.

She wanted to walk downstairs with him, but Coral and Danny stuck with her. Miss Jessie accompanied Isaiah. He didn't even look back at Shan as he went into his classroom.

Coral didn't speak until they were seated in the training area. "Shall we begin?"

"If I can do it, today, you'll let me out of my room?"

"Shan," Coral sighed, "How many times do I have to repeat myself? I don't lie to you. All I want is for you to demonstrate a willingness to do what I know you can. If I can tell the Directorate you've done that, we'll all be able to move forward."

"Okay." Shan closed her eyes and cupped her hands, forming her energy ball. She changed it to fire and ice, then back to its natural, electrical state. "I'm ready."

"This time, I want you to try to destroy the paper fully."

Shan nodded. It should be just like the bottle in her room. She constructed a line to the paper, framing it, and allowed her magic to flow through the small opening. There was a brief flash of light and the paper disappeared. Shan slammed the opening shut and dropped her line.

"Bravo!" Coral's eyes were alight. "Now the top cinder block."

Shan understood, as she encased the cinderblock in her conduit, that she didn't need to regulate the amount of power she released, if she regulated the containment field. The block exploded with a loud crack.

Coral pointed to a brick, then a large cement block, choosing targets swiftly. Shan drew and released power, building containments at the blink of an eye. Her head remained clear, her breathing steady.

Finally Coral stopped.

"I think that's enough for this morning." She stood, stretching. "I'll go report to the Directorate and see you at lunch. This afternoon, we'll work on managing the repercussion associated with larger targets. And other things."

Using the elevator to her room, Coral left Shan in the training center. Once she was certain Coral could no longer hear her, Shan let out a whoop. She and Isaiah were going to leave.

She waited outside the classroom until Isaiah exited. He didn't see her at first because he was looking back, listening to Miss Jessie. When he did see her, his eyebrows went up. "You're not grounded anymore?"

240

"I did what she wanted." She shrugged.

"So it worked?" He regarded her seriously, no hint of warmth in his dark brown eyes.

"No!" She caught his hand. "I mean…I'm sorry. I'm so sorry I got you hurt."

"It wasn't your fault." He freed his hand and ran his finger under her eye. "Don't."

"I'm not." She lied, turning away. "I hate that woman."

"I'm okay, you know."

"No you're not." She said when she could speak again. "You're not yourself."

"Shan, girl, we got to get to the dining room. We'll talk about it later."

He hurried down the hall. She followed him, scrubbing her eyes, angry at The Circle, at Coral and at herself.

Apparently Isaiah's appetite hadn't returned, since he ate as sparingly as he had in the morning. Shan chewed her own food mechanically, watching Isaiah and her aunt. Coral's face glowed. No doubt, the directorate was pleased with her success. Fury made Shan hot all over and she finished her lunch without tasting it.

She walked back to the basement with Isaiah, but he said little. At the classroom, he turned to her.

"I'm fine and I'll talk to you this evening."

Back in the training center, Coral told Shan the directorate approved her progress.

"We can move forward." Coral's eyes glittered. "Everything we've worked for is coming together."

"But at what cost?" Shan bit her tongue, too late. Starting an argument was no way to lure Coral into relaxing security enough to allow Shan and Isaiah to escape.

"How much is too much to save that little boy in your dream?"

"That boy could be saved in a lot of different ways." Shan kept her voice as level as she could. "Isaiah's right now."

"What if the boy were in trouble right now?"

"But he isn't."

"You don't know that, Shan, unless you know something I don't." Coral massaged the bridge of her nose, exhaling. "Listen. *We* know by our analysis of weather patterns, concentration of greenhouse gases in the atmosphere, seismic activity and geological data that, every day we move closer to disaster."

"I know." Shan crossed her arms, "Isaiah told me."

"Did he also tell you that once this planet can no longer support life, it's too late to change?"

"What do you expect me to do?" Shan wanted to recall the question as soon as it was asked. She knew what Coral expected her to do and there was no way she was going to do it, but she couldn't tell Coral that.

Coral's eyes narrowed and she tapped a finger against her leg. She lifted her shoulders and let them drop. "We expect you to remove enough pollutants to restore the balance."

"Meaning?"

"We've spent centuries planning this, hoping it wouldn't have to be this way." Coral began, but, probably

242

seeing the doubt in Shan's face, she stopped. She exhaled, her lips thinned and she started over. "We'll wait until the last moment, but, in the end, we will have to destroy enough targets to restore the balance and in a manner convincing enough to get people to work with us."

"That's…" clenching her teeth so she didn't voice her first thought, *that's terrorism,* Shan tried to think of a different finish. "That sounds stressful."

"Stressful is an understatement. I wish I could say no one will get hurt, but I can't. What I can say is that people will survive." Coral's eyes closed. "The situation is terrifying."

"Why don't you just tell people? Find a reporter, show them your charts?"

"Have you really had so little interest in the news?"

"No. I mean, yes. I've had the net, but…" Shan's face flamed. She hated the way her aunt made her feel like a six year-old.

"We've tried for generations. But you can buy experts to say anything you want and climate change is bad politics."

As soon as her aunt was certain Shan could contain the fallout on small targets, Coral asked her to dispatch an entire stack of cinder blocks. Shan's containment kept the backlash from touching anything in the room, but the frame stretched, throwing her to the wall. Her back slammed against the concrete, knocking the wind out of her lungs, leaving her ears ringing.

"That fucking hurts." When she could move, Shan touched the back of her head, feeling dampness beneath her hair.

"That's what I feared." Coral came over and placed her hand on Shan's head. From where her aunt's hand rested, a sudden sense of well-being flooded through Shan's body. Her aches were gone. Coral moved back so Shan could stand. "I bet you're using a two-way gate. If I were to do that when I healed, negative energy from the injuries would flow back into me. We'll work on that tomorrow. You're free to go today. No training and no classes."

Shan went back to her room immediately after Coral left. The kitten was nowhere to be seen. She looked out the open window, but there was no sign of him. Despite her intention to leave, Shan had hoped he would still be there when she got out of class.

Impatient for Isaiah to return and needing to do something she went onto the internet and opened Google Maps. Guessing at the Bellingham's location, she tried to identify the quickest route out of the city. She wished she could print the maps but she had no printer of her own. Maybe Isaiah could remember the important streets. There was no way she could.

Wearing a fleece lined, suede jacket, she met Isaiah at the elevator. His smile didn't reach his eyes. "You're out early."

"I showed Coral the control she wanted and she gave me the rest of the day off." She eyed the stack of books and papers Isaiah always carried. "Put that stuff up and walk outside with me. "

"I have a lot of work to do."

She punched his shoulder, not holding back. "Isaiah, I haven't been out of this building in twenty-four hours. Come with me."

Rubbing his arm, he agreed reluctantly. Leaving his books on the couch, he slipped on a lined leather jacket.

The weather had changed again. It had grown very cold. Bits of ice swirled in the stiff wind and heavy, low clouds gathered on the horizon. As soon as they were out of the lee of the building, she spoke. "Tell me what's wrong."

"I'm fine, Shan." He looked down at her, smiling with his mouth closed. "Why are you making a big thing?"

"I know you're not fine." Shan shoved her hands deeper into her pockets. "You're not acting like yourself."

"You mean I'm not acting goofy right now?" He snorted, "Girl, this got serious a long time ago, you've just been too busy to notice."

Shan blinked. Thinking back over the last month, she realized Isaiah had been growing more serious. Reserved even. "But you hardly ate today."

"Your aunt and Miss Jessie have been shoving fruit and granola and all that crap down my face all morning."

"How were you able to stand there talking to them like nothing happened?" Shan's hands formed fists. "I want to kill them."

"Don't you know they asked me first?"

Shan's mouth opened and closed. "What? You *let* them do that to you?"

Isaiah started walking. "I didn't know for sure what they wanted. They just asked if I was willing to do something to help get you on the right track. I said 'yeah' and your aunt asked was I sure I was willing to do anything. I said I was and Danny hauled off and punched me. It kind of got rough for a little while and, the next thing I know, there you are and I'm feeling fine. Very, very fine."

"Did you let them hurt you to please me?" Shan swallowed with difficulty. Like a movie, memories of his intense looks and his reactions to her touch surfaced in her imagination. She shook her head. He couldn't be in love with her. He was too young. Too young for *her*, but not too young, she corrected, all the strength leaving her body. "Oh, Isaiah."

"What?" He crossed his arms and that little muscle started working in his jaw. "I did it for the same reason you're doing what you're doing. To save the earth. Whatever."

"I'm not going to do what they want."

"You just got let out because you showed your aunt you *could* do what they want."

"To get freedom." She tucked her arm under his, pulling him down. He pressed her hand against his side, holding it there. "I can't...I can't hurt people the way she can."

"What if you have to? What if we all die otherwise?"

"There has to be another way." Shan would never have imagined she'd have to convince Isaiah that Coral was off her rocker. "Granny said there were two stories. Something like that."

"We don't have time for guesses." He eyed the sky, shaking his head. "This shit's going to start going down really soon."

"I can't do what she wants." Shan closed her eyes, "Please understand. I think she wants me to destroy a bunch of power plants. Do you have any idea how many people would die?"

"Less than everybody."

"But the people at the power plants have just as much right to live as anyone else." Shan dug her fingers into the flesh of his arm. "Isaiah, she wants to hold the world hostage with me as her weapon."

"It's not what she wants," He didn't pull his arm away. "It's what has to be."

"Maybe not." Shan looked directly into his eyes, "Do you think Coral's going to notify everyone around those power plants, asking them if they're willing to die to save the planet?"

"They wouldn't understand." He looked away. "They're not going to understand."

"So they die?"

"They're going to die anyway." His shoulders slumped and he relaxed the arm holding her hand. "I don't get it. You've got the dreams. You've got the power. Why don't you just do what you need to do?"

"Because, I don't see why Coral gets to choose who lives and who dies."

"Who *should* choose then?"

"Nobody." She stopped, pulling her hand free. "There has to be a way nobody has to die."

"It is what it is." He took her hand in both his, "you've got to deal with that."

"Why me?"

"Why do some people get cancer?" He shrugged looking away.

"You have something to say? Go ahead and say it."

"It seems to me you're just against everything because your aunt says it has to be. She's not like you think."

"Even if you were willing to be her pincushion, it didn't make it right for her to use you." Shan stalked toward the grove whose trees had sung to her. Why did he have to be so—so—male?

Her eyes burned and rage tightened her throat. It wasn't right that he was on Coral's side. She heard him coming up behind her, the heavy thud of his feet, the sigh of his breath. She sped up and the cadence of his steps increased.

He caught her shoulder. "Shan, wait up."

She waited, her back to him, gritting her teeth, trying to breathe away the knot in her stomach.

"Truth is I don't want *you* to die." He said against the back of her head. "I'll do anything to save you." He pulled her shoulder gently, trying to make her face him. "I know you don't want to hear that."

"You're my best friend, too, Isaiah." Shan turned but she didn't look into his eyes. She would deal with what lay beneath later. "So will you help me?"

"What do you want to do?"

"I have to leave here." She pulled on the edges of her jacket. "I want to go find Granny, make her tell me that other story."

"When Coral catches you, she'll never let you out again."

"We can't let her catch us, then." The conversation wasn't going the way Shan had expected. "I thought you'd want to leave as badly as I do."

"You've not convinced me we have a viable choice."

Shan could feel the haunting music of the trees on the wind. The song resonated in her bones, rolling over all her other emotions like a flood. Time would be up soon. She had to go, but leaving without Isaiah would be useless. He'd be the tool Coral wielded to make her come back. Maybe if she just started leaving, he would go with her.

"I'm leaving tonight, Isaiah. You can go with me or you can stay." She wheeled and stomped back toward the building.

"We have to get out the gate." He was behind her. She kept walking, not wanting him to see the relief on her face.

They made it to the other side of the building without talking. Shan glanced at the front doors as they passed. She thought she could just make out Danny's outline in the distorted shadows on the front glass.

"Danny's watching." Isaiah spoke into his folded hand, as if covering a cough.

"I know." Shan didn't look over her shoulder. "Keep walking."

They reached the corner. The gate was to their right and a line of trees followed the fence on the left. Shan veered toward the trees, Isaiah stayed beside her.

"Maybe we can use the trees to climb over the fence."

"I don't know." She said, "but we can talk in the shadows."

Shan wondered if she could touch a tree again without losing herself in the song but if it was the only way, she'd have to try. They found, however, that the fence was much higher behind the trees and that the iron bars were spiked.

In the woods, they veered toward the house. Isaiah was silent, concentrating. Shan came up with and discarded plan after plan. They needed more time to figure things out, however, if she waited, it could be weeks before she got another free day.

"They go out to buy clothes and food and stuff, don't they?" He didn't wait for her to answer. "They have to."

"Or somebody delivers it."

"What if we hide in the back of one of the vehicles?"

"That sounds too chancy." Shan bit her lower lip. Actually, hiding in a vehicle would be a great way of escaping. "Do you know when they come and go?"

"Megan goes out every day, just about." Isaiah's sideways look was not lost on Shan. He thought she might be jealous of the staff member. She had more important things to worry about than whether Isaiah had a crush on a woman old enough to be his...older sister.

"When?'

"I don't know." He scratched his head. "If she's going out, she usually does it before dinner or before breakfast. We've just got to watch.'

"Then we'll watch." She took a seat on the leafy ground, where they could see the Bellingham's garage.

Like strains of music from a distant car, the lullaby played on the air and she was careful not to touch any tree or rootling.

The clouds parted and the wind died. The sun moved slowly across the sky. Fingers of light warmed Shan's back while shadows lengthened on the grass in front of her. Isaiah sat straight at first. The pride in his bearing struck Shan. He looked older and unfamiliar. Something rippled through her and she looked away. After a while, his shoulders rounded and his head moved forward, giving him the familiar, gangly appearance that made Shan comfortable.

"What're we carrying with us?" He stretched, arching his back. "Food would be good."

"It would, but I think we should go light." Shan chewed her lower lip. "I think I'm just taking the clothes I have on, my coat, my gloves and my backpack with my laptop and stuff."

"Okay." He shrugged. "I'll pack light, too."

After a moment, he spoke again. "Are you sure about this? It's not just you and me."

"That's what makes me sure." She sighed. "I'm not qualified to hand out executions. I don't think Coral is either."

"What if your granny doesn't know what to do?"

Shan had wondered, too, what she'd do if Granny had no solution. She hadn't come up with an answer. "We'll deal with that when we have to, I guess."

Isaiah was looking ahead but she saw his eyebrows go up.

"What?" She pushed him. "Don't you see I have to try every other option first?"

"Don't *you* see," He twisted, fixing her with a grim look, "You're probably choosing who dies by not choosing."

"That's a risk I have to take." She didn't look away. "You don't have to leave with me."

"If you go, I go." Isaiah scooted back to lean against an elm. His cheek pressed against the smooth bark and he faced the garage.

When dinnertime came and Megan had not shown, Shan stood. "We'll have to watch out for our chance and try again."

"We should make a code word, then." Isaiah stood, dusting the back of his pants. "One of us hears somebody's leaving, we say the code word and meet out here in five minutes."

"Maybe someone will take off after dinner." Shan straightened her jacket. "We could have guests tonight."

"Last chance to change your mind." Isaiah's eyed her intently. She had to look up further than she remembered to meet his gaze.

"We can't stay here."

He nodded and they walked toward the Bellingham. "About that code word?"

"It has to be something that wouldn't come up in normal conversation." Shan tucked her hair behind her ear, frowning.

"Ostrich?"

"Really?" Shan stumbled, laughing. "Ostrich? It has to be something we can use in a sentence."

"Ostriches are ugly mo'fo's."

Fine." She nudged him. "Ostrich it is."

CHAPTER TWELVE

Shan went upstairs long enough to pack the painting, her computer and the picture of her mother in her backpack. As an afterthought, she added her grandmother's pearls. Coral had said they were meant for her. As she zipped the bag, little claws scratched the window and the Siamese appeared on the sill.

"Oh, what are you doing back?" Shan stared at him.

He meowed and raised a paw toward her, his posture displaying confidence she'd pick him up. She did.

"I can't take you with me." She kissed the top of his head and he climbed onto her back. She sighed. What could she do? She couldn't abandon him. She opened her pack and he crawled in, curling on the painting as if the bag had been set up just for him. When she closed the zipper, Shan left a tiny hole so he could breath. She'd ask Isaiah to let him out when he carried the bags to the woods.

Downstairs, she gave the bag to Isaiah, who had his own backpack.

"We don't have time for questions but there's a kitten in my bag. Could you please unzip the main compartment so he can get out?"

Isaiah looked at Shan as if he doubted her sanity, but he carried her backpack with his and went out to stow them in the woods while she kept watch. When he came back, he told her he had unzipped the bag but the kitten had just changed position and gone back to sleep. Together, Shan and Isaiah entered the dining room.

There were no guests for dinner but Coral's cheerful mood seemed to influence all the staff. Everyone laughed and chattered. Catching Coral's gaze resting on her, Shan turned to Liam, smiling broadly.

"Did you enjoy your break from getting beat up by a girl?"

"I did miss inflicting my usual punishment but I suppose I can make up for it tomorrow." Liam smiled.

"I look forward to seeing you try." Shan's face muscles strained with the effort of keeping her smile in place. Whether or not her sparring partner had helped Danny beat up Isaiah, he had, at the very least, stood by and watched it happen. She almost regretted that she'd be leaving. A part of her would very much enjoy using her power on Liam. This time, on purpose.

Liam asked if she'd spent her break resting and she told him she had gone for a walk around the grounds. The servers brought sorbet and Shan concentrated on eating, keeping her expression neutral.

After dinner, she waited in the hall for Isaiah, who stayed in the dining room, deep in conversation with Megan. A stab of anger made Shan huff. Boys were impossible. Megan's glowing red hair and fluttering lashes seemed to have distracted Isaiah from their desperate plan.

She was about to go back in and interrupt when Isaiah and Megan came through the door. The redhead grinned at Isaiah, saying goodnight in a voice too husky to be appropriate with someone his age.

As the girl passed, Shan turned away. Isaiah stood close to Shan, hands in his pockets. "I was just thinking you look about as happy as that ol' rooster your granny used to have. Man, that thing was ugly. No wonder he always went around looking pissed off."

Shan gaped at him. What rooster was he talking about? And why had he reverted to his annoying hillbilly patter? Staff milled around, coming in and out of the dining room, gathering in little clusters in the hall. Voices rose and fell. Laughter rang out.

"Yeah. Think that's the ugliest bird I ever seen." Isaiah went on, watching her, a little crease in the middle of his forehead. "Except for that ostrich I saw at Lincoln Park."

Shan stood straighter, her heart thundering. "He was an ugly rooster." She swallowed, trying to think of something else to say.

"Did your granny really cook him?"

"No." Shan stuck out her tongue. "We couldn't eat a tough old bird like that."

Isaiah angled his head, indicating they go down the hall, and took a step toward the door.

"What'd you do with him?" Isaiah raised an eyebrow. "It ain't like he had any pretty feathers left to make a pillow."

"I think Granny tossed his carcass into the woods for the foxes to gnaw." Shan walked with him. They

256

drifted, talking about the imaginary chicken. Isaiah claimed he never got to sleep in until the old reprobate was gone and Shan swore he pecked at her legs every time she crossed in front of him.

By the time they reached the door, there were no staff members in sight. Isaiah slipped out and Shan followed. They flattened themselves against the wall, making their way to the corner of the building and into the woods.

"One of the kitchen staff, Roger, I think, told Megan he had a date tonight." Isaiah whispered as they reached the place where he'd stowed their packs. Shan could've pinched herself for her relief that Isaiah had been talking to Megan for a good reason.

"He's taking a staff car parked out behind the garage." Isaiah said, "We can sneak into the trunk and, when he stops to pick up his girl, we'll hop out and get lost in the city."

The kitten was no longer in her bag. Shan swallowed her disappointment. Really, she should be glad. The plan was crazy enough without adding a complication.

"What if it's locked?" She didn't dare waste a moment. "Maybe we should just hide by the gate and sneak out when it opens."

Isaiah shook his head. "They have cameras on the gate and those cameras are watched twenty-four-seven." He leaned against her, grinning down at her. "If it's locked, I get to show you a skill I learned in the hood."

Shan nodded, swallowing. She sometimes forgot Isaiah once had a life away from her.

They moved as quietly as possible to the back of the garage, through the forest. Shan took long strides to keep up with Isaiah, making herself as small as possible to avoid touching the trees. Isaiah stopped and pointed. The black sedan waited next to a red smart car. The smart car's driver was just backing up, so they had to wait for the headlights to disappear before approaching the bigger car. Shan crossed her fingers no one else, including driver would show up before they could secure their hiding place.

When the red vehicle's taillights disappeared around the corner, Isaiah ran, crouching, to the black sedan. Shan followed. They squatted beside the vehicle. She hoped it had no alarm as Isaiah reached for the driver's side door. It opened easily and, still bent over, Isaiah fumbled with something inside. There was a faint click and the trunk opened.

They crab-walked to the back of the car and Isaiah lifted the lid. Shan started, feeling something brush against her leg. Bringing her hand down to knock it away, she made contact with a soft, living body. The kitten. Without another thought, she slipped her backpack off her shoulder, unzipped it and deposited him back inside. Isaiah watched until she was finished, then raised himself to look into the trunk. Shan stretched to survey the space, as well.

It was too dark to see inside. Holding out her hand, Shan called her magic, allowing a small flame to form above her palm.

"Uh." Isaiah jumped, banging his head on the lid.

"Quiet!" She shook her head, the movement making her flame waver.

"Sorry. Forgot you could do that." He rubbed his skull.

Shan bit her lip. What if he wasn't comfortable with her as a druid? She grinned when his fingers wrapped around her wrist pulling her hand deeper into the trunk.

"Yeah, here." He raised her arm a little so the entire interior was illuminated. "That's handy."

There was a small toolbox, an emergency kit, a single man's shoe and a crumpled blanket in the trunk.

"This is it." Isaiah looked into her eyes. "The minute we get in is the minute you're at war with your aunt."

"Climb in." She pulled her hand away from Isaiah's to focus the light on the blanket. He shrugged. Pushing his backpack in front of him, he crunched down to get in, then folded himself against the exposed seat backs. Shan handed him her pack, trying to keep her right hand steady. He tucked the pack at his feet, taking extra care. Letting the light go, she climbed in, pulling the lid closed. When the trunk was secure, she scooted back against Isaiah.

He moved his knees down so she could fit in front of him and pulled the blanket over them both, his arm lying over her. His spicy sent filled the small space and she could feel his heart thumping against her shoulder blade. His breath caressed the back of her neck and, despite the warmth stealing over her, chills spread across her chest. She started to move away when she heard a voice outside.

"I'll be there in about half an hour." The speaker's voice got louder as he approached the car. Roger, no doubt. Shan's own heart thrummed so loudly, she no longer noticed Isaiah's. What if Roger needed to get into the trunk?

"No, no." The man continued, and the car swayed as he got in. Shan held her breath until the door slammed. "I've got to stop at Riley's. Five minutes. 'k. Bye."

Isaiah squeezed her gently. She patted his arm. Two seconds later, the car started and with it, the jarringly loud bounce of a hip-hop beat. Shan was relieved she didn't need to worry about Roger hearing the kitten meow.

"Never would of thought." Isaiah said into her ear. "Good jams."

"You're talking about music?" She angled her face to make sure he could hear. "Let's get off at Riley's, whoever that is, if we can."

"Right with you." Isaiah blew a strand of hair back over her cheek. "They're going to know we're gone soon. The faster we're out and off, the better."

The car accelerated, slamming Isaiah into Shan. At the curve, around the building, Shan assumed, she and Isaiah slid right, then left. When the driver hit a bump, she heard Isaiah's head thud against something.

"Dammit!" His hold on her relaxed, but she had to grab his arm to keep from being thrown forward as the car slowed.

"Are you alright?" She tried to reach back, but all she could do was grasp his arm.

"I'll live."

The car rested for a moment before shooting forward. Isaiah pulled Shan to him, curling his knees up behind hers. Grateful for his support, she pressed her cheek against his arm, noticing, with a blush, that he had developed some serious biceps over the past semester. She smiled, telling herself she was just glad he'd be able to defend himself on the road.

Every time the car slowed, or stopped for a light, Shan's mouth went dry. If Coral caught her now, there was no way to predict what she'd do. One thing was for certain, though, if she were caught, neither Shan nor Isaiah would ever get away again.

Shan couldn't think too much about the possibility of being found out. Instead, she focused on trying to calculate how far they traveled by the number of times the driver stopped. After a short while, she lost count and tried focusing on her breathing. Unfortunately, thinking about her breath and the position of her body made her acutely aware of how Isaiah held her. Her face flamed as she realized he'd angled the lower half of his body away from her. She may not have been allowed out, but she did read and she'd had the internet.

Which was worse, knowing what Isaiah felt for her, or thinking about how she would feel if he were older? Wait. Could she go to jail if someone thought…No. He'd turned sixteen in November. *Damn, how could she have forgotten?*

Shan stiffened, wishing she could pull into herself like the kitten. When had Isaiah's crush on her started and how much of their friendship was based on that crush? Sometimes, it sucked being a girl.

Roger slowed the car and turned onto an uneven surface. After driving less than a hundred feet, he stopped. The music went off and Shan held her breath, hoping the kitten wouldn't meow, that Roger wouldn't come to the trunk. The car rocked. The door slammed and, somewhere nearby, heavy metal screamed into the night.

"Let me pop the latch and you peek out." Isaiah scooted on his side until he could reach over her head and fiddle with the latch. It clicked and he moved behind her.

She inched forward until she could see. They were in a small parking lot across from a row of dark buildings. She raised the lid a little further and verified they were at a bar.

There was no one in sight, but, from the shadows the bar's neon sign cast on the parking lot, it was crowded.

"Clear?" Isaiah didn't whisper. He put his hand on her back. "Go for it."

Shan raised the trunk lid enough to climb out. The kitten meowed when Isaiah handed Shan's backpack to her. She cradled it in her arms and, ducking, ran to stand behind the nearest car. Isaiah climbed out, too and shut the trunk just as the bar's double doors opened. Isaiah dropped into a crouch. From her hiding place, Shan watched a man and woman exit the bar. She had no idea whether the man was Roger. She held her breath until the couple turned right and sauntered across the street.

She hissed, "Come on!"

Isaiah, still crouching, closed the distance between them and, putting his arm around Shan, led her across the lot and up the deserted street. Once she judged they were far enough from the bar to escape Roger's notice if he came out, Shan straightened out of Isaiah's embrace.

She slipped the pack off her shoulder and opened it a little. The kitten poked his head out and his forepaws.

Watching Shan intently, he waited. She shrugged the pack onto her back and the little animal moved out far enough to rest his face against the back of her neck.

"Which way?" Isaiah spread his hands looking up and down the quiet street.

"South." Shan said, crossing her fingers.

"Okay." Isaiah wheeled and started down the sidewalk. The roar of an engine came from the main street and Shan grabbed Isaiah's arm, pulling him against a building. They watched the parking lot for a moment.

The car was long and black and it pulled into the lot just as a young man with a buzz cut ran out the door. Shan didn't have to say anything to Isaiah. He ducked into the nearest alley and she followed him. The kitten backed down into the pack with a grumpy trill as Shan's pace increased.

Sprinting from alley to alley, Shan heard voices back the way they had come. The Circle was already in hot pursuit. It wouldn't be difficult for several staff members to corner them. Shan watched for places to hide as she ran.

"There," Isaiah whispered, as if he'd read her mind. He pointed to a subway sign and they sprinted down the street until they found the steps. At the bottom, Shan blinked, looking around the brightly lit lobby. There were two other riders past the turnstiles, but one was engrossed in a book while the other glanced at his wrist and looked down the tunnel.

A uniformed agent watched Shan from his booth. His bored expression changed to mild interest. She turned her back on him.

Isaiah pulled her aside. "Remember, don't see anybody."

He indicated the corner of the room. There were several ticket machines. "Got any money?"

Shan took her wallet out of her backpack. Isaiah opened it, selected several bills and gave it back to her.

"Wait here." He said.

Shan leaned against the wall, panting, pulse racing. She thought she heard a shout.

Isaiah came back, "Got a debit card?"

Shan gave him the card Granny had let her use for internet purchases. She had no idea how much, if any, money was on it. Isaiah went to the machine and returned again with two thin subway cards. He gave her one with her debit card. "Follow me."

Isaiah walked to the turnstile, stuck the end of his card into the slot atop the divider and after a light blinked on, he pushed through. She did the same, noting the arrow and flipping her card just in time. A train roared into the station as they went through. The doors opened and Isaiah directed her onto the car.

As the doors closed, Shan looked back. Two pairs of black-clad legs clattered down the stairs. Shan moved away from the windows to watch as the train started. The two men wore green coats. She stepped back further and Isaiah grabbed her backpack.

"I saw them." He whispered, pulling her pack off her shoulders and handing it to her. "You have to hold it."

Shan followed Isaiah down the car until they found two empty seats. Isaiah sat beside the heavy man wearing a brown work coat and green overall. Shan sat on the end beside Isaiah, staring at the back door. What if the men had gotten on one of the other cars?

"They're not supposed to go between cars." Isaiah's gaze followed hers. "But I guess they're not too worried about the rules."

"Should we ride the train to—wherever it's going or switch and go somewhere else?"

"I think it's going to Manhattan." Isaiah frowned. "Maybe we should just stay on 'til close to the last stop, then switch direction."

"Won't they know where the train stops?"

"They will but there's no way your aunt has enough people to cover all the stops."

"According to what I learned from Liam, The Circle might."

They rode in silence for a few moments. The train stopped and several people got off. The workman sharing their seat moved to an empty one closer to the door. Isaiah stood to look out the window across the aisle. He sat down quickly.

"Think I saw some people in green jackets." He spoke into her ear, crouching down into his coat.

"Do they know which car we're in?"

"Duh, girl. Are they in here?" He nudged her. "They know which train, though."

"What if we didn't get off? Does the train come back?"

"I don't know."

"We can't take a risk and get stuck." Shan rested her hand against the pack material outlining the kitten's spine. He purred lightly under her touch.

"We can hope the closer we get to the Times Square, the more people get on." Isaiah sighed again. "Shan, I don't know we did the right thing."

"Trust me." She watched the blur of tunnel lights give way to winking neon and white lights as they went above ground. She wondered how many people were in those buildings. How many worked in a power plant? "This is what I have to do."

"We should get off with a crowd then, and try to switch to a different train."

"What if they see us?"

"We run." Looking around the car, Isaiah rubbed his chin. "Give me a couple of twenties."

"That's half the cash I have." She dug the money out of her wallet and handed it to him anyway.

He went to some older men sitting at the far end of the car. They were bundled in puffy jackets, wore scarves and knit caps. He traded each man a bill for his hat. As Isaiah walked back, the men whispered to each other and one tucked his scarf over his bald head.

"Put this on." Isaiah gave Shan a gray cap and pulled a dark blue one over his black curls. Shan took the used cap still warm from the previous owner's head, trying not to be obvious about examining the man who had sold it. She shook it out, off to the side, before turning it inside out and pulling it over her hair.

"Disguise." Isaiah grinned, removing his fine leather jacket. He turned it inside out, revealing the black silk lining, and shrugged back into it. He eyed her, one brow raised. "You're going to owe me big time for this one."

Shan tucked her hair up under the cap and removed her own chocolate brown coat. Any other time, she would've laughed at the idea of someone wearing a fleece lined coat wrong side out, but now, she just pursed her lips in satisfaction. The natural fleece looked quite different from the suede. With the hat on, she should be able to lose herself in a crowd.

With his jacket turned and his cap pulled low, Isaiah blended in with other young men on the subway.

"Brilliant," she said, winking at him.

"It's what they pay me for," Isaiah's color deepened, "But we're together and that's going to make us stand out unless we're in a crowd."

At every stop, they put their heads down. From beneath her lashes, Shan watched the legs of the people getting on and her heart leaped every time she saw black pants. She glanced upward each time, relieved to find regular coats and jackets, not the distinctive green uniforms of The Circle. Once the train started after each stop, Isaiah would cross the car and peer out into the station.

Sometimes he reported seeing people who could've been Circle agents, other times he was pretty certain he saw no one. He agreed with Shan that they shouldn't take chances.

Despite many people getting off at each stop, the train grew more crowded. They stood, joining the crowd near the door as the car approached Times Square. They left the train with the other passengers. Isaiah tucked his arm in hers and ducked.

Shan's blood roared in her ears, and she wished she could make shields like Coral, so they could be invisible. She almost drew magic, so she could see any wards in the area, but she worried that drawing power would lead the agents right to her. She felt strangely blind.

Isaiah kept them moving inside the crowd, out of the station, up the stairs. Shan glanced left and right from beneath her lowered head. Seeing a flash of green, she looked up. Stupid. It was just an M & M sign. Isaiah guided them left with the bulk of their fellow travelers. Signs flashed and video rolled, transforming the street into a riot of color. Music, laughter and talk swelled out of venues on every side as they reached the corner. In the circus of light and sound, Shan couldn't make out the colors of most people's clothing. She clung to Isaiah's arm, trying to keep her chin level while her eyes drank in Time Square's electric brilliance.

Her Salt Creek class would be coming to New York City for their senior trip in the spring. They planned to see *Wicked*. There were signs for *Wicked, Billy Elliot,* and *Momma Mia*. Across from the towering Double-Tree, there was a billboard for the *Phantom* Shan had longed to see.

The atmosphere was so charged, she could taste the phosphorous flavor of power. Every pore of her skin ached with the pressure of magic. Her flesh felt raw and she grew weak with the effort of holding it off. It would be an easy bet The Circle would be looking for a power stream leading to her.

"Walk faster." She pulled Isaiah's arm, pushing through people, who just allowed them to pass, acting as if they didn't exist.

"We don't want to be noticed." Isaiah held back. He was too strong for her.

"I've got to get away from these people." Speaking took all her extra effort. She clung to him, remembering Coral's explanation that her body wanted to draw power. She'd been holding off since they'd left the car and, now, she wasn't sure how much longer she could keep her control.

"Please." She exhaled, trying not to stumble.

They stopped at a crosswalk and Isaiah stretched to look over the crowd. He led them across at an angle and they followed Forty-Sixth Street to an alley between a bank and a souvenir shop. He veered into a parking area. She looked over her shoulder. No one seemed to be following and no one paid them any attention.

The passageway opened onto another street but Isaiah turned to walk along a row of parked vehicles. He stopped between a cargo van and a column that backed to the street. "They're not going to find us in this crowd. What's wrong?"

Shan held up one finger, while she controlled her breathing until the sunburned feeling left her skin. "If I release magic, I'm afraid it'll look like searchlights to any druid in the area. But my body is programed to draw in magic and I can't hold it off in crowds. If I get too much and don't release it..."

"Yeah. Makes sense." Isaiah, palms on his thighs, angled his back against the column. "Energy's energy, you know, and there's a lot of it here."

Shan didn't know, but she nodded. "We need to find someplace less crowded, but where The Circle can't find us."

"I know just about as much about New York as you do."

"At least you've lived in big city."

"All I can think is getting back in the subway and using it to get out of the city."

"They can't watch every station." She frowned. "So we just have to pick a direction they wouldn't expect."

"Come on, then. Let's go through here."

They came out the other side of the pull-through and turned away from the street with all the theatres. There were still too many people thronging the sidewalks, even under the scaffolding built around a building in mid-renovation.

The kitten cried and wriggled in the backpack, so Shan unzipped it enough to let his head through. He complained vociferously. Suspecting he was hungry, she bought hot dogs and water for them all from one of a myriad of street vendors. Isaiah held Shan's loaded hotdog, eating the bun from the kitten's, then his own dog while she fed the Siamese one bite at a time. After he'd finished his own food, Isaiah poured water into a paper food basket and they stood while the cat drank his fill.

"What's his name?" Isaiah regarded the little animal with a mixture of amusement and impatience.

"I don't know." Shan said, but as she did, she realized what it had to be. "Arlo."

"Arlo?" Isaiah looked taken aback, "Somebody you couldn't save?"

"Somebody different and brave, who deserves to be honored."

Isaiah smiled. "I like it. But," He frowned at the kitten, "You better not be trouble."

Shan feared the cat would want down after the food, but he stretched, tangling his claws in her hair, and went back to sleep.

While they walked, Shan tried to look at the signs, so, when they went into another subway station, she could tell where they had been on the map. They walked for blocks, in the crowd. Shan felt battered the whole way. Soon, she lost track of where they were. For all she knew, they could be passing the same places over and over.

Her heightened inner focus, both to avoid Coral's staff and to keep her guard up against magic, combined with the physical toll of walking concrete in ballet flats, drained her.

Finally, they crossed Fifth Avenue, but there were so many people, she drew Isaiah down the next narrow alley they found. There were a set of dumpsters, a chained bicycle and what appeared to be a back door to a restaurant. A thin, older man slouched in a metal chair at the far end of the alley. He just stared at the ground nursing his cigarette.

"We're never going to find a subway station."

"I wonder…" Isaiah sauntered down the alley, closing half the distance between him and the smoker.

"Excuse me." Isaiah drawled, employing a southern accent. "Can you tell me how to get to Grand Central Station?"

With his shoulders back, his head held high and his arms in both his pockets, Isaiah cut an impressive figure but Shan tasted her magic, just in case.

The smoker looked up, catching his cigarette between his thumb and forefinger. He scrutinized Isaiah for a second, flicked his ashes and spoke. "You go back down the avenue to Forty-Second. 'Bout half mile. Turn left and walk 'til you see the station."

He put his cigarette back in his mouth and resumed his study of the asphalt. Shan fell into step with Isaiah, hoping he knew which way "down the avenue" meant.

"We can go anywhere from Grand Central. They'll never find us." He picked up the pace, forcing Shan to pull him back.

"I can't race-walk a half mile, Isaiah." Especially not in the crowd. Power crackled all around her. Her chest felt as though it had been clamped in iron. "We need to find a map."

"I know." He shifted his bag, "I should've got one at that first station, but they'll have all kinds at Grand Central."

"Geography's not my strong suit, but won't we have to cross the Hudson or something to get out of New York? Does the subway cross somewhere?"

"Yeah, we have to cross, but I have no idea how." He patted his pockets. "And I've got no green. That twelve dollars in your wallet won't get us to Kentucky. What's on your card?"

"The last time I checked it had less than a hundred."

"Girl, it's a long walk to Salt Creek from New Jersey." He rubbed his chin. "Maybe I ought to call Mom."

"No." Shan touched his elbow to remind him to slow down again. Being short was a drag. She needed privacy, but she could only move so fast. She hated having to run to keep up with other people. "If you call your Mom, Coral will know."

"You think she's not going to be there waiting, anyway?" Isaiah spread his arms.

"I don't plan to go home." Shan stopped to gather her strength. "I plan to find Granny. Or let her find me."

"How you figure?"

"Coral knows more about Granny than I do and when she can't find me, she's going to find out how to contact Granny. Granny's not going to be in hiding anymore, so she'll let herself be found." Shan took a couple more breaths before continuing. People streamed around them as if they were statues. She could feel their energy flow over her, looking for entry. "When she hears from Coral, Granny'll know we ran off and she'll be looking for us. She'll meet us somewhere on the road."

"So we're going to head home but hope we find your granny before we get there?" Isaiah's mouth twisted. "That's the plan? And we have to dodge your aunt's security goons as we go?"

"That, and," Shan looked down. She hadn't had time to tell him about the demons, "Rome's magicians."

"What're you talking about?"

"Never mind, now." She stepped forward. "Just get us out of this crowd and find us a map."

On the outside, Grand Central Station looked like a cross between the Bellingham and the county courthouse in Hyden, only much bigger than both of them put together.

Inside, it was breathtaking. Despite her tense control, Shan couldn't help looking every which way. There was a drug store, restaurants and escalators to another building. There were great globe chandeliers hanging over the open gallery and a grand staircase. Signboards above ticket windows announced trains on specific track numbers and arched doorways led to tracks. At each end of the huge room, soaring, leaded windows were topped by ornate arches. The deep blue ceiling rose over the entire center. Curving lines depicted the night sky zodiac. Gold medallions marked stars within the mythological bodies. Shan wished she were traveling through that vast, peaceful emptiness of space.

"You coming?" Isaiah tugged her sleeve. He held a clutch of maps. "Don't look up, but I think I saw two Circle agents walking the gallery."

"Yes. We have to hurry." She rasped, instantly drawn back into her burning body. "I can't control my magic much longer."

"I have an idea." Isaiah stood on his tiptoes to look over the crowd. "This way."

They ducked around clusters of people, some, obviously tourists, looking around, dazed. Others wore that familiar New York cloak of invulnerability. They didn't see anyone or anything but themselves. Clearly, nothing existed outside their personal space. If only she could get the hang of that.

Shan focused on the muted click of her heels against the honey-colored marble floor. Exotic perfumes, sweat, cigarette smoke, body odor and urine from passing people wafted through the air, mingled with mouthwatering scents of coffee, bread, spices and searing meat. The clatter of trains formed a backdrop to the rise and fall of thousands of voices, laughing, whispering, shouting. A small, mahogany-skinned girl, clinging to an adult's hand, looked up into Shan's face. The child's brick-red lips pursed and her luminous, chestnut eyes radiated suspicion.

Shan looked away, increasing her pace. Her head swam, her stomach cramped. The child was right. What would happen to that little girl, to Isaiah and everyone else in the station, if Shan lost control of her power?

Isaiah slid his hand beneath her elbow and steered her to a stairwell. The lower level boasted restaurants and rows and rows of tracks to one side. People milled around the eateries or strode briskly along the platform, intent on cellphones, schedules and maps. Still, their presence, the energy they stirred, chafed Shan's already tattered restraint.

"If I don't find a place to hide and release," she squeezed Isaiah's forearm, "I'm going to explode."

Looking back and forth, for a place to go and, no doubt, for moss green jackets, he took her down the track, past shops, signs and commuters. Finally, he went around a steak restaurant and down a narrow corridor. They walked the passage, unmarked except for overhead lights, curving back and forth until Shan had no idea which direction was out. Finally, the hallway ended at a wall with a single door, painted the same butter color as the wall.

"Will you stay and let me go buy some food and water to carry with us?"

Shan agreed, sliding to the floor.

"Don't forget Arlo." Pulling the blinking kitten from her pack, holding him against her chest, she gave Isaiah the last twelve dollars in her wallet and her debit card.

"Can't he catch mice or something?" Isaiah shook his head, "We don't know how long we've got to eat on this, or how much we might need to travel."

"You can buy a box of dry food." Shan glared, "It has to be cheap."

"More to carry." Isaiah mumbled going back down the hall.

"Don't you get caught!" She called as he disappeared around a corner.

"You neither."

Shan considered releasing her magic into the floor right then, but there were probably Circle staff out on the main concourse. If they were near enough, they could be looking for any release or draw of magic.

Arlo struggled to get down, mewing and nibbling her hand in frustration. She distracted him with strands of her hair, rubbed his stomach and cooed to him, fearing every minute that she would let her guard down and accidentally kill them both. The kitten settled eventually, nestling under her chin to sleep. Isaiah's absence seemed to go on forever.

CHAPTER THIRTEEN

Images and ideas floated aimlessly in her thoughts. The painting, Gaiaes, the demon, the tree lullaby, flash-frozen people, drowning...

She jumped when Isaiah came around the corner. "I didn't hear you coming."

"That's not good."

He lowered plastic bags to the floor and moved his pack over to her. "I couldn't find kitten food. I got the only brand of cat food they had in a box. Why don't you sort these into our bags while I get this door? I'll carry the waters.

"Maybe," Shan opened a bag with one hand, "The door won't be locked."

Isaiah tried the door and Shan gritted her teeth. How far away would a druid have to be to detect her release of power?

"Locked." Isaiah's brows drew together. "You're not seeing me do what I'm about to do."

He took a small tool out of his pocket. It looked something like a flat pocket knife, but instead of blades, long, thin metal rods opened out. Pushing most of the rods back, Isaiah selected a few and inserted them into the keyhole. He rattled the knob, readjusted the rods and tried again. And again.

Shan sorted beef jerky, trail mix, dried fruit, peanuts and M &M's into her bag. That left three large bottles of water for Isaiah's bag and one bottle for her pack. When she started to stand, she realized she would have to make room for Arlo before they started off again.

While she put some of the food in outer pockets, Isaiah selected different rods and went back to work on the door.

"Bit out of practice?" Shan hadn't noticed any security cameras but she hadn't been looking. Her magic roiled inside her. "The gestapo could be here any minute."

"'Preciate the faith." Isaiah wiped his forearm across his brow and tried again. Shan heard the distinctive click of the lock turning. They slipped into the dim passageway and Isaiah closed the door behind him.

"We have to move." Taking her hand in his sweaty one, he started running.

She had no choice but to follow him. They ducked beneath pipes, some steaming, others exuding a distinctive petroleum smell. Arlo meowed and twisted about in the backpack. Shan felt as though she were doing everything in slow motion, leaving con-trails of movement in the air beside her.

Isaiah kept running until they'd traveled deep into the warren of maintenance tunnels. They managed to avoid workers, maybe because there were few in the section this late in the evening, but rats were everywhere—rats as big as Chihuahuas.

Isaiah stopped in a tunnel comprised of dirt on one side and concrete on the other. Without a word, Shan put both hands on the dirt wall and, as the power flowed out of her, she pressed her body against the soil, letting its cool, dry texture absorb the raw pain of control. She was unsure how long she remained against the wall, but when she became aware of her surroundings, she realized Arlo yowled in the back pack.

Isaiah had taken a seat on the concrete floor and watched her with guarded interest. She took the pack down, unzipped it and pulled Arlo to her chest. He accepted a few seconds of affection before scrambling over her back and up the passage.

"I hope he comes back." Isaiah opened a brochure on Grand Central Terminal. "Those rats will eat him alive."

"He'll come back." Shan wished she had some more hotdog instead of dry cat food, and not just to lure Arlo back. It had been a long time since their last meal, and she'd controlled and released a lot of magic in the meantime. But she didn't want to waste any of their food "Will we be away from people for a while, guide master?"

"If all goes according to plan." He looked up from the map he had spread on the floor. "Can't handle the crowds or the magic?"

"The magic, I guess. I could handle a little so I'm not starved, but only if I know I'm not going to be overloaded again."

"Shouldn't be." He mumbled tracing a line on his paper.

She extended roots into the earth beside her, finding dry nothingness at first. She pushed further and drew a little of the rich magic she found. When the sharpness of her hunger had been dulled, she cut off the entry. She was still a bit hungry, but she could think clearly.

"You never told me your idea." No longer worried about staining her clothes, she stretched out on the ground, parallel with Isaiah so she could watch Arlo who was further down the aisle, scratching at the dirt.

"There's supposed to be a secret underground section of the station." Isaiah showed her a trifold brochure, with dates and black and white photographs. "The Nazis knew about it and planned to blow up the station, but they were caught before they could do it."

"Okay. So?" Shan wriggled her fingers on the concrete and Arlo looked up before scampering in the other direction.

"So, I saw this documentary about people who live in villages under the subway." He shrugged, "Supposedly they have town councils, elected officials and everything. Anyway, I thought we could move underground awhile and throw The Circle off our scent."

"You see, Isaiah, this is why I need you." Shan smiled, "You're a genius."

"Your aunt might know about the underground, but if it's really anything like that documentary I saw, she and her people would stick out down there like a sore thumb."

"So where are we now?"

He raised his eyebrows and shook his head. "That's the tricky part. I can find that steak house on the map, but these papers don't include maintenance tunnels."

"I don't suppose you have a sense of which way's north?"

"You're the druid. You don't know?" Isaiah cocked his head, flushing beneath his dark skin. "Can't you, I don't know, ask nature or something?"

"See a lot of nature down here?" Shan flattened her palm against the dirt wall on the off chance she could feel something. She heard only the raucous hum of electricity, the mechanical rattle of machinery. "It's dead. Besides, I only listened to trees. I didn't talk to them."

"You did in your dreams."

"That was Palax Lae."

A dusty gray creature skittered across the pavement a few feet from Isaiah. Shan jumped and it stopped to turn it milky gaze on her for a second. Isaiah twisted, too, but the movement scared the creature away.

"Maybe you could talk to the rats?"

Shan rolled her eyes. "I don't think I can talk to animals. I'd have noticed with Arlo."

As she said his name Arlo galloped back down the tunnel toward her. His tail was fuzzed and his back arched. The light reflected red from his eyes. Shan might have laughed, if she didn't understand exactly how the little animal felt.

"Maybe we should move on?" She said, standing with Arlo on her shoulder. "There have to be some kind of blueprints down here for the workers, or signs on the pipes, something like that."

"Yeah. Or we can just look for doors that don't lead back outside." He shouldered his pack and she took hers. "The big thing is we don't' want to be caught by workers, so we need to find someplace to hole up."

A sense of urgency pushed at the back of her mind. Palax Lae? Her most recent nightmare came back to her; a woman driving along a high road, her daughter in the back seat, washed down the mountain in the muddy waters of a flash flood. *Thank you, I don't need the reminder.* "We don't have time to hole up."

"We can't get anywhere with The Circle on our asses, either." He pointed his thumb over his shoulder. "I think that's the way back to the station, so we'll head for the far end."

Ducking around equipment, pipes and conduit, they made their way. Arlo scrambled to get down and wouldn't allow Shan to put him in the pack. She had no choice but to release the kitten. She stopped and poured a little water into a depression in the concrete. Arlo lapped quickly while Shan took a single drink from the bottle.

They kept the dirt wall to their right. Isaiah took the lead, Shan stayed on his heels. Arlo zigzagged around her, sometimes ahead, sometimes behind, exploring small spaces and shadowy corners, always keeping them in sight.

Shan wasn't sure how far they'd traveled when they found another door. Her legs were rubbery and every joint in her body hurt. She wanted to sleep desperately, even though it meant facing more nightmares.

The door was locked and she sat down while Isaiah worked with his lock pick. Arlo bounded to her, climbed her arm and rubbed his face along her jaw. She lifted him to the floor and pulled the box of cat food out of her pack while he walked her arm and clawed at the box.

She dropped a few pieces of food onto her pants and Arlo devoured them as Isaiah got the door open. Picking up the cat, she joined her friend in an office. There was a desk, a wireless phone and a filing cabinet. A metal shelf held various mechanical objects and a padlocked tool box."

A stack of large papers were spread across the desk, some with torn edges, most curling, held in place with broken bits of concrete at each corner.

"Shi-i-zzle!" Isaiah leaned over the top document. "Motherload."

Shan examined the blueprint. Arlo curled down off her shoulder, stretched and stepped lightly across the desk before hopping to the filing cabinet where he began bathing. Isaiah frowned at the blueprint, tracing route after route with his finger.

Shan tried to find a block saying "You are here," but the tiny markings were coded.

Isaiah backed up to rifle through the unlocked desk drawers. He pulled out a magnifying glass and began scrutinizing the page.

"Look." After a while, he put his forefinger on a spot and offered Shan the magnifier. "This line and curve symbol means there's a door there. All the other doors have letters and numbers on them, but this one doesn't."

Shan looked at the door. It seemed to be in an end wall. "It opens out?"

"Yeah." Isaiah straightened up pressing his hands against his arched back, "All the other doors open in."

"It might be the way to the secret chamber."

"Or it could just be a maintenance exit." Isaiah leaned over the desk again. "All we can do is check it out."

"How do we know which way to go?" Shan scanned the blueprint. "They've not marked this office's location."

"I'm not a hundred percent sure, but I think this is the opening that we took. Here's the dirt wall. There's another room, here, that could be an office. Here's a bathroom next to it. I didn't see one near this office did you?"

"I didn't but, now that you've mentioned it, I'd really like to see a bathroom."

"Yeah, we'll find one on our way." Isaiah didn't look up. He was too busy tracing a route. "This office is closest to the dirt wall, so it must be the one we're in. If we come out the door and go left, walk past all this stuff 'til we come to another office and then turn right, we'll be in this section."

Shan nodded, hoping he'd remember the way. She could easily move about in the woods back home, but her sense of direction seemed to have disappeared once she left the hills.

"Then we just go down to this T, take a left and the next right should be the hall to our door."

"Do you want to draw it out on my notebook?" Shan reached for her pack.

"Nah. I think I got it." He put the magnifying glass back in the drawer and retrieved Arlo from the top of the tool shelf. The kitten wrapped his paws around Isaiah's thumb, but his claws were retracted. Isaiah looked surprised and pleased for a second before he schooled his face back to a serious frown and handed Arlo to Shan. She hid her smile against the kitten's fur.

Isaiah locked the door behind them when they left the office. Arlo rode Shan's shoulder for a while, before springing off the wall and bounding ahead. She worried, as it was probably getting late, that Arlo would flush out one of the huge rats.

Occasionally, they heard footsteps, the clank of metal and voices. When the sounds were nearby, they'd stop and crouch. Shan kept an eye on her magic, hoping she wouldn't be forced to use it.

Isaiah said it was unlikely The Circle would find them and Shan agreed it was probably just workers, but she didn't want to get thrown out or arrested. So, she had to be prepared.

They found the bathrooms and Shan filled her water bottle to save the purchased water. When she came out of the restroom, Arlo sat outside, like a guard. He took off before she could lift him, stopping a few dozen feet away. He looked over his shoulder as if to say, "Are you coming?"

When Isaiah came out, they resumed their trek.

The last corridor to the unmarked door was devoid of wiring, pipes or mechanical devices. There were bare bulbs swinging from the ceiling like Granny's porch light. On the left, the smooth concrete wall had given way to crumbling brick and the dirt wall on the right had grown uneven. Sprays of soil crossed the walkway, probably remnants of rodent activity. Remembering Coral's warning about the things coming for her, Shan hastened her step.

Arlo, still running ahead of them, clambered up the dirt wall, then, facing a shadowy area, arched his back and hissed. A huge, pale-eyed rat lumbered up the bank toward the kitten.

"Arlo!" Shan cried. Arlo ignored her, standing his ground, a little ball of fur against an ungainly monster. Isaiah bent to the rubble wall just as Shan called her magic. Crafting a conduit in an instant, Shan released her power before the ugly creature reached Arlo. The rat exploded with a shriek and the rebound, not contained enough, bounced Isaiah's well aimed brick back against his arm while Arlo streaked down the passage.

"Fuckfuckfuckfuck." Isaiah rocked on his feet, holding his upper arm and tucking his forearm around his waist. "That fucking hurt!"

"Is it broken?" Shan's fingers were over her mouth. She didn't want to look at Isaiah's arm.

"I don't think so." Isaiah wiggled his fingers and uncovered his wound. The brick had ripped the material of his coat and the shirt beneath. Blood trickled from a gash. A fragment of brick protruded from the pink flesh beneath Isaiah's dark skin. Shan bit her lip and pulled out the fragment.

"Damn!" Isaiah jerked away. "Can you heal?"

"No." Shan's face went hot. "All I can do is destroy. Didn't I tell you? I can blow your arm off, but not close the cut. Let me get into your pack."

Isaiah turned, looking down at the wound, his face going ashy. Shan took out a fresh water bottle and opened it. "I wish we had some alcohol. All I can do is wash it out."

"Will it hurt?"

"Most likely." She poured water down Isaiah's arm, hoping the wash would be enough. "I wish I had some eye balm or St. John's Wort."

"What?"

"Herbs." Shan closed the bottle, judging she had cleaned as much as she could. Blood oozed from the wound, soaking Isaiah's shirt and his jacket. "Granny knows plants to cure anything. Are you wearing a tee shirt?"

"Yeah," He eyed her suspiciously. "Why?"

"I think we need to bandage this." She lifted Isaiah's coat and shirt, but she couldn't tear his thick, expensive shirt. What would Granny do? Of course— cobwebs. "Don't move."

Arming herself with a shard of brick to remove any occupants, Shan searched the corners, finding an ample supply. She kept an eye out for Arlo, but he was nowhere to be seen.

She called him. "Kitty, kitty!"

No response.

She'd have to find him after she had Isaiah stabilized. Gathering the sticky silk in her fingers, she repressed a shudder, silently thanking Granny for making her practice as a child. When she had enough to cover the gash, she went back to Isaiah.

"No." Isaiah put his hand over the wound again, backing away and shaking his head. "You not doing what you think you're doing."

"I am." Shan pried loose his guarding hand and smeared the cobweb into the gash. She caught the torn ends of his shirt and tied them together to help protect the wound. "You might as well turn your coat right side out, now, anyway."

"Yeah." Isaiah carefully removed his coat. "I want to make a nice corpse when I die of blood poisoning."

"Shut up." Shan took a handful of cat food out of her bag. She shouldered the pack and tucked her arm under Isaiah's good one. "You're not going to die of anything, if I can help it."

"Making band aids out of dusty spider webs." Isaiah pursed his mouth. "You've got a scary way of helping, girl."

She un-tucked her arm and shrugged out of her own jacket, pulling the sleeves back through. Shaking accumulated debris from her coat, she put it back on the right way. Damp cold permeated everything in the tunnels and she preferred the soft fleece next to her skin. She rattled the food in her hand and called Arlo again.

Isaiah walked behind her as they moved in the direction Arlo had run, toward the door on the blueprint. The further they moved, the darker the tunnel grew. There were few working lights. Shan called for Arlo, periodically, feeling uneasy.

After calling "Kitty, kitty, kitty" for several minutes, Shan listened for some sign of the kitten. When she heard the rattle of falling rubble just behind her, she assumed she'd found Arlo. But she screamed when a tall, leathery creature stepped out of the shadows.

Isaiah tried to stand between her and the creature but she pushed him back. The thing had pointed ears and fleshy, bat wings. Its raccoon-shaped face was covered in black fur and its mouth stretched wide, showing needle-like teeth. The clawed hands attached to its wings reached for her as it moved forward.

She drew power from the earth, not knowing how much she would need, but, before she had built a conduit to the creature, it charged. A white shape flew from the wall like a bullet, landing on the creature's shoulder with a yowl. The creature shrugged violently, throwing Arlo against the dirt bank, and resumed its charge.

Arlo's attack had given Shan time to build her containment field and she released her power as the creature's hot, fetid breath blew her hair back.

It burst out of existence. The backlash only made Shan stumble, but Isaiah fell against the concrete. He raised his head, but he didn't get up. He stared at her, his expression frozen.

Arlo climbed her leg and she caught him to her chest. "Silly, brave Arlo."

She knelt in front of Isaiah. "Are you alright?"

"What the fucking hell was that?"

"I told you about the angels and demons." Shan licked her lips. "I think that was a demon."

"Where'd it come from?" Isaiah sat up and checked his arm. "How'd it find you?"

"It was sent." Shan stood. "We need to go before something else comes."

"Sent by who?" Isaiah scrambled to his feet and led a quick pace down the walk. "Why haven't we seen anything like it before?"

"It wasn't sent by Coral." Shan searched for the understanding that lay just beneath her consciousness.

"And my guess is, it couldn't get into Coral's compound. There must've been some sort of ward against it."

"How'd it know where to find you?"

"Magic." Shan sighed. Her defense. "It must've found me by tracing my use of magic."

"On the rat." Isaiah raised his chin. "And now you've done that, there's going to be another one."

"Run!" Shan leaped forward. Arlo's claws dug into her back, but she didn't slow down. Isaiah kept pace with her, frequently looking over his shoulder.

They didn't slow down until they'd traveled for what seemed half a mile. By the time they reached the door, they'd been moving in semi-darkness for several minutes. There was a light a few feet from the door, but there was not an exit sign and the door was unmarked. Shan could tell by Isaiah's grim expression that he was anxious to put as much distance as possible between them and the spot where she'd dispatched the demon.

Isaiah made quick work with the lock pick and they fell into a dark, dirt chamber. Rats chittered in every direction and Shan rose stiffly, holding Arlo, while Isaiah reached around her, shutting the door.

"I don't suppose you bought a flashlight." She whispered as they stood in the gloom.

"Can't you just use your flame?"

"Not if we think my use of magic's what led the demon to us." She considered. "But it didn't come when I released my magic into the earth and it didn't seem to be tracking us while I was holding all that power."

"I don't think we ought to risk it."

"Probably right." Shan started forward, fingertips brushing the wall on either side, shuddering at the possibility of touching rats or spiders.

"Maybe I should go first." Isaiah spoke into her right ear before she had taken half a dozen steps.

"The worst thing we're likely to meet is another demon." Shan kept walking, "and I'd have to handle him."

"True. But if we run into a person…"

"I'll move aside."

Walking through the rubble strewn tunnel was difficult. Shan stumbled, Arlo wanted down and she had to keep switching positions to stop him sailing off her shoulder. She could see nothing and had no idea what would be at the end of the tunnel, so she held on to the little cat.

"I've got to risk it." She told Isaiah, after what she *hoped* was a rat scurried over her feet.

"I'm with you."

She summoned a tiny flame above her right hand. It gave off enough light to show her arm and the dirt wall curving around them. She waited, ready to dispatch magic if a demon should appear. After a few minutes, she turned to Isaiah. His face, in the soft light, looked old and tired. Dust coated the downy hairs on his chin, upper lip and brows. Shan smiled. "You look like your own grandpa."

"You're not looking 'all that' yourself." He slapped the dust out of his hair. Shan backed away, sneezing. Arlo pawed at the larger dust motes.

Isaiah looked into her eyes, his own irises luminous and nearly black. He appeared a combination of the Isaiah she knew before and the strange new Isaiah who would

292

take a beating for a friend. Her eyelids grew heavy. His gaze pulled her toward him. His eyes widened and she leaned back, forcing herself to smile. Trying to ignore his disappointed expression, she tucked Arlo under her hair and used her free hand to brush the dirt from Isaiah's upper lip.

He accepted her ministrations for a few seconds before turning away. Her chest contracted. She wanted to tell him that, if she had to go through such a terrifying ordeal, there was no one she would rather have by her side. But knowing his feelings about her, she couldn't say anything.

They resumed their walk, Shan in front, holding the light, Isaiah just behind and to her left.

After another half hour, they found the tunnel branching left. They'd traveled another few hundred feet when Shan's light revealed a dark opening to her right. "Is that another tunnel?"

Isaiah moved into the space, feeling the air before him "It is."

"Which way?"

"Shine your light in here."

The secondary tunnel was all dirt, and looked cramped. "Keep going the way we were?"

Isaiah was already nodding before she finished. "I'd have to stoop over to go down the other one."

After another hour, Shan could see light ahead. She shut off the flow to her own light, and let her tired arm drop to her side. As they got closer, they realized their tunnel opened into a larger room with concrete walls.

When they reached the uneven doorway, framed by crumbling brick, Isaiah flattened himself against the opposite wall and motioned for Shan to follow suit. He inched forward, stretching his neck to look out. He stepped softly into the antechamber and, with one finger to his lip, curled his other hand at Shan, indicating she should follow.

They were in an unfinished room. Pieces of scaffolding, tumbled brick and work signs were strewn across the space. There was a doorway to a similar room, and a set of dusty tracks beyond. Isaiah checked the next room before they entered. At the last doorway, Shan looked out, too. There was a tangle of tracks and a large, rusted train car with no windows. A barrier had been erected past the unused tracks. She ducked back into the room when she saw a train approaching on the distant rails.

"Waldorf Astoria platform." Isaiah whispered, pulling her back into the room. "I didn't know it was open like that."

"Is this the secret room?"

"I don't know." Isaiah said. "I thought there was supposed to be a welded elevator door, but all I see is a wall. Besides, how's it secret if anybody riding a car can see it."

"We could keep looking in all these unfinished rooms." Shan rubbed her cheek along Arlo's back. "There might be another doorway, or another tunnel."

"Considering the alternative is that little tunnel, I think I agree."

Hiding when trains roared by, Shan and Isaiah went through the platform room by room. Many were nothing but walls and dusty floors. Some, though, were full of rubble or trash. The rats were very bold, staring at them, hissing like cats if they walked too close.

The back section of the structure angled away from the open railway, and, by silent, mutual consent, Shan and Isaiah took that route. The first few walls didn't reach the ceiling, so the lights from the station illuminated portions of the rooms. In one room, a pile of rags in the far corner moved as Shan came through the door. She clamped her hand over her mouth to keep from screaming when a head emerged from the pile. Isaiah put his arm around her and pushed her sideways. The red-faced, bearded man watched with sunken, bleary eyes until they were out of sight.

"Homeless." Isaiah pushed her quickly through the next few rooms. All of them were strewn with rubble, some with shopping carts and plastic bags. "We've got to be careful. We're in people's territory."

The last few rooms were built against the earth. In one of those they went through, Shan noticed a diamond patterned tile floor, partially obscured by debris, beneath the broken concrete floor. After they had explored the last few rooms, finding no other tunnels or entries, Shan and Isaiah turned back.

"I guess it has to be the small tunnel." Isaiah sighed.

"I want to check something, first." Shan brought him to the spot she'd seen.

"I think that tile goes past the concrete." Isaiah dug with his toe. Bits of brick, concrete and dirt fell over his shoe, but he made an inroad beneath the pile. The tile floor did extend behind the newer concrete walls.

Shan looked around. She saw no one. Isaiah started digging with his hands, dragging the debris onto the concrete floor. Shan transferred the sleeping Arlo to her pack, settled it on the floor by her foot and started digging. Though concrete and dirt fell from above as they worked, they had soon excavated a small, dark hole. But, when they removed the debris at a lower level they met solid earth.

The opening they had uncovered was big enough to crawl through, but did it lead anywhere?

Shan nudged Isaiah aside and stuck her upper body into the opening. Bringing up her light, she found the opening continued and, as far as she could tell through the shadows, actually widened.

"It goes through." She straightened, trying to wipe the front of her coat, succeeding only in spreading the dirt.

"Do you think it's safe?" Isaiah lifted a bit of concrete from her hair. Voices came from main tracks. Shouts.

"I'm willing to try it."

Both of Isaiah's brows went up and he exhaled with feeling before starting to climb into the hole.

"No." Shan caught the edge of his jacket. "I'm smaller and uninjured. I'll go first."

Over on the main railroad the voices grew louder. It might mean nothing, but, on the other hand, it could be The Circle on her tail. Without waiting for the protest

Isaiah's scowl promised, Shan pushed her bag into the hole and climbed in. Isaiah's back pack hit her feet, and the dim light was blocked as he followed.

"Make a light." He ordered, rolling over on his back.

Staring at him, wondering what he was thinking, Shan opened her palm, balancing her small flame. Isaiah kicked at the ceiling near the entry, loosening chunks of earth and buried brick. Within a few moments, he had obscured the way out.

"Hiding our exit." Isaiah rolled over onto his belly and got to his knees. "Can you make that light float or do you have to move with one hand?"

"I don't know and the only way I can think of doing it, means projecting magic in front of me." She watched her little flame, biting her lower lip, trying to find words to explain what she only dimly understood. "I think magic in me is just energy, like energy's in every person, the demons can't sort it out. But if I send it away from me, it's different and it draws them."

"That's possible." Isaiah nodded, his lips curling down. "Like trying to spot a single star in the sky. They all look alike, until one of them falls and leaves a trail."

Shan nodded and moved forward. When her body was over her book bag, she pulled it ahead. Arlo struggled under the canvas.

"I'm sorry, kitty." She touched him through the cloth, "I'll let you out soon."

The floor of the tunnel curved down gradually, but by the time she could stand, both Shan's arms felt like rubber. Picking up her bag, she opened a flame over the palm which had been supporting her body and let the other hand drop. As they progressed, she switched hands so she would not tire too quickly. She could no longer hear anything but her own heartbeat, Arlo's occasional meows and Isaiah's breath.

When the tunnel ended abruptly, with no opening, Shan's heart sank. They'd have to crawl all the way back. Isaiah reached over her and rapped on the wall. His knuckles made a hollow, cracking sound. He knocked on the wall beside him and the sound was a gentle, flat thud.

"There's a door there."

Shan tried digging with her fingers but Isaiah pulled a piece of stone from the tunnel wall.

"Just keep the light up for me." He told her and scraped a layer of dirt. Shan held her flame high and freed Arlo with her other hand. Arlo trotted off into the darkness, but she heard him scratching. He came back and, after conquering a piece of rock in fierce battle, sniffed at the zipper with cat food. Shan fed him, and using the defeated rock, hollowed out a small bowl in the dirt for water.

Isaiah worked for half an hour and stopped to take a drink. "I wish we had a shovel."

"And a flashlight." Shan sighed.

Isaiah went back to work and soon, removed enough dirt to reveal the upper part of a metal door.

"I sure hope it opens out." She said.

Isaiah gave her a dirty look over his shoulder. "Did you have to say that?"

"If this was a passage, it should open out." Shan hoped the statement was true. She couldn't remember being in any corridors with doors that opened in.

Isaiah glared and went back to work. It took him another half hour to find the doorframe and the hole where the knob would've gone. The frame indicated the door did open out. Shan's relief was short-lived when Isaiah pushed against the door with both feet. It wouldn't budge.

"There might be dirt blocking it on the other side." He said, lying back with his head at Shan's knees. Arlo came over to inspect Isaiah's face. Isaiah lay still, allowing the little animal to sniff his eyelids and even pat at his hair. After a few exploratory licks, Arlo started grooming Isaiah's hair.

"Could you tell if you dug out the doorknob opening?" Shan pulled the kitten back, but as soon as she put him down, Arlo went back to grooming Isaiah.

"It's your turn to dig." He said raising his eyes to look at her while he lifted Arlo to his chest.

She grinned down at him. "You hold the light and I will."

"You sure you don't want to just sleep here?" Isaiah stroked the kitten curled on his chest.

A voice in the back of Shan's head screamed *no!* Shan agreed. She didn't want to wake from one her nightmares in total darkness. But was it fair to push Isaiah?

"I'd rather not." She kept her voice level, "But if you're too tired, I guess we can."

"The things I do for you." Isaiah pulled a long face. Plucking Arlo off his sternum, he sat up dug at the opening where the doorknob belonged.

After a few moments, Isaiah grunted and leaned back against the wall. Shan saw he had scraped through the small opening, revealing light.

"At least it isn't blocked." She rubbed his shoulder.

"Yeah, but there's light, so it's another part of the station. We could've saved ourselves some time just using the regular sidewalk."

"We have to push through unless you want to crawl all the way back to the Waldorf platform."

"Help me, then." Isaiah moved over against the wall and bent his knees to put his feet against the door. Shan scooted in beside him and put her feet next to his. "On three."

"One…two…" She counted with Isaiah, bracing herself, "three!"

The door gave way suddenly after a second. Shan's legs fell outside the tunnel. Arlo ran over her face and leaped into the new space. Shutting off her light, Shan sat up with Isaiah. The room they'd found didn't look like a regular part of the station. The walls were partially crumbled brick. The floor was the black and white tiles Shan had seen at the Waldorf platform, but the tangled network of wires coming out of the ceiling looked like it had been stolen from a mad scientist's laboratory. The overhead light flickered with the distant hum of passing trains.

Strips of metal and pieces of wooden crate, separated by stacks of brick and cinder block, formed bookshelves lined with decaying books of various shapes and sizes. The air smelled of dust, mold and old paper.

Arlo stood in the center of the room facing a dim corner back arched, hackles raised.

CHAPTER FOURTEEN

Gradually, Shan's eyes adjusted to the light and she could make out a form in the corner. A little woman, head wrapped in a dirty purple turban, stared at them with small, black eyes. Dirt-filled wrinkles mapped her dark face. Her mouth was a narrow, pale gash beneath a wide flat nose.

"Who the hell are you?" A slight movement of her hand flipped aside the tattered ends of her blue, moth-eaten shawl, revealing the barrel of a rifle, pointed directly at Isaiah. Even in the weak light, the metal gleamed with well-oiled danger.

"We lost." Isaiah said evenly, without looking away. His voice held neither challenge nor fear.

"Fucking runaways." The woman sneered. "For love, looking at you." She waved the barrel. "Get out of that hole and put that door back in place. See you pile the dirt back, too. And don't try nothing."

Gathering their packs, Isaiah and Shan climbed down slowly. Arlo backed up to Shan's feet and she bent to lift him.

"Aw. You brought your kitty." The woman grinned, revealing brown, uneven teeth. "Good. I'm tired of rat meat."

Shan tucked Arlo inside her shirt and buttoned the top button of her coat. The woman cackled. Isaiah pushed the door closed and Shan helped pile dirt and rubble against it. They pressed the debris against the door with their feet.

When they were finished, the woman pushed herself out of her seat. The chair was a plastic subway seat braced on a stack of bricks. It rattled when she moved. For a moment, Shan was certain it would fall, but it settled back in place beneath the wires. Dust filtered down from the ceiling with the passing of another train.

"Walk to the door and stand."

Isaiah pressed Shan's spine, urging her forward. She watched the woman out of the corner of her eye. Demons or no demons, if the old crow so much as wiggled a finger on that gun, Shan would blow it up.

The door led to a cavernous space. The ceiling soared in irregular curves, more like a cave than a man-made structure, but concrete columns and portions of tile indicated that, at some point, the space had been part of the underground system. Lights, hung on wires of various lengths, swung gently, creating moving shadows on the uneven floor.

Furniture groups were placed at odd intervals. There were makeshift stoves in two far corners. A freezer, surrounded by patched wooden stools cobbled together out of chairs and rusted scrap metal, near one of the stoves held stacks of canned goods, plates, cups and a plastic dish pan. Several of the columns formed the basis for bizarre sitting rooms furnished with, among other things, car seats, vegetable crates and trash cans stenciled with the letters NYC and PLEASE RECYCLE.

Shan gasped when she realized what she had, at first, dismissed as dusty rags and tarps were actually human beings. There were at least forty people in the room. Males, if beards were an indication, and females of differing ages and sizes stared at her from every direction.

"Walk." The old woman barked. Shan stepped out into the space, her skin prickling.

"What've you brought, Nettie?" The question came from a burly man in the nearest sitting area. Pink blotches marred his brown face and a black-tipped gray beard spilled across his barrel chest. The shirt beneath his tangled facial hair may have been black at some point, but age and wear had faded it to a mottled charcoal. Several missing buttons left the shirt gaping, revealing a faded red t-shirt with an age crackled logo. He held an open book in one hand. The nails on his knobby fingers were long and curving, like yellow talons. He closed his book on one finger, so he could peer at Shan and Isaiah over plastic reading glasses.

"Runaways, Lord Power." She cackled. "Want me to take 'em to Archer?"

"Give me a moment." Lord Power looked over his shoulder. Two slim, ebony skinned men sidled out of the shadows. Their faces, beneath lopsided, hairless heads, sported identical broad noses, protruding lower lips and up-tilted eyes. "Help them with their luggage, boys."

The twins grinned identical grins, exposing their only apparent differences in gapped, yellow teeth.

Shan glared at them, holding her pack close. "We'll handle it ourselves, thanks."

The advancing twins stopped, looking back and forth between Shan and Lord Power.

Isaiah nudged her, speaking under his breath. "Just let them have it."

"Don't move!" Nettie shouted.

"I wouldn't dream of asking you to do that." Lord Power's eyes sparkled. Whether with amusement or fury, Shan couldn't tell. "It wouldn't be hospitable."

"We just passing through." Isaiah drawled. "We won't trouble you none."

"We almost never receive visitors, young man." Lord Power said. A few low chuckles accompanied Nettie's quack. Lord Power's eyes went flat. "You're here, so, you'll stay for dinner."

"One way or the other." A male voice, with a hint of a brogue, shouted from a dark corner.

"Do be quiet, Dylan and I might let you have the leftovers." More laughter. The high pitched giggle of a child gave Shan the shivers.

"You don't want us to stay." Shan said, arms around her pack, trying not to react to Arlo's claws digging her chest for a way out. "We're being chased by some nasty people."

Lord Power threw back his head and guffawed. His people laughed with him, their voices wild and artificial, like clowns in a nightmare.

"My dear girl, you haven't seen nasty." Lord Power wiped his mouth on his sleeve. He nodded once at the twins. "Until now."

One of the twins grabbed her bag, while the other lunged for Isaiah. Shan couldn't give up the painting and she wouldn't put Isaiah at these people's mercy.

"I beg to differ." She spoke in her most polite southern tone and released her magic to destroy a brick outcropping on the wall behind Lord Power. Within seconds of the resounding pop, as the outcropping disappeared, there was a flash of smoke and a demon, in all his leathery glory, bounded straight at Shan.

The twins fell over themselves getting out of the way. Nettie fired a shot that ricocheted off the beast's chest and pinged around the room eliciting screams from people scrambling out of the way.

Shan sprinted toward the opposite exit, hoping the demon wouldn't reach her before she was hidden enough to dispatch it. She looked back to see it fling Isaiah across the floor. There was no way she'd make it out of the room before it caught her. She swerved behind a pile of litter, pulling magic and constructing a containment field as she went. She flung her hand back, directing her magic through her improvised conduit and the demon was gone. Instantly, the debris flew into the air, crashing and splintering around her. A piece of metal caught her a glancing blow on the head and she dropped to her knees. Arlo rocketed out of her coat and sped back toward the library.

Stunned, Shan touched the place where her forehead hurt, feeling oozing damp. She stared at the blood on her fingers, trying to collect her thoughts. The demon was gone, but she must have botched the containment. She'd been angry. It had thrown Isaiah...*Isaiah*?

Lurching to her feet she looked around the room. He was by Lord Power's sofa. The twins held him between them. He shook his head slightly, staring intently.

"What the fecking hell was that?" Dylan hung onto a column. Lord Power stood beside him. Dylan was skinny, younger than Lord Power with long greasy hair and a blond beard to match. "You got the Motherfecking devil after ya?"

Shan shrugged. "I told you some nasty people were chasing us. You should let us be on our way before the next one comes."

Lord Power inclined his head and the twins released Isaiah. He straightened his jacket with a jerk and crossed to stand beside her, his arm touching hers, pressing against her slightly. She knew he wanted to go. But the people filed back into the big room. Shan noticed there were some small children and a couple of teenagers. The children stared at her as if she were a monster. She raised her chin. She shouldn't care. It stung, though, to have children look at her like that. If she found a way to save the world, and therefore, them, they wouldn't even know it was her.

Nettie glowered at Shan with open hatred. Her eyes were slits and her lips had disappeared.

"Let's go, girl." Isaiah hissed.

"I have to find Arlo."

Isaiah spun on his heel and headed for the Library. Nettie didn't look away from Shan, even when Isaiah passed within inches of her.

A large red demon appeared a few paces behind Dylan. It jerked the woman next to him out of the way, tearing off her head, and reached for Dylan. Shan reacted without conscious thought. Her hand went out and energy roared through her, blasting the demon out of existence. A thundering backlash sent Lord Power and Dylan tumbling along the floor. Damn, she needed to practice containment on the go.

Both men climbed to their feet, Dylan looking furious, Lord Power speculative.

Isaiah bounded out of the library, holding Arlo, who gnawed furiously at the fingers caging him. Shan reached for the kitten, giving Isaiah an apologetic glance. When she turned to survey the large hall, the people had reassembled. The twins dragged the woman's body between them. One of them held her dripping head under his arm. Shan's knees threatened to buckle and her stomach flipped. She breathed through her nose, trying not to wretch. But if she didn't get moving, someone else would die.

"Are you going to leave us to fend for ourselves, young goddess?" Lord Power twisted his beard in his right fist.

"She's a witch, Lord Power." Nettie's voice was hoarse with contempt.

"Now, why ever would you think that?" Lord Power released his beard, looking only mildly interested.

"My .30-06 just bounced off that first creature, then it follows her behind a stack and disappears. Another pops up, she waves her hand and *it* disappears." She looked at Shan. "You control them."

308

"Yeah!" Dylan croaked.

"Witch." A tiny black woman hissed from her place on a milk crate.

"Satanist." A male somewhere behind Shan.

"Nettie, Nettie." Lord Power clucked, shaking his head. "I think you're wrong. This girl looked pretty scared to me. And that first monster tossed her friend aside like a paper bag. But you are correct. She did get rid of them."

He pointed at Dylan. "Saving your worthless life, Dylan, I do believe."

Shan didn't feel comfortable with Lord Power's show of support. She started to walk away, but clapping stopped her. She twisted back to look at him. He clapped again, and others took up the beat.

Clap, clap. Clap, clap. Clap, clap.

One after another, everyone in the room joined the clap, except Nettie. After a harsh look from Lord Power, even Dylan clapped.

She looked at Isaiah, but he simply raised his eyebrows. She shrugged.

"You're being offered citizenship." Lord Power bowed his head. "Welcome, neighbors, to Ragville."

"Thank you." Shan took a step, "But our staying here would only put you in danger."

"You handle that danger just fine."

"This time. But there's something very important I have to do." Shan licked her lips, "Besides, I don't think they'll always come in ones."

"I see your point. It might be best if you do move on for now. But you always have a home here." Lord

Power's arm moved in an encompassing wave. "You may come and go as you like. No one will bother you."

Nettie shot Lord Power a dirty look before turning her back on Shan. As the old woman shuffled into the library, Shan thanked Lord Power and the people, before starting for the far door.

"What is your destination in the city?" The big man cleared his throat.

"We need to get to New Jersey." Isaiah spoke. Shan nodded. New Jersey would do.

She inched toward the exit. She knew Lord Power wanted to offer help, but the longer she stayed in one spot, the more likely other demons would appear.

"If you have… regular people looking for you, too," Lord Power lumbered back to his couch and took a seat. "You'll want a private boat. If you're not too fastidious, try Pier Sixty, far south dock. Look for the Day Sky, a little blue and white tourist hauler. Ask for Gazinski. Tell him you're from Ragville. He'll get you across."

"Thank you!" Shan nodded and looked around the chamber, anxiously. Where would the next demon appear?

"Go. Go. Through the next two chambers." As Lord Power spoke, Shan shot forward. His words followed her, "And at the end of the second, you'll find a hall. Take the left and it'll lead you to proper subway tunnels where you can get out. If you need to stay hidden, go right and you'll eventually find your way to the outskirts. But I'd advise you to go left. An awful lot of people live down here and most of them are not as sophisticated as us."

Already halfway across the second chamber, Shan waved her thanks. She picked up the pace, running with Isaiah behind her until they came to the hall. She didn't dare go back to the real subway so she turned right.

The new tunnel was very much like the one which led to Ragville. There were no lights in the main tunnel, but there were several branches, some of which were lit. After the Ragville experience, Shan thought it best to avoid the lighted areas.

"Straight." Isaiah suggested when they came to the first intersection. Shan agreed. The further they traveled, the darker it became.

"Reckon we're far enough away to rest?" Isaiah was out of breath, his color was dull, his eyes shadowed.

"In this tunnel?"

"I aint—sorry, habit—haven't seen anybody since we left Ragville. I'm beat. You look like you are, too." Isaiah dropped his pack and flopped down beside it. Shan sat across from him, releasing Arlo, feeding and watering him before putting her bag behind her head. She released her light, surveying her surroundings in the half light from other tunnels. Lying down felt good.

"You go to sleep first." Isaiah stretched his legs. His feet nearly touched the wall on Shan's side. Arlo explored down the hall and came back. He stepped into Shan's hair and, purring loudly, began kneading. Finally satisfied, he curled by her ear, his purr growing fainter and fainter as he drifted to sleep.

"I don't want to sleep." She mumbled, but she was so tired. Arlo's warm body leeched her tension and Isaiah was right there.

"Wake me in an hour." Maybe if she only slept a short while, she wouldn't have the nightmare, anyway.

"Sure thing, girl."

She was in the grove, but the Sentinels were quiet. The day had come and they knew it. She reminded them that the earth needed them. She promised she would keep them safe. They didn't argue and they didn't express fear, but the absence of their music was like a death blow. Nothing would ever be the same.

Heart thundering, she approached Gaiaes, desire for the contact mingling with fear, Palax Lae's hope tinged with Shan's grief at the coming loss of the spirit within the tree. No! She couldn't think of that. *Stay back!* Shan screamed, but Palax Lae didn't listen. Her hand stretched forward, morning light revealing the cold emptiness of the stones in her ring. Her fingers made contact. She heard a deafening, ululating scream. Disbelief, rage and horror blasted her. The scream stopped abruptly.

She stood in darkness. There was neither sight nor sound. Just before she realized she couldn't breathe, she felt the flutter of fingers on her arm. She tried to gulp, but she could get nothing. The fingers stiffened and held her so she couldn't flee. She clawed at the other hand, finding purchase on a ring with icy stones, tiny stars exploded in her mind and she awoke.

A strange man stood over her. When he saw her eyes were open, His own sparse brows arched and he licked his full lips.

"Tasty." He said

"Hold, Pitcher." A stocky black man with a shaved head stood over Isaiah. "Wake up, nigga."

Shan struggled to sit up, but Pitcher planted a foot on her chest. Arlo was nowhere in sight.

"Get your foot off me, asshole." Shan caught Pitcher's leg.

He laughed, pulling his foot loose, backing up. "Good thing I like flashy ho's."

The stocky man looked at Pitcher.

"My bad, Cowboy." Pitcher snapped his fist against his stomach but Cowboy had already turned back to Isaiah. Shan stood up, shouldering her bag. Two other men took defensive positions behind Pitcher and Cowboy.

Isaiah's eyes were open. He regarded the speaker. Shan could tell by Isaiah's expression, he'd come across the type before. "What you want?"

"What yo hood?" Cowboy shrugged one shoulder and a chain draping his chest slide down his upper arm. The chain's links were as thick as Shan's little-finger. She realized it wrapped around the young man's forearm.

"I ain't no banger." Isaiah sprang to his feet. He was several inches taller than Cowboy, but thinner.

"You with us, now." Cowboy twitched and the chain fell in graceful loops onto the floor between him and Isaiah. Cowboy looked Shan up and down, sucking his upper lip. "An' the b."

"I told you I aint banging."

"No skin o' mine." Cowboy moved his arm and the chain began to uncoil, rising to spin between him and Isaiah.

Shan drew magic, focusing on the chain, trying to plan an escape when the demon showed up. But, before she could unleash her power, something thudded against

Cowboy's back. He grunted, dropping the loop of his chain. He turned to see what had hit him. Pitcher, still leering at Shan, grunted and nearly fell into her.

Shapes moved in the dim light, arms raised. Lord Power, the twins and other citizens of Ragville crowded into the tunnel, clutching bricks, blocks and large pieces of concrete.

"You a dead man." Cowboy bent to collect his chain. "You all dead!"

"You know where we are." Lord Power shrugged. "Gather your friends and come on over." Lord Power examined his fingernails and added, "Oh, that's right. You don't have any friends anymore. They buried you down here. Well, you still know where we are. But unless you think you can take us now, I suggested you scamper away."

"You dead, old man," Cowboy slung the chain around his own body, casting Isaiah a nasty look. "We got unfinished business, boy. I see you again, you going to pay up or put up."

He strode between Shan and Isaiah. "Come on Pitcher. Hilo. Boys."

Shan flattened herself against the wall to let Pitcher pass without touching her. She moved down the tunnel to allow the broad shouldered, muscular boy through after Pitcher. She kept walking past the two other boys following Cowboy, until she faced Lord Power.

Before she could speak, a thin, a pre-teen girl with lank brown hair and crooked teeth stepped forward. Arlo climbed out of her arms, stretching as if he had enjoyed a long, refreshing nap. His bright blue eyes held Shan's.

Taking the cat, she smiled at the girl. The child blushed and ducked back behind Lord Power.

Shan met the man's gaze. His brown eyes were dark and serious.

"Thank you, Lord Power." She swallowed back the sulfuric taste of magic. Her words felt inadequate. She pulled her pack forward. Settling Arlo on her shoulder and taking out her copy of *Emma*, she held it out to Ragville's leading citizen. "I know you'll love it."

Lord Power's eyes gleamed. His hand came up but he hesitated. "It means a great deal to you, child. I can't take it."

"Please." She pushed it into his hands. "If I...I can always buy another copy, someday."

He took it then, holding it to her chest. "It will be one of my dearest treasures."

His breath washed over her, reeking of rotting teeth, and his body odor was overpowering at such a close distance. She remembered Lord Conway's tailored clothes and manicured hands. In a flash, she realized she'd rather have Lord Power on her side any day.

"You're welcome." She curtsied and he moved aside to let her pass.

"Thanks, man." Isaiah added as he followed her.

They walked single file for a short time. As soon as she judged the citizens of Ragville could no longer see them, Shan stopped.

"I had a dream, before the gang woke us." She looked at her wrist. There were no marks where Palax Lae's hand had grabbed her, but even now she could feel the desperate pressure. "I think something went wrong."

"In the dream?" Isaiah frowned, crossing his arms. "Something's wrong in your dream?"

"In my dreams, and I guess in real life, Gaiaes could read Palax Lae's mind and vice versa. Well, somehow, tonight, I think, I really *was* back in Palax Lae's mind and Gaiaes looked into my thoughts. She found out her tree would be destroyed."

"How could you …" Isaiah raised his hand, palm out, "No. Don't answer that. What makes you think she found out?"

Shan started walking again. The tunnel had grown dark, requiring her to hold a light over her hand.

"I—Palax Lae—we touch Gaiaes and we go instantly to some future disaster." Shan flattened her free hand on the wall for support. "This time, Gaiaes screamed and we were in darkness. Palax Lae tried to hold on to me as I woke up."

"Hmmm. Any idea what it means?" Isaiah looked down, but his expression was hard to read in the weak, flickering light.

"Coral said, or, at least, she seemed to think it was possible there are gods, maybe created by the universal unconscious or some other energy." She watched Isaiah's shadowed face, remembering that like she always had, he considered religion a load of crap. "Coral was upset, the most upset I've ever seen her, when she talked about Gaiaes's tree being destroyed without her being sent into another vessel."

"So is she just floating around somewhere or did she blip out of existence?"

"Nobody knows. Coral said there had to be a ritual to prepare a receiver for the spirits. Like the one that put Palax Lae in my ring. The Sentinels died, though. I'm supposed to have their powers."

"Why can't you just talk to Palax Lae?"

"To be honest," Shan sighed, "I'm scared of her. She wants my body. She broke my hand trying to take the ring. Remember?"

"Didn't she heal you?"

"What is it with you?" Fury bloomed inside her. "You think it's okay to hurt somebody as long as you put a band-aid on it?"

"I don't think that." She could see, even in the dusky tunnel, that he rolled his eyes. "And healing's nothing like a band-aid. Your hand's not still broken."

She clamped her tongue between her teeth, afraid to say anything. His arm was no longer broken, either.

"I'm alright." His quick smile cut her. "But it's nice to know you care."

"Don't you still remember the hurt?" There. She said it. Palax Lae's abuse had left ghost pain and fear Shan couldn't forget.

"You want the truth?" His voice was deep and different.

Did she want the truth? "Of course."

"I volunteered." Isaiah stopped walking. She faced him. "I know the earth is being destroyed. I know my Mom'll die. I know…" He hesitated, looking into her eyes and away quickly, "Everyone and everything I love will die a horrible death. But I don't have some magical power that'll let me fix it all. So, I gave what I could."

He strode ahead of her, walking with his head high. Her vision blurred but what could she say? He was her best friend. He was tall, strong, smart, handsome and funny. But he was almost two years her junior and, even if that didn't matter, who she was mattered. Was she even a whole person? Could she have babies and grow old like other people? Or would she burn like a piece of kindling after she lit the fire she was meant to start?

She followed Isaiah for a long time. Feeding power into her flame, she held it aloft, hoping it provided him with enough light. The main branch of their tunnel remained deserted. There was always the distant roar of trains somewhere far overhead, the intermittent rattle of earth falling from the ceiling and the faint moan of air passing through offshoots. Sometimes, Shan thought she heard a cough, a shout or different footsteps. Light showed at the end of some tunnels, but Isaiah set a steady course, handing out food on the go. Arlo had eaten from the pack and, long since, settled under her hair, sleeping half on her shoulder, half on the backpack.

She couldn't calculate the passing time. How long had they slept before Cowboy found them? What day was it? How far to the end of their path?

She could see nothing past Isaiah's broad, leather clad back. His backpack hung from one shoulder, the strap lost against the black of his jacket. Earth, dust, cobwebs and other bits of debris clung to the back of his head. She wanted to run her fingers through his hair, to dust away the filth as she would have a few months earlier. But it would mean something different now.

She took occasional sips from her water bottle, just as she saw Isaiah do, holding his bottle gingerly with his injured arm. What had happened to the boy who would've moaned about his pain? The boy who was afraid of the dark, and of closed spaces?

Isaiah passed a shallow opening and Shan had to call a stop. "You stay there." She ordered. "Nature."

Isaiah stopped and leaned against the wall. She set her pack down. Arlo woke, stretched and explored the small room, taking care of cat business on the way. When she was finished, Shan went to Isaiah and tapped him on the shoulder.

"Your turn, if you need to."

"If you don't mind." He motioned toward the wall.

She turned her back and clucked to Arlo. The Kitten sniffed around her feet until she gave him a small handful of food. Returning, Isaiah took a stand beside Shan, watching Arlo turn his head left and right, breaking the hard food with his sharp little teeth.

"Maybe I should crush it for him." Shan mused.

"Cats eat bones." Isaiah readjusted his pack.

"What's wrong with you?" She pushed off the wall and stood in front of him.

"Nothing." He stepped around her.

"Bullshit." She grabbed his arm.

"I've told you." He shook off her hand. "And you don't get it."

"Cut me some slack, Isaiah." She spread her hands. She didn't want to go into a whining litany. "It's been a rough couple of days."

"That's it." His gaze followed Arlo who trotted up the passage. He walked after the cat. "You think you're the only one who's having a rough time?"

Shan rushed to pace with him. "I know. I don't have the words to say how much I appreciate your being here with me. I couldn't do any of it without you."

"It's fine for me to 'be here' for you." He stopped walking and faced her. "But what if I'm here for my own reasons? What if I think it's better to take a sure path and save as many people as possible rather than take a risk and lose everybody?"

"Isaiah!" Shan crossed her arms. "I can't believe you think that way."

"Yeah." Isaiah's mouth twisted, "You don't want me to have a mind of my own. I'm supposed to be, what? Your sidekick?" He hit the wall. "And I'm here, right? Panting after you like a dog. I make *myself* sick."

He strode off into the darkness. Shan stood for a moment, stunned. Gradually one thought emerged. He was right that she expected him to think the way she did because…because he was her friend? Because he loved her? But how was she any different than Coral if she only wanted people to see things her way?

"Hey, you!" Shan stomped after him, allowing her light to glow with more power than she ever had. She'd make him understand. "I'm sorry! Wait up."

Isaiah slowed, but he didn't turn around. She could tell his arms were crossed and she saw his jaw muscle worked.

"At least talk to me. Convince me." She exhaled. "*Men.*"

A dimple appeared next to the agitated jaw muscle. "Ha!" he said over his shoulder. "Women, more like it."

Arlo passed between them, batting her leg on the way, and taking a swipe at Isaiah's shoe lace. Shan stepped up to Isaiah, switching the light to her left hand, putting her right hand in her jacket pocket.

"I'm sorry if I seemed to dismiss your opinion. I don't think I would've had the courage to let Danny beat me up."

"I was scared until it started." Isaiah ducked, his skin darkening, "then I was busy. But that's not what makes me mad. You still don't get it."

"Tell me."

"I should've argued with you." Isaiah spread his hands. "I shouldn't have let you leave. I saw somebody die today. Because of us."

"You mean because of me." Metal bands settled around Shan's chest. She found it difficult to breathe. "If I hadn't gone to Ragville, that woman would still be alive."

"You walked away like it was nothing." Flattening his palms against his temples, Isaiah stood still, sucking air through his teeth. "And I left right with you."

Shan couldn't speak. Her eyes burned, her throat burned and her mind replayed the image of the twins dragging the body into the shadows.

"You think Coral's going to ask you to kill people to save the earth." Isaiah shook his head, moving forward. "Maybe she will, maybe she won't. You think your granny has a solution. What if she doesn't? More people are going to die, Shan. Real people. No matter what you do."

"I just don't understand why Coral should be the one to choose who dies." Shan croaked, trying to keep up with Isaiah when every movement hurt.

"But it's okay for you to choose?"

"I didn't say that." Shan's nostrils flared. Fury rocked her to the core. "I'm not like Coral. I don't hurt people on purpose. That woman was an accident."

"If you hadn't been there, she wouldn't be dead, would she?"

Shan shook her head once. She bit the inside of her cheek, looking at her feet, determined not to let him see her cry.

"What if, by leaving Coral's, you lost the chance to stop the cataclysm? Won't you be the one choosing to let everybody die?"

"I have the magic, Isaiah!" Shan cringed at the shrill tone of her voice, but she couldn't stop. "I'm the one who has to be responsible! It wasn't given to Coral or Granny or you. It is in me. Nobody else!"

"That's just it. You're not alone. You've got Coral, you got Granny and you have me. Why do you have us, if you won't let us help?"

"Who's there?" A coarse, male voice called from up ahead where the tunnel widened. Shan let her light go. There was enough light in front of them to see a burly person lying half across the space and another equally bulky male sitting opposite.

Her relief at the interruption embarrassed Shan. She welcomed time to absorb Isaiah's words. To get over the pain of his obvious disappointment in her.

"Hello?" Isaiah's left hand came out, holding Shan back. Arlo went on though, alternating between advancing slowly and stopping, tail twitching, to eye the strangers.

"You all come down to get out of it, too?"

"Out of what?" Shan asked as they got closer. She detected the sour mash body odor of a drunk, even over the foul musk of unwashed bodies.

"Weather's gone crazy topside." The other man said, bloodshot eyes going from her to Isaiah and back.

"It was so hot this morning, we headed for a culvert by the river to find a cool sleep." The first continued, "Then winds just come out o' nowhere, blowing signs down, making waves in the river. Boats breaking loose."

"Then it come rain and lightening. Lightening hitting almost constant. Me and Hoyt knowed about this place and we scrambled down here. Happen that's why you all here, too?"

"Something like that." Isaiah mumbled. "Pardon." Leading Shan by the hand, he stepped over the men's legs.

"I wouldn't go out if you can help it, boy." Hoyt raised up on his elbows. "It ain't just New York. Heard the dock cop say weather's crazy everywhere."

Shan gripped Isaiah's hand, her heart pounding in her ears. It was happening now!

"Which way did you come in?" She pulled against Isaiah's momentum, dragging him to a stop.

"If I was you, I wouldn't go back up there, sweetheart."

"I've got to find my grandmother." Shan didn't need to fake a concerned expression. She was terrified. "She needs me."

"Well, in that case, take the next pass right. Go 'til you come to a fork. Take the left fork and you'll be in a rail tunnel but no trains run in it. Follow the rails and you'll come to some broke down steps. Go up careful and you'll come out in a empty warehouse."

"Empty except for trash, crack heads and drunks." Hoyt's companion added. "Be careful in the storm. You ain't got a couple bucks on you, have you?"

"I'm sorry." Shan called as Isaiah pulled her forward. Arlo shot up her legs, over her arms and dug his claws into her shoulders.

She slowed down enough to pry him loose and zip him into the backpack. As she did, she noticed the zipper coming loose on the compartment where she had stashed the little painting. Starting to close it, she saw the canvas had gone nearly black. She pulled the compartment open. A few highlights could still be seen in the leaves and in the branches of the trees, but most of the colors were dark now. She could no longer tell the painting depicted a clearing.

They were out of time. She knew it. "I'll contact Coral, Isaiah, just get us out of here."

Isaiah nodded, pulling her through the first passage at a run. They entered the tunnel with the tracks, stopping cold when they heard laughter behind them.

"Yo." Cowboy drawled. "Thought you might come this way."

Isaiah pushed her behind him, backing her against a disintegrating brick wall beneath an arch anchoring thick white cobwebs.

Trying not to imagine what might be crawling up her back, Shan pressed against the uneven wall. Crumpling Isaiah's jacket with tense hands, she stretched to see over his shoulder. Grit sifted from the ceiling with the rattling of a subway train. Much closer than where they had been.

Several lounging figures were visible across the room. One of them pushed off a pile of stones and sauntered forward, twirling his heavy chain like a lasso.

"Move. Now, Chickenshit." Cowboy stood in the middle of the room, legs spread, chain dancing smoothly. Hilo and Pitcher crept forward to flank him. Cobwebby dirt formed epaulets on Hilo's fat shoulders.

"Get 'im." Pitcher hitched his pants with the hand gripping his crotch, "I want me some o' that fine little dime."

Without looking back, Cowboy flexed his right arm and the chain cracked a stone at Pitcher's feet. Hilo sniggered.

Shan tightened her grip on Isaiah's coat. She knew what he was going to do before he did it. His spine stiffened and his shoulders pushed against her fists. One hand came back, shoving her to the wall and Isaiah walked free of her restraint.

Shan clenched her fingers. Watching Isaiah stop six feet from Cowboy, Shan called her power. She held it ready, wondering if Isaiah would hate her for using it. She would use it if she had to, though.

"Name ya hood." The chain flicked the empty air inches from Isaiah's nose.

Isaiah's shoulders stayed square. His arms spread from his body, his fingers splayed. Over the past six months, his shoulders had broadened, so his head no longer looked too large for his body. Cowboy was broader, though, and large muscles bulged beneath his ebony skin.

Shan closed her eyes, desperately forming a conduit between her power and Cowboy's chain. Would her containment hold? Cowboy stood close to Isaiah and she held so much power.

She stared at Isaiah, willing him to be wise.

"I told you I ain't part of no gang." Isaiah spoke clearly. "And I ain't going to be."

It was happening too fast. She wanted it to slow down. *Slow down!* Fiery warmth flowed through Shan's body, power rolled over every nerve. Time slowed. In his heavy face, Hilo's eyes widened slowly. Pitcher's thin nostrils flared. Dark fury crawled over Cowboy's face, his expression contorting, neck muscles bulging. With the gradual twist of his lips, Cowboy's bicep contracted. The chain undulated and floated outward, curved end moving to circle Isaiah's throat.

In slow motion, Shan flung both hands outward, releasing the magic roaring inside her, making and remaking a conduit as she watched the power travel toward the chain. The instant the tongue of magic touched metal, the links folded in on themselves, sucking air particles toward them. The chain disappeared, releasing the energy drawn with it. The particles bounced back, flaming, crashing against Shan's framework, spewing out of cracks where her joints didn't meet. The uncontained energy swelled outward, sparking the air. Isaiah, Cowboy, Hilo and Pitcher flew upward and backward.

A shotgun boomed, jerking Shan back to real time. In the weapon's flash, she watched rock explode and scatter down the tunnel where Cowboy had been standing. With the second shot, concrete, stone and dirt exploded behind Cowboy, Hilo and Pitcher. The gang bangers clambered to their feet. Still on his back, Isaiah scrambled away.

"God*damn*!" Cowboy swerved into a branching passage, Hilo and Pitcher at his heels.

"Get the hell out of here!" A familiar, raspy voice screamed. Shan blinked at Granny emerging from the smoke, cocking her weapon again.

CHAPTER FIFTEEN

Granny let off another shot, chipping the brick wall behind the escaping thugs.

"Get up, boy." Granny motioned with her gun. "Them hoods'll be back with buddies."

Isaiah lurched to his feet, dusting his hands on his pants.

Shan staggered out of the corner. "Granny?"

A pair of demons popped into the room, on either side of Shan. She hesitated, unsure how to separate her power stream. Granny's rifle went off, knocking one of the creatures back a few feet. Shan dispatched the other, pulled more power, weaving a containment at the same time, and gave the second demon full force as he loomed over her.

The backlash from her first cast had knocked Granny to the ground and sent the pile of stones flying across the tracks.

Struggling to her feet, dusting off the back of her skirt, Granny looked Shan up and down. "Let's get out of here."

Shan shook her head, blinking. "How did you find us?"

"Boy!" Granny looked up at Isaiah. "Can you lead the way out?"

Isaiah nodded and stared back at her.

"Finding you wasn't nothin'." Granny's laugh echoed through the tunnel. "I know you, you, see? I figured they wasn't going to get much out of you by force. Figured you'd get out soon as you could."

Shan shook her head again. Granny in the New York City underground. Unbelievable.

"Coral might be smart, but she don't know a thing 'bout people. She's handin' out hundred dollar bills for lies trying to find you." Granny tucked her rifle under her arm to light a cigarette. "I just told people my granddaughter had run off and I worried she took up with a pimp."

Isaiah scowled, raising his chin. "I am not—!"

"Don't get your britches in a heap." Granny's sniggered, again. "I know your face barely got peach fuzz, but people felt sorry for me and told me everything I wanted to know. It saved your skinny ass."

Shan touched Isaiah. He moved back as if she'd burned him, turned away and started walking. Shan and Granny followed him, pacing side by side. Granny, dressed in a heavy overcoat, held her cigarette in one hand and the shotgun in her other. Still, she managed to scramble around the rubble with alacrity.

"Coral told me everything." The words were spoken the instant the thought crossed Shan's mind.

"Hmph." Granny stopped to flick her ashes. The smell of tobacco mingled with the tunnel's peculiar, dank scent. She patted the pockets of her apron and pulled out a half pint bottle. Shan wanted to knock the bottle out of her grandmother's hands.

Eyeing Shan as if she could read her mind, Granny took a long swig. Then she started walking again, briskly. Shan trotted to keep up.

"Coral Morgan told you what she wanted you to know. I doubt that's everything."

"I learned to use my power."

"Did the demons show up at the Bellingham?" Granny caught Shan's forearm, stopping her.

"No."

"Circle keeps it warded." Granny tossed her cigarette butt and took another drink. She lit another smoke. "Did you learn easy or did she have to make you?"

"I learned. I broke some stuff, but I learned." Shan wasn't about to share Isaiah's sacrifice with the woman who had lied to her for seventeen years.

Granny's bloodshot eyes held Shan's. "What did you do?"

"I broke some antiques." Shan waved a hand, "But what's it like out there?"

"All hell's broke loose." Granny snorted. "We almost got blowed into the river."

Shan's thoughts whirled. She waited for Granny to talk about options. When Granny didn't speak, Shan gathered her courage.

"I've been having dreams about weird weather killing all kinds of people." She kept her eyes on Isaiah's back.

"Do you think this is it?" She glanced at Granny. "Am I too late?"

Granny exhaled loudly, coughing at the end. "You're askin' me?"

"Coral said you were there. You were part of the plan."

"The plan to raise up a reincarnation of Palax Lae? I was part o' that stupid plan. You ain't no reincarnation o' nobody." Granny said, coughing. Bringing her cigarette to her lips, she inhaled and exhaled with a relieved sigh.

"I know that. She does, too." Shan suppressed a shudder. "What am I supposed to do to save the earth?"

"Coral didn't tell you that, I guess." Granny spat.

"You said there were two stories."

Isaiah waited, ahead, leaning on the uneven doorway, arms crossed. Shan couldn't tell whether he watched them or the stairwell.

"They is two stories. About the past and what happened. And at one time they might have been more than one way to stop this craziness." Granny tucked a stray hair up under her wrap. "Coral and her crowd thought they would force the world to change their ways."

Shan waited.

"With your help o' course." Granny blew smoke with a grunt. "You would of destroyed a few targets to get attention, and then she'd have told everybody to turn off their fossil fuel cars and stop the factories."

"That's what she said."

"Factories, oil companies, something like that?"

"I wouldn't do that." When Granny didn't continue, Shan asked, "What other option did I have?"

"Don't matter now." Granny picked up the pace. Shan couldn't understand how a woman Granny's age could move so fast after all she smoked and drank.

"I caused somebody to get killed last night."

"I saw that bit o' throwback, just then." Granny stopped and looked up at Isaiah. "I guess Coral didn't show you how to keep it locked in."

"It wasn't backlash. It was a demon."

Granny laughed. "Yep. They got your scent."

Shan looked over her shoulder. They were close enough to Isaiah she could see his scowl. His arms were crossed and he stared hard at her.

"Can you do magic?"

"I used to think I could." Granny pulled out her bottle and stared at it. "Don't know now."

"In there, when Cowboy was about to hurt Isaiah, it felt like time slowed. Did I imagine that or did you do it?"

"You didn't imagine it." Granny looked up from her bottle, "and it didn't slow. You just saw things faster. That kind of magic was always beyond me."

Shan took a deep, shaky breath. She couldn't recall a different feel to the power, or any indication of how she'd done what she'd done. Except that she had wanted more time.

Granny finished off her drink and dropped the bottle onto the littered floor. "Coral Morgan never could understand people is always who they is and if you're patient, they'll do what comes natural."

"You believe it, don't you? You believe magic's in my nature?"

Granny waved toward Isaiah. "Let's get out of here before the thugs catch up with us. Or the demons or Coral Morgan. No matter what your nature is, I ain't no match for The Circle. But they's some people I want you to meet."

332

Granny clutched Shan's forearm, speaking into her ear. "That boy shouldn't be with us. He ain't one of us."

"Granny!" Shan backed up. "He's my friend."

"You can't be distracted right now." Granny's mouth turned down, "That boy can't help. The most he can do is take your mind off what it needs to be on."

"We can all stay down here and die, or he goes with me."

"'Bout time you showed some grit." Granny crowed. "Keep it. You going to need it real soon."

Shan couldn't tell whether Isaiah had heard their conversation, but, his posture seemed less rigid as he picked his way up the steps.

She heard the howling wind and the rattle of hard rain before they reached the surface. The warehouse had only a partial roof and rain bounced off the stone floor, pooling in low areas, pushed, by the wind, across the rugged space. As Isaiah stepped into the open area, water turned to hail, forcing him to duck into a protected corner. Shan stayed in the doorway with Granny. She felt Arlo struggling in the backpack and put her hand on the pack to comfort him.

The small hail stones were replaced by increasingly larger ones, until ice particles as large as Shan's fist covered the floor. The partial roof cracked and separated beneath the onslaught. But the hail stopped suddenly and the silence was deafening. Shan started out of the stairwell.

"No!" Isaiah shouted holding up one hand. "Get down!"

He broke from cover. Scattering hailstones, sliding and pitching, he ran to the stairs, "Go down! Go down!"

Granny moved faster than Shan. Hand to the wall, she scrambled over damaged steps and rubble. Shan twisted to make sure Isaiah came down, too. Behind him, trash, twigs and other debris floated in the electric air. Isaiah's eyes were wide, his mouth open. He caught up with Shan in two leaps, taking her arm and pushing her down the stairs while he stretched to close the door.

They were still on the bottom step when what sounded like a freight train roared into the warehouse they'd just vacated. The air lifted Shan's hair, as if it were trying to pull her back up the steps. Isaiah pushed her down between two of the rusted subway rails, where Granny already crouched, shotgun tucked between her chest and knees, hands over her head.

The rumbling surged overhead. A long, loud shriek split the air and there were thunderous crashes. Bricks, garbage, metal and wood rolled down the stairs. Shan screamed flattening her hands against the concrete, releasing the power her body drew against her will. Energy scraped her nerves raw and she only stopped screaming when silence descended above.

"Tornado." Isaiah put his arm over her. She let him think she'd simply been frightened, but Granny eyed her suspiciously.

"Guess it ain't easy for you to channel all that power." Granny cocked her head.

"How do you know?" Shan couldn't help asking, "Coral said no other druid used magic the way I do."

"They don't. But we all got the gist of pulling energy." Granny turned her shotgun, running her hands over the stock and barrel. "Imagine it ain't all that nice to just have it push into you, 'specially if you can't let it out."

"Another tornado's coming." Isaiah said, crouching again. They waited out three more. Head pounding, muscles cramping, Shan allowed the power to flow through her directly into the earth, cringing at the sounds overhead; thuds, crashes and shattering glass.

When they were certain the wave of tornadoes had passed, Granny insisted they venture back outside.

"My friend, Walter, is waiting for us." She frowned with concern, "and others of our friends aim to meet us at the pier."

They emerged into a nightmare world. The warehouse had been reduced to piles of rubble. An office building across from them had been twisted like a plastic toy. Structures on one side of an adjoining street were fine, while those on the other side had been destroyed. Cars and buses were overturned. People were shouting, crying and moaning. Huge, soft snowflakes fell, blurring some of the city's ragged edges.

Shan tried not to look at the injured or at Isaiah but she couldn't avoid her own heart. Would these people have been hurt if she'd listened to Coral?

"I know what you're thinking." Isaiah took her hand, standing between her and Granny's scowl. "But there's no way two days would've been enough time to stop this."

"Boy's right." Granny circled behind him, clearly agitated, "We'll talk about it again. Right now, I got to find Walter."

"Where was he?"

"Couple blocks over that way." Granny pointed past a row of metal warehouses, most now without roofs. "Parked in a loadin' zone."

A groan, nearby, caught Shan's attention. A very large man in a muddied suit lay on his side near a crosswalk. Blood seeped from a deep wound in his head.

"Granny," Shan pointed to the man, "Can you help him?"

"I ain't got no idea. Ain't tried in fifteen years," A shadow passed over her face and Shan knew she was thinking of David.

"But look at all of them," Granny indicated the people in doorways, in cars, unmoving figures in a bus bent around a light pole. "I can't heal 'em all. 'Sides, Walter could be hurt, and there's others who can heal. If I stop and help everybody here, it'll mean more bodies down the road."

Shan wished she could walk with her eyes closed. Was her life always going to be about choosing who would die?

The wind picked up and the snow came faster, almost blinding them. Shan pulled her coat tighter, placing her feet carefully to avoid slipping. They found Walter's rusted blue pick-up parked where Granny expected. It was undamaged but Walter was nowhere in sight.

CHAPTER SIXTEEN

Granny put two fingers in her mouth and whistled.

"Kat!" A man shouted from the lee of a storage facility. The snow, now falling at a forty-five degree angle, made him difficult to see. He came into view slowly, hands over his head. Not much taller than Granny, he was several times as wide. Not fat though. Walter's bulk was muscle.

"Shit." Granny spat, taking aim with her shotgun. Coral, dressed in a green and black ski suit, stepped out behind the man. A black knit cap covered her hair, and windburn highlighted her white face. Circle staff fanned out behind her. Wave after wave of them emerged from the snow screen. Shan's heart sank.

"Stop right there." A female shouted from behind Shan. She turned.

A crowd collected behind them, too. There were women, old and young, men and boys. They wore an assortment of coats, hats and scarves that didn't match, but their uniformly grim expressions trained on Coral identified them as a group. The woman who had shouted wore an orange hunter's cap over her long, gray-streaked chestnut hair. A red woolen cape blew around her shoulders, tethered to her body by a thick cord across her collar bone.

"Vivian!" Coral's voice carried the sting of bitter recognition. "What've you done?"

"This?" Vivian indicated the ravaged city block. "Weren't you the one with the plan to stop it? Where's your super druid now? Did the great Palax Lae fail to return?"

Coral's eyes didn't leave the woman's face.

"Let Walter go." Granny snarled, pumping her shotgun.

"He's been telling me all about your New Druids." Coral's mouth turned down, "And how you were going to save the earth without bloodshed."

Coral shoved Walter forward. Shan touched her magic and recognized the crawling blue dome of The Circle's heavy ward.

"How's that working for you?" With a tilt of her head, Coral indicated the twisted skyscraper.

Shan looked back at Vivian. The New Druids were warded, too. Only Granny, Isaiah, Walter and Shan were vulnerable to a magical attack. If she'd known how to make one, Shan would've created a ward for them. She wondered if it was like creating a containment field, but she couldn't figure out how to hold magic to the outside and not inside, where it would destroy everything.

The wind died for a moment and the snow stopped falling. Shan would've sworn the entire crowd held their breath as one. She tensed, too, looking for an area big enough to hold the group in the event of another tornado. But the wind came back, twirling snow in blinding circles. Ice crystals bit her cheeks. Her lips and nose were numb with cold. She hoped the backpack was keeping Arlo warm enough.

A movement at the corner of her vision told her Granny was going to shoot Coral.

"No, Granny!" She cried but Granny's finger pressed back on the trigger. Shan released magic and conduit in one reaction and the gun, along with the emerging projectile, burst. The fly back tossed Granny against Vivian, rocking them both into the people behind them.

Granny struggled out of Vivian's arms, staring at Shan with astonishment and anger.

Before Shan could speak, a demon appeared in the space Granny had just vacated. Another popped into existence beside it. As she dispatched one, she saw others appearing all over the streets. Within a few seconds, a demon army had gathered on the block.

Vivian struck one with lightening as it reached for a druid's head. Shan destroyed a third and saw another writhing in a column of fire cast by one of The Circle. Isaiah jerked her out of the way as a demon appeared behind her, she cast as she rolled, catching the creature as his talons were inches from her face. The air filled with lightening, fire and rebound explosions from Shan's magic. It became harder to pull power. She had to reach further, dig deeper and spots danced at the corners of her vision.

She threw her bag to Isaiah. Screaming, "Duck! Guard it!"

Isaiah dropped to his knees, curling over the backpack. Shan tried to keep an eye on him as she fought the monsters, but the druids were fighting just as hard as she was, falling over Isaiah in the process. The snow made it difficult to see if an approaching figure was demon or druid. The wind increased, so that Shan could barely stand against its force, but she kept destroying, learning as she went, to reach beyond for her power, to draw it from the sky as well as the earth. She became lost in world of battling winds, pulling magic and throwing power. She had no concept of time but the demon onslaught stopped as suddenly as it began. The creatures were gone. Shan stood, swaying, looking left and right, forward and back. The New Druids and The Circle were doing the same thing.

Shan, realizing the demons weren't returning at the moment, looked for Isaiah. She found him still hunched over her backpack. He turned his head. An ugly gash crossed his forehead, his arm was bleeding and the side of his face was swollen. A druid, who, with others of her group, was busy healing, placed her hands on his shoulders. Within seconds, his face was clear. He stood. Nearby, Granny panted, fists planted on her hips, staring at Coral.

Coral walked through her gathering, bending to heal, as if the New Druids weren't forming ranks across from her. The Circle showed their awareness, though. Every able eye trained on the New Druids and on Shan. Walter stood between the two parties, his face red with exertion despite the cold.

Shan blinked several times, catching her breath as much as she could in the storm. When her legs were steady, she headed for Walter, touching Isaiah's hand as she went, thanking him and willing him to stay put.

She stopped a foot from Walter.

"Go to Granny." She said, meeting her aunt's gaze. Coral didn't flinch, but she said nothing when Walter left the center of the street.

"Can either of your plans stop this now?" Shan raised her voice. Everyone watched her. "Those demons will be back and I'm guessing the weather isn't going to improve."

" Earthquakes down south. Volcanoes erupting in the Midwest and a hurricane's headed for England." A middle-aged druid with The Circle held aloft an old portable radio.

"She's right, Katherine." Coral opened out her hands. "It's too late for either of our plans to work."

"If we don't work together, we're all going to die." Shan's fists settled on her hips just like Granny's. They'd faced each other this way, many times over the course of her childhood. "Well?"

"She killed David." Hatred etched every line of Granny's face.

Shan's stomach twisted. Granny's words had the ring of truth. Besides, Shan remembered Isaiah's broken body on the couch surrounded by Coral and her friends. Coral didn't deny Granny's accusation. Shan looked from one woman to the other.

"How'd she kill your son?" Isaiah shouted, though Granny stood close to him.

Granny didn't speak at first. Shan ignored the cold creeping over her limbs and watched the woman who'd raised her.

"Tell them, Katherine." Coral spoke after a moment, her tone neither accusatory nor guilty. "Tell *her*."

"What do I care if this damned world's destroyed? I got nothing left. You took it all!" Granny screeched. She clutched her skirts with white knuckled fingers, glaring at Shan.

"If you didn't care, why did you keep her?" Isaiah, again.

Granny cast him a black look and fished for a bottle of whiskey. She downed the final half ounce and threw the bottle at Isaiah. Catching it, Isaiah kept his eyes on Granny.

"David loved her like she was his, didn't he? To David," Isaiah pointed at Shan, "That's your granddaughter."

"Tell her what happened to David." Coral advanced across the lot, her hands in her pockets.

She passed Shan, her unique fern and honeysuckle scent wafting behind her, reminding Shan of her hours in the practice room. In her mind, anger and hate warred with the need to believe someone had the answers.

When Coral closed in on Granny, Isaiah stepped between them.

"Tell her," Coral commanded, "before we all die out here. Including the child of David's heart."

Shan went to stand beside Isaiah. She made her expression as neutral as possible, but, when Granny's eyes filled with tears, Shan had trouble keeping the shock from registering.

"He died trying to get back to you." Granny spoke softly to Coral, then her volume raised. "He would still be livin' if you hadn't convinced him she needed you. And she didn't, did She?"

"David wrecked on the way to New York?" Shan's lips were stiff with cold. How long before the weather took them all?

"Yes," Coral answered. "He was coming to ask me to take you and him both back into the compound," She raised her voice, "So Shan could be raised with her inheritance, and with training. We could've averted all this."

"What makes you think your plan would've worked?" Vivian called.

"Gaiaes thought it would work. Thousands of years of training and knowledge. Your plan *didn't* work, Vivian. Nobody believed you."

"Just tell her you're sorry." Isaiah looked at Coral. "You didn't mean for David to die."

"Of course I didn't. I regret David's death." But Coral's clipped tone didn't relay the kind of sympathy Shan thought Granny would want.

"You could of left us alone."

"You brought him into The Circle."

"And I brought him out of The Circle." Granny hugged herself, shivering. "But you kept calling, you kept sending him messages. You hounded him until he thought he didn't have no choice."

Thunder rumbled and lightening flashed in the lowering clouds. Hail came down with the snow. Warm air, washed with the cold swept across Shan's face.

"We have to get out of this, now!" She yelled. Looking at Coral she motioned, "Follow us."

"Ain't no use." Granny declared, watching Shan with narrowed eyes. "It's too late. We all dead anyway."

"I would've thought you'd be the last person to give up." Shan said, only glancing at Granny before taking her pack from Isaiah.

She held out her hand, indicating he should lead the way. Warm and cold wind swirled first one way and then another, buffeting Shan, making each step on the melting snow even more treacherous. She didn't look back to see who was following her. She skirted the ice covered bodies of those killed in the first tornados. She looked away from the thick, white comma she knew to be the body of the man she'd asked Granny to heal. She gritted her teeth, refusing to allow guilt to find purchase in her heart.

There'd be more and it might be the best she could do to save the few hundred people gathered in her name.

Isaiah lifted a metal bar and kicked aside rubble to clear the entrance to the underground.

"It aint going to do no good." Granny called from somewhere behind, "The tidal waves'll flood the tunnels, too."

"And even if we could survive that," Jessie said right behind Shan, "Within days or hours, the atmosphere won't support any kind of life as we know it."

"Then we have hours or days to figure out what we can do." Shan snapped. "I'm not going to just sit and watch everybody die."

"Damn straight." Isaiah stood on the top step, holding his arm for Shan.

Lightening licked out of the clouds exploding a transformer with a deafening crack. Sparks shot from the pole the bus had hit, arcing over the druids.

Arlo yowled, clawing the backpack. Shan leaped rubble and broken stairs to make room for people crowding onto the steps behind her.

The space was tight for the large group of druids. The electric lights had stopped working, so most of the druids cast their mage lights. With a slight nod, Isaiah indicated the tunnel to Ragville had collapsed. Shan hoped her friends were safe in their deep, hidden world. Around her, the druids were forced to mingle. Uniforms mixed with shawls, camouflage and down jackets. Some people took seats on the ground, others gathered against the walls, but there was no room for the armies to define separate spaces.

Granny sat on the bottom step, Walter beside her. Carol took the short wall next to the steps flanked by Jessie, Liam, Danny and Megan. Vivian, flipping her shawls over her shoulders, stood in the middle of the room, beside Shan and Isaiah.

Shan released her frantic pet from her backpack. Arlo jumped from her shoulder, bounced off the back wall and disappeared among the druids.

Sounds of the storm rose to a crescendo, then, stopped. Whispering ceased and every hair on Shan's arms stood up with the electrical charge in the air. The tornadoes started far away, low raucous whistles, now in unison, now counterpoint. Shan listened, with everyone else, wincing at distant crashes, mechanical screeches and moans. The whistles grew to roars as the twisters approached the warehouse lot. The roars changed to a long, resounding boom. The door rattled and objects crashed against it. The raging above continued for much longer than the first storm and Shan's heart sank. What would the city look like now? How many people were dead?

"If I hadn't run away," Shan stepped up to Coral, "Could we have stopped this?"

"No." Came Coral's immediate answer.

"Not a chance." Jessie said at the same time. "Unless Gaiaes was still with us."

"Five years ago, yes." Coral's voice rang in the silence left in the wake of the storm's passing. "I had hoped…"

"We hoped there would be a chance once you were found." Jessie finished, "But it was a slim hope. We already had information that the ecosystem had become completely unstable. Once the process started, it was difficult to calculate how long it would take for things to accelerate past a point of no return."

"Tell her how you was going to stop it if you'd had her." Granny called from the steps.

"Yes, Katherine." Coral sighed. "I intended to have her destroy targets including plants where people might be working. I would, of course, have taken steps to minimize casualties."

346

"Minimize casualties?" Granny spread her arms. "What's that s'posed to mean?"

"It means less dead people than there are going to be now." Shan spoke her own understanding out loud, despite her antipathy toward her aunt. "And this is a useless debate."

She moved back to stand beside Isaiah. "Is there something we can do?"

"I'm open to suggestions." Coral looked to her people and then at Granny, Walter and Vivian. "From anyone."

The quiet in the space was tomblike. Shan could hear the constant rat-a-tat of ice hitting the metal door upstairs. Something touched her leg and she started as sharp little claws bit into her calf. She lifted the kitten to her face.

A thought made her feel that her heart would fly out of her chest, but it was the only suggestion she could offer. "What about Palax Lae?"

Several gasps rose from the New Druids. Shan exhaled loudly.

"I'm not Palax Lae." She held up her left hand so the ring would be visible. "She's in here. But Coral can call her out."

"Excellent suggestion." Coral drew power instantly, raising her hands at her sides. Shan could taste the subtle difference in the air. Her automatic response was to draw her own magic. Which reminded her:

"Wait. Will it attract demons?"

"Demons are creatures of destructive magic." Coral grimaced. "They are a by-product of Rome's attempt to

347

subvert druidic magic to gain power. Druids who tried to help Rome were twisted and stunted by their desires. At first, Rome used them to hunt other druids, though they're particularly attracted to destructive power. But Rome forgot about them. The modern Church doesn't believe in magic. So the demons live on, unable to reincarnate, constantly scenting the air for destructive magic."

"In other words…" Shan frowned.

"In other words, they were made for you." Granny snarled.

"So that's why they only bothered …" Unwilling to reveal the existence of Ragville to outsiders, she finished awkwardly, "people around me?"

Coral nodded and closed her eyes, starting to chant.

"But why didn't they bother me at the Bellingham?"

"The Bellingham, like all The Circle's compounds," Jessie whispered, "has a special ward to hide your particular brand of magic."

Except for a few people in the far corners, the druids extinguished their lights. Coral's ring of fire extended around Shan, Isaiah, Granny, Walter, Vivian and, of course, herself and her four assistants.

This time, Shan felt the psychic weight of Palax Lae slide out of her, like the last breath of an illness. Palax Lae took form between her and Coral. The instant she was fully corporeal, the priestess turned to Shan.

She grabbed Shan's forearms, her nails digging in. Arlo arched his back, spitting and hissing. Isaiah's hands came up to remove the kitten. The stinging pain of Arlo's claws kept Shan focused enough not to faint.

"Did you feel it?" Palax Lae cried. "Did you hear her realize it?"

Shan pulled back, but the woman held her tightly. She trembled with terror, but she couldn't let it show. "Feel what?"

"Gaiaes." Palax Lae's grip eased. "She read your mind."

Palax Lae released Shan and turned to Coral. "She saw her future!"

"How?"

"Shanliegh Morgan and I are connected. In her time and in mine." Palax Lae said. "We become one in our dreams and when we last stood before The Mother, she heard Shanleigh Morgan's memory. She knew her vessel would be destroyed."

Coral's jaw dropped her eyes widened. "What did she do?"

"Then? She screamed and threw us into darkness. She sent no more dreams."

"But who sent my dreams?" Something tickled the back of Shan's mind, but she couldn't name the thought.

Palax Lae floated close to Shan. Her chilly breath caressed Shan's face. She was as real and alive as anyone else in the room. Faint blue-green veins pulsed beneath, pale, translucent skin. Cobalt light flecked her indigo eyes. Her red hair tumbled behind her, her robe moved as if it, too, lived. "She sent both our dreams. At the same time. The Mother is a Goddess. Time is forward and backward to her."

"What did she do afterward?" Coral breathed, eyes sparking emeralds.

"I do not know, Coral Morgan." Palax Lae's form lost solidity around the edges. "But she knew what the Romans thought to hide from her."

Palax Lae's form pulsated. Sweat trickled down Coral's face. Vivian came to stand beside her, placing a hand on Coral's shoulder. Walter did the same thing on the opposite side. Vivian, Walter and Coral looked at each other and at Jessie. Amazement, fear and hope mingled on their faces. Even Granny's habitual frown had been replaced with a sharp, interested stare.

"She could have found another vessel." Palax Lae swept back and forth in front of the druids.

She could have found another vessel. Maybe the goddess had fled to one of the other trees in the grove. But were there others besides the ones Palax Lae's priests had chopped down? Shan tried to remember the painting of the grove.

The painting!

She swung her pack forward and wrenched the zipper open. She pulled out the picture, more careful than ever not to touch the surface. "Granny, where did you get this?"

"It's been in my family for generations." Granny took it and held it close to her face as Coral swept forward. "What'd you do to it?"

Coral leaned in, still connected to Vivian and Walter. All of their faces were tense with the effort of retaining the connection to the spirit world.

"What is it?" She peered over Granny's shoulder "It's a picture of night?"

350

"It was a painting of a sacred grove." Granny brought her hand forward to touch the surface. "Have you painted over it?"

"No!" Shan pulled the picture back from Granny. "Don't touch it."

"Why, girl, I've touched that thing a million times."

"I didn't paint over it, Granny." Shan looked into Granny's eyes, then, switching her gaze to Coral she went on, "When I touch it, I feel magic in it."

Coral and Granny's eyes met for a moment. Palax Lae hovered behind Coral.

"Can it be?" Coral's head tilted. "How could it hold her?"

Palax Lae floated beside Shan.

"Make a light." She commanded and Shan obeyed, holding it up to illuminate the painting. Though the darkened colors were indistinguishable, swirls and eddies of the artists strokes stood out in the light.

"That Daeon Olner." Palax Lae smiled her terrible smile. "That worthless, incredible acolyte. He could never memorize his histories and spent all his free time in the grove, mixing paints, making pictures. Only his devotion to Gaiaes kept me from sending him back to his clan."

"Was that frame always on it?" Coral asked Granny.

"Far as I know."

Shan exchanged glances with Palax Lae.

"The twigs from her tree." The priestess smiled, "Daeon's love for the Goddess went into every stroke of his brush and he framed it with twigs from her tree. She

351

must have spoken to him, taught him how to make a place for her."

"Hold it closer to me." Walter spoke for the first time. Shan was drawn immediately to the deep, gentle voice. She did as he asked. Palax Lae hovered behind her.

He sniffed the painting. "Flip it over."

Shan did and he sniffed again. "The material is disintegrating. She's...leaking out."

"Can't we do something?" Handling it with great care, Shan slid the painting back into her bag.

Shan sought Jessie's face. "Didn't you say we couldn't stop the planet's destructive cycle without Gaiaes? Can we find a safe place for her?

"She needs a venerable oak." Walter frowned, closing his eyes. "Somewhere perpetually safe."

"Like the original grove?" Isaiah raised one eyebrow.

"Right." Vivian smiled bitterly, "Somewhere Rome can't penetrate."

"Or wouldn't know to." Walter added.

Ice pelting the door grew louder and thunder rolled.

"Better be nearby," Granny snorted, "Way the world's turned upside down, don't think we'll be getting far."

"Release me." Palax Lae addressed Coral in her commanding tone, "Call me back for the ritual if you do not have it."

Coral hummed and Palax Lae, along with the fire circle, disappeared. Coral sagged between Walter and Vivian for a second before extricating herself and straightening her spine.

"It'll take twenty-four fully trained druids." Vivian said. "Coral, can we get twenty-four people to your compound?"

"I don't see how." Coral ran both hands through her hair. Her face was flushed, her eyes feverish. "But we must find a way."

"What about Central Park?" Isaiah held up a map. "We'd have a better chance walking there than trying to get to the compound. Unless the goddess can be moved to dirt?"

"Central Park?" Danny grunted. "We'd have to have someone there twenty-four seven. Somebody who knows how to tend the Goddess."

"In theory," Jessie said, "we all know."

"It's our only hope." Vivian looked around the room. "Can I have a show of hands? Volunteers for the rest of the twenty-four?"

Except for Granny's, every hand went up, including Isaiah's. Jessie walked to him, placing her hand on his shoulder. "Isaiah, I appreciate your offer…"

"But I have no magic." He dipped his shoulder, sliding from beneath her touch. "She's going, isn't she?" He pointed at Shan.

"I am."

"Didn't you say she could only destroy things?" He shrugged. "She'll be as useful as me, then. But if she goes, I go."

"Leave that behind." Coral pointed to Arlo, who lay across Isaiah's neck.

"I can't leave him." Shan's eyes stung with tears. "He followed me from the Bellingham."

"Did he?" Coral raised an eyebrow. "What was he doing there?"

"He didn't say."

Exhaling, Coral turned away, pointing at Circle druids while Vivian selected volunteers from among the New Druids.

"You two stay." Coral told Jessie and Megan. "I know you won't, Walter. I need you Vivian, but if you have a second-in-command, that person should stay, as well."

Vivian nodded. "Maureen."

Shan understood. Coral and Vivian were choosing replacements, people to carry on if they didn't come back. To carry on with what, she wondered? If Coral and Vivian didn't return, there would be nothing to continue.

Shan removed the food from her backpack, placing it on the floor. She handed her computer, the pearls, her notebook and the picture of her mother to Megan. She took Arlo from Isaiah. After cuddling him quickly, she zipped him into the bag and hooked it over her shoulder. While The Circle and New Druid volunteers sorted themselves, Shan and Isaiah climbed the stairs.

Isaiah pushed against the door. Veins stood out on his neck, his muscles bulged against his coat sleeves and across his back. "It won't move."

"Blast it." Granny said.

Shan looked back and realized Granny meant for her to hit the door with magic.

"I can't." Shan blinked, "Demons."

"Reckon they can fix that." Granny thumbed at Coral and Vivian. "Caught 'em by surprise, first time, I imagine."

Coral conferred with Vivian and the other druids. In a moment, Shan tasted power, and addressing her own core, recognized the muffling shield placed around the entire lower station.

"Now, Shan." Coral called, zipping her jacket up to the neck.

"Breaking the door won't help with the next tornado." Isaiah said, but Shan had already cast her magic. The door exploded and Shan had to cast again, quickly, to stop heavy debris rolling down the stairs. The rebound of her second blast pushed her backward, but Isaiah caught her by the forearms, holding her in a vice-like grip.

"Always be prepared." Isaiah whispered, "Isn't that what the boy scouts say?"

Shan checked Granny and the rest of the druids. Granny must've caught some of the blast because her back was flat against Walter's chest. Her eyes sparkled with grim delight. "Would of saved us a ton of work, if you'd a knowed how to do when you was younger."

Shan flashed a smile, glancing at Coral's impassive features before facing the storm blowing through the doorway. She and Isaiah stepped out first and narrowly missed being guillotined by a falling road sign.

Declaring she knew Manhattan best, Coral took the lead, Danny at her side. She asked Isaiah to keep his map at the ready in case weather damage blocked the routes she knew.

"Be careful," She said, "of desperate people. We have precious little time. We can heal afterward, if our efforts succeed."

CHAPTER SEVENTEEN

In the short period they had been below ground, the city had morphed into something alien. Few street lights worked and no lights showed in the nearby business. Cars, buses and trains were overturned, crunched into one another or smashed against buildings. Skyscrapers, silhouetted by the low, black sky had been truncated, hacked to pieces. From the graduated stories of a dark, otherwise uninjured tower, a yacht hung upside down, sails wafting stiffly in the icy breeze. A pristine Victorian clock, surrounded by splintered remains of wooden buildings, read three forty-five. Too early to be dark.

Coral set a breakneck pace forcing the party to navigate over and around storm-tossed machinery, automobiles, appliances and trash. Shan heard a groan, nearby.

She lurched in the direction of the sound, but found Granny's steel fingers gripping her left arm.

"Keep walkin'."

"I'm glad I can't heal, then, because I couldn't pass somebody in need."

"I hope you'll grow out of that." Granny let go and continued.

Shan addressed Walter, "Can you heal?"

"I do." He, too, refused to even glance in the direction of the moaning.

"How can you just walk on?" Shan scrubbed the ice away from her eyelashes. Tears hovered in the corners of her eyes, and she was pretty sure they'd freeze if they started down her face.

"What if you could just heal him really fast and catch up with us?"

"What if there are ten more around him?" Walter's face sagged with regret. "What if I heal them and there are fifteen more on the next block? What if thousands crowd around us and we can't finish our mission?"

"I know. I know. Everybody dies." The tears overflowed her eyes, hot streams coursing over her cold skin, freezing at her jawline. "I'm not asking why we can't heal a thousand people. I'm asking why we can't heal the ones who show up in our path."

"She's got a point." Isaiah spoke through his turtleneck which he had pulled up over his mouth. "Why can't you just help the people we run into? I'm fast. Let me go over and check on this one person."

He left before Walter could respond.

"Stupid boy," Granny snapped, "He'll get'imself killed."

"He's not stupid, Granny!" Shan fired back. "He's the smartest person I've ever met."

"Got a funny way o' showing it."

Coral had circled back with Danny, Vivian and the other druids, "What's wrong?"

"Isaiah's checking on something." Shan told her.

"We've got to keep moving."

"Go on, without us, then." Shan snapped. "We'll catch up."

Isaiah climbed a pile of bricks which had probably been a small access control center for the depot. Skidding, he caught himself with one hand and disappeared on the other side.

He climbed back moments later, waving at Walter.

"Go on. Get yourself killed," Granny snarled.

"You'd better come help me, Kat." Walter said calmly, "Make sure somebody knows where my bones are."

"We'll all go together." Coral said between clenched teeth. "The quicker we get done, the better."

Isaiah had found a worker shivering beneath a blanket of snow, bleeding profusely from several gashes on his legs and back.

While the other druids watched, Walter flattened his palm on the man's arm. The victim's eyes flew open, then, closed blissfully.

"Are you an angel?" He asked drowsily as his skin regained color beneath Walter's touch.

"Something like that." Walter whispered. He stood up and pushed the sleeping man with the toe of his boot. "Hey, buddy. You alright?"

The man jerked awake, his hands flying to his leg, feeling for his injury. "What happened? Who are you?"

"Bad weather. Think you got knocked out." Walter shrugged. "Better find shelter before you freeze to death."

The man frowned, but Walter turned away. Shan looked back as the group clambered over the rubble. The man still stared at them, frowning with confusion, working his fingers in and out of his ripped clothing.

"Are you happy now?" Granny asked as they trotted across the lot, going around stalled and wrecked cars.

"If we can't help those beside us, how can we make decisions for those far away?"

Walter chuckled wryly. "That may be one of the smartest things I've heard in a long time."

"She's smarter than she lets on." Coral said, her dark gaze resting on Shan's face for a second.

Granny snorted. "Never said she was stupid. Just bullheaded."

A smile flitted across Isaiah's face and Shan wondered what her life would be like now that Isaiah and Granny knew each other. A sudden gust of wind and roiling clouds gathering overhead reminded her there could very well be no life by the time the day was over.

Feeling Arlo wriggling in the book bag, she pulled it around to cradle him in her arms and ran to catch the rest of the druids. Isaiah loped easily beside her.

Coral stopped to survey the street they needed to cross. Cars, most with fog lights still on, had crashed into each other, or were left sitting, abandoned with open doors and windshield wipers running. Metal poles leaned over the streets. Stoplights flashed red and yellow or did nothing at all. Windows were broken on every store front. On either side of the street, people wearing hoodies under coats or knit caps pulled low, scurried in and out of businesses carrying clothing, televisions and computers. One woman, with yellowing skin and blue-gray pin curls, trotted by with hands full of jewelry, layers of pearls, diamonds, rubies and emeralds bouncing on her ample chest as she passed. Her eyes were wide, her mouth straight, giving her an avid look, as if she believed, with enough jewels, she could get through the disaster.

Shan watched her dart into the street and run along the cars trying to find a way to the other side. As the woman ran, another gust of wind threw her against a car draped with broken power lines. She jerked, her body sparking, light bouncing off the precious stones splayed across her chest. Shan clamped her mouth shut, breathing through her nose to ease the nausea.

Isaiah linked arms with her. She held close to him, pulling her bag between them so Arlo was sheltered. Ahead, the druids walked in the street, going between cars where there was an opening, staying close together. Coral's dark head touched Vivian's orange hat, their animated faces revealing they were in deep discussion, dodging cars and people, automatically. Danny shadowed Coral. Over her shoulder, Shan saw Granny and Walter following, arm in arm.

Coral and Vivian slowed as they climbed over the tangled front and back bumpers of two cars, one an SUV, the other a small hybrid. The hybrid was crushed between the SUV and a panel van. Shan noticed the driver of the smaller car was still inside, her head lying against the steering wheel.

"Walter!" She called, "Walter!"

The older druid was too far back, but Danny heard and jumped from the hood of a taxi in the next lane. The druids crowded around as Danny tried the passenger door.

When it wouldn't open, he smashed through it and stretched to touch the driver. He brought his hand out quickly, shaking his head.

None of the other people milling up and down the streets seemed to notice Danny's actions or the strange group of people moving together. Danny backed away from the car and the druids moved through the stopped traffic and crowds of looters. Wind blew so hard they had to walk nearly doubled over. Coral led them through allies and backstreets as much as possible, avoiding entering any structures. Shan was glad. The city was full of creaking, groaning and cracking noises. She kept her power ready to destroy falling electric poles, signs, buildings, anything.

The cold became a living thing, seeking egress to her skin through every buttonhole, every seam. Shan brought Arlo out of her backpack, and placed him under her shirt. For once, he didn't fight. He curled over her left breast, tucking his cold nose between his paws. She pushed her hair inside her coat collar, turning it up and lowering her head so the fleece covered her mouth.

In the thick precipitation, beneath a black sky, surrounded by the crumbling city, she could only focus on putting one frozen foot in front of the other. She stumbled again and again. Isaiah caught her each time, but she no longer felt warmth from where their bodies touched. She forced her heavy eyelids to lift so she could see his face. His skin had gone charcoal over his bones. His eyebrows and lashes were coated with ice. She had a perverse urge to tell him he looked like a Vegas transvestite, but she didn't have the energy. She wanted to stop, just for a few minutes, and sleep. Coral was far, far ahead now, and

Granny and Walter somewhere behind. She could just sleep…

"Shan!" Isaiah shook her. "Don't close your eyes."

His own eyes were slits between his frosted lashes.

"Won't if you won't." She mumbled, numb lips making her words sound more like "wannafuoron."

Gathering her strength, she rubbed her mouth back and forth against her collar. "I won't if you won't."

"It's not much further." Isaiah said slowly. "There's one of the gates."

Instead of pointing, he looked ahead and right.

"Tha's a statue."

"Still Central Park."

Either the driving snow or a lack of loot had cleared the streets of people. Cars, buses, bicycles and carts jammed the circular drive, outlines softened by the accumulating snow. But the crowd of pedestrians had either found shelter or more attractive targets. Shan could see only the druids. Coral stood beneath the tall sculpture base until the entire group had caught up to her. The sheltering stone and the press of bodies eased the sting of the cold. Granny and Walter brought up the rear. Shan's chest contracted. She'd never seen Granny's face so white.

Granny caught her stare and raised her gray brows. Dislodging her arm from Walter's grip, she dug in her overcoat pockets, pulling out a pack of cigarettes. Shooting Coral a wicked look, Granny lit one.

"We need to find the biggest and oldest tree we can. Preferably a healthy oak sheltered with other trees. I think there's some along the bridle path, so if we could just stay together." Coral's voice was pitched so everyone could hear her, but not loud enough to attract the attention of any passersby.

"Let's keep moving. Shan," Coral curled her gloved fingers, "I think it might be best if you walk with me. In case we come across an impediment."

Shan caught Isaiah's hand and joined her aunt. The druids, including Vivian, held mage lights because the park lights weren't working. The magic illumination allowed Shan to see about eight feet in any direction, but they also cast shadows on the driving crystals, making it look as though the air was nothing but snow.

Coral kept to a broad path, at first, and though there were branches and debris, nothing completely blocked their way.

Shan's neck ached from ducking to tuck her chin into her collar. Arlo remained a warm spot on her chest, despite the increasing cold. Some of the shrubbery, small statues and signs were reduced to white, shapeless forms and Shan remembered her nightmare. How long did they have before it came true?

They entered a broad courtyard, undamaged by the storm. The road connected with another but Coral continued straight. She walked beside a low, ornate stone fence which reminded Shan of a mountain overlook. It did lead to steps, but only a few going down to a fountain. Shan was confused. To their right, a fairly dense, ice-coated wood sparkled in their magic light. Why didn't they step over the little fence and use one of those trees?

Coral led them past the fountain. Its three basins were filled with snow, but the wings of its crowning angel stood out against the darkness, sheltering the children carved beneath her bowl. Shan remembered Gaiaes's branches spread over the Sentinels in the ancient clearing.

She and her companions passed the fountain and continued along a path with a wire fence. To her left, past a body of water marked by frozen ripples, great white clouds rolled past the dark sky, highlighting a set of towers. One of the towers was completely intact, its spire silhouetted against the clouds. The other tower's upper portion was missing, as if some giant hand had ripped it away.

The ground beneath Shan's feet trembled. She gasped and looked around, but no one else seemed to have noticed. She followed her aunt, recalling the earthquake she'd witnessed in her nightmare. Coral took a sharp right and, as they went through a short tunnel, Shan felt the tremor again.

"Wait!" She shouted. "Did you feel that?"

"I did." Coral said over her shoulder without stopping. "It means we're nearly out of time."

After exiting the tunnel, Coral increased the pace, angling right onto a different path. She went past a frozen pond and stepped over a low bank to enter a thick grove. Walking through the woods, Shan listened, in vain, for strains of tree song but she didn't touch the ice covered bark.

The tremors increased in frequency and strength. Before Coral found the spot she sought, Shan was rocking to stand upright. Wood snapped and branches shook, raining twigs and ice on the druids.

Dark masses of cloud roiled above the trees, cascading across to the city, dropping black, twirling fingers, which, when they touched the earth, were soaked with the lighter colors of lifted debris. Snow fell like rain, in thick, driving swaths.

"Join hands!" Coral screamed above the din. Gripping Isaiah's fingers, Shan reached back for Granny's just as a heavy limb crashed through smaller boughs. Walter shoved Granny into Shan as the large branch fell between them.

"Walter!" Shan destroyed the great limb without thinking. Granny flung herself over Walter's body as Isaiah hooked his arm around Shan's waist to keep her from going forward. Arlo scratched his way out of Shan's coat, leaving burning traces on her bare skin. He leaped into the snow and bolted past Walter's prone form.

"Help me!" Granny pressed her hands against Walter's chest.

Coral pushed past Shan and Isaiah, Vivian and Danny with her. She leaned over Walter but a demon appeared, knocking her aside. As Shan drew power to dispatch the first demon, a second and third appeared. Coral burned one. Shan blew the other away but the third reached for Granny and Danny stepped in its path. Shan threw her magic at the demon and it exploded but not before its claws had ripped through Danny.

Coral screamed. Shan retched, falling to all fours.

"He ain't gone!" Granny pushed on Walter's chest. "Walter, get back here! Don't leave me!"

Shan sat back on her knees, looking between Granny and Coral. She couldn't look at Walter or Danny.

366

Coral knelt, caressing Danny's pale, unmoving face. Images of Danny's longing looks at Coral flashed through Shan's mind. She saw now, what Danny may never have known; that Coral had loved him, too.

"He's gone." Coral dabbed each of her eyes with a gloved hand and stood. With her head high, her spine stiff and her shoulders square, she intoned a few words. She waved her hand over Danny's body. He burst into flame that produced no heat and, rising into the air, he faded away.

Isaiah pulled Shan to her feet, keeping his arm around her waist. The earth rumbled again, the wind switched direction and the trees swayed around them. Shan kept looking at the spot where Danny had fallen.

Coral, eyes glassy, looked at Walter. "Are you alright?"

"I'm okay." He sat up, taking Granny's hand, but his gaze remained locked on Coral's face. "I'm truly sorry about your friend."

Coral nodded, traces of frozen water on her cheeks sparkling in the mage light.

Staring at her aunt, Shan felt horrible. She should've hated Danny for beating Isaiah. But he had done it on Coral's orders, and, a small voice whispered in the back of her mind, with Isaiah's blessing. Anyway, his quick action had saved Granny's life. From a demon which came because Shan had acted without thinking. The tree branch had probably only stunned Walter, and now, Danny was dead. Because of Shan.

Walter pulled Granny to stand with him. Her face was set in stone. She stared at Coral without revealing any emotion. Walter nudged her.

"Sorry about 'im dying." Granny's words were measured. "But, he's a druid, an' like you told me when David passed, he'll be reincarnated."

"That's true." Coral lifted her chin and looked at Shan. "You have the painting?"

"I do." Shan hugged her book bag. "I'm sorry about the demons. I thought Walter…"

"Now's not the time to second guess your actions, Shan." She started walking. Then, she stopped. Without looking at Shan, she spoke, "He always said you were a funny little thing."

Shan's heart twisted. She wanted to get away. Peeling Isaiah's arm loose, she looked around for Arlo. She couldn't see him and there was no time to search.

Every move had become hazardous. Lightening struck random objects. Trees cracked and fell. Wind and ice turned in the air and the ground trembled continuously. In about a quarter of an hour, they'd gone only a little way into the stand of trees. Coral raised her hand, calling a halt. She stood before an older oak. The tree's trunk had split into four sections, each broader than a human, reaching in different directions. Its branches arched and tangled over the surrounding trees.

"This'll have to do." Coral waved Shan forward. Shan pulled out the dark canvas. She placed it carefully atop the book bag at Coral's feet.

The druid leader addressed those collected around her. "It'll take all of us, but Shan and Isaiah, to do the ritual. You both need to keep watch."

Coral linked hands with Vivian and Liam, who joined with other druids. Granny stood next to Vivian and Walter took Granny's hand. They formed a very large ring around the tree, erecting a ward.

"Shan, destroy anything that threatens. No demons can track through the ward. Is everyone ready to do the ritual?

"I don't know it." Vivian said.

"It's simple. I'll say it, you repeat after me. Three times. While we chant, follow my lines to make a bridge between the picture and this tree. If she's able, The Goddess will cross to the living tree."

If she's able. Shan didn't like that phrase at all.

"Do not stop. Do not break concentration, no matter what happens. Shan destroy any threats. Isaiah, help her watch.

Coral's words undulated like music "*Pates Gaiaes pa rah on ay Gaiaes rey oon.*"

"*Pates Gaiaes pa rah on ay Gaiaes rey oon.*" The druids sang, wind shrieking, lightening flickering and the earth rolling around them. A bridge of ruby fire arched between the painting and the center of the oak, near the ground. Faint at first, it grew brighter and thicker, until it seemed solid. At the painting side, it was small and thin, but nearer the oak it looked like a footbridge made of glowing rubies.

Coral repeated her spell and Shan looked sideways at Isaiah. She wished he could see what the druids were building. A cracking roar rose nearby and she whirled to trace its origin. She could see nothing but trees around her. Raising her eyes skyward, she saw what looked like a line of exploding treetops heading directly for The Circle. But as it sped toward them, Shan realized it was a whirling cloud. Could she destroy a tornado?

She had to try. Gathering magic from all around, pooling more and more, until her mind could barely take in her core, Shan aimed at the approaching cloud. She tried to form a containment, but the vortex snaked wildly, left and right. Widening her focus, Shan built a box around that portion of the wood and released her power into the storm. For a moment, the funnel stood perfectly still. Then, it exploded, flattening every tree within Shan's containment, harming nothing outside. Sweat trickled down the back of her neck and she realized Isaiah's hands were under her arms, supporting her. She pulled more power and moved forward a single step, just as the druids sang the final syllable. The painting dissolved into dust. A beam of golden light spilled from the dust and flowed over the bridge, enveloping its lines. Swelling into the oak, it changed every twig to molten gold.

The tree's radiance limned the face of every druid, softening lines, disguising scars, removing wrinkles. They were each strikingly beautiful. Shan turned to Isaiah, and lost her breath.

The gleaming light burnished the elegant planes of his face, bronzing his high forehead and gracefully sloping cheekbones. Gold traced the chiseled lines of his mouth, sparked in the topaz glow of his eyes and cast a halo around his head. He stared at her, too, stunned.

"Shan, now!" Coral's shout broke the enchantment and Shan turned to her aunt. A paroxysm of the earth threw her to the ground, along with most of the druids. Isaiah fell beside her. She scrambled on all fours, toward the oak. From the heart of Manhattan, she heard the rumbling of her nightmares and saw the tidal wave's shadow, darker than the night, creep past her fingertips. She crawled faster, unable to think what Coral wanted from her.

She only understood that Gaiaes called her. The earth shook again and she rolled against the oak. The moment she touched the bark, she fell beyond the universe. There were more stars than she could've imagined, on an infinite highway of amethyst, garnet and golden lines. Neither time nor words existed. Knowing blossomed in her mind and compelled her to look down from her great height.

There! A rotating blue orb slowly changed color to a poisonous green. Patches on the orb's surface went from emerald and brown to white, spider-webbed with black lines. She recognized her planet, dying. Oxygen overcome by carbon dioxide, land buried beneath ice, crumbling in the sudden change. In seconds, the planet, *her* planet would be dead.

A different knowing burst in her mind. The planet was closer, turned faster. She could see deposits of a viscous liquid on the changing waters, cased in stone beneath the surface of the great landmass she knew as North America. She saw black beneath stone in tunneled hills, in trucks, stopped trains and in piles. She saw it everywhere and knew it was her job to destroy the containers, break the stone, demolish the metal and burn through the tunnels.

Even as the protest sparked in her thoughts, Shan received knowing that no one would be hurt. Gaiaes loved all her children, green, flying, furry, scaled, skinned, thinking and swimming. She loved them all.

Understanding her task, Shan drew power from the blue, red and yellow lines, from the starry highway, countless suns worth of energy and it came to her, building within her, blinding her thoughts, burning her soul until she floated in a sea of power. It was time. She opened her eyes and released the flood.

In the fraction of a second before she flew outward with her magic, she saw Coral and Granny, all the druids, fall back from her. She watched horror and pain spread across Isaiah's face, his mouth open in a wordless scream, then, she was light.

From her distant sky seat, she watched it all. Oil, coal, gasoline, diesel and kerosene poured from confinement, spilling over land and sea, concrete and snow, mountain and city. As it spilled, it changed. Lifting and contracting, it all swelled, becoming craggy bark and reaching limbs. Sprouting to great leafy plants and vivid blooms, breaking through plowed fields, pushing through paved lots, rolling stones down greening hills, swallowing fenced parks and sandy beaches. When it was done, she looked down, once more, at the planet and watched it spin, casting a blue-green light out into her darkness, cooling the fire of her being, lulling her to a gentle sleep, wrapped in a mantle of peace.

But she couldn't sleep. Someone called her name. "Shan. Shan. Shan."

"I'm done." She spoke in her mind. "Let me sleep."

CHAPTER EIGHTEEN

"You are not done." It was words, not just knowing. But knowing grew, too. She'd only started. She struggled to find her way back along the star-field to the planet where she belonged.

Her body no longer burned, but hands were on it. Holding her fingers, pushing her chest, caressing her hair. A tiny, rough brush pulled at her eyebrows.

"What?" She brought her hand up to catch a soft, warm bit of fluff. The name came to her from an immeasurable distance. "Arlo?"

She opened her eyes to sparkling sunlight spilling through the green canopy of a dense grove. Was she back in the hills?

"Shan?" Isaiah's voice. Gravelly and strained, but his. She found his face in the crowd of faces around her.

"Isaiah?" She tried to sit up but too many hands held her down. It was clearly morning. A million birds, it seemed, called the early hour. "How long was I…gone?"

"The earth changed in a few minutes," Coral's voice, "But you were out all night."

All night? Shan lifted her head. The world of legs blurred and she fell back.

"Take a few breaths, girl."

"I'm fine!" Shan caught Arlo to her cheek and scooted back against someone's shins. She stood up, but she could see nothing past the people around her.

Coral and Granny stood side by side, faces different, but strikingly similar in their concern.

"Really." She sighed, "I'm fine. Could you all back off?"

The people parted and she surveyed the small forest. Among the oaks, pines and willows were trees she didn't recognize. Vines and plants as tall as trees, with leaves as broad as cars, filled the spaces between trunks. The air around her swelled with the music of the forest's new song. The chorus of hope was joyous and as powerful as each breath of fresh air.

"You did it." Walter said.

"No, Gaiaes did it. She…" Shan began knowing exactly what had happened, but as she tried to articulate it, the knowledge slipped away. "She…"

"She restored life to fossils." Coral finished. "Not just here, though. It must be across the continent at least, to have this effect. But Gaiaes never retained the power to destroy, it belonged to the Sentinels, and then, to you. You did that. You destroyed the repositories so she could remake the plants."

"Gaiaes turned fossil fuels back into plants?" Shan inhaled. "Perfect!"

"And the gases emitted by the plants restored the atmosphere." Vivian's smile nearly split her face.

"Yes, the planet is blue-green."

"You saw the planet?" Coral's eyes widened.

"Where were you? How did you get there?" Druids fired questions at her.

"What was it like to walk with Gaiaes?"

"What did she say?

"I was in a sea of stars." Shan struggled to answer. "I didn't see her. She didn't talk, just sent...knowledge."

"But how'd you know what she was going to do?" Liam asked.

"That's enough." Coral snapped. "We need to get back out into the city, to help, however we can, with the devastation."

"She did it in a way no one would get hurt."

"I thought as much," Coral nodded, "But there are still casualties from the storms."

The walk out of the grove was much easier and faster. Or would have been if Isaiah hadn't kept stopping and exclaiming over new flora.

The fountain had disappeared behind trees and plants, and only bits of brick walkway remained to indicate there had been once been a broad avenue. Trailing vines carpeted the stairway. The fence, the small pool and the pavilions were gone. Swallowed by the forest. Shan could no longer see the towers through soaring trees. The soft blue sky sported puffy white clouds and the air smelled like the mountains back home, only more so.

"Miss Jessie's going to be in hog heaven." Isaiah laughed. "Oh, you might not want to touch that." He pulled a young Circle druid away from a tall, spiked, fernlike plant. "No clue which ones are poisonous and which ones might bite you."

Granny walked with Walter, saying nothing to Shan or Coral. Shan glanced at her several times, but her lined face was set and unreadable. She simply couldn't tell whether Granny was relieved or angry.

"Is it over now?" Shan looked up at Coral.

"You did well, Shan." Her aunt's brows drew together. "And it's stopped the planet's imminent destruction. But," Coral raised her voice, glancing around the group. "It's only a temporary stop. It's bought us some time, but we still have a war in front of us."

"Didn't we just save the earth?"

"We've won a battle. The war isn't over. Some of the fossil fuels are gone." Coral spread her hands in front of her. "That means at least a portion of the flow of wealth from those industries is gone. Here are all these new plants and all this new timber. Where do you think corporations are going to find a new source of revenue?"

"Vivian and I are going to the Bellingham to gather our troops." Coral shouted, now. "Could the rest of you please go with Liam and collect those druids left in the tunnel. Heal people who really need you on the way there and back, but don't draw attention to yourselves."

Coral watched druids weave through the woods. When they were out of sight, she ran her fingers through her hair and sighed.

"People will believe you now, won't they?" Isaiah kept pace with them. "After this."

"I hope it'll make a difference." Coral shook her head. "But some ideas are hard to break loose."

"Reckon it's time for the New Druids to try their plan?" Granny came up beside Shan.

"I think it's time we all put that plan into action."

Granny nodded once "Reckon me and Walter's going to stay and watch Gaiaes's tree." She patted her apron pockets then, spat into the weeds. "But you'll have to send us some people to train, cause we spent an awful lot of time holed up. Might get a hankering to see the world.

"You've got it." Coral said. "Vivian will coordinate between The Circle and the New Druids. She'll know the best recruits."

Shan stopped walking. Coral, Isaiah and Vivian went ahead a few paces and examined some tall flowering plants. Shan imagined, for a second, Danny standing there, hands behind his back, gaze switching from the back of Coral's head to searching the foliage for danger. She shook herself. She couldn't go forward if she kept looking back.

She faced Granny and Walter. "Is this goodbye, then?"

"Nah." Granny said. "It's 'see you later.'"

Walter stuck out his hand. Shan took it and he shook hers warmly. "We'll keep in touch."

Making a sudden decision, Shan pulled Granny into a quick hug.

"Let go of me girl," She said, but she didn't push Shan away. "You're going to smash my last cigarette."

"See you soon, Granny."

"Still don't trust that city woman. If you keep company with her, do your best to keep her on her toes. If the house still stands, it's yours, though, if you want to hide out, instead." Granny turned away, but not before Shan caught the twinkle in her eye.

She wondered if she could stomach keeping company, as Granny put it, with Coral. The glow of Gaiaes's touch still permeated her being and Coral's action didn't seem so monstrous alongside the horrors of the previous night. But how could Shan ever trust such a ruthless person?

Following her aunt, she walked with Isaiah, who seemed oblivious to her struggle. She wondered, for the umpteenth time, how he could be so calm about things that drove her crazy. She was about to ask him when she noted, after they'd passed through a particularly dense bit of jungle, that a frown creases his forehead.

"What is it?" She touched his arm.

"Mom, of course." Isaiah sighed. "Aunt Jolene. My cousins."

Shan wanted to kick herself. Of course. All her family, such as it was, were in the forest of Manhattan. Safe and healthy. "They must be okay. Gaiaes made sure no one was hurt."

Isaiah nodded, but Shan knew he was thinking about the storms. "We'll find a way to get to her, to make sure everyone's okay."

They reached the circle drive where they'd entered Central Park the previous evening. The statue still stood at the entrance and cars jumbled the drive. Some skyscrapers had fallen, some leaned sideways and others stood upright. The buildings had been damaged by the storm, not Gaiaes's rejuvenation, but parking lots had been turned to verdant parks and mini-groves.

People were hanging out open windows, wandering the streets, marveling at the damage. One man stood atop a city bus trapped among the dead cars.

"This is God's warning." The man indicated the broken towers around him. He held a black book high above his right shoulder, shaking it. "The Rapture's near. Next time, the earth will be fully destroyed. Don't suffer the calamity. Repent now, and leave with God!"

"Amen!" Several people shouted.

"Rome's still fighting, I see." Coral sighed.

"It's about time we fight back." Watching Coral through narrowed eyes, Shan scratched Arlo's chin.

"Yes." Coral's eyes gleamed, though her smile was brief, "A general's work is never done."

She licked her lips. "I am a general, Shan, and I hope you understand I did what I had to do. This is a temporary stasis. Only a portion of the damage has been repaired. We need our magical army to continue healing the damage where we can. We need our intellectual army." She nodded once at Isaiah, "to convince people to preserve our environment."

Her gaze was distant for a moment. She blinked and her eyes met Shan's. "I won't promise I'll be different. I am what I am. But I'll never back down. Will you both be coming back to complete your training?"

"I will." Isaiah spoke with conviction. Shan stared at him, but her surprise ebbed as quickly as it came.

Isaiah had changed.

She had to be willing to change, too.

"I guess being responsible for the planet I live on isn't too much to ask." Shan sighed. "I hadn't really picked a college major, anyway."

"Good." Coral raised her brows. "You know you'll have to study with other acolytes?"

Shan nodded.

Coral glanced at Isaiah as she started walking again, "We'll get communications going soon to check on everybody's family."

Vivian put her hand on Isaiah's shoulder, "Your Mom'll be one of the first."

He smiled.

Shan slowed her pace to let Vivian and Coral go ahead. She glanced at Isaiah and looked at the ground. Coral had said they'd only won a battle. That meant there would be more. The demons were still out there, too, watching for her. She respected Isaiah's wish to help, but couldn't he help from anywhere?

"You don't have to stay on the front lines on account of me." She lowered her face, rubbing her chin against Arlo's head.

"Still thinking you all that? Who says I'm staying on account of you?" Isaiah took his hands out of his pockets, "I want to keep saving the world, too."

He let his hand drop to his side, his little finger brushing hers.

Walking the carpet of moss between rows of singing, reborn trees, Arlo on her shoulder, Shan thought about the upcoming months, her studying magic and sparring while Isaiah learned to tend the earth. She imagined them prowling the grounds after hours, comparing notes, talking about…everything.

Smiling, Shan caught Isaiah's hand, wrapping her fingers around his. Maybe saving the world wasn't such a terrible fate after all.

THE END

About the Author

Barbara, who grew up in eastern Kentucky, is a strong believer in preserving the environment and in the power of storytelling. Her earliest memories include forcing her younger siblings to act out the stories she wrote. In return for their cooperation, she wrote more stories. A few decades, continents and universities later, Barbara, also an artist, horse trainer, insatiable reader and avid computer gamer, holds an MFA in Creative Writing. Barbara divides her time between Halifax, Nova Scotia and Kansas City, Missouri so she can experience the world's climate extremes on a regular basis. She lives with her husband, an inventor/entrepreneur, their youngest son—a physics student—their lap-dog collie, guard-dog Chihuahua and the Siamese cat who commands them all.

www.ingramcontent.com/pod-product-compliance
Lightning Source LLC
Chambersburg PA
CBHW071157250626
47159CB00001B/123